CATHERINE HART

**Winner of the *Romantic Times*
Storyteller Of The Year Award!**

NIGHT FLAME

"Let me go. Take me back to the fort," Sarah begged. "I do not belong in your world. My life is very different."

"Your life is with me. You belong to me. You will learn the Cheyenne ways." Night Hawk's dark eyes watched closely for her reaction to his words.

Tears glittered in her eyes, turning them to sparkling starlight, but she faced him defiantly. Her small chin came up in defense. "I do not want to learn your ways. I will be very unhappy with you. I love my father and miss him. I must return to him."

Night Hawk stood firm. "You will learn our ways, as you will learn to love me. In time you will forget your life among the whites."

Dismay filled her. "No! I will never come to love you, Night Hawk. Never."

A smile lifted the corners of his sensuously sculptured lips. "We shall see, my beautiful Flame. If the Great Spirit wishes it, your heart and body will be mine for all time."

**"Catherine Hart writes thrilling
adventure...beautiful and memorable romance!"
—*Romantic Times***

Night Flame

CATHERINE HART

LOVE SPELL BOOKS ✦ NEW YORK CITY

I dedicate this book, with fond appreciation, to my many fans for their unfailing support and encouragement.

Most especially to Beckie R., who has also become a valued friend and fellow author—Good luck, Beckie!

And to Amy E. (The Great A-Me!), with thanks for the two beautiful busts of Indian chief and maiden she painted for me, which now grace my office shelf.

Last, but never least, to my wonderful family for their constant love and patience. I love you all so much!

A LOVE SPELL BOOK®

June 2000

Published by

Dorchester Publishing Co., Inc.
276 Fifth Avenue
New York, NY 10001

ISBN 0-505-52386-8

The name "Love Spell" and its logo are trademarks of Dorchester Publishing Co., Inc.

Printed in the United States of America.

Night Flame

Chapter 1

Sarah Wise was bored, just plain bored. Here she was, seventeen, the belle of elite Washington society, and little good it did her with this silly war going on! All the really interesting men were off fighting, and even when they were in town, all they could talk about was war, battles, and more war. Of course, she should be used to that, having a Union Army general for a father, but Sarah could think of a thousand more interesting topics to discuss—herself, for instance.

Sitting at the parlor window, watching the spring rain stream in rivulets down the glass pane, Sarah hoped to change all that very soon. Oh, she couldn't do anything about the war, but she could change her own circumstances, if her father would only agree. General George Wise was heading West in a few days to tour the forts in the remote Indian territories and direct summer campaigns on the western frontier. It was Sarah's intention to go along. All she had to do was convince her father.

With the lamp lit against the gloom of the day, Sarah caught her reflection in the window pane. With a smug smile, she patted manicured fingers along her freshly coiffed hair. The style was very attractive on her, with the sides pulled back and up from her face. Artful little wisps were left to frame her delicate features and accentuate her bright blue eyes. The remainder of her thick red mane was tamed into a fall of sausage curls that began high at the crown of her head and tumbled in bouncing succession to the center of her back. Let down, her hair fell to her waist, though Sarah rarely wore it loose, as it had a tendency to tangle. Her father loved her hair, and Sarah was glad it looked especially lovely this afternoon. She wanted everything to be just right when she sprang her proposal on him this evening. She had even bought a new dress just for this occasion.

Sarah cast a critical eye at her reflection. Some might say her nose was a bit too small for the fullness of her mouth, but then she had never cared for persons with thin lips anyway. They always looked as if they had been sucking lemons. Wide eyes framed by long, thick brown lashes stared back at her from a perfectly oval face. Sarah nodded. Yes, her eyes really were her best feature. Brought out by her vibrant hair, they were a light, clear blue, the color of a bright morning sky, almost piercing in their intensity at times. Her fair skin was flawless, if one discounted the small beauty mark high on her right cheek. The deep dimple to one side of her mouth merely drew attention to her tempting lips.

Sarah considered herself fortunate that, with her particular coloring, she did not have the terrible problem of freckles. Poor Becky Davis's face was peppered with them, as were the girl's shoulders and arms, and no remedy seemed to fade them in the least. Well, Sarah thought selfishly, that is Becky's problem, not mine, thank goodness! My concern is talking Papa into taking me along on his campaign this summer.

Her train of thought was interrupted by a quick tap on the shoulder, and Sarah turned to find Joey, the cook's son, standing next to her. She had not heard him enter the room, and had been too caught up in her own thoughts to notice his reflection joining hers in the window.

"Yes, Joey?" she asked, using her hands in the sign language she had learned long ago in order to communicate with the deaf boy. "What is it?"

"Mother wants to know if you want asparagus or peas with dinner," he signed back, grinning down at her.

"The peas will be fine," she told him, returning his smile.

If Sarah was a bit inconsiderate of some of the other servants at times, she always exercised patience with Joey. They had grown up together. Much of the time he had been her only playmate, and she adored him as she would have a younger

brother. While some people might pity Joey for
his lack of hearing, Sarah did not, but perhaps it
was because she and he could communicate so
well without words. Maude, Joey's mother, had
taught Joey Indian sign language learned from
her trapper father. Even before he could walk,
Joey was talking with his hands, and Sarah had
learned right alongside him in Maude's cheery,
well-ordered kitchen. It had become second nature to Sarah to speak with her hands and the
force of habit was so strong that she often used
signing by accident when speaking with hearing
friends.

Now she smiled and said, "I heard the Harpers
have a new litter of pups about to be weaned. I
told Helen I would tell you so that you could stop
by and pick one out for yourself if you want.
They should make good hunting dogs when they
are grown. Why don't you run over there now
and look at them? I will speak with your mother
about dinner myself."

Joey's grin widened, his entire face lighting up
with joy. "Are you sure your father will not
mind?" he signed.

"Trust me, Joey," she assured him, and herself
as well. "I intend to have him so well-fed and
pampered tonight that he will agree to anything."
Then she added softly to herself, "I hope!"

When Joey had left the room, Sarah took a
final, satisfied look at her reflection. Then she
rose and went to check on dinner preparations—
her father's favorite meal, of course. If there was
one thing Sarah was adept at, it was manipulat-
ing her father. She'd had the poor man twisted

about her delicate fingers since birth. He was her "darling papa," she his "pampered princess." If she was spoiled and vain, it was not Sarah's fault alone.

"Be reasonable, pet." General Wise shook his head and smiled indulgently at his young daughter from across the dinner table. From the moment he'd entered the house and smelled the tantalizing aroma of crisp fried chicken and plump dumplings, he'd known that Sarah was up to something. He'd been prepared to give his permission for a new spring wardrobe, perhaps a visit to his sister Emily's house in New York during his absence, even the possibility of a new horse. Anything but this!

"This will not be a pleasure trip, Sarah. It will be a long, dusty, dirty journey fraught with danger. Why on earth you would even entertain the thought of going is beyond me!"

Her lips pouted slightly in a naturally flirtatious gesture that brought another smile to the general's eyes. "I don't care, Papa," she said. "Anything has to be better than sitting here all summer with nothing to do."

"I'll put you on the train to New York and you can spend the season with your Aunt Emily," he suggested hopefully. "You can shop to your heart's content."

The pout became more pronounced. "Why bother?" she asked. "Who would I impress with my new wardrobe, with all the men away fighting in this dratted long war?"

George's bushy brows rose in amusement.

"What about the dashing Dr. Moore? Or has he lost favor with his princess now?"

Sarah's pert nose tilted upward as she sniffed delicately. "Indeed, he has!" she responded to her father's teasing remarks. "Handsome he may be, but there is more to life than spleens and colons. I am weary of hearing of nothing but his bloody operations and his precious patients."

George almost laughed aloud, but caught himself in time. "Been ignoring you, has he?"

"Dreadfully. Why, do you know, he had the audacity to cancel our afternoon ride the other day, merely because he had to remove a bullet from some man's leg? And the patient wasn't even an officer!"

"Sarah, you can't fault the man for taking his work seriously. God knows, we need more dedicated doctors like him."

Sarah stared at her father as if he'd gone daft. "Papa, it is not as if the wound were that serious. Any one of the other doctors at the hospital could have handled it just as well. James obviously did not want to spend the day with me when he could find an excuse to stay at his beloved hospital."

The general knew when to retreat, especially in one of these discussions with Sarah. It was his fault she was so spoiled—his and Ivy's. They had cosseted the girl terribly, simply unable to say no to their only child. It had been that way since Sarah issued her first infant cry, and had only gotten worse in the seventeen years since. Since Ivy's death six months before, George had been even more lenient, knowing that Sarah was hurting as badly as he.

Now he was trying to be both mother and father, as well as an Army general. He was a damn good general, he knew, but he feared he was failing miserably as a father. What was a man to do with a daughter on the brink of womanhood? Emily had offered to take Sarah under her wing, but George felt he would be abandoning Sarah at a time when she needed him the most. He simply could not take that way out. Truth be told, he needed Sarah as badly as she needed him. However, he could not see himself taking her with him over hundreds of miles of wilderness on his summer campaigns.

"It's simply too dangerous, Sarah," he repeated. "Not to mention uncomfortable. We'll be sleeping in tents, riding all day, rain or shine. There would be no special comforts for you."

She was not to be so easily discouraged. "It will be an adventure, Papa. What could be safer than traveling with you and your troops? If a general and his men cannot protect one small woman, pray tell me, who can? Besides," she added slyly, playing her trump card and casting wounded blue eyes his way, "I'll be with *you* all summer. I've seen little enough of you these past months as it is. I've missed you nearly as much as I have missed Mama."

She had hit him at his most vulnerable point. His work took up a good deal of his time and attention, and guilt often ate at him when he thought of how lonely Sarah must be without her mother. The big house almost echoed these days.

Sarah could sense him weakening and pressed her case. "Please, Papa. I won't be a bit of

trouble. I promise. Please let me come along."
Not for the world would she tell him that she had
reasons for wanting to go other than those she
had mentioned. She loved him and did not wish
to burden him further, but she was very troubled
these days. In fact, she was actually frightened for
her very sanity.

Sarah had told no one of the disturbing dreams
she had begun having in the past year. She
shuddered at recalling the dreams she'd had of
her mother's death. Before Ivy had even become
ill, Sarah had dreamed of her mother's illness,
her death, her funeral; and it had all come about
just as she had seen it, down to the last detail. It
was strange, uncanny, and so very frightening!

Then she had dreamed that Nan Harrod's
horse would stumble and break its leg. Sure
enough, it had come to pass. Fortunately, Nan's
groom was astride the horse when it happened,
and not Nan. The man had broken three ribs and
his arm in the fall. It was getting so that Sarah
was afraid to go to sleep at night, for fear she
would dream something else disastrous that
would then come true. She was sure that no one
else she knew was afflicted with such prophetic
powers, and she was just as certain that no one
would be able to help her. If the truth were
known, everyone would shun her. Why, they
would think she was a witch, or worse! They
would surely think she had lost her mind, and
Sarah feared they might be correct. She was not
at all certain she was not going completely crazy!

Lately, she had begun dreaming of a strange
man, someone she knew she had never met.

What did this man have to do with her? With her life? Several times now she had envisioned him, but she had no idea where he was from or what he had to do with her. In her dreams she never saw anything but his face. He had a bold face, with strong, handsome features. Dark hair framed tanned flesh. White teeth flashed in an arrogant smile from firmly molded lips. His hair seemed over-long, but this was just the impression she received, for she never saw beyond the stubborn jaw, the high cheekbones flanking a proud nose.

But it was his eyes that held her spellbound in her dreams. Oh, those eyes! So dark and glowing, so mysterious and beckoning! They drew her; they challenged, they dared. Even the thick fringe of lashes framing them, the heavy lids that half-masked those deep-set eyes, could not conceal their brazen gleam, could not hide the bold intent in their fathomless depths. That searing gaze seemed to look straight through her to the secret, hidden thoughts. Those eyes, that smile, called to her, made her quiver with chilling fear and hot, forbidden longing—and all the while, they seemed to claim her, body and soul.

When Sarah awoke from one of these dreams, she was always drenched in perspiration. Her breath came in short, hard gasps, and her heart raced as if she had run a thousand miles. She was overwhelmed with dread, feeling as if she had barely escaped with her life. Yet, at the same time, she felt compelled by the stranger's spirit, caught in the sticky web of an unknown Fate. For days afterward, wherever she went, she would

search the faces of passersby, watching for the
face of this mysterious man; fearful yet hopeful
of encountering him at last in real life. For she
felt certain they would someday meet. Why she
felt this, she could not say, but in some way she
could only vaguely sense, she knew that this
man's destiny and hers were intertwined.

As time wore on and he appeared in her
dreams more and more often, she became anxious and jittery. Her nerves were frayed to breaking. She became sharp with servants and friends,
impatient with herself and others. She prayed for
a decent night's sleep without dreams, for a
restful time of solace and peace. Her sanity
depended upon escaping these ceaseless, disturbing visions. That, more than anything else, was
the reason she wanted so desperately to accompany her father on his tour. Perhaps if she could
get away, have a complete change of scene, she
would regain her normal senses once more. Perhaps then these dreams and this man would cease
to plague her.

"All right, Missy," she heard her father say.
"You may come. But I will warn you right now
that we cannot set an easy pace for you. You must
keep up, no matter how hard the journey." Sarah
nodded eagerly in agreement, disregarding the
stern frown he attempted. "Another thing. We
have no room in the wagons for the tons of
baggage you seem to think necessary whenever
you travel. You will limit yourself to one small
trunk of clothing." When she opened her mouth
to argue this point, he wagged his finger beneath

her nose. "That, or you stay behind," he stated firmly.

If her friends thought that Sarah had been behaving strangely of late, this most recent decision of hers had them completely baffled.

"Are you thoroughly addled, Sarah Wise?" her best friend asked in open-mouthed amazement. "That's Indian territory, you ninny! There are heathen savages out there, not to mention wild animals and snakes and Lord knows what else! Besides, in case it has escaped your attention, there is a war going on!"

"Which is precisely why I have chosen to go with Papa," Sarah announced, and went on to explain her reasoning. "Addie, this town will be as dull as a dirge in a few weeks, with all the best men gone to fight. At least I will be traveling about and seeing some of the country, untamed though it may be. It is bound to be more exciting than sitting around here with no one but other women to occupy my idle hours. Gossip and tea are fine, as far as they go, but I do not want a steady diet of them for an entire summer. Besides, Papa intends to be back in Washington by fall, just in time for the revival of the social season, so I won't miss a thing of importance."

"What about James?" Addie persisted. "Won't you miss him? Surely you can't expect the man to wait patiently for you all that time?"

Sarah gave a negligent shrug. "Why, Addie, it would surprise me if he even realizes I am gone, so wrapped up is he in his hospital and his all-adoring patients. It may just do the man good to know that he cannot treat me so shabbily and then find me waiting when he finally decides he has the time for me."

"And if he doesn't wait? If he finds someone else while you are gone?"

"Then I am well rid of him, aren't I?" Sarah responded unconcernedly.

Addie eyed her queerly. "You really don't care one way or the other, do you?"

Sarah smiled. "Why, Addie, my dear, you seem quite taken with our handsome doctor yourself!" When her friend had the grace to blush, Sarah gave a soft laugh. "Take him, Addie. He is yours, with my blessing. Just be warned that you are going to have to share him with his beloved profession. I fear any woman would always come second with him, and that is not the rank I wish to hold in a man's eyes."

"You are too vain for your own good, Sarah," Addie said, "but in this case, I am only too glad that you are. With you out of the picture, I just might stand a chance with the man. Don't blame me if, by the time you return, I am Mrs. James Moore."

"Mrs. Dr. James Moore," Sarah corrected with a chuckle and a shake of her bright head.

The good doctor was not quite so glad to be relegated to the sidelines of Sarah's life.

"For pity's sake, Sarah. If this is some sort of ploy to get me to take more notice of you, it has already succeeded by mere threat alone. There is no need for you to go through with this insanity.

Stay, and I promise you I will make more time for us to be together." He looked on in dismay as the servants loaded the last of Sarah's things into the wagon. Somehow, Sarah had managed to talk her father into allowing her two trunks and a small bandbox.

"I am sorry, James, but my mind is made up. Actually, I am quite excited about this trip, and it has nothing whatsoever to do with you. In all fairness, I must tell you that I am embarking on this journey in order to get another man off my mind."

"What!" James's shout had heads turning. More quietly, but no less angrily, he said, "Do you mean to say that you have been seeing another man while I have been courting you?"

Sarah could scarcely contain her laughter as she continued her half-lies, thinking how her dream man had finally come to some good use. "Yes, James, I'm afraid I have."

"Who? Who is the rogue?" he demanded.

"That I cannot tell you. Let it suffice that you have never met him, and most probably never will."

"Is he one of your father's men? Is that why you are so insistent on this trip? Are you running away with him?"

"Oh, no. Definitely not," she assured him. Then she proceeded to confuse him further when she added vaguely, "If anything, I am trying to elude him."

A quarter of an hour later, with a befuddled James looking on, Sarah was on her way. With her father and a contingent of soldiers to guard

her, she left her home and the capital of the
war-torn nation behind. What she might find on
the western frontier, she knew not. What she
hoped to leave behind was a man far more
threatening than the one who stood there waving
good-bye.

Chapter 2

What Sarah missed first was her maid. She had never before realized how much she had come to rely upon Tilly to help her dress, to make sure her clothing was washed and ironed and laid out for her, to fashion her hair so perfectly in the latest styles. What a chore it was to struggle by oneself into a gown with thirty small buttons up the back! Especially when one's father had suddenly turned into an ogre before one's very eyes! Oh, Sarah was quite accustomed to hearing her father bark commands to his men. What she was not used to was having those gruff orders directed at her! Suddenly her patient, understanding father was all commanding general, with nary a paternal bone in his body!

Not only was she unaccustomed to this, but

she had not taken into account having to rise with the sun every morning—and the sun was rising earlier with each passing day! Neither had she counted on being handed a plate of burnt bacon and doughy hotcakes and being expected to dress, eat, and be ready to travel, all in the course of half an hour! At home, Tilly had brought her a tray each morning as she lay abed. Sarah would drink her hot cocoa at her leisure and nibble at her lightly toasted muffins while she read the morning news. Then Tilly would help her dress and do her hair.

Then, of course, there was the lack of privacy among all those men! It had never occurred to Sarah that she would have to perform her most private duties out in the open! It was either find a spot behind a concealing bush, or use a tin pot in the rear of a covered wagon. Oh, how humiliating to march past those men, carrying her little chamber pot to empty and clean it! Sarah died a thousand deaths each time she was forced to do so! Never in her life had she thought she would have to clean a chamber pot, let alone have so many knowing grins follow her on her way to do it!

Before the sleep was even cleared from her eyes, they were on their way. Usually Sarah chose to ride in front of the wagon until the noon stop. Then she would order her horse saddled, don her riding habit, and ride for a few hours with her father.

Meals were a trial to the stomach. Never had she more appreciated the delicious meals their

cook had served at home than now, when she
had to suffer Army cooking instead. She could
barely swallow the bland, heavy food, and the
coffee was so strong it nearly melted the metal
cups.

There were times in the first few days, after
riding for endless hours, enduring dust and heat
and mud and rain, when Sarah could have burst
into tears. Sheer stubbornness, and the expectant
look in her father's eye, were all that kept her
from crying. Sarah managed to hold the tears at
bay, but four days into their trip, she could no
longer curb her tongue. Her temper exploded.

Sarah marched into her father's tent that evening without bothering to announce herself first.
"Why is it," she ranted spitefully, "that you
would not allow me to bring Tilly along to serve
me, yet you have an orderly to see to your every
wish and whim?" She faced him squarely, her
hands in small fists upon her hips, and it was all
George could do not to grin at the outraged
picture she presented.

"Do I see you struggling into your clothes by
yourself, or washing your own laundry? No! Your
devoted slave does it all for you! You have warm
water delivered to your tent each morning! If you
desire food or a hot cup of that hateful brew you
call coffee, all you have to do is tell him, and it is
at your elbow before you can blink twice! Do you
have even the foggiest notion of how hard it is for
me to dress and manage my own hair? No one
heats my water! Look at my hands!" She held
them out for him to see. "My nails are all broken,

my skin red and raw! I have to wash my clothing
in the stream! I even have to empty my own
chamber pot, for heaven's sake!"

At this, the general did grin. "Jealous, pet?" he
asked with a dry chuckle.

"Yes, by God, I am!" she retorted, stomping
her foot in anger. "Why should you have all the
amenities, while I suffer?"

George frowned at this. "Now, Sarah, I will
not have you cursing!"

"Then do something!" she demanded.

The devilish twinkle was back in his eyes as he
pointed out, "You really must be quite distressed
about this. You are speaking with your hands
again, princess, and you look like an angry robin
about to fly off in a huff."

"I'd use my feet as well if it would get me some
consideration around here!" she snapped.

"What would you have me do?" he asked
curiously. "Somehow I cannot see my orderly
laundering your feminine unmentionables for
you, nor sewing the torn lace on your bodice.
Would you have him button the back of your
dress for you each morning? And I can imagine
the sight you would be if he attempted to dress
your hair! No, Sarah, I told you this journey would have its discomforts for you. You
will just have to continue to make the best of
things."

"Someone could at least heat some water for
me, as long as they are doing so for you," she
pointed out. "And it would ease my mind a great
deal to have someone tend to emptying the
chamber pot for me."

"I suspect it would ease your embarrassment more than your mind, girl."

Sarah blushed, but continued her tirade. "I would also appreciate having someone to tidy my tent a bit now and then. If you could see the way they throw things about haphazardly after hastily erecting the dratted thing! Why, it is a wonder it hasn't tumbled down about my ears! There is barely room enough for a small dog, and then they just throw my belongings into it willy-nilly! Too, if someone can bring your supper to you, they can provide the same service to me, with little trouble."

"Shall I have someone make up your cot and turn down the bedcovers for you, too?" he suggested wryly.

"Why not?" she huffed. "They do so for you!"

"I happen to be the general," he reminded her.

"And I am the general's daughter!" she shot back.

"That and a smile might get you a cup of coffee, princess."

"Hah! I'll believe that when I see it happen!"

Thereafter, a few minor services were performed for her, so Sarah assumed that her father had issued orders to that effect. She suspected she was the butt of some hearty joking, but none of the men said anything. Probably they did not dare offend her. Sarah continued to grumble, hating the constant grime, the endless hours of traveling, the lack of amenities, the bugs and the snakes. By now everyone was used to hearing her complaints and tried to turn a deaf ear.

Their brief stops at various forts along the way were the best times for Sarah. There she could usually sleep in a real bed and obtain a tubful of hot water for a decent bath. She also had the company of other women at some of the forts, mostly officers' wives. With them, she could discuss the latest fashions, the merits of marriage and children, the latest women's gossip. They rarely touched upon the topic of the ongoing war.

The months and the miles wore on. Sarah lost count of the number of forts they visited. She had made a few new friends on some of their longer stops, when her father would leave her at the fort and take his troops out into the field to encounter enemy forces. Then he would return, and they would be on their way again.

She saw her first Indians in Kansas, a ragtag band of Kiowa. They were fierce enough looking to be frightening, and the very sight of them made a shiver dance up Sarah's spine. They were a small, rather poor band, however, and presented no threat to the larger Army troops. Throughout that summer, they encountered a number of tribes. Though Sarah never had any close contact with any of the Indians—indeed, she wished none, so fearsome was their painted, near-naked appearance—she became somewhat accustomed to seeing them from time to time.

Only once did the Army unit have to flee from any of the Indians. It was while they were traveling through Wyoming territory. Suddenly they found themselves under attack by a fairly large tribe of Utes. Two of the wagons had to be abandoned in the race, but they reached Fort Bridger unscathed, and Sarah privately thanked her lucky stars that neither of the lost wagons contained any of her precious belongings.

Now it was late August, and they were on their return trip east once more. In a few short weeks, they would be back in civilization, and Sarah was ready to embrace polite society with open arms. She could quite willingly live the rest of her life without hearing the sound of wolves and coyotes serenading the night. If she never saw another snake or wild animal, it would be too soon! Oh, to be back in her Washington world of opera and balls and servants and shops! Sarah could barely wait! Why, it would take weeks just to return her skin to its porcelain perfection. Her hands and hair were a fright! The very moment she reached home, Sarah intended to burn every article of clothing she'd brought with her. Her friends would laugh her out of town if they saw the condition of her gowns, so worn and frayed were they from months of wear and laundering. Yes, Sarah was long past ready to go home!

They were approaching Ft. Laramie, Wyoming, now, and Sarah was eager for a long, soaking bath to rid her of the dust of the road. She intended to beg, borrow, or steal some lotion to soothe her thirsty skin. Despite her best efforts, long months beneath the hot sun had turned her fair skin slightly tanned, only after she had first burned and peeled several times. There was nothing she could do to correct that, but at least she would be clean and smooth for a change.

She also longed desperately for some female companionship.

Sarah knew that this journey had been a trial for all concerned, and she had done nothing to help the situation with her constant complaining and bickering. She simply could not seem to help herself. If they did not reach civilization soon, she feared her father would strangle her, for she could tell he was heartily sick of hearing her bemoan her fate. She would not have been surprised to learn that his men were drawing straws to see who would win the honor of gagging her for the remainder of the trip. But now the end was in sight, and Sarah's spirits were beginning to revive. At least she had not been plagued so much by those disturbing nightmares. Only a very few times had she awakened from her dreams, and they had all been visions of the same strange man. Always the same. . . .

Night Hawk leaned casually against the outside wall of the trading post located inside Fort Laramie, waiting for his three friends to complete their purchases within the small building. They had come, at the end of their buffalo hunt, to trade skins and furs for tobacco and coffee and other white man's goods. The young Cheyenne chief's obsidian eyes scanned the cloudless skies overhead. In a few short weeks, the skies would be heavy with clouds, and snow would blanket Mother Earth in a mantle of white. Hunting had been good this summer, despite the intrusion of more and more white men into the land of his people. They would have plenty of furs and food in the coming winter, and for this he was thankful.

Unconsciously, his lean bronze fingers played with the pretty beads of the necklace in his hand. It was a gift for Little Rabbit, the woman who was now his wife. She had been his older brother's wife, until Many Arrows' death at the beginning of the summer. Many Arrows had fallen from his horse, killed instantly of a broken neck. As Cheyenne custom decreed, Night Hawk had then taken his brother's wife into his own tipi, making her his wife and responsibility from that day forward. He would also be responsible for the child Little Rabbit was carrying, his brother's child, to be born in the coming winter. He would raise his niece or nephew as his own.

Night Hawk did not resent the responsibilities thrust upon him by his brother's death, but he did yearn for children of his own and a wife of his own choosing. While Little Rabbit kept the lodge neat and tended to his meals and clothing, she did not share his sleeping mat. There would be no intimacy between them until after the child was born, and Night Hawk was glad for that. Even then, Night Hawk was not sure he would want to bed Little Rabbit, for his brother's taste in women was not his. Though she was fair enough to look upon, Night Hawk's heart was not touched when he gazed at her; his body did not yearn for hers. Her limpid eyes did not draw him, and her voice grated upon his ears. At times she seemed almost too willing to please. Obedience was one thing, blind stupidity another, and Night Hawk often felt smothered by her presence. He wanted a woman of his own heart, a soul-mate to ease his days and soothe his nights, someone to truly share his life and his love. He wanted children of his own loins. He was twenty-four winters now, a newly elected chief of his tribe, and it was time he started his own family.

Night Hawk was roused from his thoughts by the sound of a bugle announcing the arrival of troops. Minutes later, forty riders and several wagons filed through the open gates and pulled to a halt in the open area in the center of the fort. As the dust settled, Night Hawk saw the commander of the fort hurry from his office and rush to greet the new arrivals. This drew his attention, for the commander was saluting one of the officers at the head of the column. Though Night Hawk did not know all the ranks of the white army, he was sure this new man must out-rank the major-commander. Above the surrounding noise, he heard the major address the man as General Wise. Night Hawk understood very little of the white man's language, but he assumed this was the man's name, and that he was some sort of high chief to these blue-coat soldiers.

Night Hawk heard the woman's voice before he saw her, and his gaze swung in search of its owner, for the voice, though demanding, was still as lyrical as a birdsong. Then he caught sight of her, and the breath rushed from his body as if he had received a physical blow. She was sitting atop a horse, not astride as the men were, but with both legs to one side of the saddle. She had just removed a strange-looking headdress, and the sun was glinting down on her brilliant head, making her hair glow like fire. Night Hawk had never seen such hair before in all his life. It was magnificent to behold.

As someone spoke, she turned her head, and Night Hawk saw her face. It was pale perfection, so perfect to behold that an ache clutched at his belly. Her body was swathed in yards of the white man's cloth covering, but as one of the soldiers helped her from her horse, the cloth caught about the pommel, and Night Hawk got a quick glimpse of slender legs before her skirt fell once again to cover their white length.

He watched, spellbound, as she came nearer. Though she was tall, she walked with the supple grace of a doe, her head held at a proud angle. The dress she wore did nothing to disguise beguiling feminine curves that set Night Hawk's mind to spinning wonderful fantasies. Suddenly she smiled, and her beautiful face became almost as radiant as her hair, which he could now see more clearly. It was bound up in a braid and coiled atop her head like a length of rope, but he could discern hues from the brightest copper to the deepest red, like the leaves of autumn after the frost. Unbound, he knew it would reach to her waist, like a waving, living banner of flame.

Just as she was passing where he stood, she looked up and caught his dark gaze upon her. Night Hawk found himself gazing into eyes so blue that they rivaled the morning sky, so pale that they seemed to pierce his own. To his mind, they could have been no other color, for as her hair reminded him of fire, so did her eyes. They were the exact color of the very heart of the hottest of flames.

"*S'cou-te!*" The word for flame and fire seared itself into his befuddled brain as he stared at her in wonder. Their eyes locked for what seemed an eternity, and as he gazed raptly at this beautiful vision before him, he saw her eyes widen suddenly with raw emotion. It was more than fear he saw in them, though he had done nothing to frighten her. It seemed to be startled recognition he met in her look, mingled with disbelief and fright. As her gaze traversed his features, he saw her face lose much of its color, and she swayed as if she might fall faint at what she found there.

"No! No!" Sarah's exclamation was but a whisper, as she shook her head in stunned disbelief. "It cannot be!" Even as she gaped at the dark-skinned man before her, she sought to deny what her own eyes were seeing. "You can't be real! It cannot be you!"

Again her eyes scanned his face. It was all there! The lips, the skin, those deep, black eyes that would not release hers! This was the man from her dreams, the very one who had tormented her sleep for so many weeks!

He stood before her in the flesh, and now she had a living man to put to the face in her visions. His hair was, indeed, dark, so black it gleamed with blue highlights, even bound as it was in long braids on either side of his face. Her eyes flitted helplessly over his tall, lean body, registering the bronze skin, the smoothly muscled chest and arms, the long bare legs above dusty moccasins, the brief covering of the breechclout that was his only other clothing.

Unconsciously, her hand came out as if to ward him off. "My God, I don't believe this! You are an Indian!" Again, her words were a mere murmur, heard only by Night Hawk, who did not understand. Her actions spoke clearly, however, and Night Hawk dared not move, for fear she would flee, screaming. He could sense how close to sheer panic she was at this moment.

As they stood staring at each other, from the corner of his eye Night Hawk saw General Wise approach the woman from behind. The Army man laid his hand upon her shoulder, and the woman jumped in surprise.

"Sarah, are you all right?" At the sound of the general's voice, the woman Night Hawk now thought of as Flame almost wilted with relief. Night Hawk could see this in every motion of her body and face. "Are you coming along, dear? I thought you wanted that hot bath so badly." The general glanced curiously at Night Hawk, who had moved not so much as a muscle the whole time. Night Hawk still held his relaxed pose, though by now his body was tense, every muscle tightly coiled in reaction to this flame-haired beauty before him.

"Wh-what?" Sarah stuttered, then gathered her rioting senses. "Oh! Yes! Yes, Papa. I'm coming."

The general's eyes speared Night Hawk as he put a protective arm about Sarah's shoulders. "Was this Indian bothering you?" he asked gruffly.

Night Hawk met the white chief's gaze squarely, no emotion showing on his chiseled features,
though he felt the heat of the man's glare. He
sensed, more than saw, the change come over the
woman, the disdain that now replaced the fright.
Her fiery gaze now held a frosty contempt that
aimed arrows of pure ice in his direction. This
dismayed him more than her fear.

With a toss of her bright head, Sarah gave a
small brittle laugh. "No, Papa. Why, he was
standing so absolutely still, that I thought perhaps he was made of wood. I simply had to stop
for a second and see for sure." Her chilling eyes
raked Night Hawk once more before she turned
her back to him with haughty arrogance and
walked briskly away.

To all appearances, Sarah Wise had just dismissed the dark stranger from her mind. Only
Night Hawk's sharp gaze registered the small
shiver that shook her slender frame as his smoldering eyes followed her hasty retreat. Neither
did anyone else notice the slight curving of his
handsome lips as a thoughtful smile crept over
them.

Chapter 3

Night Hawk's friends were stunned almost speechless. They could not believe what Night Hawk was planning. It was much more bold and dangerous than anything any of them had ever before attempted, and Night Hawk was asking their aid in this daring coup.

"Your brains have turned to buffalo dung!" Crooked Arrow, Night Hawk's friend since childhood, exclaimed bluntly. "Steal a white woman from beneath the noses of a fort full of soldiers? Have you been chewing too many peyote buttons? You cannot do it without getting caught, and I, for one, do not intend to swing from a white man's rope!"

"It can be done. I want this woman with the hair of flame. If you will not help me, I will do this alone, but it will be accomplished much more easily by four Cheyenne than one. Two to steal the woman, one to stand as look-out, and one to stay with the horses." Night Hawk could not explain why he wanted this woman so desperately, so he did not even try. He only knew that he must have her. His body grew hot at the very thought of her, and his heart raced in his chest like a runaway horse. The thought of leaving Fort Laramie without her was unbearably painful to him, and he had a shaky suspicion that this was the woman he had been waiting for most of his life. This woman, with the brilliant blue eyes and fiery hair, was surely his soul-mate at long last!

As his mind pondered on this, he also wondered about the look of recognition he had seen flash in her eyes. Why should this be? He was certain that they had never before met. Yet he had not mistaken that look on her face; he was sure of that now. Could it be that she also recognized him as her soul-mate, though the idea obviously displeased her? It was a mystery he vowed to unravel.

He was also curious about her relationship to this general, this white Army chief. Was he her husband? Her lover? Her father? An uncle, perhaps? The very idea that he might be her husband or lover enraged Night Hawk. It would not alter her fate, of course, but Night Hawk desperately wanted Flame to come to him as a virgin. He wanted to be the one to initiate her into the ways of love. He wanted to take her as his wife, his mate, the mother of his children. He wanted to plant his seed deep within her and watch her grow big with his child. With all his being, Night Hawk wanted a child by this stunningly beautiful woman.

"If you take her now, the soldiers will guess who has stolen her," Red Feather said.

"Then we shall wait until tomorrow night to take her. The soldiers will think that we have gone from the area. They will not know that we are the ones who have stolen her, for they will think we are many miles from here when they discover her missing."

"What if the woman and the soldiers she travels with leave the fort before tomorrow night?" This question came from Stone Face, the third member of the group.

"Then we shall follow them and steal her when they have camped for the night. But I shall have this woman."

The hairbrush halted in mid-stroke as Sarah stifled a huge yawn. Though they had not traveled again today, she had been busy. As eager as she was to be home again, she had been glad for the chance to have her clothes laundered and her hair freshly washed, and to give her backside a rest for a day. One full day of relative ease from the rigors of the trail. What a relief it was—and what a relief that those Indians had left the fort! When she had questioned the major's wife, Sarah was informed that the Cheyenne had left shortly after her arrival the previous afternoon.

Early tomorrow morning, they would be on the trail once more. All her little chores were done, her clothing repacked and ready. The outfit she had chosen to wear for the next day was neatly arranged on a nearby chair. Now she was ready for a good night's sleep in the comfortable little bed.

Sarah laid the hairbrush aside, blew out the lamp, and snuggled down under the sheet. Her last thought was of how fortunate she had been to have been given a room all to herself at this stop. The bare little room, with the bed, a single chair, and a tiny nightstand made her bedroom at home seem palatial by comparison, but it also seemed like heaven compared to some of the conditions in which she had been forced to sleep on this horrid journey. At least this room was clean and private.

A slight rustling sound disturbed Sarah's peaceful sleep. She shifted, stretching her cramped limbs. The long crescent of her lashes fluttered and lifted lazily. As her hazy gaze met that of her dream stranger, her heart lurched within her breast. Onyx eyes blazed down into hers, holding her prisoner within their inky depths. It was the dream again, so familiar now and so real—too real! This time Sarah could feel the warmth of his breath fanning her face as he bent close to her. The same taunting smile she knew so well curved his lips, but now they moved ever so slightly as he whispered, "*S'cou-te.*"

At the sound of his deep, rough voice, Sarah's eyes widened in alarm. Sleep fled on swift wings as she felt his voice ripple through her in icy waves of fear. Never before had her dream stranger spoken. Never before had she felt the brush of long dark braids against her cheek. In desperation she closed her eyes, praying that when next she opened them, the vision of this man would be gone. But when she dared to look once more, he was still there, staring down at her. The breath caught in her throat as he lifted long fingers to her hair, murmuring softly as the silky strands caressed his bronze skin. Then one long, calloused finger was tracing the shape of her lips, and she felt the heat of his touch like lightning searing through her. A whimper escaped her frozen throat, and immediately the finger was replaced by a strong hand over her mouth.

Raw terror broke through the dreamlike state that had held her motionless. This was no dream! This was real! This man was no vision, but flesh and blood! This was the Indian she had seen the day before, and he was bending over her bed! Sarah tried to scream, but it was too late. His hard hand muffled her shriek too well. With a strength born of fear, she tried to throw him off her, only to find her arms bound to her sides, his weight holding her to the bed. Thrash as she might, she could not dislodge him. Within moments, she was breathless, held helpless in his savage grasp. Tears ran heedlessly down her cheeks as she stared up into his relentless black eyes.

When he felt her strength melt away, he murmured something in that strange language of his, something soft that sounded oddly like an apology. Then, before she could comprehend what he was doing, the hand over her mouth was replaced by a crudely wadded cloth crammed between her chattering teeth; another cloth tied about her head held the gag in place. Flailing arms and legs did not deter him as he swiftly rolled her into the dark bed blanket, covering and binding her, head to toe.

Through her thick cocoon of blankets, she felt him lift her from the bed. His arms were strong about her as he carried her a few steps. Then she barely heard a low exchange of muffled words, and she was shifted about again. Sarah wriggled violently, fruitlessly. The breath was knocked from her tortured lungs as she found herself slung over a broad shoulder. A few hearty bounces later, she felt herself hefted upward, hard fingers digging through the blanket into her ribs. Then, to her utter terror, she was sailing downward, falling helplessly! Her scream echoed only in her head as she braced herself for a hard landing. Once more, the air left her body as she tumbled into another pair of waiting arms. Her pained exclamation was met with a muffled "Oof!" from whoever had caught her, and together they crashed to the ground. More soft whispers, and what sounded like laughter. Then she was hanging upside down again, jounced painfully as her captor ran lightly across the uneven ground.

"Your white woman eats well, Night Hawk," Stone Face grunted as he handed Sarah's bundled body back to Night Hawk, having caught her when Night Hawk dropped her from the top of the outer wall of the fort. "She weighs many stones."

The friends laughed softly, and Night Hawk retorted, "You are becoming as soft as an old woman, Stone Face. My woman is but a bundle of feathers."

Stone Face grimaced. "Wet feathers, perhaps, on a fat goose."

"Sshh!" Crooked Arrow warned. "Come. We must hurry away from here. Would you have us caught while you giggle like girls?"

They hurried to the place where Red Feather waited with their horses. With callous disregard for Sarah's comfort, Night Hawk slung her stomach-down across his horse's back like a sack of flour and mounted swiftly behind her. With a touch of his heels to the stallion's flank, they were racing into the night, Sarah bouncing roughly with each long stride.

Wrapped like an Egyptian mummy inside her blanket, Sarah feared she would soon suffocate. Fright had first robbed her of her breath, and then the blanket had compounded her problems. Now, bounced about upon the bony back of the galloping horse, she gasped for air. Each time her ribs connected painfully with the horse's spine, precious breath left her. The blood rushed to her head, pounding ever harder. Colored lights danced before her eyes, against a blood-red background. Terror still held her in its overwhelming grip, but even that lessened as consciousness slipped away bit by bit. The last sound to reach her ears was the frantic pulse of her heart pounding in time to the horse's hoofs. Her last coherent thoughts were, *Perhaps better to die this way, than suffer whatever this savage has planned for me.* Then, uncontrollably, her young heart cried out rebelliously, *But I don't want to die!* Finally, *Oh, Papa! I'm so sorry! Please help me!*

Sarah awoke to rude slaps against her cloth-chafed cheeks. Even as she sought to escape the light blows, her eyes flew open to behold that same dark face.

"Not again!" she mumbled groggily, thinking she was dreaming again. "Please. Not again."

The man above her shifted slightly away, the night shadows almost hiding him from her. Then he was back, holding an animal skin bag to her dry lips. As he tipped the vessel, water poured into her mouth, then down her neck when she failed to swallow fast enough. Choking and gasping, Sarah tried to sit up, only to find herself still bound in the blanket. "Enough!" she managed to croak. "Are you trying to drown me?" Her eyes flashed blue flames at him, even in the dark of the moonlit forest.

She saw his teeth gleam in a white grin at her sassy retort, even as he grumbled something at her in his guttural language. Motioning for her to be quiet, he waved the newly removed gag before her face in a threat that needed no words to be understood. Her wary gaze now moved from the cloth to his face and, swallowing hard on the fear gathering anew within her, she managed to nod. "I'll be quiet," she whispered shakily, wondering what would happen next. Suddenly, the confining blanket seemed a comforting barrier between

her and this frightening savage. As long as she
was wrapped within its folds, she would be safe
from him, from his detestable touch.

Mere seconds later, he disproved this fragile
theory. When she saw his hands coming toward
her, fingers outspread, her heart faltered to a
thudding halt. Did he mean to strangle her? Oh,
God! But his hands reached not for her slim
throat. Instead, they framed her delicate face in a
strangely protective gesture. He stared deeply
into her wide blue eyes for the longest time, his
thumbs caressing her cheekbones almost rhyth-
mically. Sarah's heartbeat resumed—and tripled
its pace. Again he smiled, and when his fingertips
rested on the thin skin of her temples, she knew
that he felt her pulse pounding madly there. He
seemed aware of her smallest reaction to him.
When a tremor coursed through her, his hands
tightened ever so slightly about her face, as if to
still her trembling.

Long bronze fingers slid upward, scissoring
into the depths of her unbound hair. With his
chest now resting over hers, Sarah felt his in-
drawn breath. Drawing long, fiery strands loose,
he sifted them through his fingers, a look of awe
upon his strong features. He crushed the strands,
wondering at the silkiness. In a move that further
startled her, he buried his face in the shimmering
mass, and she heard him sigh and murmur softly.

Oh, merciful heavens! she thought in blind
panic. He wants my hair! He's going to scalp me!

When his lips left her hair to find the sensitive
flesh of her neck, Sarah cried out in fearful
protest. "No! Oh, God! Don't do this!" Bruises

and sore ribs forgotten, she thrashed about beneath him. "Stop! Please! Let me go!" Useless arms beat against the confining blanket in frantic effort, hands clawing at the cloth as her hysteria reached new heights.

"No!" she shrieked. Using the only weapon left to her, she sank her sharp teeth deeply into his bare shoulder.

Her assailant gave a surprised grunt, but Sarah's small victory was short-lived. Fresh tears swamped her eyes as long, lean fingers tightened cruelly on her hair, pulling steadily until she was sure the roots were being ripped from her scalp. On a gasp of pain, she released her hold on his shoulder. Her head was pulled back with such force that she feared her neck would snap.

Fury blazed from his eyes as he glared down at her. One hand still gripping her hair, the other now clamped about her chin like a vise. From deep within his chest, he growled what Sarah was sure was some vile curse. She tried to escape the force of his angry eyes, but there was nowhere to go. A sob escaped her trembling lips, drawing his attention momentarily. Then his demon's gaze captured hers in a long look once more, a look that spoke clearly of his anger and supreme domination over her. Slowly, deliberately, he lowered his face to hers, taking her lips with his in a kiss of calculated cruelty. His lips ground down upon hers. With her teeth tightly clenched, Sarah felt her dry lip split and tasted the coppery flavor of her own blood. The iron grip of his fingers forced her jaws apart, parting her lips and allowing his tongue entry into her mouth, yet preventing her from biting him again.

She could barely breathe, as panic overwhelmed her. Try as she might, she could not wrench her face from his. Every nerve and muscle in her body was as taut as a piano wire, ready to snap at any moment, along with her sanity. Tears raced down her face, wetting her hair. Sobs shook her chest beneath the weight of his. Then, miraculously, something changed. The lips covering hers were no longer so forceful. Instead of insisting, they urged, they caressed. The tongue probing her mouth was now gently searching. His mouth paused to nibble lightly at hers, his tongue sweeping out to lick lightly at her wounded lip. He sipped sweetly at her swollen mouth, as a hummingbird might at a delicate flower. He tasted of her lingeringly, deeply, before finally easing his mouth from hers.

When she had bitten him, Night Hawk had been stunned and immediately furious. He had not meant to frighten her so badly; he had merely been so enthralled with the beauty of her face and the wonder of her glorious hair that he had let his senses lead him further than he would have wished. With his friends sleeping nearby, he had no intention of bedding Flame this night. Their first time together must be special, a time for the two of them alone.

That this woman had spirit to match the fire in her hair was a delight to him, but he was now aware that it must be tempered. Never would he wish to break her fine spirit, yet never must he allow her anger to be directed toward him. Flame must learn this, even if it took harsh lessons to teach her. Each time she turned her temper on him, he must be firm with her, until she learned to honor him as her husband and master. He was a chief among a noble tribe of Northern Cheyenne, and he could not afford to have his friends and fellow warriors laughing at him because he failed to control his woman.

If she allowed him, Night Hawk would lead her gently into her new life as his wife, but it was up to her whether that path would be easy or difficult. He knew it would be hard for her to adjust. She would miss her family and her life in the white world. Night Hawk wished he knew her language, or she his, for it would make communication so much easier. He hoped she could learn his tongue without too much difficulty. Perhaps she could teach him the white man's tongue while he instructed her in Cheyenne. Yes, that would benefit both, for a wise man learns his enemy's ways, and it could prove worthwhile to understand the white man's words. Little Rabbit could teach Flame much of what was expected of her as a chief's wife, but he would undertake the chore of teaching her his language himself, as he would teach her obedience to his will. This night was just the start of many lessons for his flame-haired beauty.

Many heartbeats after the kiss was ended, Night Hawk held her to him. Finally, when he felt the tension in her body ease, he loosened his grip. Her wary gaze followed as he reluctantly reached once more for the discarded gag. He tried to tell her with his eyes that he did not wish to hurt her, but she must not be allowed to cry out in the night, lest there be enemies lurking about. The cloth once more securely about her mouth, he then unwrapped the blanket from about her. Immediately her eyes filled again with terror. Swiftly he lay down beside her and pulled her into the curve of his body, her back to him, and covered them both with the blanket. With her head pillowed on his hard shoulder, he crooned softly to her. Though he knew she could not understand his words, he hoped the tone of his voice would help to calm her fears.

It was a long time before her quivering ceased. At last the measure of her breathing told him that she slept. Gradually, her limbs relaxed against him. Night Hawk drifted into a light sleep, his arms wrapped tightly about his bright prize.

Chapter
4

Sarah's lessons began early the next morning. She was rudely awakened just as the sun was beginning to color the eastern horizon. Stiff and sore from the rough ride the night before, she was not in the best of humor to start with. Then to awaken within the arms of her Cheyenne captor did not improve her temper. He did not touch her again, other than to remove the chafing gag from her cotton-dry mouth. He provided her with water and some foul mixture of what seemed to be fat mixed with dried meat and berries. Supposedly, it was some sort of food, for he placed a blob of it in her open palms and gestured for her to eat it.

Sarah stared at the unappetizing mess for several minutes before gathering the courage to taste it. Then, as hungry as she was, she was sorry she had. It tasted every bit as bad as it looked. As her captor and his cohorts were chanting what seemed to be prayers, Sarah was tempted to dump her meal on the ground behind her, but the moment she tried, her captor caught her and shook his head vehemently. "*Oui-then-e-luh',*" he commanded sternly, gesturing again for her to eat. With a grimace and a hateful look as he continued to watch her, she ate.

Her second lesson in Cheyenne ways came in short order. No sooner had she finished eating than her dark captor nearly frightened her to death as he tore a strip of cloth from the hem of her nightgown. Wetting it with fresh water, he handed it to her and directed her to cleanse the angry bite wound on his shoulder. When she hesitated, he sent her a black look and uttered some command in his gruff language that promised punishment if she disobeyed. She understood the threat, if not the words, and reluctantly did as he bade her. Then he scooped some foul-smelling ugly green ointment onto her trembling fingers, indicating that she should apply that to the wound also. Finally, he tore another strip of cloth from her gown and ordered her to bind it about his shoulder. By the time she was finished, Sarah was visibly shaking, both in terror of what he might want next, and in anger at having to obey him and having her only garment torn to shreds. She was much relieved when he required nothing further from her.

If privacy was rare among her father's troops, it was now nonexistent. Sarah was horrified when her captor refused to let her out of his sight in order to perform her morning rituals. After many hand signals she managed to convince him to let her squat behind a low bush for her necessary duties. With all but her head concealed from the view of the four grinning Indians, and her face as red as a ripe cherry, she hurriedly relieved herself.

Wrapped once again in her blanket, this time merely to cover herself from their avid gazes, since she wore nothing but her thin cotton night shift, she was hefted onto the back of the horse once more. There was another conflict when her captor insisted on putting her astride the horse. Sarah had never in her life ridden astride as a man would. She had always ridden side-saddle, and to find nearly the entire length of her legs exposed was mortifying! However, even this was preferable to riding slung over the horse's back as she had been the night before. This morning, she was to ride behind her captor on his horse, her arms tied about his waist. She could only guess that he did not want her to slip off and somehow manage to escape, though how she might have done that on foot with four mounted Indians chasing her, she could not imagine. At least he had not replaced the gag, and for that small favor she was grateful.

"You know, of course," she informed him irritably as he bound her wrists together before him, "my father will have your head for this! He will find me, and he will find you, too! He is a very important general in the United States Army!"

Something in her speech gained his attention, for he twisted about to gaze pointedly at her. "Gen-e-ral?" he said.

"Yes, General. A very important white chief."

At this he frowned severely and muttered something she could not begin to fathom.

Night Hawk recognized the word general, though the rest of her speech was unfamiliar to him. Again he wondered what her relationship to this man was. It irritated him greatly that she could not tell him. The rest of her predicament amused him as much as it did his friends. He could hardly keep from laughing at her embarrassment at having to ride with her legs uncovered, and he could tell, as they rode along, that she was doing her best to sit upright and avoid touching him. This would not last long, for they would ride hard and long this day, putting many miles between themselves and the fort. She would soon tire and rest against him. She would soon learn to save her puny resistance for more important issues.

Having her ride behind him was not for his benefit alone, and he did not lash her to him merely to keep her from escaping. The trail ahead was rough, and Night Hawk did not want to risk her tumbling from the horse's back and injuring herself. He could not carry her before him on the horse, for he needed his hands free for his weapons.

Night Hawk was right in assuming that Sarah was desperately trying to avoid his touch. Not that he was as smelly or filthy as she would have supposed an Indian to be; but she would never willingly touch this savage who had dared to abduct her. He was a crude heathen, and she would resist him at every turn. She vowed to escape him at the very first opportunity—or die trying. How she would survive the wilderness or find her way back to the fort, she did not know, but at least she would try.

Sarah wondered if her abduction had been discovered yet. How she wished she had possessed the presence of mind to scream when she had first awakened to find him looming over her! But she had mistakenly thought, at first, that she was dreaming. By the time she had realized her error, it was too late. Still, she wondered how the Indians had managed to breach the walls of the fort and steal her away without alarming any of the guards. Thinking back, she could not recall hearing any sort of alarm go up. Had they killed the guards on duty, or merely been so silent that they had entered and left undetected?

As the morning wore on, Sarah knew her disappearance must have been discovered. Her father had wanted to get an early start for Fort Kearney, which was a good week and a half's distance from Fort Laramie. Her father must be frantic with worry by now. If she knew him, he would have scoured the fort for her, and finding her gone, he would question the guards unmercifully. Heads would roll before all was done! The thought of her father's grand tirade made her smile, despite her worry. Within half an hour, he would have men mounted and a search party would be on its way, with General Wise in the lead. Sarah could only hope that her abductors had left a trail, and that her father could catch up with them before . . .

Here she faltered, not wanting to contemplate what might lie ahead, what these Indians might have planned for her. Would she be tortured? Killed? Worse? She dared not dwell on it. The fright of it all would surely unhinge her mind, if she were to think on it too deeply. As it was, tears dripped steadily down her face, and a quiver of intense fear trembled through her.

Night Hawk felt the tremor race through her, and could only imagine what Flame must be thinking. Again he wished there were some way to ease her mind, to calm her fears. Remorse tore at him when he felt her salty tears splash against his bare back. He felt her sorrow, and pitied her, yet he would have acted no differently had he to do it all again. Flame was his, as she was meant to be his from the beginning of time. Their fates had been written in the stars and carried on the winds even before their own births. No matter the pain it caused her, it must be this way, for she was his soul-mate, the one true love of his life.

Eventually, Sarah gave up the struggle to remain upright. Her arms and back ached, and her tailbone felt as if it were being driven into the horse's backside. Her head now wobbled precariously atop her stiff neck with every step the animal took. With dull capitulation, she sagged against her captor, letting his broad back support her. A whole new set of problems now assailed her weary senses, for his bronze back was bare,

the skin warm against her cheek. With each
stride she could feel the honed male muscles
move in smooth coordination with the stallion's
gait. Even a fool could tell that this man was in
prime physical condition; there was not an ounce
of fat on his well-muscled frame. Though he was
probably in his mid-twenties, about the same age
as James Moore, Sarah was willing to bet that he
was in much better shape than the good doctor
had ever been.

The direction of her thoughts turned to her
friends and family back home. What would they
think when they heard that she had been abducted by savage Indians? Aunt Emily would have
hysterics, at the least! Would her cousins and
friends miss her, weep for her, perhaps pray for
her? Would they care what became of her, or
would they shake their heads at her fate and soon
forget her? As her best friend, Addie would surely
worry, at least for a while. Of course, she would
also recall how she had warned Sarah about this
very thing happening; and she and James would
probably console one another.

What about James? How long would he remember how much he had claimed to care for
her? Or had he already forgotten her and turned
to Addie? Damnation! Sarah could have kicked
herself. She should have married James while she
had the chance! Then she wouldn't be in this
predicament. She would be safe and sound in
Washington—bored silly, no doubt, but safe. As
it was, she had gone pell-mell from the lap of
luxury to the very halls of hell!

Fresh tears stung her eyes, and Sarah sniffed in angry disgust. She, who rarely cried, was turning into a regular weeping willow! She was even beginning to wonder what would happen to all the beautiful clothes hanging in her closets back home—as if it were already certain that she would never again wear them. She had to stop thinking so negatively! Surely her father would soon find her. Surely they were somewhere close behind at this very moment. By nightfall she might be safe in her father's arms once more, hearing him rant and rave. Then again . . . A tiny corner of her mind jeered silently at her, *Well, Sarah, you wanted adventure! You've certainly got your pretty little hands full of it now!*

Sarah blew at the feather that was dangling down her captor's back. It had been tickling her nose in the most irritating fashion for the last hour! With her hands bound about his waist, there was no way to dislodge the offending object. She could neither trap it beneath her head, nor shift it from its position. She tried turning her head in the other direction, but the feather followed, as if by magic, to tickle the back of her neck. She rubbed her nose roughly against the Indian's back in an effort to alleviate the tickling sensation assaulting her.

Finally, in exasperation, she tugged at it with her teeth. She cared not if she pulled all his black hair out; she intended to rid herself of that aggravating feather once and for all. When the feather failed to come loose, she spat it from her mouth and nipped petulantly at her captor's bare

shoulder blade. Not hard enough to break the
skin, for she had learned her lesson there. Just
hard enough to get his attention.

Sarah could not see the smile that flirted at
Night Hawk's lips when he felt her fussing with
the feather. Astute as always, he soon guessed
what her problem was, but he wanted to see how
she might solve it on her own. Now, as she
nipped at his skin, he relented, twisting about to
stare straight-faced at her.

"Will you get that dratted dirty feather out of
my face?" she railed waspishly. "I don't know
why you are wearing it in the first place! It
doesn't do a thing for you, you know. It would
look a good deal better on one of my hats, if not
on the bird you stole it from!"

Her haughty look spoke volumes, and it was all
Night Hawk could do not to burst out laughing.
Before his humor could become apparent, he
turned abruptly forward again, and no matter
how she squirmed and wriggled and puffed, he
ignored her once again. He shared the joke and a
broad grin with his friends and rode on, enjoying
the feel of her breasts bouncing lightly against his
back, her hair and smooth cheek caressing his
bare flesh.

They paused briefly in the early afternoon to
rest and water the horses, and it was not until
after nightfall that they stopped for the day. As
they had the night before, they built no campfire,
and Sarah could only assume the Indians considered it unwise in case they were being followed.
They camped near a small stream, where the men

watered their mounts and refilled their water skins.

She wished her captor would remove the bonds from about her wrists, but even when he gave her food and water he left her hands tied, forcing her to manage as best she could. This greatly frustrated her, for she had begun to wonder if she might be able to communicate with him if she had the proper use of her hands. The sign language she had learned from Maude had come from the Indians originally, and Sarah understood many of her captor's signals. Still, they were very simple commands, and the gestures he used would have been common even to a white person trying to communicate to someone without aid of words. It was a moot point anyway, since her hands were never free to try.

By this time, Sarah would have sold her soul for a decent bath and a change of clothes, but considering the lack of privacy afforded her, she was not about to suggest bathing in the inviting little stream. The dirtier and smellier she was, the better, for then perhaps she would not appear as attractive to these savages. Sarah would have had to be blind to miss the lustful looks directed toward her all day, and not just from the man she rode with.

Sarah had not misjudged the situation by much. No sooner had they eaten their cold meal, of what she now knew the Indians called pemmican, than a fierce argument ensued among the men. From the numerous gestures and glances directed her way, she deduced that they were discussing her. One man in particular was arguing loudly and glaring at her captor, who returned glare for fierce glare.

"We helped you to steal this woman from the fort. Now we should share in the prize," Crooked Arrow argued heatedly. "Why should you be the only one to enjoy her white body?"

"If you, as my friends, require payment from me, I will find another manner in which to return the favor, but I will not share my woman with you. She will be touched by no man but me. I will gladly kill the first man who dares to try." Night Hawk faced his fellow warriors defiantly, ready to fight even his best friends for his right to this woman.

"If you desire her so fiercely, why have you not yet taken her?" Crooked Arrow scoffed. "Has she cast a spell upon you that leaves you unmanned? If you cannot claim her properly, do not despise us for wanting to do what you fail to accomplish, Night Hawk."

Night Hawk's eyes blazed dark fire at Crooked Arrow, but before he could speak, Red Feather said, "She is but a slave, Night Hawk. Stolen goods to be used by all. Is this not true? Why become so angry over such a small matter?"

"She is more than a mere slave," Night Hawk refuted. "I mean to take her for my wife."

Three pair of eyes stared at him in astonishment. Crooked Arrow was the first to break the stunned silence. "You have joined the Crazy Ones, my friend. Your mind has flown from your body. She is beautiful, yes, but it is crazy to think of taking this white woman to wife."

Stone Face spoke up now, with a terse laugh.

"His mind will not be all to fly from his body once Little Rabbit hears of this! I can only guess which she will sever first—his head or his manhood!"

"Little Rabbit will have nothing to say in this matter. She will accept it and abide by my wishes, as any other Cheyenne wife must do when her husband decides to take a second wife. Her status in my tipi will not be lessened; there will merely be two more hands to tend to the chores. She grows heavy with my brother's child and should be glad of the help."

Red Feather shook his head. "You are asking for trouble, Night Hawk, if you truly believe that," he predicted. "Little Rabbit has not yet shared your sleeping mat with you. She will resent it greatly to have this white woman share it before her."

"That is my concern, Red Feather."

Red Feather shrugged. "Then the woman is yours. I will not bring ruin to our friendship over this, and you owe me nothing for my help. I owed you a debt for the time you saved me from that mountain cat."

"I, too, relinquish all claim to the woman," Stone Face stated. With a grin that belied his name, for he was in truth a cheerful and humorous man despite his rough-hewn features, he added, "I may live to regret my generosity, but Shining Star would carve my heart out with a dull knife if I were to touch another woman, and I am a coward when it comes to my wife's rages."

All but Crooked Arrow laughed at Stone Face's jest. He speared Night Hawk with a determined glare. "I do not relinquish my claim, Night Hawk. I, too, wish this woman, though I am not stupid enough to want a white whore for my wife." He reached for a leather pouch at his waist. "I will match wits with you in throwing stones to see who gets her, and that will determine her owner."

"No." Night Hawk was not willing to gamble with stakes so dear to his heart. The risk of losing Flame in this way was too great to chance on a throw of the stones, a game of pure chance. "We will wait until we reach the village and let the council elders decide what we must do."

"They will decree that we fight for her," Crooked Arrow said.

"So it shall be, then," Night Hawk answered in a cold voice.

"Are you so willing to spill your blood for this white woman's favors?" Crooked Arrow asked scornfully. "Why not take her into your lodge for a time, and when you tire of her you can easily discard her. I am not so greedy that I cannot wait until then, nor so vain that I would care that you have used her first."

The tension in the air was thick as Night Hawk faced his boyhood friend with smoldering anger. "You test our friendship severely this night, Crooked Arrow. I have said that this woman will be my wife. Red Feather and Stone Face have respected my wishes in this matter. If you cannot, then we shall fight. But we shall wait until we reach the village to do so, for I would not endanger us all when we are so far from our camp, with enemies about. A Cheyenne chief must put the needs of his people above his own." This was a subtle, if painful, reminder to Crooked Arrow that his rank of warrior was below Night Hawk's status of chief in their tribe.

"Be warned, Crooked Arrow. I have sworn this night before the witness of our friends that I will kill any man who touches this woman whom I claim as mine alone. I will earn my right to call her wife. I will fight you for her, if I must; and once she is mine, I will gladly slay the first man to touch her."

Chapter 5

Rain! Cold, miserable rain soaked through the thin blanket Sarah had pulled like a tarpaulin over her head. Again, this second day of captivity, she was riding behind Night Hawk, her arms bound about his trim brown waist. She sneezed for the third time in as many minutes and huddled her shivering form closer to his, trying to absorb some of his body heat. If she lived to be a thousand, she knew she would always hereafter hate the smell of wet wool. Not for the first time, she wondered how he could ride nearly naked and still be so warm, while she was turning blue to the tips of her fingers. Goose flesh peppered her bare legs, and she kept wriggling her feet to restore feeling to her numb toes. How could an August rain be so bone-chilling?

Night Hawk could have told her that autumn and winter often came early in this land of his forefathers. Before long, snows as deep as a horse's bridle would blanket the earth. Still, the rain this day was unusually cold for late summer, for it was driven by a cool northern wind that held the bite of the winter to come. Even the four Cheyenne warriors, as used to the elements as they were, were uncomfortable. It was only their desire to reach their village as soon as possible that prevented them from taking shelter until the deluge ceased.

The driving rain made travel twice as dangerous, for the sounds of the rain and wind covered any noise of approaching enemies. It obscured vision and slowed their progress, and it turned the dry earth to mud, thus making it impossible for them to travel without leaving behind a well-marked trail, at least until the pelting rain washed out their tracks behind them.

It was mid-day when disaster nearly struck— or near-rescue, from Sarah's point of view. They were nearing a juncture of forest trails, when Night Hawk suddenly held up his hand in a silent signal to halt. The well-trained Indian ponies made no sound as they awaited their masters' commands. The four warriors sat as still as carved statues, straining their ears and eyes for signs of danger. Alert and wary, they waited with limitless patience.

Then they heard it—the sound of muffled hoofbeats, the jangle of metal on metal from horses' bridles, the soft creak of saddle leather. Knowing that these sounds were not made by

Indians, but by white men, Night Hawk reacted
swiftly and silently. Without warning, he quickly
unbound Flame's arms from about him. Before
she even realized that she was free, he leaped
from his horse. With one hand immediately
covering her mouth, lest she cry out a warning,
he dragged her down and carried her swiftly into
the concealing trees at the edge of the path.
There, he roughly shoved the gag into her mouth,
bound her hand and foot, and covered her with
the wet brown blanket. Within mere heartbeats,
he had rejoined his friends on the trail.

Sarah was confused and frightened. Why had
they stopped? And why had her captor suddenly
ripped her from the horse's back and dragged her
into the woods? Even as she struggled to free
herself from the confines of the blanket—quite a
task with her arms tied behind her—she heard
the soft sounds of horses walking away. They
were leaving! Oh, God! They were leaving her
here alone, bound and helpless in the wilderness!
As much as she wished to escape them, the perils
of this new situation were too staggering to
ponder! Was she to be left here to die of hunger
and thirst? Or to be found and eaten by some
wild animal?

Blind panic made her struggle wildly against
the rawhide thongs that bound her wrists and
ankles. Her mad thrashing dislodged the blanket
from her face, but try as she might, she could not
spit the cloth from her mouth. Tears blurred her
vision and clogged her throat, making it all that
much more difficult to breathe. She was forced to

calm her struggles just to catch her breath once more.

It was then she heard the sound of horses again. Straining to hear above the sound of the pouring rain, she thought at first that it was her abductors returning. Why? What had they done in so short a time that they had to leave her here like this? Had they done it merely to frighten her? Was it some kind of cruel game to them?

Then Sarah heard the sound of voices—voices speaking English! Oh, sweet heaven! White men! Craning her head, she caught a glimpse of blue through the trees. Soldiers! There was no denying the sight of those distinctive Union uniforms! Renewed energy poured through her at the thought of rescue so close at hand. With every ounce of breath in her body, Sarah screamed. She shrieked again and again with all her might. Wide, disbelieving blue eyes watched in horror as the soldiers passed by without hearing. She lay mere yards from them, yet they did not hear her! One of the men spat a long brown stream of tobacco juice just feet from where she struggled, yet even with his head turned in her direction, he failed to notice her.

Suddenly the column stopped, and Sarah could have fainted with relief. They must have spotted her at last! Oh, thank the good Lord! She was about to be rescued! Yet no one came walking through the trees. No one seemed to be looking her way or dismounting. What were they waiting for? She strained her ears to hear what was being said.

"Unshod horses, Captain," she heard a man say. "Four of them. Probably Indian ponies, and the tracks are real fresh."

"Looks like they heard us coming and doubled back," another voice announced.

"We gonna track 'em, sir?" a third man asked. "They's twelve of us and only four o' them."

"Didn't know you could count that high, Smitty," another man put in jokingly, causing several of the men to laugh.

Smitty took offense at this. "Yeah, well, mebe I ain't had yore edjucation, Mr. Smart Ass, but I know Injun signs when I see 'em, and I'm still alive to talk about it. One o' these days yore purty yeller hair is gonna be swingin' from some Injun's belt, 'cause you ain't got the sense God gave a goat when it comes to soldierin' out here, city boy!"

"That's enough, you two!" The sharp command cut into their argument. "We have enough problems without you men bickering at one another. Chances are these Indians are not far ahead, so I want each of you to keep a sharp eye peeled and your mouth shut. If we are lucky, they are from some friendly tribe. It seems they want to avoid a confrontation with us. Just the same, stay alert. Let's move out."

Sarah could not believe her ears! They were leaving! They hadn't noticed her at all! Crazed with panic, she wriggled and thrashed, pounding her feet against the ground and screaming until her throat was raw. She must get their attention! Why didn't they hear her? To her own ears, her screams sounded so loud! If only one of them would look her way! Surely they could not fail to see her! As if to prove how wrong she was, one of the men shifted in his saddle and looked almost directly at her. He was so close she could see the color of his eyes and count his teeth! Yet he turned about again with no sign that he had seen anything at all!

Slowly they rode off, and Sarah wanted to die. Tears flooded her eyes, blurring the last blue uniform as it disappeared from view. So close! So close to rescue! Why? Why? Devastating disappointment pierced her heart like shards of broken glass. As the last sounds of hoofbeats faded away in the distance, Sarah lay her head down in the mud and sobbed brokenly.

Stupid, stupid men! If they could see the tracks of the horses, why had they not noticed her captor's footprints leading off the forest path? In a moment of severe disappointment and anger, Sarah wished death upon all of them for their stupidity and resulting failure to save her. There was no way she could know that her rash wish was soon to be granted. Some minutes later, had she not been sobbing so hard, she would have heard the sound of shouts and brief gunfire.

How long she lay there crying her heart out, Sarah could not be sure. It seemed an eternity. When she had cried all the tears there were to cry, she lay quietly, tormented by her painful thoughts. Now that rescue was no longer a possibility, her fears of being left here alone returned. The upraised root of a nearby tree was poking her in the side, but she no longer had the strength

to move. She lay miserably, letting the cold rain
beat down upon her. The rain eased to a drizzle,
and suddenly Sarah became aware of the other
sounds about her—eerie, scuttling forest sounds,
sounds of animals scurrying through the brush.
The longer she lay there, the more frightened she
became. What if no one came? Ever?

Suddenly, out of nowhere, with no sound
preceding them, two moccasin-clad feet bracket-
ed her head. Sarah jerked violently in surprise.
Relief made her weak, but then another thought
seared through her weary brain. What if this were
not her captor, but some other Indian? Her
breath caught in her throat, threatening to choke
her. The thought was terrifying, and Sarah did
not even try to reason why she might prefer one
savage captor to another, but she did. Two days
of traveling with Night Hawk had bred a certain
familiarity. Though she feared him and what he
might do to her, to her befuddled mind he was
still preferable to yet another savage Indian.

With terror clutching at her heart, she raised
fearful eyes past the long legs, the leather breechclout, the hard bare chest. Finally, her gaze dared
to find his face, and she heaved a silent sigh of
relief. It was him. It was her Indian.

Night Hawk gazed down at her dirty, tear-
streaked face, the swollen red-rimmed eyes, and
he felt kin to the lowest of creatures. He could
only guess at how frightened she must have been,
all alone and helpless, wondering what was happening. Yet it could not have been helped. He
wondered if she had heard the soldiers pass by, if

she had agonized over not being able to call out to them.

He knew they had not spotted her, or she would have been with them when he and his friends had fought with the white men. The four Indians had gone back along the trail a short distance, then concealed themselves and waited. Had one of the soldiers not spotted Red Feather, they would have passed by without incident. But the young white man had panicked at the sight of the Cheyenne brave and tried to shoot Red Feather. In the blink of an eye, all was confusion as the other soldiers joined in the melee, shouting and shooting at everything and nothing in blind panic. Their leader could not control them or bring order to his troops.

The battle had been brief. In the confusion, it was an easy thing for the hidden Cheyenne warriors to kill the soldiers. One by one the bluecoats fell from their horses, arrows piercing their white flesh. Only two of the soldiers had fled swiftly enough to avoid death. The Indians let them go. It was not worth their time to chase after them. If the soldiers did return later with more men, the Cheyenne would be gone from this place. Where they were going, the soldiers would not be able to track them. Let the white men come and collect their dead. Let them see the death that would come to those who trespassed on Indian lands. Let it be a warning to others who dared to do so.

Night Hawk bent and cut the bonds from Flame's wrists and ankles, almost wincing at the damage she had done to her fair flesh by straining against the leather thongs. Raw red marks grooved her skin, cut to bleeding in places. Foolish woman! Why had she done this to herself? If she had lain quietly, she would not have caused herself such pain. Had she not known he would come back for her?

Because he was angered by the sight of her marked flesh, Night Hawk jerked her to her feet more roughly than was his intention. He heard her cry out in distress beneath the gag. When her legs refused to take her weight, she sagged against him for support; without thinking, his arms caught her to him and he held her close to his heart for a long moment. Then, recalling his friends awaiting him on the trail, he put her from him and removed the cloth from between her trembling lips.

Fat tears slipped down Sarah's face. She hated her weakness, but she had been bound for so long that the blood had ceased to flow in her stiff limbs. Her hands and feet tingled painfully as the blood raced back into them, and her legs would not at first respond to the command to stand.

But now that she was no longer so alone and frightened, her temper quickly flared. No sooner had the warrior removed the gag from her mouth than she lit into him.

"You abominable beast!" she croaked. She tried to shriek at him, but her throat was hoarse from screaming in vain at the soldiers. Still, it did not stop the tirade that had been building up inside her for so long. "You filthy heathen! How dare you do this to me! How dare you!" She swung wildly at him, her arms flailing, but he caught her wrists before her weak blows could connect.

The pain of his hard fingers on her chafed skin only angered her more, as did her own weakness against his superior strength. "I could have been eaten by some wild animal, for all you cared! Why did you leave me here alone? Have you no heart at all?"

Night Hawk understood her fright and the resulting anger, even if he could not understand her words. His own anger had melted, and now he waited patiently for hers to run its course. Calmly he stood holding her wrists and waiting for her to regain control of herself. If Flame had not been so intent on hitting him, he would have released his hold on her. He did not want to have to further punish her for striking him. She would have enough to endure in the coming days without his adding to her discomfort.

Her raving soon reduced itself to broken sobs. Night Hawk swung her into his arms and swiftly carried her to his waiting horse. He mounted and bound her arms about his waist once more. Quite by chance, Sarah saw the fresh scalps dangling from Crooked Arrow's warbelt. Her already dry mouth went drier still. Her eyes went impossibly wide as she stared in mute shock. Her stunned gaze swung from one warrior to the next, finally lighting on Night Hawk. Each carried several bloody scalps.

Sarah recoiled in horror. There, in the belt at Night Hawk's side, mere inches from her arm, hung three fresh scalps! She swallowed back the bitter bile rising in her throat. She counted ten scalps in all, and the one dangling so near her leg had pale blond hair.

The soldiers! They had killed the soldiers! Revulsion knifed through her. As she recalled her own recent wish for their deaths, guilt clawed at her with sharp talons. Had she somehow brought this horrible fate upon them, as her strange dreams had somehow foretold the future at other times? Could this be her fault? Was the blood of these unsuspecting men on her hands also?

Sarah went wild, like some poor demented creature whose mind could take no more torture. She twisted violently, nearly succeeding in throwing both herself and her captor to the ground in her frenzy. Mad, crazed screams tore from her raw throat, echoing eerily on the still forest air. Having no other weapon, she beat her head upon Night Hawk's back again and again, shrieking frantically all the while. By the time he finally unbound her arms and turned to subdue her, her eyes were glazed and staring sightlessly at the gruesome trophies on his belt. Her face was deathly pale, except where her forehead had hammered against his muscled back. Just as he caught at her arms to shake some sense back into her, Sarah gave a low moan and fainted.

For two endless, agonizing days they traveled on. They rode from sunup to sundown, and Sarah reluctantly had to admire the Indians' stamina. She felt like a rag doll that had lost most of its stuffing. Of course, some of that was her own fault, for she had refused to eat since seeing those awful scalps. She was weakening because of her own stubbornness and hunger. She would accept water to quench her thirst, but she would not eat.

So far, her captor had not forced the food upon her, though she knew he wanted to. She could sense his patience wearing thin, and she could only wonder why he did not force her to eat. She was sure he could have found a way if need be. She would also see his demon-dark eyes flare in anger when she spitefully wiped the mouth of the water skin free of his touch before placing it to her own lips. As it was, he offered her food each morning and evening, and when she refused, he calmly walked away and left her to sulk and suffer in silence.

Neither had Sarah spoken since the day of the killings. Her expressive blue eyes shot pale daggers at all four of the warriors, but she did not bother herself to speak to them. What good would it have done? They could not understand her any more than she could them, so why waste her breath and limited energy, especially since her hands were still kept bound almost every minute? Her only defense against her enemies was to ignore them as best she could, and this she did with inbred and obvious arrogance. When her captor spoke to her or commanded her to do something, she simply stared at him with hate-filled eyes. She complied with his orders only so far as was necessary to avoid punishment, and always in silent disgust. The one time she almost succeeded in loosening her bonds, the better to try to communicate with her captor, he had

become infuriated with her. Sarah had feared he
would strike her, so fierce was the anger blazing
from his dark eyes. But he had not. He had
berated her soundly in his strange tongue and
proceeded to tie her wrists even more securely
than before, almost cutting off the circulation to
her hands.

Sarah shed no more tears, for herself or the
soldiers. Guilt still lay heavily on her heart, but
she could not undo what was done. She could not
bring those men back to life. After wishing her
captors dead a thousand times a day, she eventually accepted that the soldiers' deaths were not
her fault; if it were possible to wish death upon a
person, these four savages would have met a vile
demise days since.

No, Sarah did not cry again. Though her throat
would often ache with the need to do so, it
seemed she had shed all the tears she was allot-
ted. Her heart was torn, her soul bleeding, yet she
could not weep. Her eyes burned with hatred and
deep sorrow, but they remained dry of tears.

Sarah was surprised that her captor had not yet
harmed her or touched her intimately again. She
could only hope that one kiss the first night had
been as distasteful to him as it had been to her.
Though he still insisted that she lie next to him
under the blanket each night, she felt it must be
only to insure that she did not try to escape while
he slept.

They were now well into the Black Hills territory, many miles from Fort Laramie. With each
passing day, Sarah grew more despondent.
Where was her father? He should have caught up

with them long since. Couldn't they find the trail? Had the Indians covered their tracks so well that the cavalry could not follow? Were the soldiers her captors killed men that her father had sent to look for her? Did any of them escape alive to report to her father?

Then an even more depressing thought arose. Even if someone did make it back to the fort, he could tell her father nothing of her whereabouts, for none of the soldiers had seen her that day. They would only report of an attack by Indians, nothing more.

That night, lying so still in the arms of her sleeping captor, Sarah stared into the night and wondered what was to become of her. Was she to spend the rest of her life like this? Would her captor never release her? If he did, would he simply let her go, or would he give her to one of the other warriors? Was this the reason he had failed to violate her? Was she being taken to someone else for that dubious honor?

Sarah had surmised that the Indians were probably taking her back with them to their village. What would it be like there? Would she be beaten? Raped? Tortured and killed? Could she possibly escape before they reached the Indian camp? Would she ever be clean and safe again?

It seemed almost impossible that her life had changed so drastically in such a short time. Just a few days ago—or was it in another lifetime?— Sarah's biggest problem was finding hot water for a bath and worrying over wrinkled clothing. Now her only clothing was a filthy, torn nightdress, and she hadn't washed in days. Her petty problems of just a few days before seemed so small, so insignificant now. How could she have complained so loudly over such trivial inconveniences? Given the chance, she would gladly trade her present situation for those small grievances and never, ever complain again, if only God would grant her that one wish. Sarah turned anguished eyes skyward and prayed as she had never prayed before.

Chapter 6

They stopped early the next day, for what reason Sarah did not know. Usually, they rode until darkness forced them to halt for the safety of the horses. Sarah was fast learning that an Indian took excellent care of his horse. In fact, he looked after his horse's needs before his own, in many cases. She wondered if they treated their wives and sweethearts with half the care and attention they devoted to their mounts and their weapons. Somehow she doubted this.

The sun was still a good hour from setting, but when they stopped, Sarah expected they would make camp immediately, as seemed their habit. She was much dismayed to discover her mistake. Her captor once again pulled her from the horse's back, replaced the hated gag, and tied her to a nearby tree beside a tiny clearing. Disregarding her renewed fright, he and his fellow warriors then rode away without a backward glance.

Sarah was more angry than frightened this time, for she felt certain that he would return for her. He had not brought her all this way just to leave her tied to a tree in the middle of God-knew-where! Still, it was unnerving to be left alone and defenseless for an indefinite time. Anything might happen to her while he was gone! Why, she could choke on this dratted piece of cloth and be dead by the time he returned. An enemy, be he white or Indian, could happen along and harm her. Any number of snakes or wild animals could attack her, and she would have no means of escaping or defending herself!

As she fumed helplessly, the bark of the tree trunk biting into her back, she heaped upon Night Hawk's head every curse she had ever heard her father or his men utter—and they were numerous. Her father would have swallowed his tongue to hear the words running through his darling daughter's mind at that moment. Had she been able to speak, she would have screamed them to the heavens.

Sarah was tired, thirsty, and irritable, and to make matters worse, she could hear the tantalizing sounds of water coming from somewhere nearby. With each passing moment, the cloth in her mouth soaked up more precious moisture from her mouth, and she could have strangled her captor with her bare hands for leaving her to endure such torture. She couldn't help but wonder if he had done so knowingly, just to torment her further.

Time passed slowly, each moment an eternity. Eventually she began to nod. She was so weary, so very tired! Though she hesitated to sleep, not knowing what peril might befall her before her captor returned, Sarah could not prevent her heavy lids from drifting shut.

She awoke suddenly, totally aware. Foreboding chills chased across her skin even before her eyes were open. Something was terribly wrong! Ever so slowly, she raised her trembling eyelids, cautiously keeping her eyes shaded with her long lashes. Every nerve in her body was screaming an alarm, but she felt compelled to see what danger lurked so near.

Had it been possible, Sarah would have swallowed the cloth in her mouth, for she found herself staring directly into the face of a huge wolf! The animal stood not five feet from her, staring at her with hungry yellow eyes. In her fright, Sarah's eyes popped open as if controlled by a puppeteer's strings, though instinct had warned her against this sudden move. A muffled shriek escaped her, and the animal snarled a warning, its white fangs bared and ready. She broke out into a cold sweat, and only the gag prevented her teeth from chattering. She was certain the mangy wolf must smell her fear, for as frightened as she was, she could smell his rank odor from where she sat quivering in total terror.

As she watched in helpless horror, the wolf

crept nearer. Its nose lifted slightly, as if it did indeed smell her fear. Saliva dripped from its large, open mouth to further mat its dingy fur. Sarah sat transfixed. Had she not been tied, she would still have sat there frozen in terror. Neither could she close her eyes, though her mind was silently screaming at her to do so. Death was inches away, and all she could do was cower and watch it stalk her! Even if she wore no gag, she could not have screamed for help, for her throat was frozen with fright.

The wolf crept closer still, evil gleaming from its devil's gaze. Its powerful muscles bunched beneath the grey pelt, and Sarah knew it was about to pounce. She tried to pray, but her mind refused to form the words, and just when it would have eased her tortured mind, she could not manage to faint! The predator's huge haunches lowered in preparation for that final, fatal leap, and Sarah could not even draw a last breath into her trembling body.

She never heard the faint whistle of the arrow winging its way through the air. Before her disbelieving eyes, the wolf suddenly stopped. It trembled for a moment, its jaw sagging, a glazed look in its yellow eyes, then toppled to the ground at her feet. Imbedded deep in its chest was a quivering arrow tipped with the blue-dyed feathers that were the unique signature of her captor.

At last her eyes obeyed her command and closed tightly. The scream that had lodged in her throat tore loose. The tense muscles of her body melted like hot wax, and she sagged in a shaking heap against the rawhide rope that bound her to the tree. Yet even now she failed to weep or faint. She just sat there quivering with disbelief and prayerful thanks for her salvation from such a horrid death.

When Night Hawk had entered the small clearing to find the huge wolf stalking Flame, his blood ran cold in his veins. Thunder's reins slipped unbidden from his numb fingertips, and the big stallion stopped immediately a few steps behind his master. Never, in all his days as a Cheyenne brave and a bold warrior of his fierce tribe, had Night Hawk known such terror. His mind almost refused to function. Thankfully, his warrior's training, second nature to him now, took over.

Almost without thinking, he reached for his bow and an arrow. As he drew back the bowstring, sighting the arrow upon his target, Night Hawk's hands were trembling. He forced himself to take a steadying breath, for he knew beyond doubt that he would not be given a second chance to save his beloved Flame from the jaws of death. The wolf was but a heartbeat from attacking her. He could see its body tensing, ready to launch itself at her delicate throat.

As he released the arrow, he prayed that his aim was true. He watched as it found its mark, and held his breath until the animal fell dead in its tracks, unable to complete that final leap. With a quick prayer of thanksgiving to the Great Spirit for sparing his chosen woman, he ran to her side.

Night Hawk ripped the gag from her mouth and quickly loosened her bonds. As he knelt beside her, Sarah threw her trembling body into his arms, gasping for breath and sobbing hysterically, wetting them both with her hot tears. Her arms wound themselves about his neck, her face nestled against his smooth chest.

Night Hawk's heart pounded madly at this welcome and unexpected reception. Even while he knew that she reacted out of fear and relief, he rejoiced. His arms tightened about her protectively, holding her tightly to him. His hand came up to stroke her bright, tangled hair. He cradled her as one would a child, soothing her with soft words and caresses.

"Don't ever leave me alone like that again!" Sarah sobbed. "Not ever! Promise me you won't! Promise me!" Her tear-streaked face lifted toward his as she sought an answer.

It was more than Night Hawk could resist. Though he did not understand her words, her shimmering blue eyes asked for comfort, and he would have had to be made of stone to refuse. Cradling her head in his palm, he bent to kiss the tears from her face. Her cheeks felt cool to his touch, and his lips lingered to warm them. His tongue swept out to lick the salty tracks from her skin, his lips drying where his tongue had washed. Gently he calmed her, reassured her with light kisses peppered across her face from forehead to chin, from one small shell ear to the other. The small beauty mark on her cheekbone intrigued him, as did her delicate little nose.

Sarah's lids fluttered shut as he tenderly kissed the last teardrops from her wet lashes. A final shuddering sigh escaped as the last of her fear

melted away beneath his warming touch. The
chill left her bones as he held her tightly, one
hand caressing the length of her spine in long,
soothing motions. The other gently stroked her
hair, his long fingers lightly massaging her scalp.

When his mouth had touched and tasted every
inch of her face, it settled at last over her
tempting mouth. Her lips quivered beneath his
for a long moment, then softened in unconscious
invitation. It took all of Night Hawk's immense
self-control to calm his racing blood, his heated
response to her welcoming mouth. With great
effort, he forced himself to go slowly with his shy
white maiden. He promised himself he would
not frighten her this time.

For the longest time, his lips merely tasted
hers, warming them while barely moving. Slowly,
so slowly, he shifted his lips over hers. Pliant
flesh grazed and clung. Gently he teased her with
soft, moist swipes of his tongue, with tiny nibbles
at the edges of her mouth. So sweet! So very
sweet! Her lips parted on a trembling sigh, and
his tongue slipped easily past the barrier of her
teeth. As his tongue touched hers in gentle greeting, he felt her shiver, though not with fear this
time. Her slim arms tightened about his neck,
pulling him nearer, and his spirit soared at her
acceptance of him.

As his tongue began a tender investigation of
her hot, silken mouth, he eased her down upon
the thick bed of grass. Eager fingers caressed her
face as his mouth searched hers. They combed
through her tangled tresses, spreading her hair
about her like a halo of flame. Gently, tentatively,

his fingers moved down her slim throat, stroking lightly as one might touch a timid fawn.

What had begun as a desperate need for consolation had become something else altogether. As Sarah's fear gradually faded, new sensations took its place. By the time his mouth claimed hers so softly, Sarah was swimming in a fine mist of rosy pleasure. A strange, warm yearning rippled through her as his tongue touched hers. This tender touching was so new, so delightful, that she forgot to be afraid. She forgot that this was her Indian captor fondling her so gently. Her mind was drifting on fluffy clouds, and all she wanted to do was prolong the wondrous feelings he was eliciting.

His fingers wandered languidly down the length of her throat and onto her chest. Carefully he laid a hand over her breast, feeling her heartbeat skip and gather speed. Through the thin cloth of her gown, he could feel her nipple push against his sensitive palm. With the greatest of care, lest he frighten her again, he gathered her breast into his hand. Knowing fingers found and fondled the rosy nipple. She stiffened immediately and began to squirm beneath him. Deliberately he deepened the kiss they shared, swamping her senses. When she calmed once more, her lips moving instinctively with his, he resumed his exploration of her breast. This time she did not protest. Within moments she was lifting her body toward his, fitting herself into his hand. The tiny moan that sounded in her throat sent a thrill of desire through him.

Sarah's mind went into a dizzying spin. The

for some reason unknown to her. Sarah sat quietly, enjoying the fire and the freedom of having her hands unbound. Some time later, Sarah came out of her daydreams of home and father to find the other warriors had bedded down. Only she and her captor remained at the fire's side, and he was silently studying her.

Once he saw he had her attention, he pointed to the fire and said, "*S'cou-te*." Then he pointed to her and repeated the word.

Sarah frowned. "Fire?" she asked hesitantly, her eyes going to the nearby blaze. What did the fire have to do with her?

Night Hawk could see her confusion. He rose and threw more wood on the fire, making it blaze up into red-orange flames. He pointed to the base of the fire and shook his head. Then he pointed to the dancing flames and said, "*S'cou-te*." His agile hands imitated the movement of the flames.

Then he took a long sliver of wood. Holding it to the fire, he lit the end. When he held it upright, a small flame wavered at the tip, like the flame of a candle. "*S'cou-te*," he repeated.

Sarah nodded. Pointing to the two flames, she then imitated his gestures. "*S'cou-te*." Then she pointed to herself and shook her head negatively, a confused look on her face. "No *s'cou-te*. My name is Sarah. Sarah," she stressed.

Night Hawk grinned, pleased that she had learned the word so quickly. Still, she did not understand that his name for her was Flame, that this was what she would be called from this day on. He leaned forward and took a strand of her bright hair in his fingers. He waved it before her, indicating its color, then pointed back to the fire. Finally he ruffled her hair until it stood out from her head, and made the hand signal for flames. "*S'cou-te,*" he insisted. He pointed to her and repeated it.

Sarah frowned, but she did not correct him. It seemed the Indian was re-naming her Flame, and there was little she could do about it. She pointed to herself and said with a sigh, "*S'cou-te.*" He nodded his approval, and she pointed to him, a question on her face.

Indicating himself, he said, "*Wamdi Te-bet-hki.*"

Stumbling over the foreign words, she tried to imitate his pronunciation and failed. After several tries, with his encouragement, she almost had it mastered. Still, she did not know what his name meant.

This was much more difficult to explain. After thinking a moment, Night Hawk picked up a small stick and began to draw pictures in the ashes of the fire. First he drew a picture of the day, with the sun shining overhead. Next to this, he drew a picture of the night, with moon and stars in the sky. Pointing to the first, he shook his head and after she had looked well upon it he erased it. Then he pointed to the second image and said, "*Te-bet-hki.*"

Sarah took the stick from him. Indicating the moon, she asked, "*Te-bet-hki?*" When he shook his head negatively, she pointed to the stars and asked again. Once more a negative reply. Finally she indicated the entire picture. This time he agreed.

Next he drew a picture of a large bird with sharp beak and talons and said, "*Wamdi*." This Sarah understood, or thought she did. It would be a few days before she would understand that his name, though literally translated to either Night Eagle or Night Hawk, was actually Night Hawk.

Her language lessons had begun. She learned that the word for horse was *tashunka*. Wood was *can. Mni* meant water. It was when he pointed to the wolf and said, "*Hokum*" that something strange and wonderful happened. Sarah's first reaction was to shiver in remembrance of her brush with death. Then, without thinking, she began to use the sign language she had learned as a child, explaining to Night Hawk in a rapid mixture of English and hand signals just how frightened she had been.

For several seconds, Night Hawk sat stunned, watching her in disbelief. Then he motioned for her to be calm. Immediately she quieted, understanding his signal. "The wolf is dead," he signed, also using his own language with the gestures. "He cannot harm you."

Her eyes did not watch his mouth form the words. Instead, they followed his hands, as if she were accustomed to this. She answered in her tongue and more signing. "Thank you for slaying the wolf and saving my life."

Suddenly Sarah realized what was happening, and her eyes went wide. They were talking! With their hands, they were communicating! They could actually understand each other's hand language! Her gaze flew to his face, where a wide smile was growing. If only he had left her hands unbound sooner, they could have talked days ago!

"How did this happen?" he asked, using both words and signs. "How do you know the hand talk of my people?"

Sarah tried to explain, as best she could, that she had been raised with a deaf child. She told him of Joey and Maude, and how Maude's father had learned the sign language from the Indians when he had been trapping in Indian territory. He had taught Maude the hand talk when they first learned that Joey was deaf, and Maude had taught both Sarah and Joey when they were small. Since she had begun to learn signing when she was only three years old, it came as naturally to her as speaking English.

Night Hawk was elated. How much easier it would be for Flame to learn his spoken language now. How much more pleasant it would be for her to be able to understand what he was telling her and teaching her—and also to make herself understood to him and his people! He had expected it to be much time before she would learn his tongue, but now, with the help of readily understood signs, she would learn quickly.

The language of the Cheyenne was very difficult. Within the Cheyenne nation, there were many tribes and bands, spread across much distance and many lands. Even within the Cheyenne nation, many tribes had difficulty understanding one another's spoken language without the aid of hand signals. His own tribe lived near their brothers, the Sioux. Over the seasons, many

Sioux words had taken the place of the original Cheyenne words. Now their language was a confusing blend of old Cheyenne, Northern Cheyenne, and Sioux.

Sign language was also a means of communication between other Indian nations throughout the plains. The Sioux, Cheyenne, Arapaho, Utes, Kiowa and many others used the same signs when speaking with one another. It was good that Flame knew these signs. Now he must teach her the spoken words, and have her teach him her native tongue.

That night Night Hawk conveyed to Flame that he would not tie and gag her if she would promise not to cry out in the night or try to escape. He warned her that if she should defy him or break her word to him, she would be bound each night and day until she learned to obey.

When she had given her word, they lay down together under the blanket. As Sarah lay curled into his embrace, his arm lying possessively across her waist, sleep was a long time coming. Her day had been long and full of unexpected shocks. First that harrowing experience with the wolf, then the equally unsettling episode in Night Hawk's arms. Her lips still tingled from his kisses, and just the thought brought a shameful tightening to her stomach and breasts. Now to learn that she and her captor could communicate! It was all too much for one day! She couldn't help wondering what surprises might await her tomorrow.

Chapter
7

"Let me go. Take me back to the fort," Sarah begged.

"No." Night Hawk's answer was quick and firm.

Sarah continued to plead. "Please. You must. My father will be so worried about me. He and his men must be looking for me."

Night Hawk eyed her speculatively. "This *gen-e-ral*, he is your father?"

Sarah nodded. "Yes, and he will be very upset over my disappearance. He will try to find me. He will not give up until he does."

His smile was almost smug. "Your father will not find you." He was very pleased to learn that the white chief was Flame's father, though he had already determined that she was still a maiden by her shy responses to his touch. He, Night Hawk, would be Flame's first mate, the first man to touch her heart with love.

Now that they could communicate, Sarah had hoped to gain Night Hawk's understanding, but she was fast losing confidence in her ability to persuade her captor to release her. "He will find me," she insisted. "He must. I do not belong in your world. My life is very different."

"Your life is with me. You belong to me. You will learn the Cheyenne ways." His dark eyes watched closely for her reaction to his words.

Tears glittered in her eyes, turning them to sparkling starlight, but she faced him defiantly. Her small chin came up in defense. "I do not want to learn your ways. I will be very unhappy with you. I love my father and miss him. I must return to him."

Night Hawk stood firm. "You will learn our ways, as you will learn to love me. In time you will forget your life among the whites."

Dismay filled her. "No! I will never come to love you, Night Hawk. Never."

A smile lifted the corners of his sensuously sculptured lips. "We shall see, my beautiful Flame. If the Great Spirit wishes it, your heart and body will be mine for all time."

Their discussion was at an end. Night Hawk had spoken, and so it would be. He refused to listen to any more of her feeble arguments. He placed her behind him on his horse once more, and they were on their way. Before *Wi* slept again behind the western rim of the mountains, they would reach their village. There he would at last be able to claim Flame for his own before his tribe and make her his by tribal law.

Night Hawk was not the only one of their group eager to reach the village. Crooked Arrow was still determined to challenge Night Hawk's claim to the white woman. He left no doubt of this, and the tension between the four warriors was thick, especially between Crooked Arrow and Night Hawk. Their friendship was becoming more strained with each passing day.

Stone Face was very disturbed over this. Once more he tried to talk to Night Hawk. "Is it worth destroying your friendship with Crooked Arrow over this white woman?" he asked. He went on to point out, "It is not just Crooked Arrow. By taking a white woman as your wife, you will be asking for ridicule from the entire tribe. It is not done for a chief to take a white captive for his wife. I fear our people will not accept this, Night Hawk."

"They will come to accept it, and her, if not at first, then with time. They will see that the Great Spirit has led me to her, that she is meant to be my mate," Night Hawk insisted. "That she is my second wife will ease matters greatly."

"Perhaps, my friend," Stone Face agreed, "but what of your sons? Our people would not want the firstborn son of a chief born of a white wife. It is possible that Flame will conceive your first son, since Little Rabbit has yet to deliver your brother's child, let alone one of yours. Have you thought of this?"

"I have considered all of the problems you have mentioned, Stone Face, and I do not take them lightly. As a chief I know what my responsibilities to our tribe entail. Yet I am led to claim this woman. She is of my heart. This I know. I can only leave it to the Great Spirit to clear the path for us. It was He that brought us together, and He will find a way to make Flame and our children accepted. She must be in His plans for our lives, for I did not ask for her to come into my life so unexpectedly. I did not ask for my blood to call out to hers, for my spirit to yearn for hers."

"What if the council decrees that you fight for possession of the woman, and what if Crooked Arrow should win her?" Stone Face questioned.

"If she is truly meant to be mine, then I shall win her," Night Hawk answered calmly.

"This could end your life-long friendship with Crooked Arrow," his friend warned.

Night Hawk nodded, his face serious. "I would be saddened if this should happen, but I must follow my heart. It will be up to Crooked Arrow whether or not we remain friends afterward. If he chooses not, then I can do nothing but grieve for the good times between us that are lost."

As they rode, Sarah tried to sort through her muddled thoughts. What did Night Hawk mean when he said that she belonged to him? In what way? As a slave? As his woman? He had said that he would not free her, that she would learn the

ways of his people. Sarah swallowed the rising
lump in her throat. It sounded as if he intended
to keep her for a very long time! How would she
ever survive such a life? She was used to being
pampered. She was meant for a life with servants
and silks and carefully prepared food served on
fine china and crystal goblets! Her delicate hands
were meant to do nothing more strenuous than
flutter a fan, her feet to dance the night away in
dainty satin slippers. She knew how to flirt
playfully, to be a gracious hostess, to gossip and
giggle with her friends. She could run a house
and command a bevy of servants in their tasks,
but little else. She could converse about the
ballet, the opera, poetry, the latest fashions, and
other polite topics, but she somehow doubted she
would find anyone with whom to discuss these
things where she was now going.

What was she to do? Would she never again see
her dear father? Would she live out her days in
some Indian encampment? Would she wear
clothes of animal skins instead of silks and
satins? Would she never again wear bows and
pearls in her hair, jewels at her throat, lace on her
dresses, darling little bonnets upon her head?
The very thought made her want to cry in
despair.

Even more disturbing was Night Hawk's comment that she would come to love him. How
utterly ridiculous! Yet, a tiny corner of her mind
immediately mocked this denial. Was that some
other girl who just yesterday lay beneath him on
the cool green grass and clung to him so fiercely?

Was it someone else who quivered beneath his touch, who returned his heated kisses and gloried in his intimate caresses? Could she deny that she thought him handsome, in a dark, uncivilized way? Didn't his black eyes draw and hold hers until she feared her very soul would leave her body and fly away? Didn't the very thought of his firmly molded mouth send tremors to the pit of her stomach?

But love was something else entirely. He was an Indian, a heathen savage! Never in this lifetime could she truly come to love this man. If she could not love James, who was a gentleman, who treated her with utmost consideration and professed undying love, who was from her own elite corner of society, how could she ever love this savage in deerhide? The idea was simply preposterous! It would never happen! Night Hawk was dreaming if he thought otherwise.

Ah, but therein lay the crux of her turmoil. Dreaming! Dreams! Hadn't she first seen Night Hawk in her dreams? Hadn't she feared to meet him, feeling instinctively that he would play a major role in her life? Could she deny that this man of her strange dreams and Night Hawk were one and the same? Hadn't her queer dreams been the start of all her problems, since before her mother's death? Wasn't that why she had come west with her father, to avoid those disturbing dreams that so frightened her? Was it Fate that she had come all this way just to encounter Night Hawk, as if he had been here waiting for her arrival all along? Did she have no control over the events of her life, over her dreams? Was her life guided by an unseen hand? Everything preordained? Did she have nothing to say in this at all?

It was a sobering thought. No, it was an absolutely terrifying one! Would she continue to have these strange dreams? Dreams that foretold the future? Sarah's blood chilled to the marrow of her bones at the possibility. Oh, why did she have to be so cursed? Why her? Why now? Why here? And why with this man, whose destiny was undoubtedly linked to hers through her damnable dreams?

It was late afternoon when Night Hawk gave the signal to halt. Whatever explanation he gave to his fellow warriors was lost on Sarah, for he spoke only in his gruff language, and not in hand signals. Confused, she followed when he indicated that she do so. They went a short distance downstream, and there, hidden from view of his friends, he directed her to remove the filthy blanket she wore about her. This she did, but when he further ordered her to remove her tattered night dress, Sarah balked.

"I will not!" she exclaimed, clutching the thin cloth to her chest.

Night Hawk simply glared at her with cool dark eyes, his arms folded implacably across his hard bronze chest. Finally he signed, "Remove it, Flame, or I will remove it for you."

"Why?" Sarah's voice trembled on the word.

"Because I command it."

She stared at him with wide, incredulous eyes.

"That's it? That is all the reason you have to give? Because you command it?"

"It is all that is needed, Little Blue Eyes. You are the captive; I am the master. You are the woman; I am the man. I am a chief, and you are the one who must learn to obey without questioning why. Now remove your clothing, or I shall rip it from your back. Do you wish to enter my village unclothed, for all to see?"

Angry tears shimmered in her eyes as her shaky fingers fumbled with the tie at the neck of the gown. She made no sign language as she proceeded to curse him roundly, with every vile word she could call to mind. Night Hawk must have heard a few of them before, or perhaps he guessed their meaning, for his stern lips twitched with restrained laughter. Then, as the gown dropped to reveal the alluring curves of her body, the half-smile dissolved. Without touching her, his midnight eyes devoured and ravished her.

Closing his eyes briefly and praying for control over his rising passion, Night Hawk took a steadying breath. With one last, long look at her long-legged perfection, he ordered hoarsely, "Go into the water and bathe."

Sarah did not need to be told twice. Not even considering the depth of the water or the fact that she could not swim, she ran into the stream, thinking only of hiding her blushing body from his view.

Torn between laughter at her hasty compliance and the almost overwhelming urge to join her in the water, Night Hawk seated himself upon the bank to watch. Hot blood pounded through his veins. How beautiful she was! Never had he thought to behold such a woman! Her voice broke through his musings, and he forced himself to concentrate on what she was saying with those fluttering little white hands of hers.

"I have no soap," she repeated anxiously.

"Soap?" he asked, not understanding either the word or her gestures for this thing.

"Soap," she said again. "To wash with." With her hands she made a lathering motion, then scrubbed at her arms in imitation.

"Scrub your skin clean with the sand," he instructed gruffly, his voice gone scratchy at seeing her rose-crested breasts bobbing in the water with her movements.

"Oh." Much to her surprise, Sarah found that the sand worked very well. It was when she attempted to wash her long, tangled hair that she ran into trouble again. Sand did not work here. It only put gritty grains in her hair and on her scalp. Rather than ask his advice on this, she did the best she could and rinsed her hair in the cool stream until it felt as clean as she could manage, all the while trying to keep her naked body below the surface of the water.

By the time she had finished, Night Hawk had endured all the torment he could stand and still refrain from mating with her. He almost threw the clean blanket at her when she timidly edged her way from the water. He turned his back to her while she dried herself and dressed in the torn nightgown. When he dared to look once more, his eyes instinctively noted the damp spots where her body had wet the thin cotton. The shadow of her womanhood beckoned, and the turgid tips of her breasts teased him. Her wet hair was rapidly turning the entire top of her gown transparent.

Night Hawk suppressed a ragged groan and prayed for strength beyond his own. He did not want to take her now. He wanted to take her for the first time as his wife, but his resolve was fast weakening. Quickly he wrapped the clean blanket about her and waited impatiently while she tried to comb shaking fingers through her tangled hair. With her hair so matted from days of abuse, it was an impossible task. His patience at an end, he roughly turned her about and proceeded to braid her long wet tresses himself into one long plait down the center of her back.

He was beginning to regret this impulsive stop. They should have gone on to the village, but he had listened to his inner urgings instead. His pride demanded that Flame look her best when first seen by his people, not dirty and disheveled. He wanted her soft white skin to glow, her flaming hair to catch and reflect the sunlight. Night Hawk wanted to be the envy of every brave and warrior in the tribe when he presented his captive bride for their viewing. He could only hope all this self-imposed torture would be worth it.

A short while later, with her breasts rubbing tauntingly against his back and his manhood aching for relief within her, Night Hawk devised a game to distract his thoughts from her body. As they rode along, he would point to items along the trail, and tell her the names of them in his tongue. When she had pronounced the word correctly several times, and he was certain that she knew what it meant, he would then ask her what it was called in English. Then he would practice the white man's word for it. This went on for some time, accompanied by laughter and jibes from his friends, who thought it quite humorous.

The sun was just beginning to set when they at last approached the Cheyenne village. Sarah's first glimpse of her new home was disheartening. Before her she saw what must have been hundreds of tipis, arranged in ever-widening circles from the center of the village outward. They were all cone-shaped, skin-covered dwellings, each with a different design painted upon it. Poles stuck out from a hole at the top of each cone. Bronze-skinned women milled about everywhere, occupied at a variety of tasks. Naked brown children played happily almost beneath the hoofs of horses staked outside the tents. A few bone-thin dogs ran about barking and trying to steal meat from campfires and drying racks.

While most of the children ran naked, Sarah was relieved to see that the adults were clothed, at least partially. The men were mostly bare-chested, wearing only breechclouts and moccasins. When cold weather came, they would wear buckskin shirts and leggings, but for now they wore very little. The women were more fully clothed, in modest deerskin dresses. Sarah saw no cloth clothing. She wondered if she, too, would soon be required to wear the heavy-looking hide dresses. Were captives even allowed clothing? As she looked around, Sarah saw no other white persons, so she could only guess at this. Was she the only white person in the entire camp?

Never in her life had Sarah felt more conspicuous. As they rode through the maze of tipis, every eye turned their way. Women stopped stirring pots, men stopped talking, children ceased to play. All eyes followed their progress to the center of the village. Many of the curious onlookers dropped whatever they had been doing and followed along. A buzz of conversation began, and Sarah was sure she was the main topic. From what she could see, most of the Indians thus far seemed only curious. Only a few faces glared at her with outright hatred.

They halted their horses near the center of the village. Even as Night Hawk pulled her to the ground, Indians began to gather about them. From one of his wrists, Night Hawk took a copper wristband. He placed it about her arm, shoving it onto her upper arm until it would stay, since her own wrists were so small. Though Sarah did not know what this meant, Night Hawk was marking her as his personal property before the entire tribe, thus preventing anyone else from mistreating her.

Immediately Crooked Arrow took offense. "The woman should not be marked as yours until the council decides it is so, or until you win her," he objected.

"She is mine until they declare otherwise," Night Hawk said with a warning glare. "I will not have her harmed while this is being decided."

"Let it be," Stone Face said, his gaze going from one friend to the other. "The council will give their decision before long. It does not matter for now. One of you will own her soon, and the entire village will know of it. If it is acceptable to both of you, I will have Shining Star watch over her. My wife will see that no harm comes to her until one of you can claim her." Once more Stone Face was playing the role of peacemaker.

Confused, and more than a little frightened, Sarah was led away to Stone Face's tipi. The man with the stern face turned her over to his young wife with a few words of explanation, and promptly left the two women alone. Sarah and Shining Star stood staring at each other in mutual curiosity, and it was Shining Star who made the first move. Unable to curb her natural inquisitiveness, she reached out to touch Sarah's bright hair. It took all of Sarah's courage not to back away from the woman's touch, but Shining Star looked as if she meant her no harm. By now, Sarah was becoming accustomed to the fact that the Indians seemed fascinated with her red hair.

"*S'cou-te!*" the woman exclaimed in awe, bringing a reluctant smile to Sarah's face. Everyone seemed to think the same thing upon seeing her hair. It seemed they were all reminded of flames.

It seemed almost natural to return the woman's compliment. Before she thought about what she was doing, Sarah quickly signed, "You are very pretty. You have lovely eyes."

The Indian woman seemed surprised, then

delighted that Sarah could speak with her, even if not in the Cheyenne tongue. There was much Shining Star was curious about, for this was the first white woman she had ever met. Within moments, they had exchanged names and were chattering away like magpies.

It was from Shining Star that Sarah learned why Night Hawk had put the copper band about her arm. It was also Shining Star who explained that there was some dispute over whether Night Hawk would remain her captor, or whether Crooked Arrow would soon own her. This disturbed Sarah greatly. While she wished to be no one's property, she would much rather belong to Night Hawk than to Crooked Arrow. Perhaps it was because he was more familiar to her, and she now believed that he did not wish to hurt her. Then again, perhaps it was because she was fast becoming attracted to Night Hawk, despite all the lectures she gave herself. Too, there was something in the way Crooked Arrow looked at her, and in the tone of his voice when he spoke of her, that frightened Sarah. He had a cruel look that made shivers run up her spine, and she could only hope that he would not be chosen as her captor.

It seemed a very long time before Stone Face returned with word of the council's decision. They had ruled that Night Hawk and Crooked Arrow must fight each other that night in a public contest. Whichever of them won the contest would also win Flame. The fight would be with knives, and it was up to the combatants whether or not it would be a fight to the death. Finally, Flame was required to be present at the contest and watch it throughout.

When Sarah heard this, she was revolted. But she had not been given a choice in the matter. She was to be brought before the tribe, as the evening's prize, with her hands bound. She would be closely watched, and there would be no chance for escape. At the end of the fight, the winner could take her and do whatever he wished with her. He could keep her for as long as he wished and treat her in any manner he liked, and no one would object. If he so desired, he could beat her, and no one would stay his hand. And if, in time, he no longer wanted her, he could trade or sell her to someone else. All this Stone Face revealed to her, and the last vestiges of Sarah's safe, sane world collapsed around her. The general's pampered princess was no more.

Chapter
8

Forced to sit between Red Feather and Stone Face, her two other abductors, Sarah knew a fear beyond all others. The scene before her was one that rivaled hell itself. It had turned dark, and against the night sky, fires blazed brightly, their flickering flames throwing eerie shadows over the faces of the Cheyenne savages. Drums beat out a rhythm that sent shivers chasing over her skin, and Sarah pulled the blanket more tightly about her.

Her gaze darted over the faces of those who had gathered to watch the contest between Night Hawk and Crooked Arrow, and it seemed to Sarah that there were hundreds of Indians here tonight, more than she, in her innocent ignorance, had ever imagined existed. The mere sight of so many savages gathered together was enough to strike fear into the stoutest heart, and Sarah's was no exception.

She tried to calm her racing heart by assuring herself that they meant her no harm—at least for now. Most of them, aside from a curious glance at the white woman who had caused dissension between two of their warriors, chose to ignore her. They were here to witness the fight. The white woman with the hair of flame would be here for many moons, and they knew they would all have the opportunity to appease their curiosity about her later.

There was one woman who caught Sarah's attention, however. The Cheyenne woman was seated almost directly across from Sarah, staring at her with unveiled malevolence. The raw hatred glowing from the woman's dark eyes speared across the space that separated them, burning into Sarah like a brand. *Why should she hate me so, when we have never met*? Sarah thought. *I have done nothing to her, yet her look tells me that she would kill me if she could.*

But there was no more time to wonder, for the fight was about to begin. Night Hawk and Crooked Arrow each entered the circle formed by the onlookers from opposite ends of the ring. They approached each other until they stood face to face, a mere two feet separating them. The drums stopped, but Sarah hardly noticed, for her heart was pounding a drumbeat of its own. Each man held a long knife, its cutting edge honed razor-sharp and glistening in the firelight. Sarah could not tear her gaze from the sight of those lethal weapons.

Another man stepped forward, putting his body almost between those of Night Hawk and Crooked Arrow. In his upraised hand he held a single feather. He spoke a few words to the two contestants, then dropped the feather and stepped quickly out of the way. As the feather lightly touched the ground, it was the signal for the combat to begin.

Both men had crouched in anticipation, and Night Hawk was the first to lunge forward, his knife blade slicing out at Crooked Arrow's arm. His rival moved swiftly out of the way, earning himself only a slight scratch on the upper arm. Once again they circled each other warily. Sarah felt the breath rush from her body as Crooked Arrow came forward with lightning speed, his upturned knife aimed directly at Night Hawk's stomach. But Night Hawk had seen the attack coming. With a graceful twist of his body that rivaled the supple movement of a ballet dancer, he avoided the gleaming weapon. His foot lashed out to sweep Crooked Arrow's feet from beneath him, but Crooked Arrow came back up onto his feet in one continuous motion.

The contest wore on and on, each man scoring small victories over the other. They were well matched. Together, as small boys, they had learned the arts of fighting and had often pitted their skills against each other in playful combat, practice for their later lives as braves and warriors. Both were skilled and well-trained, each of a build and size that gave him no true advantage over the other. As children, and later as braves, one would win a practice match one time, the other the next. Now it was anyone's wager which would conquer the other in their first real contest of animosity.

Tense minutes passed, and Sarah could not tear her eyes from their sweat-glistened bodies. She cringed inwardly each time Crooked Arrow's knife sliced into Night Hawk's skin. Both were tired now, but neither man showed signs of weakening. Varied cuts decorated their bodies, and blood stained their heaving sides, but their faces showed no sign of pain or hesitation as they launched themselves at one another time and again. Sarah choked on a scream as Crooked Arrow narrowly missed driving his knife into Night Hawk's heart. All around her the crowd of Cheyenne muttered their approval of the swift feints and calculated attacks made by each of the two worthy opponents.

Night Hawk determinedly blocked the pain of his wounds from his mind, concentrating solely upon his adversary. Crooked Arrow was tiring, but so was he. Their attacks were slower in coming, the time between them longer now. Night Hawk had one advantage. As Crooked Arrow tired, his intentions showed more clearly in his blazing eyes, allowing Night Hawk to anticipate Crooked Arrow's moves. Night Hawk was careful to control his own features, lest Crooked Arrow gain the same advantage. He also took care not to allow his gaze to waver from that of his rival. It mattered not what Crooked Arrow's hands or legs were doing, as long as he could read those moves first in Crooked Arrow's eyes.

Crooked Arrow's arm flashed upward, the sharp tip of his knife directed at Night Hawk's chest. Night Hawk's arm came up to block the blow, even as his own knife drove toward Crooked Arrow's stomach. The knife flew from Crooked Arrow's hand, aided by the slippery blood dripping steadily down his arm from the deep wound at his shoulder. The weapon flew through the air, well out of Crooked Arrow's reach. In the space of a heartbeat, Crooked Arrow felt the point of Night Hawk's knife at his belly. With his life at Night Hawk's mercy, Crooked Arrow still showed great bravery. Knowing that his next breath could be his last, still he did not flinch from the touch of cold steel. He waited, his dark eyes holding those of his former friend.

The contest was over. Night Hawk had won. No one could dispute this, for all had witnessed it. "Yield all claim to *S'cou-te*, and you shall live to fight at my side yet another day, Crooked Arrow. I do not wish to claim the life of my friend this night."

Crooked Arrow's eyes hardened and his nostrils distended in intense hatred. "I yield the white woman to you, Night Hawk, but from this day forward we are no longer friends. No longer will I ride by your side into battle against our enemies. You will be my chief and fellow warrior, but never again will we be as we were, as close as brothers born of the same womb."

"It saddens me to hear this, Crooked Arrow, for I have long valued your friendship," Night Hawk answered. He slipped his knife into its sheath and stepped away. "If you regret your hasty words once your anger has cooled, do not let pride stand in your way. I will gladly accept your friendship again, though I will never forfeit Flame in order to regain it."

It was over! Sarah was weak with relief. Though he had suffered several wounds, some of them rather nasty, Night Hawk had won the fight. Sarah would not be turned over to Crooked Arrow. But now that the most pressing issue was settled, new worries surfaced. What would happen now?

Sarah did not have long to ponder this. As she watched, Night Hawk approached the woman who had glared at her with such hatred. He spoke a few words to her, and then Sarah saw the woman give Night Hawk a beguiling smile. She turned and left the circle, walking toward a nearby tipi.

Night Hawk turned, his searching gaze finding Flame almost immediately. Their eyes locked in a long look of exchanged relief, and then he came toward her, ready to claim his flame-haired prize. For a long moment he stood over her, black eyes staring down into blue.

When she finally found the strength to tear her gaze from his, her eyes wandered down his lean bronze frame, noting every wound, and somehow feeling each as her own.

"Are you wounded badly?" she asked softly,

having some difficulty signing with her hands bound as they were before her.

"Would you care?" he countered, surprising her with his blunt words.

She immediately bristled. "Yes," she answered tartly, "but only because I would hate to be turned over to Crooked Arrow if you should die from your wounds."

A sardonic smile hardened his features. "Is it only that you prefer the known threat to the unknown evil, then, little firebrand? Are you so sure that you have chosen wisely?"

"I had no choice, or I would have chosen my freedom from both of you."

"That choice will never be given you," he assured her gruffly. "You are mine for all time, and would do well to remember it. Do not cast your eyes toward freedom; do not yearn for your father and friends, for you will only prolong the pain of separation."

They battled a silent war of wills, and Sarah's eyes were the first to turn from the intensity of his. Satisfied that she understood and would come to accept his absolute rule over her, he bent to sever the bonds at her wrists. He slid the copper wristband from her arm and replaced it on his own wrist. It was no longer needed now that the contest and Flame's ownership was decided. She was his, and the entire tribe knew this. No one would dare to harm their chief's newest woman.

"Come," he told her, and walked away without looking to see if she would follow. Where else would she go?

He was right. As much as she longed to defy him, Sarah could not sit where she was all night. Grumbling to herself, she followed him to the very tipi the other woman had entered a little while before.

Sarah had been too nervous to notice much about Stone Face and Shining Star's tipi when she was in it, but she saw at first glance that Night Hawk's tipi was larger. This was all she had time to notice before Night Hawk presented her to the woman with the flashing black eyes. Her name was Little Rabbit, and she offered Sarah a malicious look that boded ill for the white woman. The Cheyenne woman's attitude reeked of superiority and spite, yet her cold black eyes turned soft and limpid when she gazed up at Night Hawk, making Sarah wonder at their relationship, especially since it was obvious that Little Rabbit was with child.

Night Hawk said something else that Sarah did not catch at first. She had to ask him to repeat it. "Little Rabbit is my wife," he said again, watching Flame's face intently. He saw the shock of his words register on her features, but could do nothing to ease the blow. He continued to speak as if all this was of little consequence to any of them. "As such, her authority is second only to mine in our tipi. She will instruct you in your woman's tasks, and you will obey her without argument. Your place will be to help ease Little Rabbit's burden of work as the time for her child advances. You will do all that she tells you quickly and efficiently. Little Rabbit will report any defiance to me, so do not risk my anger by being disobedient, or you will be promptly punished. Do you understand what I am telling you?"

Sarah was stunned, and so angry she could barely see straight. How dare this barbarian steal her away from her own life, only to make her his wife's slave! Was this what he fought that savage contest with Crooked Arrow for? Just to make an unwilling servant of her? Sarah did not know whether to laugh or scream. She did neither. She stared first at Night Hawk, then at Little Rabbit, who sent her a gloating sneer behind Night Hawk's back.

"Do you understand?" Night Hawk repeated impatiently.

Sarah nodded, still stunned.

"Then I will leave you in Little Rabbit's care."

No! Don't! The woman hates me! Sarah screamed silently. *Can't you see that she is just waiting to take her spite out on me? Are you so blind that you fail to see how her eyes glow with the wish to kill me?*

Ignorant of Flame's silent plea, and of Little Rabbit's malicious thoughts, Night Hawk issued terse instructions to his wife. As he was leaving the tipi, he turned to Flame with one last command. "Do not attempt to escape, for the punishment would be greater than you could withstand. For your life's sake, Flame, do not defy me in this."

During the next few days, Sarah seriously considered trying to escape, regardless of the consequences. What could be worse than this menial existence? Surely even death would be preferable! Little Rabbit was the most demanding of mistresses; and to make matters worse, it was like living with two entirely separate women, for with Sarah she was hateful and mean, but when Night Hawk was near, she was all honey and sweetness. It was sickening to watch.

Deep down, regardless of her higher status in Night Hawk's life, Sarah was sure Little Rabbit was jealous. Perhaps it had something to do with the woman's present ungainliness. Yet somehow Sarah suspected, not without some pride, that Little Rabbit had never possessed a waist as small as her own, nor hips as shapely, nor breasts as firm. Every time Sarah was made to endure one of Little Rabbit's many rages, she soothed herself with the knowledge that Little Rabbit was just a hair's breadth from being homely, and that the other woman's hair was the dull, lackluster color of coal dust. Her nasty attitude did nothing to make her any prettier, either. Sarah could only hope vindictively that her face would one day freeze in one of her ugly fits and remain that way for the rest of Little Rabbit's life.

More confusing was Night Hawk's attitude toward both women. While he had not touched Sarah since bringing her into his tipi, for which she was profoundly grateful, his eyes often strayed toward her. His gaze told her he still desired her, but he wore an attitude of anticipation. Just what he was waiting for, Sarah could not imagine, but she hoped it would not come about. Being Little Rabbit's personal slave was bad enough, without having to endure Night Hawk's advances as well.

While Night Hawk did not approach Sarah, neither did he touch Little Rabbit. At first, Sarah thought it might be because of her presence in the tipi, but neither Night Hawk nor Little Rabbit had much modesty about undressing in front of her, much to Sarah's embarrassment. Perhaps it had something to do with their religious beliefs. Perhaps marital relations were forbidden while a woman was with child. Still, it seemed to Sarah that Night Hawk went out of his way to avoid any kind of physical contact with his wife.

All of this seemed strange to Sarah, who had been raised in a loving household. Her father was forever shocking the servants by kissing her mother in front of them. Of course, many of the Cheyenne customs seemed strange to Sarah, especially that of a man taking more than one wife. Sarah had been dumbfounded to find that this was quite an ordinary circumstance in the tribe, but what astounded her more was that most of the wives did not seem to object to the arrangement at all! She just shook her head in bewilderment and thought she would never understand these people.

Most of the time Sarah was much too busy and much too weary to contemplate these trivial matters. She, who had never worked a day in her life, was now busy at the most menial tasks from before sunrise until long past dark. Of course, Little Rabbit took sadistic glee in ordering Sarah to perform the dirtiest, smelliest, hardest chores her twisted little mind could conjure up. There was wood to gather, water to fetch from the stream, animal skins to scrape and tan, strips of meat to dry for the winter ahead.

All this was made much worse by Sarah's complete ignorance of the simplest tasks. Then, too, Little Rabbit never let an opportunity pass to belittle her pretty new slave for her stupidity, and she always pointed out Sarah's shortcomings to Night Hawk when he was around to hear her many complaints. "The wood was wet," or "She ruined the hide I was going to use to make your winter leggings," or "She burned the venison," or "She is so stupid and slow."

Much of this was true, but much of the blame was Little Rabbit's. She deliberately showed Sarah the wrong type of wood to gather for the fire. She refused to help the white girl learn the proper way to prepare Night Hawk's meals, leaving Sarah adrift in her own ignorance. Sarah tried, but she had not so much as boiled water for herself before this. Little Rabbit ordered her into the thickest brambles to pick fall berries, then ignored Night Hawk's directive to provide balm for the severe scratches on Sarah's body. She would knowingly instruct Sarah to use the wrong tools to scrape a skin, then berate her when the hide was ruined beyond repair.

If Little Rabbit was hateful while she considered Sarah a mere slave, she was unbelievably malicious once she was informed that Night Hawk intended to take Sarah for his second wife. She worked the girl until Sarah almost dropped in her tracks. Then, when Sarah's muscles ached so badly from the unaccustomed work, she would beat her with a stick for moving too slowly. She would send Sarah on some task outside the tipi while Night Hawk ate his meal, then throw what she herself could not finish to the dogs, leaving Sarah to go hungry.

Large, raw blisters rose and broke on Sarah's hands, then festered when they went unattended, as did those on her bare feet. Though Night Hawk had instructed Little Rabbit to provide clothing for her, the dresses never appeared, and Sarah was forced to carry out her daily tasks in her old ragged gown and dirty blanket. There was never enough time between chores for Sarah to have a bath or to wash her hair. She was soon as filthy as any orphaned urchin, and her once-bright hair hung in lank tangles down her back. The constant work and lack of proper nourishment made her almost faint at times.

Sarah trudged through the long days, dreaming of freedom and wondering what she had ever done to deserve such a vile fate. Tears gathered in her eyes as she viewed the bloody blisters on her palms and the bedraggled state of her hair and clothing. She wrinkled her nose in disgust at her own body odor, and would have done just about anything for a decent bath. She laughed ruefully as she recalled her mother's words. "Ladies do not sweat, Sarah," she could almost hear her mother saying. "They glisten." *Oh, Mother, if you only knew*! Sarah wailed silently, blinking back her tears. *If you could see your darling daughter now, you would run screaming in dismay*!

Chapter
9

Sarah's mistreatment continued undetected by Night Hawk for more than a week. He had been preoccupied with his chief's duties for several days, often staying late in the ceremonial lodge listening to speeches or talking with the other chiefs about the problems concerning their tribe. By the time he returned to his own tipi, both Little Rabbit and Flame were asleep. During the day, when Flame was being instructed by Little Rabbit in her duties, Night Hawk did his best not to interfere. In truth, he stayed away much of the time merely to avoid Little Rabbit's continual complaining and whining.

A few days later, Night Hawk was much relieved to put Little Rabbit in charge of Flame while he went on a short hunting expedition with his fellow warriors. He was very disappointed that Flame was not adjusting as well as he had hoped. According to Little Rabbit's reports, Flame simply was not applying herself to her tasks. She was lazy and slow to learn. She was also very belligerent. Though Night Hawk had yet to witness one of her tirades, he had no reason to doubt Little Rabbit's word on this. Perhaps in his absence things would improve. Little Rabbit was certain that she could soon teach Flame to obey, and Night Hawk was loathe to interfere in her woman's domain. He sometimes thought that Little Rabbit was severe in her punishments, but as long as Flame did not seem to be suffering any ill effects, he said nothing and let the women work it out between themselves.

Had Night Hawk known what was going on in his absence, he would have been angry beyond belief. His future bride was filthy and weak with hunger. While he was away hunting, Little Rabbit made Flame sleep outside the tipi, bound by a short tether to a stake driven into the ground. Not only were her wrists bound behind her back, but the end of the rawhide leash was tied tightly about her throat. She had but the one thin blanket to ward off the night chill, and she was still dressed only in the ragged nightgown she had arrived in. She was covered with bruises from the many beatings Little Rabbit administered, and she could barely walk or use her hands, so raw with blisters were they.

Even the other Cheyenne were appalled at the

treatment Flame was receiving from Little Rabbit. Some of the women tried to talk with Little Rabbit about this, but she promptly told them to mind their own concerns and leave the business of training Flame to her. They walked away shaking their heads, but could do nothing. With Night Hawk gone, Little Rabbit was in charge of her own tipi and all that went on there.

Only Shining Star dared to try to help Flame, and this she did secretly. When she could, she would sneak Flame a bite of food to eat, cringing in shame as she watched the white woman devour it hungrily. On occasion, when Little Rabbit was not aware, Shining Star would instruct Flame on the proper way to conduct some task which Little Rabbit had deliberately shown her incorrectly. This she did not only out of pity, but because she had liked Flame upon meeting her. The girl was bright and curious, and no doubt would have done much better under guidance other than Little Rabbit's.

Shining Star was ashamed and angered at the way Little Rabbit was treating Flame. One would think that the white girl was a common slave instead of Night Hawk's intended bride! Surely Night Hawk did not condone Little Rabbit's behavior! Chief or not, when he and Stone Face returned from their hunt, Shining Star was going to see that Night Hawk was taken to task for going off and leaving Flame in such misery.

With Night Hawk gone, Little Rabbit was in her glory. She relished every physical and mental hurt she could administer to Flame. Had she been able to arrange it without being blamed, she would have killed the white woman. As it was, too many of the villagers were aware of her actions, and many openly disapproved. Many also knew that Night Hawk intended to join with his white captive in marriage soon, and they watched Little Rabbit with wary eyes.

Though she could not slay the girl, Little Rabbit made certain that Flame wished she were dead. Every day was a living agony. Jealousy drove Little Rabbit to extremes, and she could have shouted with glee as the weight dropped from Flame's already trim body and dark circles appeared beneath her eyes. Her flame-red hair no longer shone; her hands were rough, and the nails were torn and ragged. She wouldn't seem so beautiful to Night Hawk when next he saw his captive!

In addition to the physical abuse and humiliation Little Rabbit heaped upon Flame, she goaded her constantly with hateful words and spiteful remarks. Guessing that Flame knew nothing about her coming union with Night Hawk, Little Rabbit reveled in reminding Flame that she was but a lowly disgusting slave, while she, Little Rabbit, was his revered wife. Correctly assuming that Night Hawk had not revealed the circumstances of her previous marriage to Night Hawk's brother, or their resulting joining as a result of Many Arrows' death, Little Rabbit deliberately encouraged Flame's misconception that the child she was carrying was Night Hawk's. She flaunted her distended belly before Flame, taking great delight in telling her what a wonderful lover Night Hawk was, how happy Night Hawk was with her as his wife, and how thrilled he was that she was carrying their child.

The hunting was good, and the warriors were on their way back to their village much sooner than they had thought. Night Hawk was eager to return and learn how Flame had fared with her lessons. He missed seeing her, and hoped she was learning rapidly now. The main reason he had not joined with her in marriage as yet was to give her time to adjust to the Cheyenne ways and her new life, but now he was becoming impatient to teach her the joys of physical union. The closer they came to the Cheyenne camp, the more eager he became.

The hunting party was late getting into the village that night, but they had been such a short distance from the camp at sundown that they had chosen to ride on rather than stop where they were for the night. With storm clouds gathering, even these courageous warriors preferred a warm, dry tipi to sleeping in the rain.

The first hard pellets of rain were coming down as Night Hawk made his way quietly through the sleeping camp to his tipi. The skies opened all at once with a roar of thunder, a blinding flash of lightning, and a deluge. Night Hawk chuckled softly to himself. Despite the long ride, he would still be dripping wet by the time he gained the shelter of his lodge. Little good all their efforts to reach home had done.

As he bent to tie his horse to the stake outside the tipi, another flash of lightning split the dark night. It was then that Night Hawk saw Flame huddled miserably against the side of the tipi. In just the short time it had been raining, she had been drenched to the skin and was shivering. With her head bent and her hair dripping about her face, she had not seen him approach. The driving rain and thunder had covered the sound of footsteps.

Night Hawk was furious! What was Flame doing outside the tipi? What was going on? "Flame?"

At the sound of his voice, her head came up, and it was then that Night Hawk saw the leash tied so tightly about her slim throat. His gaze then noted her bound hands, and anger speared through him like a thousand arrows. Not trusting himself to speak, he bent and swiftly released her. Sweeping her into his arms, he carried her inside and set her gently on her feet. The soft flow of the banked fire showed Little Rabbit sleeping peacefully on her comfortable mat.

Night Hawk's incensed roar was stronger than the thunder outside. "Little Rabbit!"

The woman nearly leaped from the mat in her fright. Her startled gaze found Night Hawk standing by the firepit, Flame huddled at his side. Her heart sank heavily; her mind raced to find excuses for her actions, but sleep still smothered her dull thoughts. "Night Hawk, you are back," she said stupidly.

"Yes, I am back!" he shouted, his black eyes snapping angrily. "And what do I find when I return, but my betrothed shivering in the rain outside our tipi! What is the meaning of this, wife?"

"She has been very disobedient, Night Hawk," Little Rabbit commenced to whine. "You would not believe the problems I have had with her since you went away!"

Night Hawk's eyes narrowed dangerously as he continued to glare at this stupid woman he had inherited for his wife. "You have gone too far, Little Rabbit. Flame is not some slave to be mistreated so. She is soon to be my wife, the wife of your chief, and should be honored as such."

Flame shivered at his side, drawing his attention to her. "Why is she dressed like this? Where are the clothes and moccasins I instructed you to provide for her?"

Little Rabbit stuttered the first lie to come to mind. "She refused to wear them."

"Bring them," he commanded. "Now. She will be dressed properly, as befits my intended bride."

Little Rabbit fidgeted nervously. What was she to do now? There were no clothes for Flame, for she had flagrantly disregarded Night Hawk's orders about the clothing. In an effort to cover her own disobedience, Little Rabbit hurried to the pegs where her own clothes hung. Quickly she selected a dress and a pair of fairly new moccasins.

Her hasty ruse did not fool Night Hawk. "This dress is not Flame's, it is yours," he accused her, holding on to his rising temper by a slim thread. His shrewd gaze noted the slightly worn places on the doeskin dress and the quill decoration that was Little Rabbit's favored design. Flame was taller than Little Rabbit, and the dress was much too short for her. Even the moccasins showed signs of previous wear and were too small. "Bring me Flame's clothing."

Little Rabbit had the good sense to hang her head in shame. "I have not gotten any for her yet," she admitted. Then she added slyly, "I did not feel that she deserved them until she learned to obey."

The long, strong fingers were twisted tightly in her hair before she saw his hand move. "You take it upon yourself to counter my commands, woman?" he hissed. "Who is the husband in this lodge? Who is the chief here? Does your word suddenly carry more authority than mine, that you disregard my orders so readily?"

Never had Little Rabbit seen Night Hawk so angry. "No, Night Hawk. I beg your forgiveness. I wished only to teach the woman to obey."

"You do not teach obedience by being disobedient yourself," he told her sternly. Taking the clothes from her, he said, "Flame shall wear your clothing for now, but you will see that she is decently clothed in her own things soon. I give you three suns—no longer." His angry eyes pinned her where she stood. "I shall also think of a proper punishment for you for daring to lie to your husband."

At Little Rabbit's frightened nod, he turned to Flame. By now she was leaning weakly upon him for support, and even in the dim light of the dying fire, he could see the violet circles of fatigue beneath her eyes. She was half asleep on her feet, barely aware of what was going on around her. Propping her up with one hand, his other reached for her sodden, dirty gown. As he ripped the offensive rag from her trembling body, he said to Little Rabbit, "You claim she does not work. Why then is she so thin and weak, with dark smudges beneath her eyes?"

Sarah came wide awake with a shock as Night Hawk tore the gown from her. With a shriek, she tried to cover herself with her hands, horribly mortified by her sudden nakedness. What was happening? Oh, sweet heaven, what was going on? Just moments ago, Night Hawk had been shouting at Little Rabbit, and suddenly Sarah found herself standing in the altogether before both of them!

As she opened her mouth to protest, Night Hawk spun her about. She barely caught a glimpse of the rage building on his face before he was exploding once more. "Explain these marks on her body, if you can, Little Rabbit!" he roared. "You have beaten her!" Night Hawk was livid as he viewed the purple, green, and yellow welts that covered Flame's back and shoulders and buttocks.

Not able to understand his words, Sarah was badly shaken, not sure if he was angry at her or Little Rabbit. She twisted against the hold he had on her arms, trying to evade him, wanting to run and cover herself. Tears welled up in her eyes. Frightened whimpers escaped her trembling lips. Suddenly, Night Hawk turned her to face him once again. The red line about her throat where the leash had choked her stood out vividly against her pale skin, and her eyes were wide with fright. She cringed from his gaze as it traveled the

length of her body, noting every scratch and
bruise. His grip loosened and she pulled free.
When he took a step toward her to pull her near
once more, her hands came up as if to ward him
off, and he saw the festering wounds that covered
her palms.

The look of the Devil was in his flashing eyes as
he turned on Little Rabbit. His rage knew no
bounds. "You jealous, lying bitch!" His hand
whipped up to strike Little Rabbit hard across
the face, and the Cheyenne woman tumbled to
the floor of the tipi in a heap. Her hand rose
reflexively to cover the red marks already showing on her cheek, and she stared at Night Hawk
with a stunned expression.

Sarah watched in horrified fascination as
Night Hawk loomed over the fallen woman, his
hands clenched into tight fists. "I could kill you
for what you have done! If it were not for the
child in your belly, I would see your worthless
hide flayed from your bones! Never again are you
to strike her. From this night forward, you have
no authority to punish Flame. She will be properly fed and clothed, and her injuries tended; and if
you value your life, you will see that she comes to
no more harm! Never again will you lie to me and
ignore my commands, or by the stars that shine
above, I swear I will see you suffer worse measures than any Flame has endured at your
hands."

Leaving her to crawl back to her bed, Night
Hawk now turned to Flame. With a tenderness in
direct contrast to his fury of moments ago, he
lifted and carried her to her sleeping mat. There

he laid her down and covered her with a robe from his own bedding. He tucked the robe about her, anger clawing at him again when he saw her abused feet. Then he sat at her side and spoke quietly to her, soothing her with gentle words and touches. "Forgive me, Flame," he signed. "I did not know. This will not happen again. Tomorrow you will have fresh clothes and moccasins for your feet. Your injuries will be tended, and you shall have a bath in the stream. You need not fear that Little Rabbit will harm you again. All this I swear to you on my honor."

He sat with her until she had fallen asleep, and for long afterward, gazing into her pale, thin face and wishing a vengeance he could not administer upon Little Rabbit for her crimes against Flame. Until Little Rabbit delivered his brother's child, there was little he could do to punish her as he wished to, for he dared not risk the life of Many Arrows' child. All he could do was try to be more observant and shield Flame from any more of Little Rabbit's malevolence.

The sun had long passed the mid-point in the sky before Sarah awakened the following day. Night Hawk had been adamant that she be left to awaken on her own. To insure that this was done, he spent much of his day in and around the tipi. After Little Rabbit had prepared his morning meal, he commanded her to bring fresh water and sufficient firewood to the tipi. Then, because he could not trust himself to be near her and not strangle her, he ordered Little Rabbit from the tipi for the day. She could go elsewhere to clean and prepare the hides and meat of the kill he had brought back.

The sounds of children playing and camp dogs barking at last roused Sarah from her exhausted sleep. The first thing her eyes touched upon was Night Hawk seated near the tipi opening, quietly mending a bridle. Even without looking, he seemed to know the moment her lids fluttered open.

"You are awake," he said softly. Putting the bridle aside, he rose and came to her side. "Do you wish to eat first, or to bathe and dress?"

"A bath. Please." Her eyes searched his and found none of the anger of the past night. Sarah saw only what she thought was concern. "May I have my nightgown back now?" She was supremely conscious that she was naked under the covers, and that he had placed her there and covered her himself.

"Your night dress has been burned," he informed her. Before she could become too upset, he hastened to add, "You can cover yourself with the blanket until after you have washed yourself in the stream. Then you will wear these, until clothing of a proper size can be made for you." He placed Little Rabbit's dress and moccasins next to her.

He waited outside the tipi until she had wrapped herself in the blanket. Without a word, he suddenly lifted her into his arms and began walking through the village to the stream.

"What are you doing?" she gasped in surprise. "I can walk."

"I have seen the condition of your feet, and I

will carry you. When you have bathed, I will give you ointment for your hands and feet, and soon they will heal. Until then, you will rest and do nothing to irritate your wounds further." His tone told her that this was a command, not merely a wish.

It was the first time in almost two weeks that Sarah had had a bath. Even with Night Hawk standing guard over her, it was the most pleasurable experience imaginable. Of course, Night Hawk was there for more than to see that she did not escape; he also insured her privacy throughout her bath. When she had cleaned the grime and sweat from her body, she proceeded to wash her hair with a gooey substance Night Hawk had thoughtfully provided. From his gestures, she concluded that it was made from the fiber of some sort of plant, and to her delight, it not only cleaned her hair, but left it soft and shining and nearly free of tangles.

Dressed in the soft doeskin dress, the pliant moccasins on her feet, Sarah felt almost human again. It did not matter that the dress was too short, or that it had been worn by someone else before her. It mattered not that the moccasins were a bit too tight. They were clean, and so was she. She was decently covered for the first time in weeks, and it felt absolutely wonderful! Her freshly washed hair hung about her shoulders in fragrant waves. Best of all, Little Rabbit was nowhere in sight.

Sarah looked about her as Night Hawk carried her back to the tipi. The sun was shining in a brilliant blue sky. Children were laughing and darting about in play. She was clean and decently dressed and being carted about like a princess. After the horror of the past days, she could scarcely believe it. Perhaps God had not deserted her entirely after all!

She looked up into the handsome face of the man who carried her, and suddenly he did not seem as fearsome as before. His face was relaxed; his black eyes glowed with contentment. Below that straight, noble nose, his firm, masculine lips curled in a slight smile, showing even white teeth. Feeling her watching him, he glanced down at her with a look that spoke of supreme satisfaction and pride. His strong arms tightened about her possessively, and Sarah's heart took flight. *Would it be so absolutely awful,* she asked herself, *if her knight was bronze-skinned instead of white, and wore buckskin in place of shining armor, and lived in a tipi rather than a castle? Would it be so bad that his horse was black instead of white, or that he wore his hair in long braids decorated with feathers, or that he had actually captured her rather than saved her? Would it really be so unthinkable to lose her heart to this man who could be as kind as he was cruel, whose strong arms made her feel so protected, who was so handsome that her breath caught in her throat and her blood raced whenever he was near? Would it really be so terrible to be loved by such a man?*

Chapter 10

The next days were vastly different for Sarah. Night Hawk had ordered her to rest, and he was there to make certain that she did so. While Little Rabbit, under Night Hawk's relentless black glare, sullenly did the numerous chores she had previously assigned to Sarah, Sarah practiced the Cheyenne language and taught Night Hawk the English words. When her new clothes were finished, and her feet had recovered to Night Hawk's satisfaction, he took her for walks about the village and the nearby woods. He taught her about the plants and the animals; everything was a lesson for her further learning.

"The Cheyenne revere the land and all that grows upon it," he told her seriously. "We are of the land and must do nothing to harm it. We take only what we need to survive, and waste nothing. Unlike the white man, we do not carve open the breast of Mother Earth with iron plows or cut down her trees to make fields and forts. We take what she offers, and it is sufficient for our needs.

"Never would we scar the land with roads as your people do, yet now they wish to deface our land with tracks for their iron horses. They bring soldiers and build more forts and drive the buffalo from the best grazing grounds. They seek the yellow rocks in our hills, and defile our burial grounds in their lust for these stones."

His dark eyes glowed with both pride and malice. "This we cannot allow. They tell us they will pay us for the land, and it will then be theirs, but how can a man sell his heart? The Great Spirit has given us, His children, this land to live upon and care for. It is ours to use, but not to sell. It provides us food and shelter. Without it we would surely die. Yet the white man comes and takes it as if it were his. Are we to stand idly by and let this happen? Who are these men to boldly take what belongs to the Great Spirit and His chosen ones?"

For the first time, Sarah began to understand. Would she meekly allow someone to take what had belonged to her and her family for countless generations? Wouldn't she, too, fight to hold it and protect it from any and all intruders? No wonder the Indian fought so fiercely against the invasion of the white man into his territory, particularly when their views were so different.

To the whites, forts and fields and roads were progress; to the Indians they were a desecration of their hunting grounds and homelands. Would these two peoples ever see eye to eye and resolve their differences?

Sarah could see both sides now. While the Indian fought to hold the land free of intruders, the white settlers were desperate for fresh farmland, land for ranches and cattle and new towns. More and more immigrants came pouring into the country every day, seeking new lives. They needed room to spread and grow, and the cities in the east were becoming more and more crowded, unable to hold the continual influx of newcomers. They looked to the west for their salvation, and uncaringly pushed the Indians aside in their rush and their greed. Sarah could see no easy resolution. The battle had barely begun and was sure to be long and bloody.

Despite herself, the more Sarah learned about the Cheyenne way of life, the more she came to admire these people. The very simplicity of their life made her ashamed of all she had previously taken for granted. If she ever got back to civilization, she promised herself that she would appreciate it that much more. After living here, Washington would be like heaven. Her home would seem a palace.

When she thought of all the silk and satin gowns in her closet, Sarah vowed to be thankful for them and not constantly be begging her father for new dresses, merely because she had already worn all of hers at least once. Here she had but two dresses and a single pair of moccasins, and she was grateful to be clothed decently. They were made of doeskin, and though they could not compare with the colorful fabrics of her former life, at least they were soft and warm and comfortable.

After the past weeks, and all the labor she had done, Sarah pledged never again to be so sharp with servants. Now she realized what a spoiled, obnoxious little witch she had been. How she had looked down her nose upon those who had served her! Having had a liberal taste of such abuse herself, she would never again treat someone below her with such callous disregard. Theirs was honest labor, and they could not help that being less fortunate, they had to work for someone else to make a living for themselves and their families.

Sarah saw many things differently these days, even while she still prayed for deliverance from her own captivity. While she was grateful that Night Hawk had put a stop to Little Rabbit's vengeance, she still yearned for her home and her father. Perhaps she always would, for with each passing day she came to realize that rescue might never come. And with each day, despite the ache in her heart, she came to admire and respect Night Hawk and his people more and more. Would their ways, in time, become hers?

"No, Flame. You must move in the other direction when I move this way." Night Hawk was teaching her one of the Cheyenne dances.

Sarah tried the steps once more, again nearly tripping over his feet as she chose the wrong direction. Tossing her long braids over her shoulders, she looked up at his disgruntled expression and laughed aloud. "I am sorry. I will try again."

Her delighted laughter pleased him, as did her words, spoken in Cheyenne without benefit of sign language. His betrothed was learning fast, now that Night Hawk had taken over much of her instruction. Her smiles were few, her laughter more rare, but they were like priceless treasure to his heart, and Night Hawk did everything in his power to make Flame happy in her new life.

He was courting her, though she had yet to realize this. He had not told her that she was soon to be his bride. When she had fully recovered from her ordeal at Little Rabbit's hands, he would tell her; he wanted her to come to him willingly when the time came for her to be his wife. He did not want to see her face cloud with sadness or fear. He did not want to feel her draw away from his touch, or close her mind to his words.

"Place your toe to the ground first, and your heel will follow," he instructed her, a grin tugging at his lips.

Flame frowned up at him in mock severity. "Do not laugh at me, Night Hawk, or I shall tromp on your toes as hard as I can, and you will limp about like a lame dog for many days."

Now he did indeed laugh. "You will have to eat more than a sparrow, if you hope to harm me with those bony feet of yours!" he taunted.

"I wonder if you would do much better trying to learn my dances," she countered smugly. "Shall we try and see?"

As he accepted her challenge, Night Hawk could only hope none of the other warriors came upon them in this remote clearing he had chosen for her lessons. They would surely laugh and taunt him endlessly, if they could see him now, trying to learn what Flame called a waltz. Their graceful leader did not seem so sure-footed as he tried to follow Flame's lead.

Sarah was humming a waltz tune and trying to teach him the graceful turns of the dance, so different from his own. "One, two, three. One, two, three," she counted softly. Suddenly their legs tangled, and down they went into a heap, her fall broken by his big body beneath hers. Helpless giggles assailed her as she viewed the surprised expression on his face. "That is not the way this dance is supposed to end, Night Hawk," she pointed out as tears of mirth made her eyes dance like merry stars.

He was entranced by her laughter and her joy-filled face. Her eyes smiled down into his; her body was light and deliciously inviting on his. He knew the moment she realized their position, her legs lying half over his, her hands braced on his broad chest, their faces so near. Her smile faded gradually; her eyes grew large and round; her breath came in short spurts. Before she could retreat like a frightened fawn, his hand closed over the back of her neck. With the slightest of pressure, he brought her head down to his.

Lips touched as softly as the velvet petals of a flower floating to the ground. They shared a trembling breath. Her fingers unconsciously curled into delicate claws, then uncurled to slide up his bare chest and twine about his neck. Night Hawk was surprised and delighted; his heart was warmed by her gesture. Words were not necessary now, for they spoke the language of lovers the world over, with lips and tongues and hands.

While one hand held her head to his, the other spread out upon her back. As the kiss lengthened and deepened, he caressed the length of her spine, pressing her smaller body into his, and he sighed softly into her open mouth.

His tongue made a gentle foray into her mouth, and Sarah felt butterflies take wing in her stomach. Why was it that every time this man touched her, her body thrilled to life? Her lips tingled against his, willing captives of his warm possession. "Night Hawk," she whispered. "Oh, Night Hawk." Then her mouth surrendered to his once more.

This kiss, and those that followed, lasted an eternity—yet only a few heartbeats. Spun of dreams, they were sweeter than honey, more potent than peyote, richer than any wine. Only immense willpower held Night Hawk's passion in check. Flame was responding so sweetly, so innocently, but he knew that if he allowed himself more than these few kisses, she would withdraw into herself again. Better to tempt and tease at this point in their relationship. Better to show her but a glimpse of the joys to come, to leave her yearning for him. How much more ready she would be then, to learn all he longed to teach her on their wedding night.

With trembling hands framing her delicate

face, Night Hawk slowly broke off the kiss. Her flushed lips seemed to want to cling to his, and a soft sound of disappointment came from her throat. Quickly, before he should change his mind and take her there and then he lifted her body from his. With one last, swift kiss, he brought them both to their feet.

"It is late, Flame. We must return to the village." He smiled secretly as she ducked her head in shy embarrassment, and he could not stop himself from saying, "You may kiss me again another day, Little Blue Eyes, and teach me to dance."

"Not if I can help myself," she murmured, then thanked heaven she had spoken in English so that he could not understand her words.

Night Hawk presented her with a porcupine quill hair brush and a carved comb, the first of many gifts he was to give her. So happy was she with them that had they been made of the finest ivory she would not have cherished them more. No longer would she have to tear the tangles from her hair with her fingers, and labor to twine the twisted, frazzled mass into unkempt plaits. Little Rabbit wore a sour look for days after she learned of Night Hawk's gift to the white woman.

He brought her ripe fruit and pretty stones. On their walks, he plucked flowers to decorate her hair. Eventually it dawned on Sarah what was happening, and she hastened to Shining Star's tipi to seek her friend's advice.

"What should I do, Shining Star? Should I

accept his gifts? What will he expect of me in return? Please help me, for I know so little of your customs."

A soft smile lit Shining Star's face. "He courts you, Flame," she explained in her quiet way. Ever since Night Hawk's unexpected return from the hunt that night, the entire camp had been abuzz. It was no secret that their young chief had been angry when he had learned of Little Rabbit's actions. His outrage had been heard by many over the sounds of the storm. Now they watched in avid curiosity as he openly courted his bride-to-be. Only a few dared to jeer at him behind his back. Others, knowing of Little Rabbit's vindictiveness, nodded in silent approval of Night Hawk's kindness. The white girl had done nothing to them. She would soon be their chief's wife. The girl was a beauty. Who could blame Night Hawk for desiring her? Better that he win her heart and have a willing mate than a second spiteful wife.

"Courting me?" Sarah was astonished. "Courting me for what?"

"For marriage, silly girl. Is that not what men do in your white world? Do they not bestow gifts upon their intended?"

"Yes, of course. But why would Night Hawk court me, when I am his by tribal law already?" Sarah could not understand.

Shining Star shrugged. "Who can understand the workings of a man's mind? I would think that he would rather have a happy bride than a sad one. He seeks to win your heart, not merely your body."

Sarah raised shaking hands to her flushed cheeks. "Oh, Lord!" she breathed. Then, "What would happen if I did not accept his gifts?"

Her friend looked aghast. Shaking her head, she said, "Flame, you truly do not understand your situation, do you? As you have said, you are Night Hawk's property, willing or not. He is merely doing you the honor of courting you before you marry, as he would have done with any of the Cheyenne maidens. It is a gesture only, my little friend, to show how honored he will be to have you for his wife. You have no choice but to accept his gifts and his offer of marriage, for he will have you even should you dare to refuse. But it would only do you harm if you should be so bold as to try to reject him, for he would lose face before the tribe, to be turned aside by a mere white woman. Flame, you must see how this would anger him."

Sarah nodded. "I see, I think. Are you saying that I will be forced to marry him, like it or not?"

"Yes, Flame. Night Hawk has decided that you are to be his wife, and so it will be, regardless of your wishes. Now you must make up your mind to accept what you cannot change. A wise woman would accept his gifts and her place in his life without complaint. A wiser woman would decide to make him happy in all ways, for a happy husband is ten times worth an unhappy man. A woman such as you should have no difficulty making Night Hawk as contented as a well-fed mountain cat; and you will reap the rewards of his joy rather than the sharp edge of his tongue."

Shining Star watched her new friend digest this

advice. "He is a Cheyenne chief, Flame. Think twice before wounding his pride. It is an honor to be chosen to be his wife."

"His second wife," Sarah inserted bitterly. "You are forgetting Little Rabbit." The sharp twinge of jealousy surprised and annoyed her. What should she care how many wives Night Hawk had? Why should it bother her to think of Little Rabbit lying in his embrace at night and conceiving a child by him? Why should her heart ache and her soul die a little at the thought of his loving another woman?

"I forget nothing," Shining Star told her. "Night Hawk does not love Little Rabbit. This I know. I know also that Night Hawk loves you. His heart is in his eyes each time he looks at you."

Torn between disbelief and exasperation, Sarah shook her head. "You see what you wish to see, Shining Star. Night Hawk could not love me. We have only just met, and I am a white woman. He would not give his heart to a white woman."

"Why does he not keep you as his slave, then? As a hated captive? Why does he bother himself to court you? To marry you?"

Sarah stared at her friend, baffled. She had no answer for this. "He has not said that he loves me," she argued feebly, a seed of hope sprouting in her heart, despite her efforts to choke it before it bloomed.

Shining Star smiled a wise and wily smile. "Perhaps he does not realize it himself yet," she suggested slyly. "It will be up to you to bring it to his attention."

Sarah could not help but return the smile. "You are a wise and devious woman, Shining Star," she said, smiling warmly at her friend. "It is a wonder Stone Face can maintain his stern demeanor. His face should be wreathed in smiles from sun to sun."

The other woman giggled and confessed, "But, it is, my friend. You should see him when he scowls! He is truly fierce to behold then!"

A further surprise was to find that Shining Star had already begun sewing Sarah's wedding dress for her. "Night Hawk asked me to make it for you. I think he does not trust Little Rabbit not to ruin it. I am glad that you now know that you are to wed with him, for I need to know your size. I would hate to make the dress too small or too short for you."

In the end, Sarah wound up helping Shining Star sew and decorate the dress. It was a golden opportunity to learn the correct way to size and cut and stitch the soft doeskin. This dress, however, was not of deer hide. It was the hide of a young female antelope. It had been tanned and cured to the soft creamy color of freshly churned butter, and when it was finished it would be beautifully decorated with dyed quills and beads and yards of long, whispering fringe. There would be new moccasins to match, and Shining Star informed her that Night Hawk would himself make the special headband Sarah was to wear on her wedding day.

It was then that Sarah took the first step toward her own destiny. By offering to help with the dress, she was, in effect, agreeing to marry Night

Hawk. She reinforced that acceptance by agreeing to make Night Hawk's wedding headband, as Shining Star told her was traditional for the bride to do. By accepting the gifts he gave her, she was telling Night Hawk, without words, that she accepted him as her future husband.

Sarah was preparing for her wedding. No, *Flame* was doing so. Sarah was a spoiled, pampered Washington debutante. Flame was a Cheyenne chief's captive—a young girl who was rapidly becoming a woman, who was daily learning the Cheyenne language and customs and was even now losing her heart to the proud, handsome captor soon to be her husband. Bit by bit, in the ensuing days, Sarah ceased to be, and Flame was born in her stead.

Chapter
11

The days until her wedding sped by. They were tumultuous days, spent veering between severe bouts of homesickness and anxious anticipation, reluctance and strange yearnings. If she were home in Washington, a suitor would have brought her candy and roses and sonnets. He might have quoted poetry to her on the porch. It was different with Night Hawk, yet much the same. They walked, they talked, they learned about each other. They exchanged soft words, laughter, and occasional stolen caresses. At night, when the stars were bright in the clear night sky, he would sit outside the tipi and play sweet, haunting melodies for her on his flute, wooing her with his music.

Only the gifts differed. Instead of sweets or

flowers, he brought her feathers and beads and pumice stone to soften her skin. He brought her fruit and pretty stones. Once, he brought her a great handful of glowing yellow stones. When Sarah looked closely at them, she nearly swallowed her tongue. They were gold! Solid gold! The whole lot of them! As she stared at them in open-mouthed amazement, it almost made her swoon to think what this much gold would buy in Washington. The gowns! The jewels! The bonnets and slippers! A new carriage and horses to match! Of course, she had no real idea exactly how much the gold nuggets in her hands would buy. Her father had paid all her bills, and she had never paid any attention to prices. Nevertheless, the gold must be worth a small fortune.

When she had overcome her initial shock, Sarah gave a rueful laugh. Oh, the irony of it all! Here she sat, her palms laden with gold, and there was not a shop or a store or a stable for miles! Sarah laughed until the tears rolled down her cheeks, and when she had composed herself once more, she put the nuggets safely away in a little leather pouch and turned her back on them. Gold would not buy her freedom, and that was the only thing she wished for now.

One day, Night Hawk surprised her with a special gift that stole her heart immediately. He brought her a darling baby raccoon. The little animal was so soft and so furry and so funny-looking, with his small black-masked face, that Sarah fell in love with him on sight. Night Hawk told her that she could keep him as a pet, and she promptly named him Bandit, a name he was soon to live up to.

Though she continued her studies with Night Hawk, Sarah also soon resumed some of her previous duties about the tipi. As Night Hawk's wife, she would be expected to share these chores with Little Rabbit. Little Rabbit was appeased somewhat by Flame's help, but still irked that Night Hawk was strictly supervising their tasks, watching to make sure that Little Rabbit did not put more than a fair share of the work onto Flame.

In addition to such duties, Sarah found time to finish the headband she was making for Night Hawk to wear at their wedding. With Shining Star's help and guidance, she flattened and dyed quills, then sewed them carefully onto the leather headband in an intricate design of her own choosing. In the center of the headband was the silhouette of a hawk flying across a full night moon. At the edges of the headband, she affixed the small, fluffy under-feathers of a hawk. These Shining Star had gladly donated. The finished headband was very well done, and Shining Star complimented her, telling Sarah that it was one of the finest she had seen, and truly worthy to be worn by a chief.

Without telling him why she wanted them, Sarah asked Night Hawk for the teeth of the wolf he had slain in saving her life that day on the trail. Though he had collected them from the dead animal, he had not put them to any use as

yet. If Night Hawk wondered why she wanted
them, he did not ask, and gave them to her
without qualm, though they were his prize and
not hers.

Sarah wanted to give Night Hawk some sort of
personal wedding gift, besides the headband, so
she secretly worked the wolf's teeth into an
intricately braided necklace made of long strands
of her own bright hair. It would be a gift to
remind him of her always, a personal apology for
bringing with her no dowry, as most Cheyenne
maidens did. She also laboriously heated and
pounded several of the gold nuggets into two
shiny hair discs. With these, his hawk and eagle
feathers could be fastened in his dark hair. Sarah
was well pleased with the final product, a fine gift
for her husband on their wedding day. She liked
them so well that she made a pair for herself, to
wear with the redbird and bluebird feathers
Night Hawk had brought her, telling her that they
matched her hair and eyes. She would wear them
and the feathers in her hair at her wedding.

Much of this extra time to make her gifts was
spent in the women's lodge. When Sarah awoke
one morning to find she had gotten her monthly
flow, she was surprised to learn that she must
now go into seclusion in the women's lodge until
her bleeding had ceased. She and her friends
back home had sometimes referred to this time
as "the curse," but it seemed the Cheyenne truly
considered it to be one. They believed that if a
woman prepared a warrior's meal, or touched his
weapons or any of his personal apparel during
her time of bleeding, it was considered a very bad

omen. Even should she do this inadvertently, he could be killed in battle or meet with some horrible accident or other disaster.

To prevent this, a woman was temporarily banished from her family's tipi during this period, spending it in the women's tent with others similarly afflicted. Sarah came to learn that a woman was not actually considered to be cursed, as such, at this time of her moon month. She was just considered to possess powerful magic that could counter the protective powers that surrounded the warrior and his weapons, powers bestowed upon the warrior by the tribal shaman through prayers and chants.

Sarah also learned that this special tipi was used not only for the seclusion of women having their monthly flow. It was the place where the Cheyenne women came to give birth to their babies. When a woman went into labor, she came here to be attended by her Cheyenne sisters and an old woman specially trained in aiding with births—a midwife of sorts, as best Sarah could figure. To Sarah's vast relief, no one went into labor while she was in seclusion. After living all of her life in a society where doctors delivered babies, she was horrified to think of having a child in such a crude environment, miles from the nearest doctor or medical attention of any kind. She trembled at the thought that she might one day be forced to do just that, should she conceive a child by Night Hawk.

While she was in the women's lodge, Sarah found to her delight and relief that many of the Cheyenne women were prepared to accept her as

Chief Night Hawk's wife. They were not all of a mind with Little Rabbit. Many of them expressed their shame at the way their Cheyenne sister had treated her, asking her not to think that they were all so mean-hearted.

Of course, there were others who remained cool, if not outright disdainful, but Sarah could accept their snubbing with a lighter heart now that she knew she was genuinely accepted by many. Then, too, during her time in the women's lodge, she did not have to endure Little Rabbit's sour looks or snide remarks, which the woman continued whenever Night Hawk was not around to notice. For this alone Sarah was thankful, but it pleased her even more to know that she might have women friends here after all, besides Shining Star. She badly missed her female friends back home. She missed talking about fashions and parties and gossiping with them. The thought of spending years here and never having other women to talk with had weighed more heavily on her than she realized.

Her wedding day soon arrived, and Sarah was as nervous as any young bride. Taking advantage of Flame's frayed nerves, Little Rabbit did her best to taunt the girl with tales of horror about wedding nights. Luckily, before too much damage was done, Night Hawk sent Shining Star and several other Cheyenne women to the tipi. They were to prepare Flame for the ceremony.

Besides allaying most of the fright Little Rabbit had instilled in her, by telling her what she should expect of her groom on the wedding night, they also instructed her in her part of the wedding ceremony itself. This they did while grooming her. By the time they were half done, Sarah was wondering whether they were being kind or cruel. She was washed from head to toe, pummeled and prodded, and literally scrubbed raw. The roughened skin on her hands and feet and knees and elbows was softened with pumice. The hair on every inch of her body except her scalp was plucked, and Sarah was glowing with embarrassment and pain long before they were finished. Then she was liberally rubbed with some sort of fragrant lotion that made her skin feel like satin. Even her freshly washed hair was brushed dry and rubbed with a flower-scented lotion, which made it shine like the setting sun.

At last she was dressed in the lovely doeskin wedding dress and moccasins that Shining Star had made for her. The discs and feathers were fastened in her hair, which was left long and loose according to tradition. Last of all, the beautiful headband that Night Hawk had made himself, was tied about her forehead. Of a color to match her dress, it was decorated with blue, red, and white quills. Across the front of the band, three copper discs, each shaped like a flame, were evenly spaced. It was a beautiful finishing touch.

Night Hawk was waiting for her outside their tipi. Most of the tribe had gathered about to witness the joining of one of their chiefs with this white woman. But after one look at Night Hawk, Sarah had eyes for no one else. A flock of hummingbirds had taken wing in her stomach, and the sight of him did nothing to calm her. He was standing tall and proud, his dark eyes blazing as she walked toward him. He was dressed in heavily fringed, light-tanned buckskin breeches and shirt. The shirt and ceremonial breechclout were ornately decorated, as were the moccasins on his feet. His hair, too, had been left loose, except for one thin side braid adorned with feathers. About his forehead was the headband Sarah had made for him. Around his throat was a bone-link necklace of several strands and a bone disk on a short leather thong. He was handsome beyond belief, and Sarah's heart fluttered madly as she slowly approached him.

Before the actual joining took place, Night Hawk asked his friend Stone Face to bring forth the bride price payment. Flame, who knew nothing of Night Hawk's plans, was surprised when Stone Face led forward a pretty little brown-and-white pinto mare. Night Hawk presented Flame with the pony, telling her and everyone else that the pony was hers, since he could not pay a bride price to her father for her.

Touched nearly to tears, Flame then shyly presented Night Hawk with the wolf's-teeth necklace, asking him to take this in place of the dowry she could not bring to him. He accepted it with grave sincerity, saying that her beauty alone would have been dowry enough.

Night Hawk now placed the marriage blanket about both their shoulders. The tribal shaman blessed them with chanted words and prayers for long lives and fruitfulness. Flame and Night

Hawk then took their places on mats placed side by side outside the tipi. Shining Star placed before them the food that Flame had earlier prepared, food provided by Night Hawk for this purpose.

Their bridal supper consisted of roast meat, acorn bread, honey, and fruit. Following ceremonial custom, Flame chose a piece of meat from the bowl for herself and one for Night Hawk. Handing him his, she quoted, "I offer this meat, which you have provided, to strengthen our bodies for our life together."

When they had eaten the meat, she then took a piece of bread and broke it in half, giving him a portion. "I share with you this bread, made of my labors, to soothe our souls and give us peace together."

Now it was Night Hawk's turn. With great dignity, he lifted the small bowl of honey. Dipping his fingers into it, he took a taste. Then, holding the bowl below her chin to catch any drips, he brought his honey-sweet fingers to her lips. As she shyly licked the nectar from his fingers, he said, "This honey I offer to you, to sweeten your heart toward me always." His black eyes twinkled with delight as a rosy flush crept over her face.

Last came the fruit. Again Night Hawk took the lead. Choosing a ripe fall apple, he took a bite from it. Turning the fruit so that her lips would touch the same portion of the apple his had, he placed it near her mouth. "This fruit I share with you that we also may be fruitful and have strong sons and beautiful daughters." Embarrassment almost choked her as Flame bit into the juicy apple before so many spectators.

Love, strength, peace, and children—they were the joys of marriage, the blessings wished upon couples everywhere, regardless of race or religion, country or culture. For the first time, Sarah truly believed in this strange ceremony that was uniting her with Night Hawk. It was a marriage as real and binding as any, and she was shaken to her very soul to realize what a momentous step she was now taking by joining her life with his, even though she had been left little choice in the matter.

Murmurs of approval came from the witnesses as Night Hawk rose and pulled his blushing bride to her feet. Upon each of her slim wrists he placed a beautifully engraved copper wristband, similar to his own but smaller. These marked her as his wife, for all to behold. The etchings on the bands read, "You are mine from this day forward, as I am yours."

Now that they were man and wife, he bestowed upon her another wedding gift. She could not suppress her gasp of delight as he fastened a gleaming gold necklace about her throat. It must have taken him a great deal of time and effort to fashion the gold links of the chain. Dangling from several of the loops were seven golden ornaments, each hammered into the shape of a flame. With a sweet smile, she thanked him and in return presented him with the gold hair discs she had made for him. His black eyes shone down into hers as he praised her efforts, and told her how much the gift pleased him.

In the final act of the ceremony, Night Hawk took her hand and gently led her into their tipi. Shining Star stepped forward then and laced the tipi closure shut, leaving the two newlyweds in privacy. Little Rabbit had for this night been banished to her mother's tipi.

Outside their tipi, the crowd quietly dispersed, some softly discussing the ceremony, the bride's great beauty, the fact that Chief Night Hawk had chosen a white woman for his bride. Others commented on the fact that Little Rabbit had not been present to witness her husband's second marriage. This was an open affront to Night Hawk, but not one which he could punish. It was the first wife's decision whether or not she would attend the ceremony joining her husband with a second or third wife, but most wives chose to attend. Most also helped to prepare the new bride before the ceremony, and publicly welcomed her into their home. They had been raised since they were young girls to accept their husbands' wives as sisters and helpmates. Obviously, Little Rabbit was not prepared to accept Flame with an open and generous heart, but given the woman's jealous nature this came as no real surprise, and it did not reflect badly upon Flame.

Inside the tipi, Flame was facing Night Hawk shyly, her face feverishly colored, her bright eyes not quite able to meet his. As she stood there quivering, half wanting to run, half wanting to have him teach her what it was to be a woman, he took the few steps to close the distance between them.

"Come, wife," he said softly, taking her cold hand and leading her to the sleeping mat. "Come let me hold you, see you, touch you. Come give yourself to me and become a woman in my arms."

Slowly, as if he were uncovering some priceless hidden treasure, he undressed her. Kneeling at her feet, in a manner strangely subservient for him, he removed her moccasins. Her dress fell into soft folds about her bare feet. For long moments his midnight-black eyes caressed her and, impossible as it seemed, they turned even darker. Twin forces pulled at her, making her at once supremely embarrassed as she stood naked before him, and oddly proud upon seeing the open desire and admiration on his face.

He rose and took her hands, placing them on the lacings of his shirt front. Without words, he was asking her to return the favor, and Flame's hands trembled so badly she was not certain she could do as he bade her. Gathering all of her shaky courage, she unlaced the shirt and pulled it over his head as he bent to help her in her efforts. With mouth gone dry, she hesitated; he waited anxiously, but patiently, until she finally reached out and tugged at the lacings of his leggings. First one, then the other, came loose and fell to the ground. Flame could not yet bring herself to remove his breechclout, and it was with profound relief that she noticed that Night Hawk still wore his moccasins. Sweeping the discarded leggings aside, she knelt and slowly removed his footwear.

The time had come. She had delayed as long as possible. He wore nothing now except the breechclout. Forcing herself to rise on trembling legs that barely held her weight, she stood before him once more—vulnerable, embarrassed, shy of her own nakedness before him. Unable to meet his intense gaze, she stared at his broad bronze chest. Her hands felt like ice, her fingers gone numb. She swallowed shakily at the lump lodged in her throat, but could neither dispel it nor bring any moisture to her parched mouth. She could hear nothing over the sound of her own heart beating in her ears.

Night Hawk waited, hardly daring to breathe, as she stood before him. He stood as if carved of stone, knowing her fear, feeling it. Her timid gestures touched his heart as she went against everything she had previously been taught in her efforts to please him. After what seemed a lifetime, she reached out to him again. Her trembling fingers touched the ties of his breechclout, then suddenly drew back as if burned. He heard her small gasp, and watched, his gaze falling on her bright bowed head, as she fought to overcome her timidness. Once more her hands reached for him, and now she did not draw back. Quickly, as if she feared she would lose her courage, she loosened the ties. Her gaze flew back to his chest and locked there as his final garment fell between them.

She stood as if frozen—unable to move, to

breathe. Then Night Hawk reached out his hand
and gently tilted her stiff face upward toward his.
Her eyes were huge, and they clung to his,
pleading with silent eloquence for him to lead the
way, for him to teach her tenderly. Slowly he
lowered his head until his warm, firm lips covered hers. The kiss was as soft and easy as a slow
summer rain. With his tongue he moistened her
dry lips, parting them with his own. He breached
the barrier of her teeth, and laved her parched
mouth, offering solace for her thirst. Her lips
softened beneath his, and he felt her tremble as
she leaned against him for support, skin against
heated skin.

When her knees threatened to give way beneath her, Night Hawk lowered her slowly to the
waiting mat. There he gathered her tenderly into
his arms, doing no more than to kiss and hold her
for the longest time. His long hard body warmed
hers where it touched, his hands framed her face
as his lips slowly worked their enchantment upon
hers.

Flame felt her resistance melting like the last
snow on a warm spring day. Her lips responded
to his, tentatively at first, then more fully. Before
she realized it, her arms had crept of their own
accord to twine about his neck. Her fingers
delved deeply into his thick black hair, holding
his lips more firmly to her own. His long, loose
hair brushed teasingly where it fell across her
shoulder and chest, and she found the sensation
very pleasant, very intimate. It drifted about
their faces in a warm, dark cloud, enclosing them
in a world all their own.

His hands left her face, to be replaced by his wandering lips. Oh, so softly did he cover her face with delicate kisses, until she quivered beneath him with mounting desire. His warm breath teased at the shell of her ear as he gently nibbled at her lobe, sending goose flesh racing across her bare body. Warm, strong fingers caressed her shoulders, steadying her in this rising storm he was creating. His lips slid down the length of her slender neck, his tongue sliding along her heated flesh. He found the sensitive dip of her shoulder, nipping gently and causing her to shiver in delight. His mouth closed over the racing pulse at the base of her throat and lingered there, then came slowly back to claim her hungry lips as his palms tenderly cradled her throbbing breasts.

With his lips, Night Hawk silenced her gasp as his hands found and fondled her waiting breasts. Calloused fingers gently worried the rosy crests, and they pouted prettily beneath his knowing touch, springing to life like rosebuds in the morning dew. Flame mewled softly, and her body arched upward like that of a cat demanding to be petted, pleading for more of this magical wonder.

Flame was adrift on clouds of desire. Her body knew only an intense longing for his touch, his tender caress. Warm fingers teased at her breasts; his tongue glided across hers, inviting it to join in the sensuous dance, an invitation she was powerless to refuse. One large hand drifted slowly down her ribcage, then meandered across her quivering belly. There it lingered to lightly knead and soothe, before traveling the length of one long, slender leg. When his hand gently parted her thighs to caress the soft inner skin there, she did not resist; she found no wish to stop his tender foray.

Only when that warm hand covered the mound of her femininity did he at last meet with resistance. With soft words and tender kisses, he lured her back under his dark spell. His fingers found that small button of her sensuality, and she lurched beneath him. His fingers moved to taunt and tantalize, and she trembled violently. Relentlessly, he tormented her, until she was moving against his touch, small moans issuing from her arched throat as she writhed and thrashed. Long fingers entered her and found her moist and ready, and so very hot.

Parting her thighs further, he lowered himself over her, his mouth ever enchanting hers lest she panic now and cause herself more pain than was inevitable. Slowly, carefully, he introduced his body into hers. He felt her stiffen at this strange invasion, and he stopped until he once more had her calmed and yearning for him. Then with one swift, merciful lunge, he broke through her maidenhead. Her startled shriek was muffled by his mouth over hers. Buried deep within her, he lay motionless, giving the pain time to subside. His hands stroked her body until she relaxed beneath him again, quivering and pliant. Slowly, easily, holding his own immense needs in check, he began to move within her silken sheath.

The sudden pain startled her half out of her blissful state. She yelped in surprise and distress, and stiffened beneath him, though she had been warned what to expect. As the pain subsided, other sensations came to the fore. It felt so very strange to be filled by him, to feel him move within the body that until now had been strictly hers. His hands caressed her breasts, his fingers brushing lightly over her nipples, and she felt the sensation deep within her, where he now lay so firmly entrenched. As he began to move within her, her entire body tingled to life. His tongue imitated the gestures below, and a silken mist enshrouded her once more, making her senses spin. The yearning built and built, and she clung to him, soon matching him move for move, naturally, unconsciously.

"Yield to me, Flame," she heard him whisper against her lips. "Yield all to me."

His hands moved to her hips, guiding her into his rhythm as he plunged into her receptive body again and again. She was so warm, so hot and wet and tight that he nearly lost control before he could bring her pleasure of her own. Gritting his teeth to stem his overwhelming passion he slowed his strokes, feeling her arch against him in search of the ultimate splendor just beyond her grasp. Then she went wild beneath him, and his blood coursed through his body like wildfire. He felt the tremors begin to quake within her. She cried out, and her passionate cries were sweet music to his tortured senses, a temptress's song luring him to join her in her ecstasy, even as her hands clawed furrows in his back.

She was flame and fire, tinder set to the torch. Never had she felt such glorious, burning torment; never would she have dreamed it possible. Her body was ablaze with desire, writhing in the need for some elusive grandeur. With every movement, he ignited more and more sparks within her, until she was aglow with passionate yearning, her pulse pounding madly, her breath coming in short, urgent spurts.

Then the fire blazed out of control, hurtling them both into a raging inferno, consuming them, branding them, melding them as one. Ecstasy engulfed them in dazzling, dancing flames that carried them higher and higher into an endless fire-filled sky. Eternity passed before they slowly drifted down to lie replete in each other's arms, smoldering embers waiting helplessly for the next passionate breeze to fan them into flames once more.

Chapter
12

In the days that followed, Night Hawk was amused to see how shy his young bride remained, even while she turned unbelievably passionate in his arms each night. He had only to touch her, and she burst into flames. This ecstasy to be found between a man and a woman was so new to her, but already she was a willing student, learning eagerly all that he could teach her.

As a part of her punishment for treating Flame so badly and for deliberately defying Night Hawk's commands, Little Rabbit was banned from their tipi for the week following Night Hawk and Flame's joining ceremony. She was not to have any contact with either of them for seven suns. It was a small punishment, but it was all he could do to teach her obedience and still not harm the child she carried. It served its purpose, in that Little Rabbit was denied his presence, which she craved above all else; and it also provided the newly joined couple the privacy they desired.

Flame, especially, was glad that Little Rabbit was not there to taunt her, for the burden of her own confusion was great enough to bear. To wake each morning enfolded in Night Hawk's embrace, or with her head pillowed upon his broad shoulder and her bright hair streaming across his chest, their limbs entangled, brought embarrassment flooding through her. Recalling the wild passion of the previous night, Flame could scarcely bring herself to face him. She could not deceive herself into believing that she had not thoroughly enjoyed their lovemaking. Not even to herself could she deny craving his touch upon her heated flesh, and this both angered and dismayed her. Humiliation and guilt assaulted her, for this man had not needed to resort to force to bed her. Quite the contrary! She fell quite willingly into his embrace each night, and she was ashamed and disgusted that she could surrender her body so readily to her enemy, her captor, her husband.

Was he really still her enemy now? Yet, if he were not, what was he? Was he her friend? He had been her captor, but he was also her protector. He had stolen her away from all that was familiar to her, yet now he was patiently teaching her to survive in his world. He had abducted her, then saved her life. Thrust into this strange new

environment, she was now reliant upon him
for all her needs. He was her provider, all
that kept her safe and warm and fed and
clothed.

Flame wondered at her own sanity these days.
How had she come to trust so readily this man
who had captured her? Where once she had
feared him, she now turned to him for guidance.
She found herself admiring not only his
magnificently formed body, but his quick mind,
his bravery, even his devotion to his gods. His
skills as a hunter, a warrior, a leader in his tribe,
drew her reluctant respect. Night Hawk was a
man of honor and pride, and she could not fault
him for this. In her heart, she knew that if she
had met him in Washington, if he had been a
white man of social standing, with all these
qualities that were so admirable, she would have
fallen deeply in love with him in short order. And
that, above all else, was her greatest fear—that
she would come to love this man she now called
husband, this savage who was strong enough to
be tender, this bronze warrior who had changed
her life and her name and claimed her for his
own.

The days were easier than the nights in some
respects. Then, at least, she had chores to occupy
her mind and her time. Night Hawk was often
gone for much of the day, attending to his duties
as chief, hunting or training with his friends. It
was when the sun began to set in the west that
Flame's nerves began to dance, her eyes straying
every few seconds to the tipi opening, her heart
thundering in anticipation of his arrival.

She would serve him his meal, trying not to look at him, blushing wildly when she felt his eyes on her. When he had had his fill, she would eat, as was the accepted custom. Women and children rarely ate with the men, and the men were always served the choicest portions, for they needed their strength in order to provide for and protect their families. After the meal, Night Hawk sometimes resumed their language lessons. Though she tried to concentrate on his teaching, Sarah's mind kept wandering to what was to come. Sometimes they sat in awkward silence, she sewing and he working on his weapons, while the tension built to an almost unbearable level.

Then, finally, when Flame thought she surely could not stand the strain a moment longer, he would calmly walk to the sleeping mat. Without words, his glowing black eyes would beckon her, and she was helpless to refuse. Quickly she would bank the fire and go to stand awkwardly before him, her body already quivering to feel his touch.

That was all it took—one touch, the merest caress of his hand or sensuous lips, and her limbs would turn to hot jelly. Her eyes, with a will of their own, would fly unbidden to his, entranced by the desire that shone there. Her hands would seek his hard, hot body—and she would be lost in their mutual passion from that moment on, giving no thought to anything else, until she awoke next to him the following morning.

Often, she would awaken to find him watching her, a strange smile pulling at his lips, a warm glow in his dark eyes, and she would know without being told that he desired her again.

Before the fire was built or the morning meal was begun, before he rose to chant his morning prayers, he would claim her again. With their bodies still warm and relaxed from sleep, with tender caresses and sighs, they would again seek those high cliffs of rapture, where only he could lead her.

That first week of being his wife passed, and Little Rabbit once more shared their tipi. If Flame had thought she was embarrassed before, it was nothing compared to now, for Night Hawk still required her to share his sleeping mat each night. Never in her wildest dreams had it occurred to Flame to consider that their mating would continue with Little Rabbit there to witness it! Flame was mortified. Little Rabbit was none too pleased either. Only Night Hawk seemed unperturbed with the arrangement.

That first night, when Little Rabbit had sullenly sought her bed, Flame turned with relief to her own solitary mat. She had taken perhaps two steps when Night Hawk's deep voice halted her in her tracks. "No, Flame," he told her. "You shall share my sleeping mat this night."

Shocked, Flame could scarcely believe she had heard him correctly. With stunned eyes, she turned to stare at him, certain he was not serious. One look told her that he was very serious. Still, she tried to change his mind, her upbringing making the arrangement unacceptable to her. "Surely, you jest, Night Hawk." Her eyes darted to where Little Rabbit was watching them with a malevolent glare. "I wish to retire to my own mat."

"I am your husband, Flame. Do you dare to deny me my rights?" If he felt the least bit of pity for her, it did not show in the cool, inky depths of his bold gaze. "Take yourself to my mat, as I bid you."

Her face flaming, she gathered her courage. "No."

The single word seemed to hang in the air over them. His face darkened in warning, his eyes narrowing as he glared at her. "Go. Now." He pointed a long finger to his mat. When she stood her ground, he growled, "Do this of your own accord, or I shall force you to do so."

Her chin quivered, and she wanted to burst into tears. Only Little Rabbit's presence and Flame's pride prevented it. Mutely, she shook her head.

They stared at one another for long minutes. Then, with a sigh of regret, Night Hawk tightened his grip on her arm and dragged Flame to his mat. Struggling uselessly against his superior strength, she could not tear herself from his hold.

It had been many days since Flame had had cause to fear him, but the grim set of his mouth and the anger blazing from his onyx eyes sent quivers through her. She could not prevent a smothered screech as he pulled the dress roughly over her head and left her standing naked before him. He shoved her to the mat, following her down and pinning her to the mat with his body. Rough fingers grazed her cheeks and clamped about her head, as he captured her one long braid in his hand and forced her frightened eyes to his. "Cease your struggles, wife," he warned softly.

"Do not fight me, Flame, for you have no hope of winning this battle."

"Let me go," she implored on a quavering whisper. "Please."

"I cannot. Nor do I wish to do so." His face held no mercy as he loomed over her.

Tears rolled from her eyes and plopped upon his wrists. "Why must you humiliate me this way?" she choked out.

"It is you who humiliate yourself by your rebellious behavior," he informed her firmly. "Why are you suddenly so stubborn?"

A look of genuine bafflement creased his brow, and Flame could not believe he did not see the problem. "Do you truly not know, Night Hawk?" she asked in astonishment. "Can it be that you do not know the cause of my distress?"

"If there is a reason for your disobedience, you must explain. You can not expect me to read your thoughts." He waited in tense silence for her reply.

"First answer me this," she requested. "Is it common for a Cheyenne man to take a wife to his mat, while the other wife is present to hear and see their mating?"

Night Hawk nodded. "Yes. Where else would she be, but in her own tipi? Does the white man send one wife from his lodge when he beds the other?" He was truly puzzled by her question, for it seemed so odd to his thinking.

"Night Hawk, a white man takes but one wife," Flame explained earnestly. "Never is that wife required to display her body to anyone but him, and certainly not to mate before anyone else's eyes. In my world, it is a very private thing, meant only for the husband and wife to share between themselves."

Amazed to learn this, Night Hawk was beginning to understand. "Ah, I see," he said softly. "When Little Rabbit was not here these past nights, you thought it was because we were mating, and when she returned this night, you believed I would no longer require you to share my mat. Is this not so?"

"Yes," she nodded, relieved that he no longer seemed angry with her.

"Little Rabbit was being punished for her treatment of you, Flame. That was the reason she was not sharing our lodge. Her return does not change things between you and me. Her presence does not lessen my desire for you, and as my wife you must obey me in this, as in all things. I regret that this bothers you, but it is the way of things, and you will soon become accustomed to it."

"I think not," she answered tightly. "Perhaps you have no modesty, no shame, but I do. I can not help feeling the way I do. It is the way I was raised. Mating before another's eyes goes against everything I have been taught and believe."

Tension shimmered between them once more, their wills battling with one another. Finally Night Hawk suggested softly, "That you may preserve your modesty, Shy One, and not shame yourself, I shall grant you the right to hang a blanket between my mat and Little Rabbit's. In this way, she may not see what we do, and you shall have your precious privacy." At Flame's dubious look, he added, "This is all I will concede, wife. It is either a blanket to shield you from her eyes, or none at all. I care not, for I intend to have you either way."

A blanket was better than nothing, and Flame was wise enough to realize that she could not bargain further with him. As she gazed up at him, she was sure no other man would have granted her this much, and that it was a great concession. It was still humiliating to know that Little Rabbit would hear them and know what they were about, but it was all Flame could hope to achieve for herself. Swallowing her own pride, she said humbly, "I will accept your offer of the blanket, Night Hawk."

"Husband," he corrected with a taunting, superior smile.

"Husband," she murmured.

It was with immense relief that she found herself released to string the blanket across the interior of the tipi. Too few minutes later, she had to force herself to return to her place at his side, and all through their lovemaking, she was excruciatingly aware that Little Rabbit lay mere feet beyond the barrier of the blanket, listening to every sound they made. Nevertheless, try as she might, she could not still the small moans that crept from her throat as Night Hawk worked his dark magic upon her senses, nor her ecstatic cry when together they found that shattering release among the stars.

That Night Hawk's desire for Flame did not diminish did nothing to improve Little Rabbit's hateful disposition. Rather, it stirred the fires of resentment that bristled between the two women. However, now much more secure in her position as Night Hawk's wife, though still second in rank to Little Rabbit, Flame found herself responding in kind. After what she had endured before at Little Rabbit's hands, Flame swore she would never allow the Cheyenne woman such liberties again. The fact that Night Hawk had forbidden it made Flame even more sure of herself, for Little Rabbit would not dare to anger him again.

Little by little, almost without her realizing it, Flame regained her former confidence. With head held high and eyes blazing, she dared Little Rabbit to overstep her bounds. Arrogance put a new bounce to Flame's stride, a bite to her tongue. No longer was she a mere captive slave, to be beaten and whipped and trod upon. She was Chief Night Hawk's wife, and her attitude now reflected this, much to Little Rabbit's aggravation. That Flame might be overstepping her own bounds never occurred to the haughty young bride. The tension between the two wives soon became a source of amusement among the other Cheyenne women, who watched and waited and giggled behind their hands, wondering and making sly bets on just how long it would take before one or the other pushed a bit too hard and set off another confrontation.

Night Hawk was not blind to their petty squabbles and kept a sharp eye on both his wives. Often he had to rebuke one or the other for their sharp words and willful attitudes. As the bickering continued, he had to wonder at his own madness, to have saddled himself with two such stubborn wives. Yet even as he drew on every bit of his patience, he had to admire Flame's spirit. No longer was she a timid little mouse, and his heart was glad for this. Released from Little Rabbit's tyranny, Flame was blossoming before his eyes. Her newfound confidence brought a glow to her cheeks and her bright blue eyes. Rather than cower before Little Rabbit's hatefulness, she stood her ground proudly and defiantly— perhaps too defiantly sometimes, but she would soon learn her place in the scheme of things. Meanwhile, she was holding her own against her rival, and when it was not trying his patience too severely, Night Hawk found it greatly entertaining to behold.

A mere two weeks after Flame's wedding, the Northern Cheyenne tribe pulled up stakes and moved to their winter campgrounds. This was yet another new experience for Flame, for she had never dismantled a tipi before. It was quite an undertaking, and Little Rabbit did not make it any easier with her constant complaints and back-biting.

The sturdier poles were lashed together to form a kind of sled, or travois. The skins were rolled and tied to this, along with their sleeping mats and other robes from their bedding. Their few cooking utensils and personal items were carefully packed in parfleches and loaded on the travois or tied to the backs of packhorses, as was their clothing. Leather bags of food, water, medicine, and other necessities were put within easy reach in the packing order, as were Night Hawk's extra weapons.

Flame was amazed at how quickly and efficiently the other women dismantled their tipis and packed their various belongings, and she tried to emulate their work. Her ignorance of the proper procedure and Little Rabbit's reluctance to help did not make things go smoothly, but eventually all was in readiness.

Just preparing to move was a major chore, and Flame felt she had done a day's work within an hour's time. The sun had barely cleared the top of the mountains as they left the old campsite. Seeing many women trudging along on foot beside their travois and pack horses, Flame suddenly realized how fortunate she was to be the wife of a chief. Night Hawk owned many ponies, and she was grateful to have one to call her own. Of course, even had he not given her the little pinto at their wedding, she could have ridden astride one of his other ponies. Still, she was proud to own one of her very own, especially since Little Rabbit had her own horse.

Flame settled the wriggly little raccoon more securely in his carrying pouch hanging from the pommel of Dancer's saddle, and gazed about in mounting interest. She giggled to note that Bandit was suspended in much the same manner as other women had secured their babies' cradleboards.

As she looked ahead and behind, the ragged line of travelers stretched out almost as far as the eye could see. Behind lay their old camp, the grass now whithered and battered down by many footsteps. It was hard to believe that by spring, there would be no sign of their having camped there. Ahead lay rocky hills and jagged mountains, and many days of travel to reach their destination. Once again Flame marveled at the stamina of the Cheyenne people, especially the women and children.

They were headed deep into the hills, far beyond where the white man traveled. There, Shining Star had explained, they would set up their camp in a safe, secluded location. There were many prime locations from which to choose, but always they tried to find a place where they were sheltered from the harsh winter winds, a place where their enemies would not think to look for them and where they could wait out the long, snowy winter until spring once more awakened the land.

As she rode along, two emotions warred in Flame's breast. She found herself curious about what lay ahead even as she felt deep sorrow that each step took her farther from her father's reach. Would she ever see his dear face again? While a part of her was almost resigned to her new life, a larger part of her still yearned for what was lost. Even now, despite the joy she found in Night Hawk's embrace—or perhaps because she found such delight in his arms—she longed to return to her former life. If she was not rescued soon, she feared she was doomed to lose her heart to her handsome warrior chief, and God help her if that should happen.

Chapter 13

Two long weeks of arduous travel finally brought them to their destination. Looking about her, Flame could see why the Cheyenne might choose such a place. The secluded little valley was nestled securely in the hills. On the north and west, high hills sheltered the site from winter winds. A forest bordered the eastern edge of the vale, but it was not so near that an enemy could attack the village without having to cross a large stretch of open ground first. Wood and meat would be easily obtained here for their winter needs. To the south ran a mountain brook, and beyond that the valley stretched out in endlessly rolling hillocks. It was a lovely place, where God's beauty was undisturbed by the hand of man. Standing there admiring it, Flame could well understand why the Indians wanted to keep it this way.

There was a great deal of work to accomplish in setting up the new camp. The tipis had to be erected in their proper order and a meal prepared for the weary travelers. While some of the warriors and braves went in search of fresh meat, others would help to corral the vast herd of extra ponies. Meanwhile, the women would fetch water and firewood and set up their new homes.

Tired and bone-sore from the weeks of travel, Flame was not in the best of moods. As she worked to erect Night Hawk's tipi, with little help and many rebukes from Little Rabbit, her temper rose. It did no good to remind herself that Little Rabbit was just as weary as she, and that the other woman was undoubtedly irritable from her advanced pregnancy. Flame knew from bitter experience that Little Rabbit was bad-tempered by nature, and lazy as well. While Flame labored to erect the poles and tie the many skins over the conical framework, Little Rabbit barely stirred herself, except to criticize Flame's efforts.

Finally, the tipi was in place. Now came the task of unpacking the travois and transfering their belongings to the tipi. The lodge fire still had to be set up, and fresh water brought from the river before their evening meal could be cooked. Resentfully, Flame noted that Little Rabbit was selecting her own items from the travois, not bothering to carry anything else into the newly erected tipi. Weary beyond belief, it was all Flame could do not to kick the other woman in her wide behind.

Leaving the tipi, Little Rabbit stood deliberately blocking Flame's path into the lodge. With her arms full of heavy robes, Flame gritted her teeth and muttered, "Move from my way, Little Rabbit."

The other woman stood where she was, an insolent look on her plain face. "When you have finished unloading the travois, we need wood for our fire," she said commandingly. "Then we must have water from the river." Little Rabbit was at her bossy best this day.

"I am well aware of that, Little Rabbit," Flame retorted smartly. "Perhaps you could stir your lazy bones to do some of the work yourself, as you have done little enough this day." With a gleam of fire in her bright eyes, she dumped the armload of robes at Little Rabbit's feet. "You might start with these, since you refuse to let me pass with them." Grabbing several water skins from a nearby pile, Flame marched off toward the river, pausing once to shoot Little Rabbit a nasty glare over her shoulder. The woman was still standing there doing nothing but staring after her with a haughty smile. Flame almost roared with anger. Damn that lazy, hateful woman's hide, anyway!

Taking her time with the water, and hoping her temper would cool in the process, Flame finally turned back to the tipi. She ground her teeth in frustration when she saw that Little Rabbit had not deigned to pick up the robes. They still lay before the entrance in a heap. Setting aside the heavy skins of water, Flame glanced inside the tipi, where Little Rabbit was humming to herself and calmly putting her personal belongings in their accustomed places. There was no firewood in evidence, nor any sign of the cooking pot and utensils. They were still on the travois, along with the sleeping mats and all the other things, waiting to be unpacked.

Too angry for words, Flame stalked off toward the nearby woods. After filling her sling with enough wood for their evening fire, she again returned to the tipi. One swift glance told her that Little Rabbit had still done nothing more. The woman was primping in the small sliver of mirror that was her prize possession.

Fuming, Flame dumped her load of wood inside the tipi entrance, startling Little Rabbit, who had not heard her approach. With a deadly calm that did little to hide her mounting anger, Flame warned, "If you do not help me with what still needs to be done, all will not be ready when Night Hawk returns, and he will be very displeased."

Little Rabbit gave a negligent shrug. "I will simply tell him that you are slow, and that I am too tired with the burden of his child to do it myself. He will do nothing to me." Her sly smile irritated Flame further. Her small, close-set eyes darted to the pile of firewood. "We will need more than that to keep us warm throughout the night. Return to the forest and bring another load or two. Then, perhaps, I will prepare our meal, since my cooking skills are much superior to yours."

"I will fetch the wood to keep you warm, Little Rabbit," Flame agreed with a snide smile of her own. "No doubt you will need it more than I, since I have Night Hawk to warm me the night long. I suggest you busy yourself with unpacking the things you will need to prepare our meal."

Three times more, Flame made trips to the woods to bring firewood. Each time she returned, Little Rabbit had accomplished little. The Cheyenne woman had set up her own sleeping mat and robes, and had removed from the travois only those few items she would need to begin her cooking. The firepit had not been dug, nor the rocks collected to surround it. With an exasperated sigh, Flame proceeded to do these tasks herself, and she soon had a small fire going inside the tipi.

Tired and grimy, she finished this chore to find Little Rabbit blithely chatting with her sister outside the tipi. Under the force of Flame's irate glare, Little Rabbit turned to say imperiously, "Finish unloading the travois, and be careful not to damage any of Night Hawk's weapons, unless you want the beating you so deserve."

Flame exploded. In a blazing fury, she bared her teeth and screamed, "You lazy, good-for-nothing bitch!" She stomped into the tipi, and seconds later she emerged with her arms full of Little Rabbit's belongings. These she flung into the startled woman's face. The neglected pile of robes followed close behind. Then, to everyone's amazement—for by now a crowd had gathered to watch—she shrieked, "You want the travois unloaded, Little Rabbit? So be it!" In a fit, she began to unload the travois item by item, flinging each at Little Rabbit, regardless of size or shape, weight or fragility. Arrowheads and lances, bowls and pots, skins and mats all went sailing through the air.

Ducking and screeching, Little Rabbit fended off the assault. "Night Hawk will hear of this!" she wailed.

"He sure as blazes will!" Flame retorted furiously. Then, finding no more on the travois to pitch at the cringing woman, she plucked a water skin from the ground where she had previously left it. "You wanted water, Little Rabbit! Here! Have some water!" Untying the end of the skin, she tossed the contents on her enemy, laughing gleefully as Little Rabbit shrieked. It delighted her so to see the woman wiping the water from her hair and face that she threw a second skin of water at her.

Turning her attention to the firewood, Flame feigned surprise. "Oh, my! You wanted a big fire to warm yourself, did you not, Little Rabbit? Oh, yes!" Her eyes gleaming demonically, she carried a huge armload inside the tipi. Through the opening the others watched in stunned amazement as Flame dumped the entire load upon the fire. It smoked a moment, as though smothered, then promptly burst into flames. Long tongues of flame shot toward the roof of the tipi. "I'll give you a fire the likes of which you have never seen before!" she declared with a wild laugh, reaching for yet another armload of wood.

Night Hawk stopped short, staring in stunned disbelief at the scene before him. A large crowd had gathered about his tipi, in the center of which were both his wives. Little Rabbit looked like a bedraggled hag, her mouth hanging open even wider than his was at the moment. However, it was Flame who drew all eyes. She was screaming oaths at Little Rabbit, even as she gathered firewood into her arms, and it was plain to see that she was in a fine rage. Her brilliant blue eyes shot sparks. Every gesture betrayed her anger. All their belongings were strewn on the ground about her, and to Night Hawk's shock, he saw that the lodge fire was blazing almost out of control, about to set the entire structure afire! Even as he strode rapidly toward her, Flame dumped another armload of wood on the roaring fire.

"Flame! Cease at once!" he bellowed.

Either she did not hear him or chose to ignore his command, for she turned to pile yet more wood upon the blaze. "Flame!" he roared again. Still she did not heed him, but continued to heap invective upon Little Rabbit's head. Night Hawk heard the words "lazy," "worthless," and "conceited."

With his lodge about to go up in flames, Night Hawk wasted no more time trying to get her attention. Marching up to her, he picked her up and swiftly slung her over his shoulder, head first. "Little Rabbit!" he shouted angrily. "Do not stand there doing nothing! Douse the fire quickly before it consumes the tipi. Then make some

order of this mess! I will attend to you later."
With Flame cursing and bouncing upon his
broad shoulder, he strode off in the direction of
the river.

"Let go of me, you beast!" Flame ranted, not
yet ready to relinquish her anger. With her fists,
she beat upon his back. "Release me, I say!
Before I am done, I will tear every stringy hair
from that woman's head!"

A broad hand swatted her raised rump with a
mighty slap. "Ouch!" she yelped. "How dare
you! Put me down immediately! I am not yet
finished with that ugly hag!"

He landed another sharp blow to her bottom.
"You are finished now!" he informed her sternly,
though his lips twitched at her description of
Little Rabbit. "You have made a ruin of our
possessions and nearly set fire to our lodge. You
have done quite enough damage for one day with
your temper."

Flame was forming another scathing retort,
when she suddenly found herself sailing through
the air. She landed with a mighty splash in the
chilly river. Before she could understand what
had happened, she sank completely beneath the
surface, bobbing up seconds later, soaked and
sputtering.

"You . . . you beast!" she wheezed. "You cur!
You snake! You could have drowned me! You
know I cannot swim!"

Night Hawk laughed. Angry as he had been, he
could not help himself, for the sight of her was
too much. She looked like an angry red hen

pheasant caught in a rainstorm. Her hair was straggling about her face in dripping strands, her doeskin dress was clinging to her, and one moccasin had come loose and was drifting away on the current. She sat there sputtering at him, the cool water swirling about her.

"Don't you dare laugh at me!" she shrieked in outrage.

When he could speak, he said, "The river is very shallow here. There was no chance that you would drown. I was merely attempting to put out the fire of your raging temper, for what better way to douse a Flame?"

Her eyes blazed up at him. "How very clever of you!" she spat back scathingly. Indeed, he looked quite proud of himself, looking down at her from the bank, his hands braced on his hips.

Wading clumsily toward the shore, her wet dress dragging her down, she attempted to pull herself out of the water. She had almost succeeded, when Night Hawk calmly and deliberately pushed her back into the river again. "Drat you! Why did you do that?" she fumed. "The water is cold, and I wish to get out now."

He grinned at her and slowly shook his head. "No. You will stay where you are until your temper has cooled."

Squinting her eyes at him, she said, "You are enjoying this, aren't you?"

He nodded. "A great deal. It is time you learned to curb your temper, Flame, as well as your serpent's tongue. You are well named, for your temper matches your coloring. However, I am weary of all the squabbling in my tipi."

"Then I suggest you do something about Little Rabbit as well."

His dark brows lifted in censure. "We are speaking of you at the moment, Flame."

The water was, indeed, chilly, for autumn was well advanced here in the mountains. Flame clamped her jaws tightly to prevent her teeth from chattering. "I am freezing, Night Hawk," she complained through her teeth.

Again he shook his head. "Remove your dress, Flame, and toss it to me. As long as you are already wet, you can put your time to good use by bathing. Before long, the river will be frozen, and you will not have the opportunity again for many moons."

For a moment he thought she meant to defy him. Then, a sopping moccasin barely missed his head as she threw it at him. Her dress followed. Glancing about to assure himself that they were alone and unobserved, Night Hawk divested himself of his own garments and waded into the cool stream to join her.

"What are you going to do?" she squealed, backing away from him and shielding her breasts with crossed arms.

"I am going to bathe, wife," he told her with a taunting grin. He proceeded to do just that. Watching from the corner of his eye, he saw her give him a curious glance. Then, satisfied that he did not mean to provoke her further, she turned away and began to wash her own quivering body.

His deep voice broke the silence as he commanded, "Wash my back for me, wife." Flame's head jerked up and she stared at his broad back in surprise. He did not look at her; he merely stood there and confidently waited for her to comply with his demand.

Flame glared daggers at him, but she knew that if she ever wanted to get out of the freezing river, she must control her temper and do as he wished. Mumbling to herself about pompous husbands, she took a handful of sand and scrubbed vigorously at his back, hoping she was scraping off his skin in the process. She did not see the wicked smile that creased his face. At length, he turned and said, "Now I shall return the favor, wife." A devilish light danced in his dark eyes.

Instantly, she regretted her hasty actions, and wished she had not been so rough with him. "I—er, I can manage on my own, thank you," she stuttered.

"No, Flame. I insist." Determined hands turned her about.

Awaiting his first touch, she tensed, her face screwed up in anticipation. His touch, when it finally came, was gentle, even caressing, as he bathed her back. Long, sensitive fingers glided along her back, making her shiver, but not with the cold now. They traced the line of her spine, lingered over her ribs, spanned her small waist as he pulled her near to the naked warmth of his body. Just before his hot lips met with the tingling flesh of her neck, she thought dazedly, *How can he be so warm in this freezing water?*

Then further thought was impossible as his sharp teeth nibbled a path to her earlobe. She shivered again as his breath warmed the inner shell of her ear, and a soft moan escaped her trembling lips. This man was like a potion in her veins, a rare and potent drug.

"I want you, Little Firebrand," he murmured darkly. "I want you more than my next breath."

"Then take me," she whispered in return, her blood on fire for him. "Take me. Here. Now." So impatient was she for him, she would not have cared at that moment if the entire tribe were gathered on the bank watching them. Turning about in his arms, she clung to him, her lips seeking his with an urgency that startled them both. Her water-slick skin melted over his. With her arms entwined tightly about his neck, instinctively she trusted him to keep her afloat. Her slender legs wrapped themselves about his trim hips like insistent vines. Taut nipples grazed his hard chest as she wound herself about him and pulled him nearer still.

His strong arms came about her hips, lifting her higher, then slowly, tauntingly lowered her over his throbbing staff. The heat of her satin chamber seared him, almost sending him over the edge with that first silken thrust. His hands locked about her buttocks to hold her still until he could regain command of himself. The sound she made in his ear was the closest he had ever heard a human come to purring, and it drove him mad with desire. As he once again began to thrust within her, she leaned back in his arms, trusting him to support her. Faster, deeper, he drove into her, until the earth began to spin about her head. Together they were caught in a whirlpool of desire, swirling faster and faster until it swallowed them both in its hungry eye.

A keening cry came from deep within her and wound its way up her taut throat. Caught tightly in his embrace, she could scarcely breath, yet she did not care. She was drowning in a sparkling spray of rapture, and taking him with her, deeper, wider, more wondrously than ever before.

When it was over, she lay limp in his arms, quivering with ecstasy. Not by word or gesture did she demur as he carried her up the bank, threw her wet dress over her to cover her, and bore her swiftly through the maze of tipis to their lodge. She simply clung to him and hid her face against his shoulder, admitting defeat to a power stronger than hers. Night Hawk had succeeded in stilling her temper and her tongue. What shouts and brute force could not accomplish, gentleness and passion had managed with ease. With tenderness he had overcome her fury.

Flame sighed and snuggled closer, wearily but contentedly ceding the victory to him. Ah, but what sweet surrender it was!

Chapter
14

Winter, when it descended upon them, did so with a vengeance. Never had Flame seen snow so deep, or heard the wind howl with such fury. Never had she experienced a cold so deep that it settled into her bones and seemed to make her blood chill in her veins. She was soon thankful for the many thick robes that she and Little Rabbit had labored over. In the long, dark nights she would huddle beneath them, tugging them up over her head as she snuggled as close as possible to Night Hawk's body, welcoming the heat radiating from him, while outside the wind whistled and tugged at the edges of the tipi, trying to force its way within.

Night Hawk brought her six thick fox pelts, and under Shining Star's direction, Flame fash-

ioned them into a warm hooded winter cloak for
herself. Little Rabbit was green with envy, but
there was little she could do or say about it, since
she had her own winter garments and Flame had
so few.

When it became nearly impossible to navigate
on foot through the deep, drifted snow, Night
Hawk made Flame a pair of snowshoes. Never
having had such things before, she was very
awkward on them at first, and Night Hawk poked
fun at her.

"You walk like a lame duck!" he laughed.

"I may not be as graceful as you, but I'm
prettier," she retorted, sticking her tongue out at
him playfully.

This was not necessarily true, for in all honesty
Flame could not recall ever having met a man
more handsome. Used to his bronze skin now,
she much prefered it over the pale, pasty
complexions of some of her previous beaux. She
adored his noble, hawklike nose, and the proud,
prominent cheekbones. His sleekly muscled
body put all others to shame, as did his wide
shoulders and broad chest. His perfect teeth
shone white in his copper face, and he had the
most wickedly sensuous mouth she had ever
dreamed of finding on a man. His eyes were the
deepest, darkest of black pools, fathomless
depths she nearly drowned in each time she
gazed into them. Whether snapping in anger,
twinkling in glee, or simmering with passion,
they held her spellbound. Altogether, he was
marvelous to behold.

Back in Washington, when she was a child, Flame had often gone sledding with her friends. She had never expected to find such sport here, among the Cheyenne, and she was delightfully surprised when Night Hawk appeared at the entrance of their tipi one morning with a long toboggan. Created by the Indians to haul burdens across the snow, the toboggan was also used for sport when they had the time and inclination to play.

The many hillocks around the camp were ideal for sledding, and Flame was amazed to find that the adults, men and women alike, were just as fond of the winter activity as the children. With a sincere apology to Little Rabbit, Night Hawk explained that it would be too dangerous for her to go sledding in her advanced condition. Her child was due to be born soon. Thus, Night Hawk and Flame had the day on the slopes to share without Little Rabbit's depressing presence.

Dressed in her warmest clothes, her new fox-fur cloak, and thick rabbit-fur mittens and boots, Flame followed him happily from the tipi. Settling Flame before him on the toboggan, Night Hawk explained, "You guide it by shifting your weight from side to side."

"And to slow it?" she asked, tilting her head back to look at him.

Distracted by the snowflakes sparkling and melting on her thick lashes, it took Night Hawk a moment to answer. "You drag your feet over the sides."

His arms wrapped tightly about her, he gave a mighty push and they were off, flying at an amazing speed down the steep hill. Shrieking with delight, Flame grabbed hold of the curved front of the sled and held on for dear life. They streaked past other tobogganers, weaving their way precariously past rocks and trees. Flame bobbed when she should have weaved, and together they went tumbling off the sled into the drifted snow. Cushioned by deep drifts, their landing was as soft as crashing into a cloud. Breathless, her cheeks blooming with color, Flame lay where she landed and laughed with sheer joy. Beside her, Night Hawk lay chuckling, delighted that he could bring such bubbling laughter to his beautiful young bride's lips.

He rolled onto his side, bracing himself on one elbow, and gazed down into her flushed face. With one hand he gently brushed the snow from her face. "You are the most beautiful wife a man could want," he told her tenderly. "Your eyes shine out of your face with the brilliance of a thousand stars. Your smile lights up your face, and your laughter makes my heart sing with gladness."

With soggy mittens, she stroked his cheek, but he did not notice the wet or the cold, for her eyes were shining up into his. "Oh, Night Hawk! In all my days, I have never had the honor of having such fine words bestowed upon me."

Their lips met in a cool kiss that soon became heated. Only when the joking laughter and friendly jeers of their fellow tobogganers penetrated their hazy minds did they remember where they were. They resumed their sledding with a promise of passion to come glowing in their eyes.

Flame had a few things to teach Night Hawk as well, when it came to snow games. They built snowmen and snow forts, and staged tremendous snowball fights. She could not believe he had never made a snow angel before, and she promptly showed him how. Chuckling and feeling more than a little like a fool, he followed her example, and the unmarked area they chose was peppered with male and female angels by the time they were done.

Of course, Night Hawk's vast curiosity made him ask her what angels were, and she had a difficult time finding the words to convey the meaning. When he finally caught on, Flame was surprised to learn that the Cheyenne believed in similar beings, though they called them spirits. According to their beliefs, every living thing—plant, human, animal, or mineral—contained its own spirit. Before killing an animal, the hunter asked the animal's spirit to forgive him for the kill, explaining that he needed its hide and meat for his own survival. Many of their ceremonies, their songs and dances, dealt with these spirits, asking their blessing and expressing thanks for their bounty. It was a strange and touching thought to Sarah, and it made her consider how much more devout these so-called heathens were than most of her former "civilized" acquaintances. Her own curiosity aroused, she made a vow to herself to learn more of the Cheyenne beliefs—not, she told herself, because she wanted to live among these people forever—but to better understand the differences and similarities between their culture and hers.

Flame had lost track of the days since her capture. Though she knew it was winter, she did not know for sure what week, or even what month it was. Knowing it must be close to the Christmas season, she fell into a deep depression that even Little Rabbit's harping could not penetrate. Nor could all of Night Hawk's loving attention. Even Bandit's funny antics failed to cheer her. She was dreadfully, tearfully, heartrendingly homesick! Finally, after much pressuring, she confided her problem to Shining Star. Though there was nothing to be done about it, just sharing her problem with her friend made Flame feel a little better.

Several evenings later, much to her surprise, she and Night Hawk were invited to share the evening meal with Stone Face and Shining Star. After the meal, Shining Star presented Flame with a gift, wrapped in a hide and decorated with beads. Her dark eyes aglow with gentle understanding, Shining Star explained that it was a Christmas gift from her and Stone Face.

"But I have nothing to give you," Flame protested guiltily.

Shining Star merely smiled. "It is your holy day, not ours," she reminded her gently. "Open it."

Her eyes filled with grateful tears, Flame opened the gift. Inside she found new moccasins, beautifully beaded. "May your feet always walk happy paths in these moccasins," Shining Star intoned softly.

"Thank you. Thank you so very much." Flame was touched to the depth of her heart at her friends' thoughtfulness.

To her further surprise, Night Hawk also had a gift for her, which he then set gently in her lap. His dark eyes watched anxiously as she opened it. Flame gasped in delight to find dangling gold earrings, shaped like flames to match her wedding necklace. She thanked him profusely, and tried to swallow a sigh of disappointment that she could not wear them, for they were made for someone with pierced ears, and she had never had the courage to have the necessary holes punched in her lobes.

Her dismay was still obvious to Night Hawk, and he immediately wanted to know the reason. When she hesitantly admitted that her ears were not pierced, Shining Star offered to do the deed for her. "It will not hurt. This I promise you. We will numb your lobes with snow first, and you will never feel the needle as it pierces your skin."

Flame's gaze lingered for long moments on the beautiful earrings before she regretfully declined the offer. "Thank you, but not now. Perhaps at a later time."

"One should never shy away from one's desires because of a little discomfort," Night Hawk advised her with a frown. "Would you have me give the earrings to Little Rabbit instead?"

Flame could scarcely stand the censure in his black eyes. She knew she had hurt and disappointed him badly. Mustering all her courage, she drew herself up and answered. "No, husband. Forgive me for being such a silly goose."

Turning to Shining Star, she said softly, trying not to wince at the very thought of it, "You may pierce my earlobes if you still wish to grant me this favor."

Rising, Shining Star went immediately to gather her needle and a small block of wood. Then, as Flame waited with cowardly thoughts, Shining Star went outside the tipi and gathered fresh snow. Packed snow soon numbed Flame's earlobes, just as Shining Star had promised. With Stone Face and Night Hawk watching avidly, for they rarely had the opportunity to observe such feminine rituals, Flame strove to keep the fear from showing on her face.

Much to her relief, she felt only the slightest twinge of pain as Shining Star braced her lobe on the wooden block and poked the needle cleanly through her flesh. The second lobe met with the same swift measures, and the deed was done. Finally, Shining Star swabbed a soothing salve on Flame's lobes, giving her some to take back with her to her tipi, and instructing her to apply it for the next few days to prevent pain and to keep the holes from closing again. Then she aided Flame in threading the thin gold wires through the holes in her ears, and handed her a small, cracked looking glass in which to view the results.

Flame stared in fascination at her own image. In the past weeks she had paid scant attention to her own reflection on the surface of the stream, and she owned no mirror of her own. Now there was a stranger looking back at her from the glass. Her hair hung in long braids alongside a tanned face, and across her forehead was her beaded headband. Her features seemed leaner and more mature. A woman stared back at her, where she had expected the familiar face of a girl. She wore a serene countenance, which was totally unfamiliar, in place of the haughtiness that had always marked Sarah's face. There was a new softness about her mouth. Only her eyes seemed relatively unchanged, although they glowed with a new spark of life.

She stared so long and hard without saying anything that Night Hawk had to ask teasingly, "What is it you stare at so intently, my vain little wife?"

Softly, still half in shock at what she was seeing, she murmured, "I can find nothing of the old Sarah in this glass. I see only the woman known as Flame."

She would never know what joy leapt into Night Hawk's heart at her quiet words of awe. As he shared a proud look with his friends, he answered simply, "That is as it should be, my love. Now, I ask you, are you pleased with your gift?"

It was only at his prompting that she recalled why Shining Star had given her the mirror in the first place. Blushing prettily, she looked closely at the earrings and the odd little holes in her earlobes. "Oh, yes!" she sighed, loving the sight of the golden flames dancing on their thin wires. "They are lovely beyond measure!"

"As are you, wife of my heart," he assured her,

causing her to blush even more brightly as Stone Face and Shining Star exchanged knowing glances.

It was late January, as near as Flame could make out, when Little Rabbit gave birth to a son. Thankfully, Flame had received her monthly flow the week before and was not in residence in the women's lodge when Little Rabbit went into labor. Flame had already had the misfortune of being present when a woman birthed a child in the lodge. The labor had been long and hard, and Flame had winced in sympathy for the poor mother each time the pains came. Of course, once the child was born, all soft and wrinkled, with a thatch of dark hair, everyone, the mother included, seemed to forget the pain and struggle in the miracle of the tiny babe nestled in his mother's arms. Still, Flame had no wish to repeat the experience soon, especially in this case; as Little Rabbit's sister-wife, she would have been expected to attend to Little Rabbit during the birthing.

As they awaited news of Little Rabbit and the child, it struck Flame as odd that Night Hawk was not more concerned. Most of the expectant fathers she had known, both here and back home, were a mass of nerves once their wives went into labor. Night Hawk seemed not worried at all. Where others would be pacing the tipi and dashing out to the women's lodge every few breaths, Night Hawk sat calmly braiding new feathers onto his war lance. Only once in a while did he look up and frown, as if he were wondering how much longer it would be, or if anything had gone wrong.

Flame was the one who began to fidget as the time dragged on and no word came. As much as she detested Little Rabbit, she could not in good conscience wish either her or her child any real harm. She fixed their meals and fussed about inside the tipi straightening things ten times over, until Night Hawk had to ask her to please be still. For a while, she tried to concentrate on her sewing, but finally she gave up and settled herself before the fire, where she sat staring into the flames and stroking Bandit's soft pelt.

From this she gained a measure of comfort, for she had come to adore the little raccoon. He was a real comfort in her life when her trials weighed heavily upon her heart. At times he would lie quietly in her lap, content to snooze as she petted him. At others he was a clown to cheer her and send her into fits of giggles. Often he was a rambunctious little pest, his immense curiosity getting him into much trouble. Always he was darling, with his black-masked face and bushy tail.

It was the small animal's insatiable curiosity that got him into the most trouble. Flame could not count the times she or Little Rabbit had to rescue a pouch of nuts or dried berries from his clutches. He had a particular fondness for bright, shiny objects, and they tried to put everything of value far out of his keen eyesight. It did no good to hang items from the lodge poles, for Bandit was a skilled climber. He was also a nocturnal creature, and many were the nights he awakened them clattering about the tipi, rattling bowls and climbing lodge poles.

Little Rabbit claimed to hate the raccoon, threatening time and again to skin him, but Flame knew the woman resented Bandit only because he was Flame's pet, a gift from Night Hawk. Many a time Flame came upon Little Rabbit unannounced and caught her gently scolding the little creature or offering him tidbits. They had all burst into uncontrollable gales of laughter the evening Bandit discovered Little Rabbit's sliver of mirror. He sat upright, holding it before him in his front paws. Then he proceeded to chatter and coo and make faces at his image. He was fascinated with the creature in the glass, trying time and again to reach through the flat surface to the animal beyond. He poked and prodded, chattering beguilingly, then angrily as the twin raccoon mimicked his actions but refused to come forth to play.

"I think he is in love," Flame said incredulously.

Night Hawk agreed. "He must think his image is a little female raccoon."

This brought a snort from Little Rabbit. "The little fool admires only himself! He is as vain as his mistress." This time, however, her sharp words were tempered with laughter as she shook her head over Bandit's antics.

This deeply into winter, however, Bandit was not all that energetic. Though raccoons did not actually hibernate during the winter months, as did bears and woodchucks, they were known to sleep soundly during severe weather, awakening periodically during thaws and milder weather to forage for food. With the advantage of the warm tipi, Bandit was merely lethargic most of the time. When he was not drowsing by the fireside, he could be found curled up in the small section of hollow log Flame had found for him and brought into the tipi. Occasionally, when the sun shone brightly and warmed the air, he would stir himself enough to waddle down to the river and poke about an unfrozen area of the stream for an unsuspecting fish or two.

At least none of them would have to worry about Bandit disturbing Little Rabbit's newborn baby. His curiosity was greatly dimmed these days, so they did not fear that he would harm the child in his inquisitiveness.

At long last, word came that Little Rabbit had delivered a fine, healthy son. She would remain in the women's lodge for a few days, until she had sufficiently recovered. Even as Flame breathed a silent prayer of relief for the reprieve, and for the safe arrival of the babe, she puzzled over Night Hawk's lack of joy at the birth of his first-born son. He seemed no more than mildly relieved that both Little Rabbit and the child had come through the ordeal without harm. She could not help but wonder if he would behave in the same manner should she bear him a child. Then she chided herself for her foolish thoughts and wayward wishes. If she were fortunate, she would be rescued before she could conceive a child by him, and the question need never arise.

Chapter
15

Little Rabbit's son was called Howling Gale, in honor of the storm that immediately followed his birth. He was a darling baby, with a mop of dark hair, and Flame adored him on sight. The tiny tyke could not help having Little Rabbit for a mother, though Flame had to admit that Little Rabbit doted on her baby son. She could not fault her treatment of him at all. Of course, it was quite a shock the first time she saw Little Rabbit pinch Howling Gale's nostrils shut and place her hand over his mouth when he began to cry. Flame almost panicked, thinking Little Rabbit had lost her mind and was trying to smother her small son. To her vast relief, she learned that all Cheyenne mothers did this with their newborn babes in an effort to teach them from the start not to cry unless hurt. Crying babies could alert passing enemies to their position and endanger the entire tribe.

Flame had expected Night Hawk's unconcerned attitude to change once he had seen his new son, and it confounded her further that he showed little interest in the baby. Upon seeing the child for the first time, he said, "He is a fine son, Little Rabbit. He will grow to be a brave warrior like his father." After that one small compliment, he all but ignored the child. Flame was baffled by Night Hawk's behavior, for she knew that many Cheyenne men cherished their sons, just as fathers the world over had done for centuries. It was not some tribal law of behavior that held him from showing much affection for Howling Gale, but something lacking in himself, for Flame thought the child perfect in every respect. True, Night Hawk would ask after the child's well-being, and he was not totally unconcerned, but he lacked the joy and enthusiasm most men showed toward a firstborn son, and Flame simply could not comprehend the reason for this.

She tried her best not to show it, but Flame was hurt that Little Rabbit would not allow her to help with the care of the baby. She could scarcely walk past Howling Gale's cradleboard without Little Rabbit screeching at her to get away from her son.

Flame tried to tell her, "I will not harm him, Little Rabbit. He is but an innocent babe." But there was no reasoning with the woman, and Flame's words fell on deaf ears.

If Little Rabbit had done little work around
the tipi before, she did even less now, but Flame
clamped her mouth shut and was determined not
to complain. Little Rabbit had a son to care for
now, and her infant took much time and care.
Flame did not want to seem small in Night
Hawk's eyes by constantly complaining merely
because Little Rabbit's energies were taken with
the care of his new son. She did not want him to
think that she was being petty and jealous, even
though she often found herself envying Little
Rabbit her beautiful child. The Cheyenne woman and Night Hawk now shared a very special
bond between them, one that Flame could not
hope to match. A man could have but one
first-born son, and Little Rabbit had given him
that precious child. Envy became a familiar
emotion to Flame in the days that followed,
though she tried her best to crush it from her
heart.

In all this time, Flame and Night Hawk had
continued to share his sleeping mat. His desire
for her was as strong as ever, as was hers for him.
Now that Little Rabbit had recovered from the
birth of their child, Flame wondered if things
might change. Would Night Hawk now split his
time between them? Would he share his mat with
her one night, and with Little Rabbit the next?
Flame tried to tell herself that she did not care,
that it did not matter to her in the least—but it
did. The thought of having to share her husband
with another woman was like a knife driven into
her heart. That it was the custom among the

Cheyenne did not ease her pain, nor did her constant lectures to herself that she did not love him so it should not bother her. She came to dread the night when Night Hawk would choose to sleep with Little Rabbit instead of her. No, he could sleep next to Little Rabbit all he wanted; it was the thought of their mating that hurt so badly.

The day soon came when Little Rabbit put her son aside for a time and busied herself with primping. With a sinking heart, Flame watched the woman bathe and wash her hair in water she'd had Flame fetch and heat for her. Little Rabbit brushed her long black tresses until they gleamed and crackled with life. With scented oil she smoothed her skin and perfumed her hair. For once she left her hair unbound and flowing about the shoulders of her best doeskin dress. Her finest headband adorned her forehead; her newest moccasins covered her small feet. No doubt about it, the woman was planning a seduction.

If Flame had any lingering doubts, they were erased when Little Rabbit arranged for her sister to take Howling Gale to her tipi for the night. If she could have arranged for Flame to be gone also, she surely would have—or perhaps not. Flame suspected that if Little Rabbit succeeded in luring Night Hawk to her mat, she would, in her vindictiveness, want Flame to witness their mating just to hurt her more. Surely, she would gloat afterward, and miss no opportunity to cause Flame humiliation.

Little Rabbit went to great pains to prepare Night Hawk's favorite meal. This was, indeed, a familiar scene to Flame, who had done the same for her father many times in the past. She recognized the scheme immediately. She watched in dismay as Night Hawk ate the dish with great relish. Little Rabbit chatted to him pleasantly the entire time, smiling and telling him all about Howling Gale's latest accomplishments and relaying bits of gossip she had heard. Each time Flame dared to try to enter the conversation, Little Rabbit deftly and unobtrusively cut her off.

The evening seemed to go on forever as Flame waited for the inevitable. At long last, Night Hawk stood and walked to his mat. Not wanting to watch what was about to happen, Flame took her time banking the fire. When she finally arose, it was to find Night Hawk alone on his sleeping mat, his dark eyes watching her with obvious desire. Little Rabbit stood in the center of the tipi, her black eyes snapping with intense hatred as both women watched Night Hawk reach out his hand in a welcoming gesture toward Flame. The loathing on Little Rabbit's face was almost frightening to behold, and Flame had never been so glad for the blanket that shielded her and Night Hawk from Little Rabbit's malevolent glare.

Matters between the two women went from bad to worse after that, as each night Night Hawk continued to ignore Little Rabbit's attempts to make herself desirable to him. Each time he chose Flame over her, Little Rabbit's vile hatred nearly choked her. Not wishing to fan the fires of the other woman's loathing, Flame carefully avoided Little Rabbit as much as was possible in the close confines of the tipi. With frigid temperatures and deep snow surrounding the camp, it was impossible, however, not to spend a great deal of time enclosed together, and the tension was as thick as smoke. Still, Flame took pains not to prick Little Rabbit's pride further. She went quietly about her work and tried her best not to give Little Rabbit cause to complain, for regardless of their differences, she knew how she would feel if the situation were reversed.

Woman-Who-Frowns approached Flame as she was returning from gathering firewood. "Night Hawk wishes you to join him at the river, where the big rocks stand," she informed Flame.

Flame's brow creased in confusion. "I thought Night Hawk was conferring with the other chiefs in the council lodge this morning."

"I know nothing about a meeting of the chiefs," the other woman said irritably. "I know only what I told you. Night Hawk wishes to see you now at the bend in the river near the big rocks."

Flame watched as Woman-Who-Frowns walked away. "How strange," she muttered to herself. "I was sure he told me this meeting was very important and might last all day." With a shrug, she dropped her sling full of wood outside the tipi entrance and headed toward the designated point.

The closer she came to the area where Night Hawk was waiting, the more she felt sure that something was not right. The feeling lingered and grew with each step she took, but she told herself firmly that she was being silly. What possible danger could befall her while Night Hawk was there to protect her?

She rounded the bend in the river, but Night Hawk was nowhere in sight. Her eyes scanned the rocks that encircled the bank, but did not find him. Now the fine hairs on the nape of her neck rose alarmingly. "Night Hawk?" she called, softly at first, and then more loudly. "Night Hawk, are you here?"

When he failed to respond to her call, the eerie feeling grew even stronger, and Flame could no longer deny its warning. As she turned to return to the camp, she suddenly found herself face to face with Little Rabbit. The woman was brandishing a sharp, wicked-looking knife. "He is not here, Flame, but it was very obedient of you to come running so quickly," Little Rabbit hissed venomously.

Eyeing the knife in fascination, Flame slowly backed away. "Little Rabbit, what is the meaning of this?"

"I mean to rid myself of you for all time," Little Rabbit said darkly. "I mean to kill you. I should have done so long ago, before you worked your white magic on Night Hawk."

Blanching at Little Rabbit's bald words, Flame asked, "Have you gone mad, Little Rabbit? Night Hawk will surely slay you if you harm me. He has warned you against this."

The smile on Little Rabbit's face was pure menace. "He will not know of it, white bitch. You will simply fail to return to the village. Your body will not be found. I have removed several of your belongings from the tipi, to make it look as if you have run away. Night Hawk may search for you, but he will never find you. I will be there to console my beloved husband on his loss, and soon he will forget you ever entered his life."

"Woman-Who-Frowns knows where I am. She will know that all is not as you would have it seem." Flame's heart was thudding in her chest as Little Rabbit waved the knife tauntingly before her.

Little Rabbit gave a demonic laugh. "Look behind you, foolish woman. Tell me what you see."

Flame risked a quick glance over her shoulder, careful not to take her full attention from the gleaming knife in Little Rabbit's hand. With a gasp of fear and dismay, she saw three women standing at her back. All of them held large sticks, and one of the women was Woman-Who-Frowns. Another was Little Rabbit's sister; the third was her closest friend.

A shiver of fear raced through Flame as she realized fully her peril. There was nowhere to run. In front of her stood Little Rabbit with the knife. Behind her were three other Cheyenne women who meant her harm. On the one side steep rocks blocked her path, while on the other was only the half-frozen river, wide and treacherous along this particular stretch.

"Do not look so dismayed," Little Rabbit consoled her with false sympathy. "I shall offer you a choice of deaths, though I would much prefer that you choose my knife, for I long to feel it twist into your body at my command. You may choose a death by beating, but it will be much less quick. That, too, has its merits," she said, as if reflecting on the idea. "Yes, perhaps that would be best. If you choose that method, I might throw away my knife and join my sisters in clubbing the life from you. Does that not sound fair? Or, you may choose to try to escape us by throwing yourself at the mercy of the river, but I warn you that it is very swift and deep here, and I know that you cannot swim."

Her crazed laugh bounced off the rocks and echoed across the water. "Which shall it be, Flame? You must decide quickly," she warned, evil glinting from her dark eyes, "or I will make the choice for you."

When Flame failed to respond, Little Rabbit continued almost conversationally, "Are you aware that the women of the tribe are much more vicious in tormenting their victims than the men? We are well versed in methods of torture. Under our hands, it can last for many suns. I regret that we have not the time to demonstrate our skills to you, for it would give me the greatest pleasure to hear you scream and beg for mercy, to plead for the death that lingers always just beyond your grasp."

The woman is mad! Flame thought, her panic growing. For a moment she had thought to try to reason with the other three, but one look told her she would find no help there. These were Little Rabbit's sisters, and they shared her deep hatred —perhaps her madness as well.

Weighing her options, Flame leaped forward, hoping to dash past Little Rabbit while she was yet talking and run to safety. Despite her apparent lack of attention, Little Rabbit was prepared. Her knife flashed outward, cutting the side of Flame's cloak and leaving a long gash in her upper arm.

Flame gasped in pain and stumbled to her knees, not daring to look as she felt the blood well to the surface and begin to stream down her arm. By the time she lurched to her feet, the other women had moved to surround her again. This time she tried to break past the two who were armed with sticks. They landed vicious blows on her head and shoulders, shrieking with glee as she stumbled backward. She whirled to find Little Rabbit close behind. Flame barely sidestepped in time to avoid having her face sliced with the arcing blade. As it was, the cutting edge of the knife cleaved through the hood of her cloak, slicing across the top of her shoulder.

The wound burned like wildfire, but Flame had no time to wonder how much damage was done. Eyes wide with fright, she watched the women advancing on her. More blows rained down upon her from all sides, and she cried out in pain. In a corner of her mind, she thought she heard a bone crack, but she knew not which, for her whole body was wracked in pain. Several hard blows to her back sent her again to her knees.

Frantically, she somehow managed to scramble upright once more. A third time the lethal knife connected, slicing through the butter-soft doeskin dress and glancing along her ribs. With a wild scream, she lurched away, only to meet with a blow to the back of her knees that sent her tumbling forward. Dizzily she rolled over. Four faces blurred before her eyes as the Cheyenne women stood over her, their evil grins distorting their features, their demonic laughter assaulting her ears. Dark shadows gathered at the edges of her vision, and she prayed she would faint before she felt the final thrust of the knife Little Rabbit waved above her tauntingly. Surely she was breathing the last few breaths of her young life, for the look on Little Rabbit's face was deadly even to Flame's pain-clouded eyes. Little Rabbit was through playing with her. Her evil game was nearly finished.

"Are you prepared to die now, as you deserve to do for stealing my husband's attentions from me?" Little Rabbit sneered.

A strange whistling sound accompanied her words. Suddenly, inexplicably, Little Rabbit yelped in pain. Simultaneously, the knife flew from her hands, and she leaped back from over Flame's prone body. Vaguely, Flame was aware of the other three women crying out in surprise and trying to flee.

All was confusion as men's voices joined those of the screaming women. From somewhere, Night Hawk appeared above her, a long whip dangling from his fingertips. Flame heard him bark stern orders to the men and bellow in rage at Little Rabbit, but in her stunned state, she could not discern his words.

Then he was bending over her, tenderly examining her wounds, crooning something to her in his deep, velvet voice. As gentle as he tried to be, she cried out in agony. She thought she heard Shining Star's soft voice among the others, but she could not be sure. A scream of pure anguish left her lips as Night Hawk scooped her into his strong arms. He cradled her against his chest, trying to cushion her from further injury as he carried her swiftly back toward the village.

"Do not die, my little Flame," she heard him whisper fervently. "I know I failed in my vow to protect you, but please do not die now, my own true heart." Whatever else he murmured was lost to her as the dark mist swirled over her and claimed her in its grey grasp.

Flame awoke to pain such as she had never before experienced. Gone was the blessed oblivion that had held her in its grip. A low moan escaped her, and at once a wet cloth found its way to her lips. Gentle fingers caressed her brow, easing the lines furrowed there. Carefully she opened her eyes to find Night Hawk bending over her with an anxious look.

"Do not try to move, dearest wife," he said softly, as if he knew how very badly her head was aching. In truth, it felt as if a thousand drummers were beating on her skull.

"I do not think I could move if I wanted to," she answered on a thready whisper, then after a moment asked, "How did you come to find me in time to save me?"

"Shining Star was getting water at the river when she thought she heard you call for me," he explained. "Knowing that I was in the council lodge, and thinking this strange, she went to see. She found you and the others and heard Little Rabbit vow to kill you. Rather than attempt to help you herself, and perhaps endanger both your lives, she slipped away without being seen and ran to the lodge to tell me what was happening." He brushed the hair from her face, his eyes solemn and dark. "The great Spirit smiled upon us, for we reached the river before Little Rabbit could complete her evil mission. I am just very sorry that you were injured so badly before I could get to you."

Not knowing if she was really ready to learn the truth or not, she asked, "How badly am I hurt? I seem to ache all over."

His black eyes blazed in his face as he scowled in remembrance of the beating she had received. "You were severely beaten, Flame. One of your ribs is cracked, but the medicine woman does not think that it is broken through. She has bound it for you. Do not attempt to draw too deep a breath, but I must ask you if it hurts to breathe normally."

If she had not been in such agony, Flame might have laughed at this. "It hurts to blink!" she confessed. "But not so badly to breathe. What else is broken?"

He grinned at her attempt to jest with him. "You have no other broken bones, but your body is covered with lumps and bruises from the beating. There are several large lumps on your head half the size of my fist."

"That explains why it throbs so, and why

everything is a bit blurry. What of the knife wounds?"

"None of them are truly serious or deep," he told her gratefully. "They, too, have been treated and bound, my warrior wife."

A ghost of a smile touched her lips. "I am not much of a warrior, Night Hawk, though I may bear nearly as many scars as one soon. I am not the one who wielded that knife so deftly."

His face darkened again. "This time Little Rabbit will pay dearly for her crime," he promised.

"Where is she? What have you done with her?" Though she dared not move her head, Flame's eyes darted around the tipi in search of her enemy.

"Fear not, Flame. You are safe here. Never again will she enter this tipi."

"Do you intend to kill her?"

"Is that your wish?" he asked, watching her face intently.

Flame hesitated, then answered honestly. "I do not know. My first thought is, yes, I want her slain for all the misery she has caused me." After a moment's pause, she said with a tired sigh, "No, I do not think I truly wish her death on my hands. I know she meant to slay me, but her jealousy drove her mad, I believe."

"You are most generous in your thoughts toward her after all she has done," he told her.

"I pity her more than I hate her, Night Hawk. Little Rabbit carries her own demon within her, and it eats at her. She is a very unhappy woman, for I think she hates herself as much as she

despises others, and that is a sad thing indeed.
My only wish is to have her somehow removed
from my life, in a way less drastic than death."

She looked up at him solemnly. "You did not
answer me. Do you intend to kill her?"

He shook his dark head, his braids swaying
with the motion. "No. As much as it would
please me to do so, I will not. She will be whipped
as soon as you are well enough to witness her
punishment. Until then she will be confined in
the women's lodge. Then I intend to put her away
from me."

This Flame did not understand. "Put her away
from you?" she echoed. "What does this mean?"

"She will no longer be my wife. You will be my
first wife after that, as if Little Rabbit was never
my wife before you."

"A divorce?"

He nodded. "Will this please you, little firebrand?" he asked with a teasing smile. "Will you
miss having someone on whom to sharpen your
serpent's tongue?"

Though her face ached with the effort, she
returned his smile. "I will still have you to argue
with, husband. And, yes, it will please me greatly
to be your only wife and have you all to myself."

He bent and kissed her gently on her lips. "You
must rest now and regain your strength. Your
body needs time to heal itself."

As he started to move back from her, she said,
"Wait. What will become of Little Rabbit after
the divorce?"

"She will be sent to the harlots' lodge, where
she will live out her days in shame and disgrace."

His harsh words sent a shiver through her. "But Night Hawk, you must not do such a thing to the mother of your child!" she exclaimed, earning a sharp pain in her head for her efforts. "Think of Howling Gale. What will he think of his mother as he grows older? And what will he think of you, to do such a thing to his mother?"

Night Hawk stared at her, stunned. "Where did you get such thoughts? How did you come to think that Howling Gale is my son?"

She frowned up at him in bewilderment, wondering if her throbbing head was muddling her mind. "Little Rabbit told me, but I guessed as much as soon as you told me she was your wife and I saw that she was with child."

"Oh, Flame! Does Little Rabbit's treachery know no bounds? The child is not mine, but my dead brother's! As is our custom, when Many Arrows was slain in battle, I took his wife for my own. From that day, she came to live in my tipi as my wife, though I would never have chosen her for my bride under other circumstances. Because she was already with child, there has been no intimacy between us in all this time. Even had she not been with child, I do not know if I could ever have brought myself to mate with her. She and the child she carried became my responsibility from the day my brother died. It is only out of loyalty to my brother's memory that I do not slay her now, but let her live."

"Then neither can you condemn her to a life in the harlots' lodge, for this same reason," she pointed out gently. "If his father is dead, then Howling Gale will need his mother even more.

There must be a more honorable way to deal with
her after the divorce."

"Your heart is much too tender, Blue Eyes. I
will offer her to any man in our tribe who would
still have her for his wife or mistress after wit-
nessing her treachery. If there is one who will
have her, she is his with my blessing. If not, she
must enter the harlots' lodge. If it were summer, I
could trade her to a brave from another tribe and
remove her from our presence entirely. Still, the
harlots' lodge is a kinder fate than banning her
from the tribe entirely, for she would surely die
on her own. Once someone is banned from his
own tribe, no other tribe will accept him. Such
outcasts are doomed to wander the land alone,
until they die of hunger or meet death at the
hands of an enemy or some wild animal. It is rare
to survive the banning, when one lacks the protection of the tribe."

Flame nodded her understanding of this. "If
she weds another warrior, will you allow her to
keep your brother's child with her?"

Sighing heavily, he agreed. "It would be well
within my rights to take the child from her and
raise my nephew in my own lodge, but I will
allow her to keep the child, if you wish."

"I love Howling Gale dearly, Night Hawk. You
know that I would gladly raise him as my own,
but the child belongs with his mother. She loves
him. He may be the only person on this earth she
does truly care for, other than you."

"If she cared for me, as you claim, she would
not have tried to slay the person dearest to my
heart," he countered.

"You are wrong, Night Hawk. Little Rabbit adores you. That is why she became so angry when you brought me into your tipi and made me your wife. Her jealousy is a sickness within her. Please believe me. Just being torn from your side, to no longer be your wife, will be a lifelong punishment almost too much for her to bear. To tear her son from her, too, would surely kill her."

"If what you say is true, then it is a just and fitting punishment for her crimes against both of us. Let us just hope that we will not live to regret our leniency one day," he said solemnly.

Chapter 16

On the morning of the seventh day following her beating, Night Hawk led Flame from their tipi. Through the gathered throng, he led her to the center of the crowd. There she caught her first sight of Little Rabbit since the woman had tried to kill her.

Little Rabbit and the three women who had aided her in her attack on Flame were gathered together in a small group, all awaiting their public punishment before the entire tribe.

"Does she know what is about to happen?" Flame asked.

Night Hawk nodded, then qualified his answer. "She knows only that she is to be lashed. I have said nothing of her further punishment yet."

He left her then, to step to the very center of the circle, near the pole where the women would be tied to receive their whippings. Holding his hand up in a signal for silence, he then told those gathered why these women were being punished. "They will each receive five lashes," he announced, then asked, "Do I now hear any arguments for leniency?"

Little Rabbit's mother stepped forward hesitantly. "I fear this may be too much for Little Rabbit," she said in a quavering voice. "She is yet nursing her small son, and this could sour her milk and harm the child."

A look of disgust showed clearly on Night Hawk's face. "Mother, if your daughter's evil nature has thus far not soured her breast milk, I doubt that a mere five lashes will do so."

There came no other pleas for the women, the tribe seeming to agree as one that the punishment was just. Because it was Night Hawk's bride who had been so severely attacked, he would be the one to wield the whip and administer the lashes. Saving the worst offender until last, the other women would receive their lashes first. Woman-Who-Frowns was led forward. Her arms were stretched over her head and bound to the pole. Then her feet were likewise tied. This done, Night Hawk took his knife from its sheath, slit the back of the woman's dress from neck to waist, and tore the material away to lay bare her back.

Stepping away, he accepted the long, braided rawhide whip that the woman's husband handed him. As he shook it from its coils, it slithered along the ground near his feet like a deadly snake. With his eyes upon his fleshy target, Night Hawk drew back his arm and flicked the whip into action.

As it whistled through the still air, Flame's eyes widened. This was the strange sound she had heard that day on the beach! Night Hawk had used the whip to fling the knife from Little Rabbit's hand. She could not help but wince as the whip bit into Woman-Who-Frowns' back, leaving behind a wide welt. The woman cried out in pain, her head snapping back as she arched away from the source of her misery. Four more times, in evenly measured strokes, the leather sliced into its victim. Other than Woman-Who-Frowns' outcries, there was no sound from anyone. All watched in censuring silence as the punishment was meted out.

Five separate stripes decorated her back by the time it was done. When she was cut down at last, her knees buckled beneath her. Her husband had to help her walk to the edge of the circle, but his face held no trace of sympathy for his mate. Woman-Who-Frowns was made to stand there in agony and witness the punishment of her friends before she was allowed to return to her tipi and have her wounds treated.

Yellow Quail was next, then Little Rabbit's sister. Finally, there was only Little Rabbit's lashing left to witness. Having viewed the whipping of her friends, and knowing she could expect even less sympathy, Little Rabbit's eyes were wide with fright. Her face was blanched almost as pale as Flame's. To her credit, she did not try to resist as Night Hawk jerked her arms high over her head and tied her hands. She did not plead for mercy as he cut her dress away from her back.

At the first sharp crack of the whip against her skin, she did cry out. By the third, she was writhing against the pole, trying in vain to evade the bite of the whip. Now she did beg for mercy, but to no avail.

Forced by tradition to watch each whipping, Flame knew that Little Rabbit was receiving much more of a beating than her friends. Though she was to be given only the stated five lashes, Night Hawk was applying the whip with more force in this case. The long leather strap sang through the air with a vengeful whine. It bit sharp and deep with each stroke, hungrily tearing away skin and flesh.

By the fourth stroke, she was shrieking and wailing like a mad animal; on the fifth, Little Rabbit fainted.

Night Hawk instructed Stone Face to cut her down from the pole, and before the crowd could disperse, he asked them to remain. Then he sent a young boy for a water skin, and as all watched, he poured the cold water directly upon Little Rabbit's lacerated back. The sharp pain jerked the unconscious woman back to an agonizing reality, and she gasped loudly in anguish.

Ruthlessly Night Hawk pulled Little Rabbit to her feet and by the very force of his hold upon her arm, held her upright. Then, to all assembled, he announced, "Before all my people, I now reject this woman. From this day forward, Little Rabbit will no longer be my wife, for she has dishonored that position. By her own vile actions, she has brought this shame upon herself."

A murmur ran through the crowd at Night Hawk's announcement. Little Rabbit's head jerked up in surprise. Fresh tears tracked down her face as she stared up at the man who had just formally and publicly divorced her.

"No! Please do not do this thing, Night Hawk! I beg of you!" she pleaded, all pride deserting her.

Ignoring her plea, Night Hawk spoke again, his strong, deep voice ringing out clearly. "If there is any man among you who wishes her for wife, slave, or whore, speak now. If not, it is within my rights to take her child, my brother's son, into my own tipi and condemn Little Rabbit to the harlots' lodge for the remainder of her days on this earth."

"Oh, no! No!" Little Rabbit was shrieking wildly, vainly trying to break Night Hawk's hold on her arm. "Do not take my son from me! I will do anything you ask!"

The murmuring of the tribe had grown louder now, but no one stepped forward to claim the wailing woman. If any thought the penalty too harsh, none spoke up in Little Rabbit's defense. "So be it," Night Hawk proclaimed. As everyone looked on, he started to drag the protesting woman away, in the direction of the harlots' lodge.

Suddenly a voice rang out. "Wait! I shall take Little Rabbit to wife!" All heads turned to watch as Crooked Arrow strode swiftly to the fore.

When he reached the place where Night Hawk and Little Rabbit stood, he said contemptuously, "If you do not honor your dead brother any better than this, I will take the responsibility of caring for his wife." A collective gasp ran through the crowd at Crooked Arrow's bold words.

Night Hawk returned his former friend's scorn in full measure. "If I did not honor Many Arrows' memory, I would have slain Little Rabbit for her crimes," he said clearly. "She has him to thank for her worthless life."

Roughly he shoved Little Rabbit toward the other man. "Take her, and may you have better fortune dealing with her sharp tongue and evil ways than I."

Supporting Little Rabbit's limp body, Crooked Arrow turned to leave.

"Wait." Once more that single word rang out, this time from Flame. Straight and proud, her eyes sought her husband's. "The child, Night Hawk. Remember Howling Gale."

His dark eyes assessed his wife, then swung toward Crooked Arrow and Little Rabbit. "Will you accept my brother's child, as well as Little Rabbit?" he asked of Crooked Arrow.

At Crooked Arrow's nod of agreement, Night Hawk turned to Little Rabbit. Hope mingled with the pain and misery on her pale, wet face. "I grant you your son, woman, but only because my wife, in her kindness, asks it of me. Even now she begs favors for the very woman who would have

slain her. Her mercy is greater than mine would
have been, I assure you."

Spring arrived, and with the first soft breezes,
the tribe was again on the move. Streams gushed
to overflowing as the mountain snows melted
beneath the warm glow of the sun. Fresh green
leaves sprouted upon bare tree limbs, flowers
budded, and the grass became a velvet carpet
once more. As they traveled through the hills and
valleys, Flame saw an abundance of new life.
Everywhere, nature was busy replenishing itself.
Fawns danced on wobbly legs at their mothers'
sides. Newborn rabbits twitched their tiny noses
in delight of spring. Ducklings swam crooked
lines behind their proud parents. There were
even a number of new foals born to the herd of
Indian ponies.

The buffalo herds were gathering once more on
the vast, open plains, and the Cheyenne soon
followed. With their supplies of food perilously
low after the long winter months, fresh meat and
skins were of primary concern among all the
tribes, and often they banded together when they
met, combining their efforts to the betterment of
all. Sioux, Cheyenne, Arapaho, and Kiowa were
all to be found in search of the buffalo, the very
backbone of the Indian way of life.

These buffalo hunts were a new experience for
Flame. The entire tribe was involved in some
way, for once the braves had spotted a large herd,
the women had to follow close behind and remain on hand to butcher the slaughtered animals. They stayed to the rear until their skills

were required, but just watching the hunt was exciting.

Most of the time the braves crept quietly as near to the herd as they could manage without causing the enormous animals to bolt. Concealing themselves behind small bushes, rocks, and clumps of grass, they got as close as possible, encircling the herd, then lay in hiding while those braves mounted on ponies advanced as near as they could. At a prearranged signal, the entire group of hunters would charge the herd at once.

Unlike stampeding cattle, the buffalo, once on the run, tended to charge ahead in a single direction. This worked to the Indians' benefit, as their fleet ponies could outrun any buffalo. The braves would ride alongside the herd, killing one buffalo after another and leaving the carcasses for the women to tend to later. A single, well-placed arrow, or a well-aimed lance, could kill one of the huge beasts. As long as he had arrows in his quiver, a brave could continue to slay animal upon animal.

Often the tribes tried to encircle the herd and get them to run in one endless and repeated circle. In this way, they did not have carcasses spread out for miles along the prairie, but neatly confined to one area. Also, a mounted hunter could easily exchange his tiring pony for a fresh mount held in readiness by one of the women or a youth too young yet to join the kill himself.

Another favored tactic, especially in early spring when the ice on the rivers was just beginning to break, was to run the herd into the river. The huge beasts not only ran in a single direction, but once stampeded, they charged ahead as one, in blind determination. If an animal to the front fell, the others charged on, trampling the fallen one. Knowing this, the hunters would drive the herd into the river, and once the front runners had pointed the way, all the others would follow like sheep to the slaughter. Accustomed to crossing frozen rivers all winter, in spring the heavy beasts would readily break through the thinned ice. Pressed tightly together and relentlessly pushed on by those following behind, hundreds of buffalo would meet their deaths in a single catastrophe. This method met with favor by the women, for the meat kept well in the frigid water, until they could get all the animals skinned and butchered.

Yet another trick was to stampede the herd over the edge of a steep cliff. Many beasts could be killed at once in this way, too, for once started, they continued to push one another over the edge, those in the rear shoving those to the front over the cliff in their panic to escape the hunters following close behind.

Watching these proceedings was very interesting, but Flame wished she could have been spared all the disgusting labor she and the other women had ahead of them once the beasts were slain. Butchering and skinning the huge animals, often beneath a blazing sun, with flies and gnats gathering in swarms, was soon one of her least favorite tasks. The odious chore was long, tiresome, bloody work that seemed never to end. Her arms red to the elbows, Flame would finish stripping one carcass, only to find several more yet ahead of her. The stench and gore were overpowering, and many were the times she thought she would lose her stomach. But she forced herself to continue, knowing that the buffalo were the mainstay of survival for the tribe.

Nothing, it seemed, was wasted. Almost every part of the animal was put to some use or other. Various foods were obtained, other than the obvious steaks and stew meat. Choice dishes included buffalo tongue, brains, raw liver, kidneys, and sausage made by stuffing the animal's intestines with a mixture of bone marrow and pounded meat. A favored dessert was made of buffalo blood and berries. Hides were softened in boiling water and then scraped. These scrapings were dried and used as flour for berry cakes. If Flame could force herself not to think of the ingredients, they were quite tasty. Dried buffalo meat and grease derived from the bone marrow were combined to make pemmican, which was then stored in grease-soaked bags made of the skins of unborn buffalo calves. The bags themselves could be eaten if the necessity arose. Some of the leaner strips of flesh were dried and packed between layers of fat, peppermint leaves, and berries in a parfleche, which was a large, decorated rawhide envelope made of the hide of the buffalo and used to store food and other small, loose items.

The skins and hides had various uses also, other than as covers for the tipis. Robes and articles of clothing were made of these, though the winter buffalo yielded the thickest, warmest

robes. Those hides obtained in summer were
usually pegged flat to the ground or tied to
upright racks and scraped free of fat and hair.
Then the women would soften them by rubbing
them with fat, brains, and liver, also taken from
the buffalo. Fresh, untanned rawhide made excellent thongs, and the longer, seasoned strips were
woven into rope. Sinews were worked into
thread, or fashioned into bow strings, or used as
bindings with which to tie arrowheads and feathers to shafts.

The hair of the buffalo was braided into bridles
and halters, or used as stuffing for saddle pads.
Tufts of the coarse hair were used as paint
brushes to decorate the outsides of the tipis,
while the women often used porous buffalo bones
to paint the more delicate designs on clothing.
Even the beast's gallstones supplied the yellow
pigment for the paint. The buffalo's paunch
made a handy bucket. Spoons and ladles and
flasks were made from the horns. Even the skele-
ton was put to use in making various useful tools.
The tails made excellent swatters for hitting flies
and bugs.

As much as Flame detested the endless, back-
breaking task, she did not shirk her share of the
work, for the livelihood of the tribe depended
upon everyone's united efforts. Though she tried
not to think of herself as a permanent member of
the tribe—for she hoped still to be rescued one
day—the fact was that she lived with the tribe
now, and if everyone else went cold and hungry,
so then would she.

When they were not busy skinning buffalo or

other game that the hunters brought into the camp, the women found time to pick spring berries and wild vegetables and bulbs, and a number of other nutritious plants to supplement their food supplies. Sometimes they would set snares for smaller game such as rabbit and squirrel. They replenished their supply of herbs and leaves and roots. Some of these were used in cooking, or simply provided necessary pigments for their paints. Others supplied the essential ingredients for curatives, remedies, healing ointments, and all manner of medicines.

It was a busy time for all, but regardless of how tiring or mundane or distasteful the work, Flame was thankful that she could return to her tipi afterwards and not have to contend with Little Rabbit's complaints. There was no one there to chide her, or sneer, or make cutting remarks. There was no more need to string a blanket across the tipi to shut out censuring eyes. She and Night Hawk had all the privacy they desired now. At long last, peace and contentment reigned supreme in Night Hawk's lodge.

Flame was completely recovered now from her ordeal, and their lovemaking had long since resumed. With Little Rabbit gone, their passion seemed to flare to new heights, more wonderful than ever. Enclosed in their own private little hide-covered world, they teased and tantalized and played love games with each other with unrestricted joy. Long into the night they would whisper and fondle and please each other, until they both fell into sated slumber. It was a glorious time of love and learning for both of them.

There was another lesson, which Flame was much more reluctant to learn. Night Hawk insisted upon teaching her to swim. "How many times have you been frightened in the water because you cannot swim?" he reminded her. "If Little Rabbit had chosen to attack you in summer, you still could not have escaped her or the others because you cannot swim. She knew this. You have told me so with your own words."

"The situation will probably never arise again," she argued.

"You do not know this. There are other times you may have to escape danger from a raiding tribe or a wild animal. This land, though it provides well for us, is not always kind, especially to those who are weak. Your lack of this skill makes you weak, and very vulnerable. A thousand accidents may occur. You could be thrown from your horse while crossing a stream. We could be caught in a flood. No," he insisted with a shake of his head, "like it or not, I am going to teach you to swim."

It was one of the most difficult things Flame had ever tried to learn. To begin with, she had a terrible tendency to float like a rock—straight to the bottom! She had always thought herself fairly coordinated, but suddenly she could not seem to get her arms and legs to move together in the proper order. She was about as graceful as a mudbound ox! She simply could not remember to breathe at the proper times. As a result she swallowed gallons of river water, always muddy from her floundering about and stirring up the sand and silt from the bottom. She would come up sputtering and spitting, coughing and cursing, only to have Night Hawk tell her to try again.

The first time she actually stayed afloat, she was ecstatic. If she never learned the rest of it, perhaps she could float along until someone rescued her or she drifted to the bank. When she suggested this to Night Hawk, he laughed. Then he shook his dark head and pointed to the river. "Swim!" he ordered, as if merely by commanding it, he could make it happen.

If it were only that easy! "I will be old and gray by the time I learn this," she muttered grumpily. "I am already as wrinkled as a raisin." She studied her prune-skinned fingers balefully.

"Swim!" came the reply.

"Swim!" she mimicked resentfully as she waded reluctantly back into the water.

Finally, after what seemed a lifetime, Flame was swimming. Not gracefully, by any stretch of the imagination, but swimming nonetheless. After a few more lessons, Night Hawk was satisfied enough with her progress to be reasonably assured that she could save herself if the need arose. For Flame, this moment came none too soon, for she was sure that if she had been forced to spend one more minute in the water, she would have grown fins and a tail. She trudged back to their tipi with a smug smile adorning her lips, and a reluctant sense of pride in her hard-won success.

Chapter 17

A child! Flame did not know why she should be so surprised at the discovery, but she was. She had been having dreams again, dreams of a child with copper skin and hair as black as midnight—and her own brilliant blue eyes. Now, as she rose shakily from her knees, having just emptied her stomach of her morning meal for the sixth morning in a row, she could not deny it any longer; she was carrying Night Hawk's child within her.

With the tribe constantly on the move now, and all the unending work each day, Flame had given no thought to the amount of time that had passed since she had last been confined to the women's lodge for her monthly flow. Now, as she calculated, she realized with a start that it had been more than two months, and she should have had her flow twice over by now. She would have liked to believed that the beating she had endured and the constant traveling were responsible for the lapse, but she knew in her heart that this was not so. She was, indeed, carrying Night Hawk's baby. Already her breasts seemed more full and tender to the touch, though her stomach was as flat as it had always been.

Stumbling to the river, Flame splashed the tepid water over her flushed face. She cupped her hands and rinsed the foul taste from her mouth. Then she sat staring stupidly at her own reflection in the clear stream. "What am I to do?" she asked herself. "What am I to do now?"

A thousand thoughts flew through her mind, like a startled flock of birds beating their wings in desperation. Varied emotions assaulted her from every direction at once. Did Night Hawk know? Had he somehow guessed before she had? Flame hoped not, for then he would never let her go, if he knew she was to bear his first child. And it would be a son. Of this Flame was certain, for she had seen as much in her dreams. By now she knew better than to dispute what she saw in her strange dreams, for they had never yet been wrong. Always they foretold what was to come with uncanny accuracy.

"I've got to escape! I have to get away, somehow, before he finds out, before this child is born!" This one thought stood out above all the rest, for Flame knew that if she did not escape soon, she would be lost. Already she spoke their difficult language fluently. She had made friends among the women. She had learned so many of the tasks that had been completely foreign to her upon her arrival. She could skin an animal, tan its hide, sew the skin into clothing; she could take the meat and dry it or cook it, and present her Cheyenne husband with a nourishing, tasty meal. In less than a year's time, she had become almost completely adapted to the Cheyenne ways, absorbed into their culture and their habits. The longer she stayed here, the more she became like them, one of them, often forgetting her former life for days at a time, and this frightened her.

Something which frightened her even more, however, were her growing feelings for Night Hawk. In all honesty, she could no longer claim to be unhappy with him. Night Hawk was a tender, passionate lover. He was a wonderful husband and provider. Now that Little Rabbit was no longer tormenting her and disrupting their lives, she and Night Hawk had grown very close. He made her laugh; he made her learn and want to learn even more about him and his people; he made her love. Oh, sweet heaven, yes! He had made her love him with ridiculous ease! Even now the thought of leaving him was like a hot spear driven through her heart. How much more would it hurt if she came to love him more, as she was sure to do if she did not escape him soon. How much more difficult to leave him once they had shared their son's birth?

The thought of trying to escape was not a new one to Flame, especially now that the tribe was following the buffalo across the plains. Often they came within mere miles of forts or trading posts, and Flame's heart would yearn anew for freedom. Her thoughts would turn to her father. Where was he now? Was the general still at Fort Laramie, or had he been forced to give up the search in order to lead his men in the war that was still going on beyond the boundaries of Flame's small world with the Cheyenne? Did he think she was dead by now? Had he given up hope of finding her alive? Was he still alive, or had he been killed in some battle, while she remained ignorant and in hope of an eventual reunion with him? What would he think of her now, if she were to escape? Would he be happy, or would he be embarrassed and enraged that she now carried a Cheyenne warrior's child?

For that matter, Flame's own feelings about her recent discovery were still new and confused. Shock, dismay, anger, fear, even a fledgling joy and instinctive protectiveness—all these things did she feel, and more. Already she knew that she would love this child, would cherish him and do anything and everything to protect him with a fierce maternal pride. She would raise him to be strong and proud, as his father was, but she also yearned for the very best her own white world could offer her son. He must have a proper education, befitting the intelligence both she and Night Hawk would surely bestow on their offspring. If she could escape soon, before she gave birth, her child would be born into wealth and comfort, with the finest clothing and carriages and horses and tutors. Never would he know hunger or lack for anything.

But Flame knew that she must escape before Night Hawk suspected her condition if she hoped to accomplish any of this. Too, the very thought of having to birth her baby in the crude confines of the women's lodge terrified her. So many things might go wrong, and there would be no one to help her or the infant; at least no one in whom she had much confidence, no one qualified as a midwife or having any degree of medical knowledge. Once her son was born, escaping with a tiny infant would be twice as difficult, if not totally impossible, and she could never go alone, leaving her baby behind. While Night Hawk might some day consent to let her go, never would he part with his son; this Flame knew without doubt. This child would chain her to Night Hawk's side forevermore, as not even her own growing love for her warrior husband could do.

It was with these thoughts foremost in her mind that Flame sought some means of escape. Day after day, she watched for any opportunity to present itself, only to end the day discouraged and downhearted, lured more and more deeply into the web of enchantment that Night Hawk was relentlessly spinning about her. To make things worse, though she was very careful not to give her handsome husband any indication of her discontent, Night Hawk seemed to sense that something was amiss. Often she would look up to find him staring at her with a bemused expres-

Thrill to the most sensual, adventure-filled Romances on the market today...

FROM  LOVE SPELL BOOK

As a home subscriber to the Love Spe Romance Book Club, you'll enjoy the best today's BRAND-NEW Time Travel, Futuristi Legendary Lovers, Perfect Heroes and othe genre romance fiction. For five years, Lov Spell has brought you the award-winning high-quality authors you know and love read. Each Love Spell romance will swee you away to a world of high adventure...an intimate romance. Discover for yourself a the passion and excitement millions of reac ers thrill to each and every month.

Save $5.00 Each Time You Buy!

Every other month, the Love Spell Romance Book Club brings you four brand-new titles from Love Spell Books. EACH PACKAGE WILL SAVE YOU AT LEAST $5.00 FROM THE BOOK-STORE PRICE! And you'll never miss a new title with our convenient home delivery service.

Here's how we do it: Each package will carry a FREE 10-DAY EXAMINATION privilege. At the end of that time, if you decide to keep your books, simply pay the low invoice price of $17.96, no shipping or handling charges added.   HOME DELIVERY IS ALWAYS FREE. With today's top romance novels selling for $5.99 and higher, our price SAVES YOU AT LEAST $5.00 with each shipment.

AND YOUR FIRST TWO-BOOK SHIP-MENT IS TOTALLY FREE!

IT'S A BARGAIN YOU CAN'T BEAT! A SUPER $11.48 Valu

Love Spell ⊕ A Division of Dorchester Publishing Co., Inc.

GET YOUR 2 FREE BOOKS NOW—AN $11.48 VALUE!

*Mail the Free Book
Certificate Today!*

TWO FREE BOOKS

Free Books Certificate

YES! I want to subscribe to the Love Spell Romance Book Club. Please send me my 2 FREE BOOKS. Then every other month I'll receive the four newest Love Spell selections to Preview FREE for 10 days. If I decide to keep them, I will pay the Special Member's Only discounted price of just $4.49 each, a total of $17.96. This is a SAVINGS of at least $5.00 off the bookstore price. There are no shipping, handling, or other charges. There is no minimum number of books I must buy and I may cancel the program at any time. In any case, the 2 FREE BOOKS are mine to keep—A BIG $11.48 Value!

Offer valid only in the U.S.A.

*Name*_____

*Address*_____

*City*_____

*State*_____ *Zip*_____

*Telephone*_____

*Signature*_____

If under 18, Parent or Guardian must sign. Terms, prices and conditions subject to change. Subscription subject to acceptance. Leisure Books reserves the right to reject any order or cancel any subscription.

A $11.48 VALUE

Get Two Books Totally
FREE —
An $11.48 Value!

▼ Tear Here and Mail Your FREE Book Card Today! ▼

PLEASE RUSH
MY TWO FREE
BOOKS TO ME
RIGHT AWAY!

Love Spell Romance Book Club
P.O. Box 6613
Edison, NJ 08818-6613

sion knitting his brow, as if he were trying to discover just what was not quite right these days, what it was about her that was different.

It was most difficult, when Shining Star joyously announced her own pregnancy, for Flame to hide her gripping reaction to this news. More than anything, she wished she could share her own news with her dear friend. Instead, she was forced to smile and congratulate Shining Star, all the while keeping silent about her own impending motherhood. To hear Shining Star speak so tenderly of the child she and Stone Face expected made Flame yearn to share her own secret with Night Hawk, knowing how proud and delighted he would be. It would be wonderful to share this with the man she loved, but Flame bit her tongue and clamped her lips tightly against the urge to do this. It would surely seal her fate.

Guilt ate at her, knowing all she was denying Night Hawk with her silence and plans to escape. Never would he know the joy of holding their child in his arms, of teaching his firstborn son to ride his first pony, of gazing with wonder into the small face that was to be a replica of his own features, but with Flame's bright blue eyes shining out of his little bronze face. If all went as she wished, Night Hawk would not even suspect that he had fathered this wondrous child within her womb, and she could not help the twinges of regret that nagged at her. There would be no chubby little legs making moccasin tracks behind Night Hawk's, no tiny bow and quiver of arrows standing proudly next to Night Hawk's larger weapons in their tipi. How her heart ached at denying Night Hawk all this! Yet to tell him, to give up her dreams of escape, would be the final surrender, and Flame could not do this, no matter how her heart cried out for love of him.

Flame had nearly given up all hope. Fate seemed determined to keep her here with the Cheyenne. She wondered that Night Hawk had not noticed the small changes already taking place in her. Even her waist was beginning to thicken now, though slightly. He gave no indication that he had observed these small differences in her body, though he did eye her oddly from time to time, as if curious, or waiting for her to do or say something.

Flame had almost decided to reveal her condition to him, when Night Hawk and his fellow warriors went out on a raid against an enemy tribe. There was no telling how long they might be gone—perhaps a week, maybe two. Meanwhile, Flame's secret would remain her own until he returned to the camp.

She was greatly relieved that he would not be constantly about to tease her with his body and torment her with his bold lovemaking. Though she soon missed him more than she had thought possible, it was good to have the tipi all to herself for a change. Her thoughts and worries were her own, without his curious dark gaze continually raking her and making her feel so awfully guilty. If she could escape now, while he was away from home, perhaps she could overcome her love for him in time. Perhaps, many years from now, he would be no more than a pleasant memory, marred by no pain or remorse. Even now, she wondered if she would ever cease to love him or yearn for him, with their child as a constant reminder of the love they had shared.

In the end, escape was ridiculously easy. It came right to her doorstep, in the form of a half-breed trader, come to exchange his wares for thick robes and tanned skins from the tribe. Trader Jack's small, two-wheeled wagon was more of a covered cart, but it was filled to brimming with all manner of goods. He had cast-iron pots and skillets, bright beads and colored ribbons, ready-made knives and tempered steel from which to make blades, for those who wished to make their own. He brought blankets, both those made by the white man, and those colorfully created by tribes to the south. There were sacks of flour, sugar, corn, tobacco and coffee; even bolts of cloth and thread, and packets of shining silver sewing needles.

If Flame had intended to stay with the Cheyenne, she would have gladly found something to trade for some of Jack's goods. She longed for the taste of coffee, sweetened with real sugar. Cooking would have been so much easier with one of those skillets, and perhaps a new spoon or two. And she would have sold her eye teeth for a packet of those needles! But Flame's most pressing need was to purchase her freedom. She needed, somehow, to convince Trader Jack to

take her away from here, to take her back to Fort
Laramie or the nearest white settlement or fort.

Forcing herself to be patient, Flame gathered
together her few precious belongings into a tidy
bundle. Then she waited and watched discreetly
as the other members of the tribe bartered and
traded. When she was certain she was not being
observed, she tucked her bundle under her arm
and crept cautiously away from the camp, hiding
in a clump of trees at the side of the trail the
trader would have to take out of the village. If she
could have stolen a horse, even her own mare, she
would not have had to rely on the trader, but
Night Hawk was not so foolish as to leave this
opportunity open to her. Always her horse, and
the others as well, were well guarded, and Flame
was not allowed to ride without her husband's
approval.

It seemed hours that Flame hid there, before
she finally heard the tell-tale creak of the wagon
wheels. Then, because she was so frightened that
someone might yet prevent her escape, because
she was hesitant to place her life and trust in the
hands of this strange trader, because guilt and
love for Night Hawk cried out against this, Flame
did not step out of hiding until the wagon was
almost abreast of her. It took all her courage to
do so then, before the trader's cart should pass
and be gone.

Flame stepped into the path so suddenly that
even the tired old nag of a horse pulling the cart
shied and would have reared up in the traces. The
trader pulled at the reins and cursed. He turned
wary eyes upon the young woman in the path, his

gaze narrowing in suspicion. "What do you want?" he asked in Cheyenne.

For a moment she could not speak. Then she blurted, "Take me with you—away from here. I need to get to a fort, a white man's fort."

His small, close-set eyes raked her from head to toe, noting the fiery hair, the blue eyes. "You are white." It was more a statement of fact to himself than a question of her.

She responded nonetheless. "Yes. I must escape. I can pay you to take me to the nearest white settlement. Will you help me?" Reflexively, she glanced about, fearful of someone finding her here. Her voice and hands shook as she begged, "Please. I must go now. You must help me."

"If you are but a captive, how will you pay me to do this?" Again his eyes raked her, this time with a deliberate interest gleaming from them. His meaning was clear, and revolting.

She drew herself up, shaking though she was, and faced him squarely. "I will pay you in gold to deliver me safely into white hands, trader. I will not barter my favors."

For one so desperate, she certainly was haughty. Trader Jack's interest aroused, he damped down his immediate feelings of lust for her, concentrating instead on her offer of gold. With luck, he could have both in the end. "Show me your gold, woman, for I would know that you do not try to trick this old trader."

Flame hesitated, but knew that she must convince him. He was her only chance. Warily, she unfolded her bundle and held the wedding necklace and matching earrings out for him to see.

She watched as his beady eyes took on a covetous gleam. When he reached out for the shining pieces, she hastily pulled them back from him. "No. I have shown you my payment, but you shall not have them until I reach safety. Then, and only then, shall they be yours."

The question he would have asked next had been answered as she reached out to show him the jewelery. She wore the marriage bands of a chieftan about her wrists. This, and this alone, made him hesitate still. "Who is this husband you run from, woman?" he asked bluntly, gazing pointedly at her wrists.

"His name is Night Hawk." Flame held her breath, knowing that this alone could sway the trader's decision against her.

Cold dark eyes stared down at her. "I know this chief. He is a great warrior, and much feared for his war skills. Why should I risk my life that you may escape him through me? If he were to catch us, he would kill me. Even now he might be searching for you."

She shook her head. "He is gone from the village with several of his warriors. With luck, we could be far from here and safe before he knows of my escape."

Trader Jack's gaze lingered on the golden jewelery as he considered her words. Only he knew that he had already been well-paid to take this white woman away from here. Even now, he knew that Crooked Arrow and Little Rabbit were probably hiding in the shadows and watching. They had known the woman would come to him, and they had paid him to take her with him. He was to sell her to some distant tribe, where Night Hawk would never find her. Why they wished this, Trader Jack did not know. Nor did he care. He could triple his profits and then some, if he handled this properly. He could have what Crooked Arrow had already paid, what another warrior would pay to gain this woman, and the gold she offered. And, somewhere along the way, before he sold her, he would also enjoy the woman for himself. His only concern was Night Hawk, for he truly did fear the warrior's wrath if this plan failed and Night Hawk discovered who had stolen his wife from him.

As Crooked Arrow and Little Rabbit had known, and Flame had hoped, Trader Jack's greed soon overcame his caution. "I will take you," he agreed, managing to stifle his lust and sound properly reluctant. "For the gold." Then he motioned toward the rear of his cart. "Climb in and hide yourself well, until we are far from the Cheyenne village."

Flame did not question his orders, for she was anxious not to be seen. She could not believe she had convinced this man to aid her, and not wishing to risk having him change his mind, she scurried quickly into the back of the cart. It was many miles before her heartbeat steadied once more and she found herself able to breathe properly again.

With her heart about to fly out through her throat, it took quite a while for Flame to calm down enough to actually believe that she had made good her escape. Her ears strained to hear sounds of pursuit, sounds she thoroughly expected and was relieved not to hear. Finally, her thoughts turned to her present situation, and she began to wonder at the wisdom of begging assistance from this half-breed trader, a complete stranger. She could only hope she had not compounded her problems. After all, what did she know of this man? He might rob her, kill her, rape her; he might trade her to other tribes or take her directly back to Night Hawk for a reward. How could she be sure he would honor his word and take her safely to the nearest fort, when she was not even sure in what direction they were headed or whether it was the right route to the fort? She could only hope she had not jumped straight from the frying pan into the fire by trusting Trader Jack.

As she lay huddled in the rear of the cart, grateful for her escape, at least so far, she could not help but think of Night Hawk. How angry he would be to arrive back at the village and find her gone! She knew, without doubt, that he would be in a fine rage and that he would set out immediately to try to find her. If only she could reach the fort before he could track her! If only this blessed cart and half-dead horse could move faster! If only she did not have this horrible feeling that she had betrayed Night Hawk—and herself in the bargain!

Tears stung her eyes, and she fought to blink them back, trying to deny the sorrow and heartbreak. With stern resolution, she turned her thoughts forward to the future, a future in her own world once more, with her baby in her arms and her father to look after them both. To look backward was too painful, for the past held Night Hawk and all the joy and passion they had shared, and a love she had slim hopes of ever finding with any other man.

Chapter 18

Eventually, as the morning passed slowly into afternoon in the cramped, stuffy interior of the little cart, Flame slept. It was a restless sleep of exhaustion, of release from nerves too tightly strung. Haunting images began to form in her mind, flitting about like ghosts in the night. Faces, places, at first in no particular order, no sequence. Then the mists began to clear and the pictures became much more crisp.

She saw herself in the back of the cart, huddled there with tears drying upon her cheeks as she slept. How strange to look upon herself, as if from outside her own body! She felt the cart swaying and bumping along, heard the wheels creaking and the pots jangling against one another. She heard Trader Jack curse the old horse when it stumbled, and she saw the open lust in the quick glance he cast toward the sleeping woman in the back of his cart. Shivers raced through her, of fear and self-recrimination for having placed herself in this predicament.

Flame could see it all very clearly now in her dream. She saw Trader Jack for the greedy, devious man he truly was. Somehow, impossible though it seemed, she could even see into his thoughts now, in this strange dream of hers. He was thinking of the gold she carried, and how he might spend it on a better horse, whiskey, women. He was thinking of the profit he would make when he sold her to a Ute warrior he knew. Again Flame trembled, with both anger and fear now, and she was glad for the knife she had strapped to her thigh before leaving the Cheyenne village. At least she would not be completely defenseless against this unscrupulous beast in trader's garb! And she would be wary—yes, she would be well prepared for the lecherous desire she'd seen gleaming in his small, close-set eyes!

It came as a surprise, however, as she continued to raid the trader's mind, to learn that he had collected a fee from Little Rabbit and Crooked Arrow to take her from the village. How had they known she would flee this day? Why had they aided her in her escape? What could they possibly profit from her disappearance? Oh, she understood that they had paid Trader Jack to sell her off to another tribe. That much she had gleaned from Jack's thoughts. It was clear that they wanted her gone, far from the village and away from Night Hawk—out of their lives forever. What she failed to understand was why they had gone to all the trouble of paying Jack. If they wanted her gone that badly, why hadn't they arranged to kill her, instead of devising this manner of getting her out of the way? It made little sense.

The dream scene shifted then, as if in answer to her unspoken question, and to her absolute horror, she saw before her the charred wreckage of the very wagon in which she was now traveling! The cart lay on its side, goods melted together and still smoldering. The old horse lay still in its traces, literally roasted alive. To one side of the wagon, Trader Jack lay rigid, his face still twisted in the agony of his last moments of terror. Flame gagged at the gruesome sight of his throat and stomach sliced open, his missing scalp. Flies and buzzards already gathered to feast on his carcass.

With chills of dread tickling down her spine, she surveyed the scene, searching against her will for evidence of her own body among the remains. It was with a mixture of fear and relief that she failed to find any proof of her own death there. Still, if she was not destined to die with Jack, what had become of her? Had she escaped, or had whoever was responsible for this carnage taken her away from here? She could only guess who had done this terrible deed, but she had a very strong feeling that she herself had only escaped through her own devices. This was a warning to her of things to come, as her other dreams often were—a warning to her to get away from this wagon and its driver as soon as possible!

Flame awoke suddenly, the terror of her dream still strong upon her. Foremost in her mind was the imperative need to escape before Trader Jack met his impending doom! Tremors shook her frame, and despite the heat inside the tiny cart, she was chilled to the marrow of her bones. Beads of cold sweat dotted her forehead and dampened her doeskin dress. Stealthily, she gathered her few belongings together and hid the small bundle beneath the folds of her dress. Her fingertips brushed the hilt of the skinning knife resting along her thigh, and she drew some small comfort from the weapon. She would escape at the first opportunity, and save herself and her child.

Warning Jack would do no good, she knew, for either he would not believe her, or he would disregard her words. He was doomed to die, as her dream had foretold, and nothing in this world or the next could prevent it. She could not change what she had seen in her vision. It would come to pass, whether she wished it or not. She could only try to save herself from the same end.

As if he sensed that she had awakened, Jack turned a burning look toward her, his beady eyes glowing with an evil intent he could not mask. "There is a shallow stream crossing just ahead," he told her in the Cheyenne tongue, making her wonder if he spoke any English at all, despite his mixed blood. "Once we have crossed, we will make camp for the night."

Absorbed in her awful thoughts, Flame had not noticed how late in the day it was. Now she saw that the sun rode low in the sky. She must have slept for longer than she had first assumed. In less than an hour, it would be dark. *Good,* she thought, nodding to herself. Eluding Jack would be much easier in the dark. It mattered little if she lost her own way, for she had no idea where they were now, anyway. Yet, nagging at the edge of her mind was the reasoning that, if the sun was now setting left of the cart, they were traveling north, and she was almost sure the nearest fort would lie to the west of the Cheyenne village they had left that morning. Jack had never meant to deliver her there. He was taking her deeper into Indian territory with every turn of the cart wheels! Damn his dirty eyes! The greedy devil deserved his fate tenfold!

This was her penalty for being so foolishly trusting! It was mostly her own fault for asking aid from the first stranger at hand, but what else was she to have done? Well, now she would have to make her own way to civilization. She must fend for herself and her unborn child somehow, and trust God to protect them along the way.

A few minutes later, Jack had pulled the cart a small distance from the far bank of the sluggish little creek. Without delay, Flame hopped from the rear of the cart, stomping about and stretching to restore the flow of blood to her cramped limbs. She eyed Trader Jack warily as he tended to his horse.

He did not seem to notice her leery look, but threw his words carelessly over his shoulder.

"You will find the fixings for supper in a bag under the seat. There should be a couple of biscuits left over from my breakfast, and a small chunk of cured ham. That will do for now. If you want one of those potatoes in the sack, you will have to eat it raw. We can't risk a fire yet. Later, when we are farther away from your husband's people, I can take the time to hunt for fresh meat, but not now."

Until he mentioned the food, Flame had given no thought to provisions. Now, realizing how thoughtless she had been, she was thankful he had reminded her of this. She must manage to take some food with her, or she might starve before she could reach safety. She would also need a water bag.

As if reading her mind, Jack added, "You will find a water skin next to the food. Take it and refill it at the stream before it gets too dark to see what you are doing."

Hastily retrieving what little food she could carry with her, and hiding it from his view, she grabbed the water bag and started toward the stream. As she walked, she called back to him. "I must make a trip into the bushes first, so do not worry if I take a little longer than I should to fill the skin."

As he caught her meaning, his crude chuckle followed her, then the admonition, "Just do not delay too long, woman. Soon the wild creatures will come out to drink, and I would hate to lose you to a hungry wolf."

As she ducked behind the first sheltering tree, Flame recalled that frightful time when Night

Hawk scarcely returned in time to rescue her from the jaws of that mad wolf. A quiver of fresh fear washed through her. Still, she thought she would rather take her chances with the forest animals than with Trader Jack. Forcing herself to tread softly until she was out of his hearing, she went slowly at first. Then, throwing caution to the winds, she ran as if all the demons of Hell were on her heels.

Blissfully unaware of what awaited him, Night Hawk rode calmly into his village with the returning warriors. They had been victorious over their enemies, and there would be great revelry and celebration among his people this night. He was feeling triumphant, having been personally successful on this raid. He looked forward to the chants and the dancing—but more than that, he looked forward to a loving greeting from his beautiful wife, whom he had not seen for nine long suns now. His heart and his loins ached for the very sight of her flaming hair and her sky-blue eyes. They would have a private reunion before tonight's tribal festivities, and again afterward. He would make certain of it!

Shining Star scanned the returning warriors. Joy and relief touched her features as she spotted Stone Face among them. Then dread returned as she sighted Night Hawk and recalled what she must tell him. If she kept silent, he would soon learn of Flame's disappearance from the others, but she felt it only right that she tell him, since she had been the first to realize that Flame was missing.

It had been three full suns now since Flame
was last seen. No one knew where she was,
though by now they had a few ideas what might
have happened to their chief's wife. No one
could recall seeing Flame since the morning that
Trader Jack had arrived in the camp. In the midst
of the frantic trading, no one had given a thought
to Flame's absence. It was not until much later
that day that Shining Star had visited her friend's
tipi. Finding the tipi flap tied down across the
opening, a sign for the wish for privacy, Shining
Star had called softly to Flame. When she received no answer, she tiptoed quietly away, not
wanting to disturb her friend.

Still, she wondered why Flame had secluded
herself in the tipi. Was she ill? Did she miss Night
Hawk and need to hide her tears from the others?
Still another distressing thought occurred to
Shining Star—had Flame found nothing with
which to barter for goods with the trader, and
thus felt saddened at being left out of the fun and
frivolity of the morning? At the time Shining Star
had not thought of this, but she could now see the
possibility and felt shamed that she had not
watched over Flame more closely, for she knew
that Flame had few possessions of her own as yet
and was still new to their ways. Perhaps the
woman was unsure of what was permissible to
trade or how to go about such things.

It was almost dark when Shining Star returned
to Night Hawk's lodge again. Still the tipi flap
was secured. No smoke issued from the smoke
hole, though Flame should have been preparing
the evening meal. Again she called softly, but

heard nothing save whining noises from within. Afraid that Flame was truly ill, Shining Star disregarded polite custom. She untied the tipi flap and peeked inside. When her eyes had adjusted to the dim interior, she saw only the little raccoon inside. The pitiful noises were coming from the small animal, for he was tied to a central pole and could not free himself. Evidently, he had tipped over the bowl of water Flame had left for him, and from the mess at the base of the pole, he had been tied for some time now.

Frowning, Shining Star considered this. How long had Flame been gone from her lodge? Where could she be? Had she gone for water or to collect buffalo chips and met with an accident earlier in the day, with no one to notice her absence? But why would she tie Bandit and leave him behind? Had she gone to bathe in the stream and not wanted the raccoon to disturb her with his antics? Had she perhaps wanted to gather roots or berries along the river or in the small stand of trees and bushes near the camp?

After investigating all these places and more, Shining Star still had not located Flame. There was no sign of her anywhere. None of the other women had seen her, and Shining Star was becoming more and more worried. She and several of the other women of the tribe searched until it was too dark to see any longer. Finally admitting defeat, they went to inform the Cheyenne warriors and braves who had not gone on the raid. They also insisted that Little Rabbit be questioned, for they remembered her treacherous attempt to kill Flame not so long ago. Little

Rabbit claimed to know nothing of Flame's disappearance, and Crooked Arrow assured them that his wife had been busy in and about his tipi all day. He professed concern for the missing woman, and even offered to head the search party the following morning, if Flame had not yet returned by then.

There was little to be done until the next morning, and it rained that night, adding to the problem of tracking her. Soon after sunrise, a small party of warriors set out in search of their chief's missing wife. All day they searched, returning in defeat just before nightfall. They had found no sign of Flame, no sign of any other tribe having been in the area, no sign of a struggle or an accident of any kind—not so much as a strand of bright hair or a bead from her moccasin.

All but Crooked Arrow agreed to try again the next morning, for they knew beyond doubt how upset Night Hawk would be to return and find his bride gone. With half-hearted apology, Crooked Arrow declined, saying that he was taking Little Rabbit and Howling Gale north to visit the tribe of his sister, having promised his new wife that they would do so. He would delay his own trip no longer to aid Little Rabbit's enemy and his former friend.

This third day of Flame's unknown fate had begun in much the same way as the day before. The search party had left as soon as there was light enough to see, and they had not yet returned, though the sun had passed its zenith. Now the raiding party had returned, and Night

Hawk with them, and Shining Star dreaded having to relate the distressing news to her husband's friend; but she must do so immediately, for Night Hawk was even now striding toward his lodge.

Gathering her courage, Shining Star called out to him. "Night Hawk!" He turned, and she hurried forward. "Night Hawk, there is something of great importance which I must tell you."

"Can it not wait, Shining Star? I admit I am most eager to greet my wife after my long absence." His smile melted upon his face at the solemnity of her answering look.

"Flame is not there, Night Hawk," she said hesitantly. Knowing no way to break such news to him more gently, she added hastily, "She is gone."

Stone Face had joined them in time to hear Shining Star's blunt announcement. Now both men stared at her and asked, "Not here?" Shaking his head in bewilderment, Night Hawk asked, "What do you mean by saying she is not here? Where is she?"

"We do not know, Night Hawk. Flame has been missing from the camp for three days now. The men are even now searching for her, as they did yesterday—as I myself and the other women did the day before that."

Night Hawk looked as if he had just received a lance to the stomach. His face paled, his muscles tensed, and the air whooshed from his throat. "How? Why?" With effort, he regained his composure somewhat. "You must tell me all that has happened, Shining Star, that we may make some sense of this."

She told him all that had transpired during his absence. When she related that Flame's disappearance had coincided with the appearance of the trader, Night Hawk frowned, a seed of suspicion beginning to grow. "Did our men try to find this trader?" he asked.

"Trader Jack?" Shining Star nodded. "Yes, but the rain had washed away the tracks of his wagon, and no one knows where he went to trade next." Her big brown eyes shone with dismay as she stared up at him. "Do you truly think he might have stolen Flame away? Surely he would know that our warriors would search for him. Surely he would not be so bold as to steal a mighty war chief's wife! To do so would mean his death."

"Very foolish, indeed," Night Hawk agreed, his dark eyes turning hard as stone, "but a greedy man might dare as much, if he thought he could escape before being caught."

"Unless Flame has met with some other accident, I must agree that Flame is most likely with Trader Jack," Stone Face told his wife. "You have said that the search party has found no sign of her near the village or along the stream."

"Is her horse still here?" Night Hawk thought to ask.

"Yes, and none of the other horses appears to be missing either."

"And Flame's personal possessions?" he questioned.

The look on Shining Star's face reflected her

confusion. "I have not thought to look," she admitted. "Why do you ask this? Surely, if Flame has been taken, her abductor would not have stolen into your lodge and collected her belongings. I do not understand what you are thinking, Night Hawk."

Stone Face and Night Hawk shared a grim look. "Our chief is suggesting that his young bride might have decided to return to her own people, Shining Star—that her disappearance might be of her own doing. Am I not right, my friend?"

Shining Star saw the truth of this on Night Hawk's face, even before his words confirmed it. "You are wrong, Night Hawk. Surely this cannot be, for Flame adores you. She has missed you greatly while you were gone from the village. Her eyes have not been truly happy since you rode out with the raiding party. They have been like rain clouds covering the sun."

"Come then," he suggested softly, his heart aching at what he might discover within his tipi. "Let us see what we find inside my lodge."

As he had feared, many of Flame's things were gone. Missing was the small bag containing her gold earrings and matching necklace, and the many small treasures he had given her. Also gone was her favorite dress, and one other. Night Hawk's face was fearsome to behold as he stared about his tipi with smoldering eyes.

"I shall find her," he swore. "I shall find her and she shall feel my wrath for daring to make a fool of me before my people. And if Trader Jack has aided her, he too shall pay, with his life's blood. If he has dared to touch Chief Night Hawk's wife, I shall take great pleasure in taking his life in the slowest, most painful manner I can devise. This I swear, upon the graves of my great and mighty ancestors!"

Chapter
19

The night was dark and wild and filled with frightening noises. Flame's ears echoed with the sounds of animals slithering through the darkness, heard but not seen. Her heartbeat matched her erratic footsteps as she forced her weary legs to go on just a few more steps, then a few more, promising herself that she could stop and rest soon. But where? Where could she hide herself and be safe from all predators?

That first night alone in the dark, she thought she would die of fright. On and on she had run, through the tangle of brush and small trees that hid her from Trader Jack's eyes, feeling him always behind her as he tracked her relentlessly. When she stopped, she could hear him somewhere behind her. Luckily, the darkness had slowed his search. Then it had begun to rain, washing away her tracks. As Flame crouched hidden in a clump of bushes, her heart thundering like a war drum, her mouth as dry as cotton, Trader Jack passed right by her hiding place. Quelling the urge to run again, she stayed hidden, trying to quiet the sounds of her tortured breathing. It was fortunate she had done so, for before long, Trader Jack had returned, on his way back to his camp.

Flame had waited long after the sounds of his passing had faded away. Finally, stiff and wet, she had crawled out of the bushes. Again she fled, as quietly and as swiftly as her legs would carry her, praying that the rain would continue to cover her trail.

At first, she followed the river line upstream, as close as she dared, allowing herself only brief stops to rest that first long night. The sun was peeking up over the horizon before she allowed herself to believe that she was not being followed and could rest at last. Shaking with fatigue and fright, she somehow managed to crawl into the lower branches of a tree and nestle herself firmly against the fork of the trunk and two sturdy limbs. Even then, as her eyes drifted shut on a wave of exhaustion, she did not relax, afraid she might fall and harm herself or the child she carried. Also, she could not help but wonder what kind of danger might lurk nearby, what sort of predators could climb trees, whether Trader Jack might find her here while she slept, and whether Night Hawk had yet returned to the Cheyenne village and discovered her missing. Was he even now trying to track her?

By early afternoon of the next day, she was on her way again—and completely lost. Nevertheless, she trudged doggedly on, for she feared that she was leaving a trail a child could easily follow. The afternoon warmed, and for a time she walked in the river itself, knowing that her footsteps could not be traced as long as she did so. Too soon the river narrowed, the current becoming swift and dangerous, and she was forced to leave it. She climbed up the opposite bank and followed the river in the direction of the setting sun. As long as she followed the river, she felt safer, hoping that at some point she might come upon a cabin or fort or white settlement of some kind. With this reasoning, she drew upon her flagging energies and forced herself to walk on long after the evening shadows had turned to the deep purple of night.

The nights were the longest and most frightening part of her journey, for she had a constant fear of being attacked by wild animals. Now, on this third night, she sat shivering, curled into a small ball. Only sheer determination held back the whimper rising in her throat as the bushes beneath her precarious tree-perch rustled. She was more frightened now than she had been earlier that day, when she had hidden from a band of Indians, not even daring to breathe until they had miraculously passed by mere feet from where she had huddled behind a large tree. She had not recognized any of the braves, nor were the markings of their tribe familiar. It mattered little, for regardless of who they were, her life would have been in peril had they discovered her.

Sitting there on a low limb, with branches lightly brushing her face in the night breeze, Flame tried to gather her courage. Surely she had traveled many miles in the last two days, since her successful escape from Trader Jack, though she had no sure way of estimating just how far she had come. She could only hope she had not been wandering in circles, as many were known to do when lost. Surely she had not, for though the trees and land all began to look alike after a while, she had faithfully followed the river all the way, veering away from it only when necessary. Of course, this would make her much easier to track, if someone were following her, but it was her sole guideline and she was loathe to wander too far from it.

Slapping at an annoying mosquito, Flame wished she could build a small fire, but she dared not lead anyone toward her. God only knew what sort of creatures it might attract, animal or human! Still, it would have been a comfort to have light to break the deep darkness of the night. The same animals roamed the land in the day as did at night, but at least she could see about her then, not just imagine the dangers that lurked in the dark.

Carefully unwrapping the last of her small store of food, Flame nibbled at it sparingly, wondering what she was going to do when it was gone. As miserly as she had been with it, there would be only a small portion for breakfast in the

morning, and then she would have to find some
other means of providing food for herself. Just
one more thing to worry about until she happened to stumble onto some semblance of civilization, if she ever did. For that would be what it
would amount to—pure accident! Already it felt
as if she had been wandering lost in this wilderness forever. She had never been so eager to hear
another human voice, never been so afraid of
being alone. At this point, she would even have
welcomed Night Hawk's appearance with a glad
cry and open arms.

Morning followed a restless night. Flame ate
her meager meal, licking the last of the crumbs
from her fingertips, and worried when or where
her next meal might come from. Her limbs were
cramped, her energies almost depleted, and her
stomach still rumbled with hunger. It was all she
could do to make herself go on.

The sun had yet to reach the midpoint of the
day when the stream, which had been gradually
diminishing, disappeared altogether. It simply
was no longer there. Without it, what would she
use as a guideline? To add to her dilemma,
without the stream there was no longer the cover
of trees. Ahead of her lay the open grasslands of
the prairie, and once she entered this flat, unbro-
ken ground she would be exposing herself, easy
prey to whoever might come along. On the
prairie there simply was no place to hide from
one's enemies or pursuers. However, other than
going back the way she had come, she had few
options but to forge ahead.

It was late in the afternoon when Flame's luck

ran out. At first, it was only a vague feeling of uneasiness, which gradually escalated into a prickly sensation along her spine and scalp. No matter how often she glanced behind her, however, she could see nothing to cause such alarm. Still, it was there and she could not deny it. As the tension increased within her, she fought the urge to sit down and cry. She was so very, very tired. What was the use of it all? Why had she been so foolish to think she could cross miles of wilderness by herself, with few provisions and absolutely no protection? Her weary brain failed to bring forth her original purpose in this escape. Her weakened, hungry body cried out for rest and food and comfort.

In her present state, life in the Cheyenne camp seemed so pleasant by comparison, and the pain of her separation from Night Hawk was almost unbearable. With each passing day she missed him more, longed for him until thoughts of him filled every waking hour, loved him beyond measure. What would she not give to see his handsome face now! How she regretted leaving the shelter of his loving arms! If she thought, even now, that she could make her way back by herself, she would retrace her steps and return to him, but she was so lost by now that she was certain she could never find the village again on her own.

Almost numb with fatigue, Flame dragged one plodding foot ahead of the other. One more step; just one more; just one more after that. No longer did she bother looking about for that elusive shadow that seemed to be dogging her trail. She concentrated solely upon placing one worn, muddy moccasin before its mate. It passed through her mind that the moccasins were of almost no use at all anymore as protection to her bruised feet. Her dress was little better, for it was filthy and torn in several places. Her hair was a sweaty, dirty mass of tangles, barely bound in braids that had long since come loose. Her bare arms and legs were terribly scratched, as was her face, and without the protection of the trees, and despite the way her skin had darkened during her time with the Cheyenne, she could feel it tightening with sunburn.

Finally, she could go no farther. She simply stopped and sank wearily into the tall prairie grass at her feet. There she sat, staring dejectedly at the lowering sun and feeling more sorry for herself than she could ever recall. Even when she had first been captured, she had not felt this tired, this emotionally drained, this defeated. Tears of exhaustion and self-pity streaked muddy paths down her dirty cheeks.

Even when her befuddled brain finally recognized the sound of hoofbeats behind her, she could not find the energy to run. Her trembling legs simply collapsed when she made a feeble attempt to rise. They would no longer obey her command to support her own weight, let alone flee approaching danger. With fear clogging her throat and her heart running away with itself, she dared to look. Already huge eyes grew larger as she saw two warriors fast closing the distance to her. She sat helplessly awaiting her fate, her body quivering, tears racing down her face until they blurred the image of the approaching warriors, small whimpers issuing from the depths of her quaking soul.

She recognized his stallion first, through the salty tears that filmed her eyes. Relief and despair warred with the joy in her heart as her eyes focused at last on Night Hawk's beloved features, features now frozen into a bronze mask of stern disapproval and scorn.

He drew his horse to a halt almost directly above her. There he sat, silently staring down at her until she had to lower her gaze, unable to meet the anger and disdain in his dark eyes. For an eternity of heartbeats, neither spoke. At last he ordered gruffly, "Get up, woman. Rise and mount behind me."

By now she was shaking so badly that every bone in her body was knocking against the one next to it, and when she again attempted to rise, her legs had turned to jelly. "I—I cannot," she admitted, her voice quavering as she sank back into the tall grass.

He did not even bother to dismount. He merely leaned down from the horse and, grabbing a huge handful of her hair, yanked her roughly to her feet. Her yelp of pain and surprise had barely cleared her throat when his hard hand clamped about her arm and he pulled her onto the horse behind him. Instinctively, her arms encircled his waist, and for just a second she thought she felt him flinch from her touch. Then, to her further shock and shame, he quickly bound her wrists together with a rawhide thong, just as he had done when he had first captured her.

"Night Hawk, it is not necessary to tie my hands," she said with a soft cry of dismay. "I will not try to flee from you."

He twisted about to glare at her, and she could have died at the look of contempt he directed at her. "I will do as I see fit, woman. Do not attempt to sway me with your honeyed words, for you have broken the trust between us. If you are wise, you will silence your tongue and speak only when asked to do so, for my anger cries out to be eased, and you alone will be the target of my wrath."

Fresh tears welled in her eyes, but she managed to nod her understanding of his command before he faced away from her again. From the corner of her vision she saw a similar look of disdain in Stone Face's eyes before he hastily averted his gaze. Only then did it dawn on Flame that she had lost more than Night Hawk's trust and respect by her unwise flight.

Much to her surprise, Night Hawk headed his horse in the same direction in which she had been traveling. Could it be that she had become so confused that she had lost all sense of direction? Shouldn't the Cheyenne village lie behind them, the way from which the warriors had come?

They rode but a short distance, topping a small rise not far from the place where Flame had collapsed in exhaustion. Huddled against Night Hawk's broad back, Flame paid little attention until he spoke commandingly. "Look, Flame. See how close you came to your freedom, only to be denied it."

Her confused gaze followed where he pointed, and she gave an involuntary gasp of dismay. Before them, not a mile distant, stood a fort. In fact, this particular fort looked strangely familiar. "Fort Laramie?" she whispered in disbelief.

"The very fort from which I stole you," he confirmed cruelly.

"Oh, Night Hawk!" she exclaimed softly. "If you have any pity in your heart at all, please release me now. Let me go back to my people, to my family and my father. He must be sick with worry, if he still believes that I am alive. He may be down there now, thinking about me, wondering what has become of me. I am his only child, and his heart must be aching. Please let me go to him."

The sneer that marred her Cheyenne husband's features was frightening to behold. "I will never let you go back to your people," he vowed darkly. "This I have told you from the moment I claimed you, long before I planted the seed of my child within your belly. You are mine for all time, or until I no longer have want of you."

Again she gasped in surprise, her eyes widening. "You know," she said simply.

"Did you think I would not notice even the smallest change in your body?" he challenged. "Did you not suspect that there were times when I was waiting for you to tell me your glad news and wondered why you kept silent? When I arrived back at the village and found you gone, I knew then why you did not tell me. You never intended to tell me, did you, my deceitful little

wife?" he snarled. "You fled and took my unborn
child with you, that I might never know of his
being or gaze upon him with my own eyes. For
that I may never forgive you. Your treachery is no
less than Little Rabbit's in my mind, and you will
have your punishment before I am done with
you."

His threat went straight to her heart, as did his
pain, for she felt it as her own and was deeply
shamed. "I could see no other way, Night Hawk.
Please believe that I would never have done this
if there were any other way. It hurt me very
deeply to leave you and know that I am carrying
your child within me, for I *do* care for you and
the babe."

"Save your lies for other ears," he advised
callously. "Mine no longer believe your soft
words which hide a deceitful heart." As her hot,
salty tears bathed his back, he added, "And save
your tears, also, for you will soon have better
need of them."

"What . . . what are you going to do to me?"
she asked hesitantly. "Will you put me away
from you as you did Little Rabbit?"

"I have not yet decided what your punishment
will be, so you would be wise not to tempt my
anger any further. Perhaps you can yet redeem
yourself in my eyes if you are truly repentant and
properly docile. I will abide no disobedience or
sign of rebellion from you. You have broken the
faith between us and angered me too greatly. If
not for the child you carry, I would have beaten
you by now, or perhaps worse. There have been

times since I discovered your treachery that I have wanted to slay you with my bare hands. Even now I am tempted to place my fingers about your throat and choke the life from you, but for the life of my child within your body."

"Night Hawk, I am truly sorry," she sobbed shakily.

His face taut with suppressed anger, he grated through clenched teeth, "Say no more, Flame. For your own safety and that of our child, hold your tongue."

As they turned to retrace their route, Flame gazed longingly at the fort, so near and yet so far away. One hearty scream might be heard by the soldiers and bring help, but could she hope to escape Night Hawk even then? Would her freedom be worth the risk of her life, or Night Hawk's, or that of their child? If anything happened to this magnificent warrior, whom she had come to love so disastrously, she would never forgive herself. Nor would she forgive herself if any harm came to the babe nestled beneath her heart. A sigh shuddered through her as she pressed her damp face to Night Hawk's back and bit her lip hard to stifle the cry that rose to her throat. God and father forgive her, but she would not summon aid that might mean Night Hawk's death, even if it meant forfeiting her freedom forevermore.

If Night Hawk wondered at her quivering silence, he said nothing. If he wondered why she did not try to call out for help from the white soldiers at the fort, he held his own counsel. He kneed his big horse into a fast trot that carried them swiftly away from the fort.

It was a long, tension-filled trip back to the Cheyenne village. Little was said, even between the two warriors, each keeping his thoughts and worries to himself. Each night, when they camped, one of the men would hunt for their supper while the other stood guard over Flame lest she attempt to escape again. Not once throughout the entire time did Stone Face say a word to her, and she knew that she had disappointed him almost as greatly as she had Night Hawk.

At each camp she would gather wood or buffalo droppings and make their evening fire. When given the meat, she would silently and obediently skin it and cook their meals. Upon retiring, she offered no objection when Night Hawk sullenly tied her wrist to his with a short rawhide strap, though it tore at her heart each time he did so. No longer did he gather her tenderly into his arms as in nights past, but kept his distance as if loathe to touch her. Not once did he make any loving gesture toward her. If he still held any desire at all for her, he did not show it, and he did not make love to her even out of revenge. If he awoke to find her cuddled next to him in the night, he would carefully disengage himself and heartlessly push her away from him, ignoring her hurt look and the tears that came so readily to her eyes these days.

One day's ride from the village, not far from the spot where Flame had last seen Trader Jack, they came upon the burned wagon and Jack's lifeless body. It was worse even than her dream of it, if that were possible. The stench of burned horsehide and decaying flesh, both animal and human, was almost more than Flame could bear. Yet the mutilated body and overturned cart were exactly as she had envisioned them. Her stomach lurched in rebellion, and for a brief moment she feared she might faint. All color fled her face, leaving it ghostly white.

Seeing her turn her gaze hastily from the gruesome sight, Night Hawk mocked her. "Do you grieve for the man who aided you in your escape?" he taunted.

Slowly she shook her head in denial. "No, but did you have to kill the poor horse as well? Could you not have released it to find its own way?"

Returning her look with one of curiosity, he answered. "I am not responsible for this man's death, wife, though I would have been if I had found him first. Stone Face and I passed this place in our search for you, and the trader was already slain. We wasted much time sifting through the ashes of the wagon looking for your body."

"Did it dismay you not to find it?" she burst out before she could control her sharp tongue.

"No, wife," he assured her softly, his tone chilling her. "I would then have been robbed of my revenge against you and felt cheated. Also, I would have grieved the loss of my child."

Swallowing her hurt, she asked, "If you did not do this, then who did? When I envisioned this in my dream, I could not determine who would kill the trader. I only knew that I must escape him if I were not to meet a similar end."

"You dreamed of this?" Night Hawk asked sharply. "When?"

"That first afternoon, while I slept in the back of the wagon," she explained. "Trader Jack did not stop until it was nearly dark, for he wanted to put as much distance as possible between us and the village. It was then I ran away from him."

"Am I to believe that you escaped him before he could lay claim to your body?" Night Hawk questioned, his keen gaze searching her face for the truth of her answer.

Her face blanched even more, but she faced him squarely. "He never touched me in any way, Night Hawk. This I swear to you on my life, on the life of my child." Embarrassed, she admitted, "I could see in his face that he wanted me, but I escaped before he had the opportunity. My dream had warned me of my foolishness, for not only did he desire me, but he was planning to sell me to another tribe."

"How do you know this? Did he tell you so?"

She shook her head. "No, Night Hawk. I have said that my dream warned me of this, just as it told me that Little Rabbit and Crooked Arrow had paid him to aid in my escape. I know not how they knew what I planned, or their reasons for doing as they did, but they paid him to take me away and sell me to a distant tribe where you would never think to look for me."

She saw the disdainful disbelief cross his face and regretted having told him of her dream. Surely he would think her crazy now. She should have kept silent about her dreams, just as she always had in the past. It was foolish to think that anyone, even Night Hawk, would ever believe such things.

"Do not take offense if I choose not to believe such a wild tale." His lip curled up scornfully. "If you can show me any proof that you speak the truth, I would see it now."

"Any proof I might have shown you has died with the trader and his wagon," she told him wearily. "I have only my word for it and my vision, and it is plain that you do not wish to believe me."

Her head lowered to hide her tears from his view, Flame failed to see the curious look that passed between the two warriors. Little did she suspect that for the duration of their ride to the Cheyenne village each man was wondering how much truth there might be to her story of her dream vision. Still ignorant of much of the Cheyenne religion and customs, Flame was unaware that, unlike her own people, most Indians placed great faith in dreams and visions. They readily believed that they often foretold the future, warning of things to come. If Flame were telling the truth about this, and not just creating a story to gain their sympathy, Night Hawk dared not discount what she had said. Also, if Flame were to prove to be one of those rare persons who had visions often, Night Hawk dared not harm her in any way, for fear of bringing disaster down upon the entire tribe. Their faith strictly forbade the harming of any true dreamer.

As they neared their village, Night Hawk had

much more to consider than the escape and recovery of his runaway wife, or her imminent punishment. Important decisions must be carefully weighed and determined, decisions that involved more than just himself and Flame now and could affect the entire Cheyenne tribe. As a chief, he must think on all of this calmly and cautiously before acting. Above all else, he could not act hastily, or let his heart rule his head as it had too often done in the past. He must set aside his personal feelings of hurt and anger and try only to consider the good of his people.

At this moment, however, Night Hawk was having difficulty feeling like the wise Cheyenne chieftan he was supposed to be. Rather, he felt more like a very confused, betrayed husband with a troublesome wife on his hands, a wife who carried his first precious child within her womb. Her dreams, or possible visions, only served to complicate matters further. What *was* he to do with this woman of his?

Chapter
20

Every head turned to watch as Night Hawk
rode into camp with his recaptured wife. Dark
eyes noted their chief's stern demeanor, Flame's
resigned look, her arms bound about his waist.
All knew that the young woman would soon
meet punishment before them all. They could
only imagine what form it might take, for the ex-
tent of it would be up to Night Hawk to determine.

Flame almost cringed at the looks that followed her as they rode through the maze of tipis.
When Night Hawk at last drew his horse to a halt,
she gasped in horror, her eyes growing wide with
fear as she saw that he had stopped before the
women's lodge and not their own tipi. Was her
fate to be the same as Little Rabbit's? Had Night

Hawk decided to rid himself of her?

She could not still her small cry of dismay as Night Hawk unbound her wrists and shoved her roughly to the ground. She fell at his feet. It took all her courage to look up at him as he spoke. "You will remain in the women's lodge until I have determined your punishment," he told her. "You will speak to no one, and you will not leave the lodge for any reason, until you have been summoned."

His dark eyes blazed down into hers as she gazed up at him imploringly, silently begging him not to leave her there. "Do not attempt to escape again, Flame," he warned coldly, "for if you are so foolish, it will surely mean your life."

With his dire words ringing in her ears, she watched as he rode away, his back stiff and unforgiving. Head hanging to shield her tears and flaming cheeks from those who watched, she bent and silently entered the lodge. Huge sobs locked in her chest and stuck there, making her heart heavier than ever as she sank to a mat and turned her face away. Hope could not find a way through the fear that enshrouded her now. Wrapping her arms about her waist, she sat shivering and praying, waiting . . . waiting.

Knowing only one person to consult about his wife's dream, Night Hawk sought a private audience with Owl Eyes, the tribal shaman. The shaman's powers of interpretation were great. He was very wise in the ways of visions and their meanings.

"Should I believe what she tells me of this

dream?" Night Hawk asked after telling Owl Eyes everything that Flame had related to him. "It might be that she seeks only a way to lighten her punishment and put blame on others."

Wise Owl considered this, then asked. "Has she ever had dreams of this kind before?"

"She has told me of none other," Night Hawk replied.

"If there have been other visions that have come to pass, we must know this. Bring the woman to me. I would talk with her on this matter."

It had been but a few hours since their arrival in the camp, but to Flame, sitting alone in the women's lodge and worrying herself sick over what terrible fate might befall her, it seemed days. So distraught was she, so wrapped in her own thoughts, that she nearly shrieked aloud and fainted when Meadow Grass touched her shoulder to gain her attention. Not speaking, the other woman gestured toward the tipi opening, beyond which Flame could see Night Hawk awaiting her. Her heart thudded in her chest and her knees wobbled precariously as she slowly rose and walked toward him. *So soon?* she thought irrationally, her throat going dry, her entire body atremble.

Gesturing for her to follow him, Night Hawk strode ahead of her, leading her to the lodge of the tribal shaman. With each step, her fears increased, and when she recognized the tipi of Owl Eyes, so great was her fright that she stumbled upon entering and would have fallen if Night Hawk had not grasped her arm. "Sit," he instructed, placing her opposite the wise old man.

For many heartbeats, all was silent. Peering at him through the veil of her lashes, Flame thought perhaps the shaman had fallen asleep. He sat before her, his head bent, his long gray braids bracketing his weathered face, his eyes closed. He began humming softly. Suddenly, some minutes later, his dark eyes opened to spear her sharply. "Tell me of your dreams," he commanded quietly.

"The . . . the one of Trader Jack and his wagon?" she stammered.

"All of them. Tell me of all of your visions. Leave out not the smallest detail. Let me see them as you have."

She told him first of her dream of Trader Jack. When she had finished relating what she could recall, he questioned her. What did she hear? What had she smelled and felt?

"How long have you had these visions that tell of things to come?" he asked. "When was the first, and what did it foretell?" His voice and his eyes seemed to cast a spell about her. It was impossible to deny the shaman that which he wanted to know, impossible for her to tell anything but the truth in his august presence.

She told him of the dream that had predicted her mother's illness and death, and how it had all come to pass. She related the tale of Nan Harrod's horse, and how it had broken its leg. a few days after she had dreamed that it would. In embarrassment, since Night Hawk was seated near and listening to every word, she admitted that she had dreamed of Night Hawk.

At this the old man chuckled, eyeing her flushed face. "It is quite common for a wife to dream of her husband," he told her.

"No," she corrected hesitantly, blushing even more greatly. "You do not understand what I am telling you. I saw Night Hawk's face in my dreams many times before I first met him. I saw only his face, nothing more, and he never spoke to me in my dreams, but I knew that he and I would someday meet, that he would play some part in my future. You cannot imagine my shock upon first seeing him that day at the fort! Immediately, I recognized him from my dreams, but I had never envisioned him as a warrior! I had always thought that he would be one of my people, a white man. It came as a great surprise to discover that he was a Cheyenne warrior, for I could not fathom what fate would link this Indian's life with mine."

Night Hawk was shocked and secretly delighted to hear this admission from her, that she had dreamed of him before their meeting on that fateful day at Fort Laramie. Now he recalled the look of shock on her face when she had first seen him watching her, the way her face had paled at the sight of him standing there. For the first time he understood the recognition he had glimpsed on her face. This only served to reinforce his original thought that the two of them were destined for each other, that the spirits had decided their meeting and their marriage long before their births.

He was further stunned to learn that she had dreamed of the birth of their child, and that it was to be a son with his own dark hair and Flame's bright blue eyes. This she admitted reluctantly, her head bent in shame before him. Could it truly be? Even as he delighted in this revelation, his anger grew to new heights that she would have denied him his first son, the very pride of his life!

Considering all this, he knew that there was no way he could ever put her away from him, as he had done with Little Rabbit. Flame would remain his wife, the mother of his children, for as long as the two of them lived. Her impetuous flight from him had been doomed to failure, for she would never escape from him unless, and until, the spirits decreed that it should be so. Her life's path was entwined with his, his destiny with hers.

The shaman questioned Flame at length about her mysterious dreams and their meanings. Finally he seemed satisfied with her answers, requesting that she wait outside his tipi while he discussed his conclusions with Night Hawk. When she had gone, he turned to Night Hawk and asked, "What is your opinion of your wife's dreams now, my brother?"

Night Hawk hesitated, and then confessed, "I am not completely convinced, but I feel she may speak truly of these visions. When first we met at the fort, I could see the shock of recognition on

her face, and I wondered over it then. Her telling
of her dreams of me would explain this. Of the
other things, her mother's death, the birth of our
son, I have no way of determining. You know
much more of these matters than I. What do you
think, Wise One?"

"There is much to consider. I know that she
must be punished for attempting to flee from
you, and I know that she has angered you greatly
in doing so, yet I must urge you to temper your
wrath. Flame may truly be one of the Dreamers,
and as such, she must not be harmed lest we call
down the rage of the spirits upon our tribe. You
must search for a way to chasten her without
bringing harm to her or the child she carries.
Flame must learn to accept her life with us, and
to obey you as her husband, but you must take
care in the manner of her correction, Night
Hawk."

The warrior nodded in agreement. "But what
of her visions, Owl Eyes? How do we know if
they are true?"

"We must wait," the older man advised. "We
must wait and see if she has other dreams, and if
these dreams, too, foretell things to come. Each
time she has such a vision, you must bring her to
me, so that I may try to interpret the meaning of
the dream. By her own tongue she has said that
often she does not understand much of what she
sees in these dreams. It would be dangerous to
disregard even the smallest detail of her visions,
should they prove to predict what is to pass."

"I can think, then, of only one way to punish
this disobedient wife of mine," Night Hawk

determined. "She will be confined to the women's lodge until the next moon. If she desires to set herself aside from me and from the tribe, so it shall be. For one moon she will not exist to us. No one will speak to her or look upon her face, and she will be forbidden to speak to anyone during that time. Perhaps after being shunned by everyone and treated as if she does not walk within our midst, she will better appreciate our company when her punishment is done."

The shaman offered a smile to the young chief who sought his counsel. "A wise decision, Night Hawk," he agreed. "As she has spurned us, so now will we spurn her. She is an intelligent woman and will soon see the error of her ways." He gave a dry chuckle. "By the next moon she will be begging for the pleasure of your attentions," he predicted.

So it was that Flame found herself bearing the humiliation of having her offenses and punishment publicly declared before a gathering of the entire tribe. Her only consolation was that neither Crooked Arrow nor Little Rabbit was there to witness her embarrassment; they were still gone from the village, supposedly visiting his sister's tribe. Pride alone saved her from collapsing beneath the weight of Night Hawk's dire pronouncement, though she knew that she was getting off extremely lightly. Her punishment would have been much greater, she was sure, were it not for the child she carried.

Still, an entire month in the women's lodge, shunned by everyone for the whole time! Already she yearned to speak with Shining Star, to apologize and explain and ask her friend's advice. Even now she regretted her rash actions and desired only to return to Night Hawk's tipi and resume their life together as it had been before she ran away. She longed for his forgiveness and a return to his favor once more. Would he ever truly forgive her? Could it ever be as it was before between them, or had she forever destroyed that fragile love and trust?

Flame had plenty of time to ponder these questions in the days that passed so slowly in the confines of the women's lodge. Each day seemed longer than the one before, and as the weather warmed, so did the interior of the lodge. Flame's only relief from the stifling tipi was her brief trips to the stream and those times when the tribe was on the move to another location. Where once she had disliked the constant traveling, the dismantling and re-erection of the tipis, she now treasured these times.

Her lonely sojourn had other benefits, though she did not relish these lessons in childbirth to which she was a reluctant observer. During her confinement, several women gave birth. Though no one spoke to her, or she to them, though all looked through her as if she simply did not exist, they could not close Flame's ears and eyes to what was going on around her. She was witness to the miracle of birth, to the pain and the glory of it, despite herself.

In the end, it served to set some of her worst fears to rest, for these women stoically bore their pain to reap the reward of holding their newborn babes in their arms. Oh, the looks on their faces as they beheld their children, still wet and warm from the womb! It brought tears to Flame's eyes, and a tug to her heart, knowing she would one day soon hold her own child to her breast and touch its tiny toes and feathery black hair.

Flame came to fear childbirth less than she had before, seeing the joy of it in the faces of those new mothers. She gradually came to see it as a natural, normal function, the culmination of the act of love between husband and wife, the ultimate reward of womanhood. If most of these women could endure it and successfully deliver healthy babies, there was no reason to believe that she could not. After all, hadn't she already dreamed of her son? Hadn't she seen him as a healthy, happy baby in her own arms? Surely there was nothing to fear in giving birth to her own child, even in these primitive surroundings —not if she were to believe in the power of her own foretelling dreams.

Time lay heavy on her hands, for she had no chores to perform here in the women's lodge. In her own tipi she would have had much to busy herself with, but here she was so thoroughly ignored that even the few chores here were tended to by others. Flame needed only to wash and mend her own clothing, which Night Hawk had sent from their tipi, and to cook her own meals from the meat he continued to provide her. Otherwise, her husband did not deign to recognize her existence in any way. At least he still *was* her husband, and for that alone Flame was thankful. There had been no suggestion that he intended to divorce her, and she lived with the hope that when her time in the women's lodge was done, he would accept her back into his lodge and his life.

With nothing much to occupy her time, Flame began to fashion clothing for her baby from remnants of two of her older dresses, and from the skins of the small animals Night Hawk delivered daily. She took great care to skin and tan the hides properly, until they were as soft as butter to the touch. Tiny fur-lined moccasins soon rested by her sleeping mat, meticulously sewn and decorated with beads from her discarded clothing. Small blankets and coverings and little garments began to collect alongside the moccasins. It eased the pain in her heart to make these things ready for her unborn son. It gave her hope and served to take her mind from her problems.

Almost three weeks had passed when Flame suddenly awoke one night in a cold sweat. The dream lingered, brushing icy fingers down her spine. She sat shivering on her mat, not knowing what to do, afraid to say anything to anyone, and at the same time afraid not to do so. Even if she did gather the courage to tell someone, who would listen? Everyone had been instructed to ignore her. Yet she knew in her heart that she could not let this pass without alerting someone. The warriors were due to leave the village at dawn on a raid, and lives might be forfeit if they were not warned of what she had seen in her dream. Of course, she did not understand all that had been shown her, but what little she did understand frightened her. The dream had been

filled with bloodshed and violence, laced through
with danger.

Finally she crept quietly from her mat, willing
to risk Night Hawk's anger if only he would listen
to her this once. Silent as a ghost, she slipped
from the women's lodge and made her way to
Night Hawk's tipi. Once there, she almost lost
her courage and turned back, but her conscience
would not let her. Afraid to enter the tipi without
first being bidden to do so, and also just a bit
afraid that she might not find her husband sleeping alone in her absence, she knelt outside the
entrance and called softly to him.

"Night Hawk! Night Hawk, please hear me! I
beg of you, do not ignore me now, for this is of
great importance or I would not break the terms
of my punishment so near to its finish."

He appeared so silently and suddenly that she
jumped in fright. Staring at her with fire in his
eyes, he warned, "Your reasons will match your
actions, or you will answer to me, wife. Explain
yourself."

"I have had another dream, husband, and I
dare not hold my silence, for I fear it will cost
many lives if I do. Please heed my words."

He looked surprised and slightly doubtful.
"What is this dream of?" he asked cautiously.

"I am not absolutely sure of all of it, but I think
it has to do with the raid you plan to lead
tomorrow. Oh, Night Hawk, I saw such bloodshed, so much death! I am truly frightened by
this vision!"

Even in the sultry heat of the night, he saw her
shiver violently. Her face was unnaturally pale,

and he was forced to believe that something had, indeed, greatly disturbed her. She could not be pretending this reaction so well. "Come," he told her. "We will speak with Owl Eyes. You will tell him of your dream, and we will see what he makes of it."

Relief flooded her that he had not dismissed her frantic plea. Gladly she followed him to the shaman's lodge and waited while Night Hawk summoned him.

Though abruptly awakened, the old man's eyes glittered with avid interest as he listened to Flame's description of her dream and questioned her about the details. "Describe again the place in which this battle takes place," he urged. "Tell me once more where the bluecoat soldiers are hiding. Is it morning or evening? Does the sun cast long shadows or shine fully upon their faces? Do you recognize the markings on any of the soldiers' uniforms, on the clothing or faces of the warriors? Close your eyes and envision it again more clearly. Tell me, can you see the mountains in the distance? What do they look like to you?"

On and on it went, Owl Eyes dragging from Flame's reluctant mind all those minute details she had failed to note without his persistent questioning. Only once did he cease his probing, just long enough to instruct Night Hawk to tell the other warriors to delay their departure until he could discern what warning Flame's vision might hold for them. It was past dawn when the old shaman was at last satisfied that he had gleaned all he could from the weary woman. Flame was dismissed and sent back to the women's lodge, while the chiefs and the shaman held a hasty conference.

The wise old shaman stood in the center of the gathering of chiefs. "Chief Night Hawk's wife has had a vision, which she has told to me. From her words, I believe that to the south of us, perhaps one sun's ride, Roman Nose and his Dog Soldiers are soon to ride into a trap set by the white soldiers. That it is a snare of their own carelessness and foolishness, I do not doubt, but we, as their brothers, must warn them. Without this woman's dream, we would have felt this same trap closing about us, for our warriors would have entered the area unwary, never suspecting the bluecoats to be so near. With her vision to warn us and guide us, we can now approach more cautiously, and perhaps set a trap of our own, as well as save our brothers from certain death."

He proceeded to give them more details. Soon they were all involved in a discussion of which war strategies would be best used. Armed with advance knowledge and a sound plan, the warriors rode from the camp several hours later than they had previously hoped, but wiser for the delay. Some might doubt Flame's vision, but being supremely cautious and superstitious about such things, they dared not discount the warning. Time would soon tell the truth of the matter.

Five days later the warriors returned, all much more respectful of Chief Night Hawk's wife and her visions. Night Hawk himself was no exception, for he had seen the proof of her words with his own eyes, just as she had forewarned. Many lives had been spared because of her warning. There had still been a battle, with much bloodshed. Many men, both soldiers and Cheyenne, had been wounded. Some had died, which was to be expected, but the toll would have been much greater had the bluecoats surprised them instead of the other way around. The victory belonged to the Cheyenne this day, and Flame was responsible for much of the glory.

This went a long way in restoring Flame in the eyes of the Cheyenne. Because of her warning, they were willing to forgive her foolish attempt to escape. She had willingly risked the ire of her husband and the ridicule of the tribe in order to save the lives of their warriors—and to the detriment of her own people! No longer would they question her loyalty to the tribe. By her own actions, she had declared herself one of them now, and they would accept her gladly. She was one of the chosen few, a True Dreamer, and they were honored to have her living among them.

By order of the council, and with the permission of her husband, Flame was released from her punishment three days early, that she might attend the celebration of this victory. She was to be seated beside Night Hawk, who had led the attack on the white soldiers, to be honored for her part in their triumph over their enemies.

That evening, as she sat beside her husband, Flame was awed at the respect shown to her, when just days before she had been scorned by one and all. Among her own people, she would have been shunned for her visions, not revered for them. Here, among the Cheyenne, she had gained a new and honored status for her strange dreams. Life was constantly throwing surprises her way!

Now if she could only find a way to restore herself in Night Hawk's eyes, all would be well again, but Flame feared this would not be so easily accomplished. Her husband was a proud man, and she had wounded his pride severely by her actions. Even now he sat stiffly next to her, his face an unrevealing mask. Neither by action nor word did he hint at what he felt for her at this moment.

Was he proud of her gift of these visions, or dismayed by it? When the celebration was ended and they returned together to the privacy of their tipi, how would he react to her then? Would he still desire her as before, or would he send her to her own mat to sleep? And in the days to come, would he treat her with aloof disdain and distant courtesy, or perhaps open anger and hatred? How long would it be before he would once again bestow upon her those heart-melting smiles, those gentle looks and sweet tenderness that had won her heart despite herself? How long before she could regain his trust and respect—and his love?

It would take all her efforts to convince him of her love and loyalty, she knew, but here and now she determined to do so—if it took the rest of her life. She would win his heart from him and replace it with her own, for she loved him beyond all else. He was the sun in her sky, the light in her life. She had been a fool to run from him, when he was all she wanted in this world. Now she had the monumental task of assuring him of this. It had taken nearly losing him to make her realize how absolutely she loved him. She had not wanted to believe it herself, yet now she must convince him of the very thing she had rejected for so long. If only she could know that she had not destroyed all the feeling he had for her, if he still cared just a little bit, she would cling to the hope of one day winning his love in full measure —to match her own love for him.

Chapter
21

Flame needn't have worried whether or not Night Hawk would still desire her. He wasn't quite the gentle, tender lover of days past, but the passion was still there, as hot and wild as ever before. Their first night together after her punishment set the pattern for those that followed. As nervous as she was, one look at Night Hawk's unsmiling, watchful face was enough to set her knees quivering, but she held his gaze with one of her own, refusing to cower before him now. It somehow seemed important that she hold her ground with him, some inner sense telling her that this was the first step in regaining his respect.

They stared at each other for some time, until he finally held out his hand to her, and when she placed her smaller one within his, he led her silently to their sleeping mat. There, still without words, he first undressed her and then himself. Gone were the sweet words, the patient urgings, the tender praise, but it mattered little when his knowing hands began to swiftly stoke her desires to flaming heights.

Flame could not have lain silent if her life depended upon it, not when Night Hawk was stroking her with light, teasing touches in all those secret, sensitive places that only he had discovered. The body he had tutored so well now eagerly answered its master's commands. In a pitifully short time, she was arching into his touch, whimpering softly, begging him with words and more to take her. Her own hands could not get enough of him, roaming hungrily over his bronze form, urging him ever nearer as passion flared between them, a passion so hot it seemed to sear her flesh to his.

His lips burned against her breasts, his teeth nipping lightly and sending fiery signals throughout her body. Her fingers dug deeply into his muscled shoulders, clinging tightly to him. Then he claimed her fully, his body coming into hers and making them one again, in flesh if not in spirit.

And then the storm began to build in earnest. Round and round they spun in an ever-faster whirlwind, tossed and tumbled like helpless leaves in a fierce, blazing gale. Bright flames danced around them, sparks flying about like glimmering fireflies in a dark night. Then it was as if the sun had exploded around them, over them, within them, consuming them in a white-hot fireball. The force of it hurled them upward, until they were as twin comets soaring through the sky, united and twirling out of control, great swirling tails of fire creating a brilliant pinwheel about them.

Afterward, when she again feared he might reject her now that their passion had cooled to embers, he surprised her by drawing her close to him. With her head pillowed on his shoulder, and his hand curved protectively over her stomach, where his child lay nestled, she listened to the thundering of his heartbeat in her ear and her heart overflowed with love. She cried then, her hot salty tears drenching his smooth chest. All the tension of the past weeks, the waiting and wondering and worrying was now released in a torrent of healing tears.

Even as her sobs shook them both, she felt him stiffen beneath her, his muscles tightening as if in preparation for battle. In the quiet of the tipi, his voice sounded like a great drum as he asked gruffly, "Why do you weep so, wife? Is my touch so vile to you that you must drown us both with your tears after our mating?"

Unable to answer him for the sobs still locked in her throat, she shook her head in denial of his words. When she was at last able to speak, she answered softly, "No, Night Hawk. I weep with relief that you still desire me after all that I have done. I weep tears of happiness that we are together again as husband and wife, and that you did not divorce yourself from me as I deserved.

And I cry because our coming together was so wondrous, and because I love you with all my heart and soul. I can only pray that one day you will find it within your heart to forgive me and to return my love."

In the silence surrounding her declaration, he lay very still. At last he said, "The words flow easily from your lips to my ears, Flame. Yet how can I believe them when such a short time ago you wanted only to flee from me?"

"I ran because I knew I was losing my heart to you, Night Hawk," she tried to explain on a shaky sigh. "I thought that if I could escape to my own people, I could also escape my love for you, for my feelings frightened me greatly. It was a foolish thing to do, for I could not escape myself as I ran. With each step that took me away from you, my heart grew more heavy with sadness. You will not believe me, I know, but by the time you found me, I cared only about how to find my way back to the village, back to you."

His hand came up to cradle her chin, and he tilted her face to his, gazing intently at her by the faint light of the banked fire. "I want to believe your words, Flame, but it is too soon after you have run away, taking my unborn child with you, that I might never know my own son."

"Then tell me what it is that I must do to prove my love to you," she implored, "and I shall do it most gladly."

Slowly, sadly, he shook his head. "Only the passing suns will mend what you have so thoughtlessly rent apart. We must rebuild that which you have destroyed, and restoring a broken trust is not easily done. Faith does not come so readily a second time."

Fresh tears glittered in her eyes. "In time, then, I will prove myself to you. I will prove my loyalty until you are no longer able to deny it. Endlessly, I shall strive to be a loving wife, worthy of your love and respect. But for now I would be happy just to know that you do not despise me, for I do not think I could bear your hatred."

A ghost of a smile hovered over his lips. "To hate you would be to hate myself," he said softly. "You carry our child within your body, a child of my blood and yours. Our lives are joined by this child, and by the crossing of our destinies."

"But will I ever have your love?" she whispered sorrowfully.

"Pernaps one day, when my heart is assured that your love is true, it will be yours to claim." With these solemn words hanging in the air about them, he gathered her close to him once more and held her until at last she slept.

To Flame's dismay, even Shining Star was reluctant to resume their former friendship at first, though she did at last relent when Flame explained her reasons for running away. "It was as if to admit my love for Night Hawk would be to give up forever all hope of ever seeing my father again," Flame explained. "The more I came to love him, the more accustomed I became to Cheyenne life, learning and accepting your ways and adopting them as my own, the more frightened I became. Then, when I learned that I carried Night Hawk's child, I knew I must try to escape to my own people, or resign myself to becoming Cheyenne for all time."

Perhaps it was because Shining Star was also a woman that she better understood and accepted what Flame told her. Perhaps it was that she, too, was expecting her first child, and knew how irrational and emotional a woman could become at that time in her life. After hearing Flame's explanation, Shining Star welcomed Flame back into the circle of her love and friendship, and soon it was as if there had never been a rift between them.

Because of her visions, almost the entire tribe opened their arms to her, readily forgiving her foolishness and accepting her more fully than before. There were exceptions, however, and Crooked Arrow and Little Rabbit were two of those. When they returned to the village to find Flame there, whole and well and most revered for her dreams, their animosity grew. Little Rabbit was especially outspoken, claiming that Flame deserved to be whipped and cast off from Night Hawk and the tribe. Her spiteful words were largely ignored, for the entire tribe knew of her jealousy toward Flame. Knowing what she did of Little Rabbit and Crooked Arrow's dealings with Trader Jack, Flame cautiously avoided both of them, seeing the vile hatred that gleamed in their eyes for her.

A few days later, Flame experienced her first Sun Dance ceremony. For this event, the tribe traveled north into the Black Hills. There they

joined with many other tribes, both Cheyenne
and Sioux, who had convened near the fork of
two great rivers.

Flame had never seen so many Indians gathered together in one place, and at first it was a
little frightening. Among this sea of dark faces,
dark hair and eyes, she stood out like a speck of
salt in a pepper mill. There were only a handful
of other whites among the tribes, and those
mostly captive slaves. One woman, a beautiful
little blonde, was the wife of one of the Sioux
warriors, and a couple of smaller white children
had been adopted by Indian families. They and
Flame were the fortunate ones, for the others
were no more than pitiful slaves.

It would not have surprised Flame to be looked
down upon by most of the Indians for her white
heritage. In fact, she thoroughly expected to be
shunned. Therefore, she was delightfully shocked
at her acceptance. It seemed the tales of her
visions had already spread among the tribes, and
she was given due respect as a chosen Dreamer.

The festivities of this special gathering of the
tribes were to last several days, with various
activities throughout. The actual ceremony of the
Sun Dance itself would be held on the final day,
after much preparation.

First the warriors went in search of just the
right tree to use as the central pole of the Sun
Dance. It must be straight and strong as a warri-
or. This was a unique and separate part of the
tradition, one which the warriors enjoyed thoroughly. The tree they sought was looked upon as
an enemy. Together they stalked it and "killed"

it. When it had been properly felled, with great ceremony, they dragged the trunk back to the camp, shouting and dancing in victory. It was then erected in the Sun Dance lodge, or in the center of an open area designated for the festivities and blessed by the head shaman. This was done to ward off any evil spirits that might be lingering in the area around the pole or hiding inside the pole itself, and to induce the good spirits to preside over the Sun Dance and bless the proceedings.

In the days preceding the Sun Dance, the major participants, and often their families as well, would seclude themselves. They would fast, refusing all food and drink until the Dance was finished. They would pray and chant and seek visions and guidance from the spirits, asking for endowments of courage and strength or sometimes for special favors or means of revenge against an enemy. They would seek special insight and powers, often by smoking prayer pipes filled with the powder of the peyote button. In this they were joined by many of their fellow braves and warriors. A good number of the men also joined in the fasting and spent periods in the sweat lodge to purify their bodies and minds, making them receptive to and worthy of the spirits they sought. Through it all, the shaman would bless the men in special ceremonies unseen and unattended by the women. In fact, many of the men shied away from contact with their women while undergoing these male purification rites.

While all this was going on, many other activi-

ties were taking place around the camp, many of
them for the women and children of the tribes.
There were games of skill for males and females
of all ages, and games just for pure pleasure.
Much gossiping and trading took place, and
adults and children alike gathered to listen to the
silvered tongues of the storytellers. There were
even productions that reminded Flame of puppet
shows she had seen in the East. Then there were
the singing and the dances, so colorful to behold,
with many different and elaborate costumes.

Flame was fascinated by the puppet shows and
the storytellers, who wove lore and legend into
marvelous stories. She would sit for hours listening to their tales. Often the legends, especially
those having to do with religious beliefs and
characters, closely paralleled some of the Bible
stories she had learned back home in Sunday
school, and she was both shocked and delighted
to find such similarities. How could this be, when
white civilization considered the Indians to be
heathens? How did it happen that they, too, had
an account of twins, one good and one evil, the
evil one slaying the good twin? Why, it was
almost exactly the story of Cain and Abel! According to tribal belief, there was one Supreme
Being, the Creator of all good things, who had
made man from earth and sand. Was this not the
same God she had worshipped in her own
church, the Creator of Heaven and Earth? And
the tale of the Great Flood—was this not the
story of Noah in Indian form?

Of course, there were also differences between
Indian beliefs and her own, but was this not so

even among the so-called civilized religions the world over? The Cheyenne and Sioux believed that the Great Spirit, the Creator, entrusted divine tasks to lesser deities—the sun, moon, thunder gods, Mother Earth, the Master of animals, the four winds. This explained their worship of the sun, the moon, and the earth, which the white world found so difficult to accept.

Also interesting to Flame was the fact that tipi entrances always faced east, toward the rising sun, according to Indian religion; but this was also the direction from which the Christian Bible said that Christ would come upon his second coming. Where the white religion warned of Satan, most of the Indian tribes also believed in an Evil Spirit. According to some, this Evil One helped the Great Spirit develop the world after the Creation. Competition with the Great Spirit caused this Evil Spirit to fall from grace, and now he ruled the underworld and all that was evil.

Another point of interest was the Indian belief that the Milky Way was the path of all souls to the land of the dead. The path forked, one way leading to a sort of heaven and the other to the underworld ruled by the Evil Spirit. Was this so different from all that she had been taught as a child? The more she learned, the more fascinated Flame became. When she thought about it, there were more similarities than differences in their religions. Why was it that the white man and the Indian could not see this and find a way to reside in peace? If her God was his God, his Great Spirit the same as hers, didn't He care for them all alike, red or white?

Within the next few days, Flame was forced to see that, regardless of their similarities in some ways, there were vast differences in their rites and rituals and the way they chose to celebrate them. The Sun Dance was a supreme example of this. Night Hawk had expressed the wish that Flame observe this sacred ritual so important to his people, and as distasteful as it was to her, she felt obliged to do so, if only to please her husband.

Within moments of the start of it, she wished she had politely declined, for while it was colorful and fascinating, it was also barbaric and bloody. Seated beside Shining Star, who helped to explain some of the intricacies of the rite, Flame watched in horror as skewers of wood or bone were laced through the flesh of several young men, literally driven through the skin and muscle of their chests, with both ends of the skewer protruding. This was done on one or both sides of the participant's chest, and thongs were tied to the ends of the skewers. These, in turn, were attached to long rawhide ropes, the other end of which was secured to the top of the sacred Sun Dance pole.

Much to her alarm and revulsion, these men were now hoisted several feet above the ground, supported only by the line and skewer, while they dangled helplessly in pain and agony. *How barbaric!* Flame thought, swallowing the gorge that rose to her throat as she continued to watch the bizarre spectacle before her—men swinging in the air like human puppets attached to the ribbons about a maypole! She could not bear to

contemplate the pain those men must be enduring. Only her wish not to embarrass either herself
or Night Hawk kept her seated there to watch this
strange celebration in which man sought to bring
himself into closer spiritual contact with the
spirits and to test his own strength and endur-
ance.

"If this is what it takes to prove one's bravery,"
she whispered to Shining Star, "I much prefer to
be a coward!"

Shining Star laughed and said, "How fortunate
for us that the women of our tribe have no such
ritual!" One delicate brow rose on her bronze
face, and she added thoughtfully, "Still, I wonder
if any man has ever endured what we women
suffer during childbirth? Surely this cannot compare!"

Flame paled at this, not really wanting to think
of it. "I suppose we must be thankful that both
rituals last only a short time then, though at this
moment it seems forever."

The men suspended from the pole continued
to dangle there as others danced and chanted
below them. This went on until each of the men
successfully wriggled and tossed himself about
until the skewers cut through the fleshy pocket in
his chest and allowed him to drop to the ground.

All this took quite some time, and bones were
often broken when the men landed upon the hard
ground beneath them. By this time, they were
usually so weakened from thrashing about and
hanging for so long, and from loss of blood in the
process, that they had to be carried away to their
tipis. There their wounds were properly tended

and they could rest at last. For the next few days they would eat and drink and regain their strength before the tribes split and went their individual ways once more.

No one was more glad than Flame when this year's Sun Dance ceremony was ended. Afterward, she crept quietly off by herself and allowed herself the luxury of emptying the contents of her stomach in privacy.

Summer faded gently into autumn, the changing season giving no hint of the increasing hostilities between the Plains Indians and the United States soldiers. The war between the states dragged on, and the tribes were feeling the repercussions of the battles between the North and South as each side sent portions of their troops to the western frontier. More and more often bands of Indians were inadvertently thrown into contact with Army troops, often with disastrous result.

Some of the conflict was deliberately aimed at the tribes, though they did not know it at the time. Colonel Chivington of the Colorado Volunteers was anxious to make a name for himself, and protecting so-called innocent settlers from hostile Indians seemed the fastest way to do this. With the support of Colorado's Governor Evans, who turned a deaf ear and a blind eye to Chivington's actions, the colonel proceeded to aggravate an already sensitive situation. Every tale of hostile activity by an Indian that reached the man's ears, whether true or not, was immediately taken as cause for action. Often Chivington exaggerated these stories himself, all for an excuse to send his troops into action and snatch some glory for himself. He initiated many raids on peaceful Cheyenne and Arapaho villages, maiming and killing women and children in the process. Though he primarily aimed his attacks at the Southern Cheyenne and Arapaho tribes, those nearest his reach, he even dared to send troops into the plains of Kansas, far out of his jurisdiction.

While the Sioux and Northern Cheyenne, Night Hawk's tribe among them, knew nothing of this man and his devious actions, they were aware that, more and more, they were coming into conflict with soldiers. They were forced to post more guards about their camps at night—camps they selected with greater care these days. Hunting parties went about with more caution than before, and raiding parties did not have to search far for white scalps.

All this had little to do with Flame, however. As the forests blazed with vibrant shades of gold and red and orange, she had problems of her own. Her once trim figure was but a dream of yesterday. It helped little that Night Hawk continued to tell her that her eyes were more blue than the clear autumn skies, or that her hair was the color of the autumn leaves. She felt like a mud-stuck buffalo, just as fat and half as graceful. That Shining Star shared her predicament was little consolation.

Additionally, Flame was trying to cope with the problem of how to deal with Night Hawk. Having watched Little Rabbit humiliate herself by fawning over Night Hawk, Flame was not willing to use the same tactics in regaining her husband's affections. While she dutifully prepared his meals, collected the firewood and water, and kept the tipi in order, she did not attempt to ingratiate herself by blatant means. She did not continually cast doe eyes in his direction, or flutter her lashes like some demented butterfly.

In fact, due to Little Rabbit's failure with such maneuvers, Flame adopted an opposite attitude. She took particular care not to be caught in a state of undress while Night Hawk was near, except at night when he called her to the sleeping mat. She never bathed or washed her hair when he might chance upon her. Her vanity did allow her to brush her long, thick tresses in his presence, though she feigned indifference to the admiring looks he cast her way all the while. Because she knew he loved the way her bright hair flowed in waves down her back, she took to wearing it loose most of the time now, rather than in braids, and thanked heaven that the weather was cool enough to allow her to do so in comfort.

She did not chatter to him continually, as had been Little Rabbit's habit, but shared the silence of the evening with him. When he preferred to spend an evening with his friends or to attend a meeting in the council lodge, she did not berate him, nor nag at him to stay, though often she had to bite her lip in order to hold her silence. The smiles she cast his way, the gentle sway of her hips as she passed by, the quiet comfort of her presence were enough to convey her feelings. They spoke eloquently by themselves.

Still, she knew she had to do more to bring them closer, so she urged him to continue his lessons in English. In addition, she offered to teach him how to read and write in the white man's language.

"Why would I need to know such things?" he objected when first she suggested it.

"Because it is wise to know as many of the ways of your enemy as possible," she countered, unknowingly using his own argument. "Do you not wish to know if the man at the trading post is cheating you? Would it not be better to know that what is written on the treaty paper is what you have agreed upon, and not something entirely different? Would you have your enemy steal from you simply because you cannot read his words?"

Seeing the sense of her argument, he agreed, and they began to have lessons together as often as his duties as chief allowed. He proved a quick student, soon copying the letters and numbers she drew for him in the dust. Within a short time he had mastered the most elementary words. Soon, his curiosity whetted, he began to look forward to their lessons with an endearing eagerness.

Day by day, as they worked together, Flame could sense that he was softening toward her, learning his lessons and also learning to trust again. He did not guard his words or his heart so fiercely now. His smiles were more ready, his laughter more carefree. The looks he sent her way

were warmer, encouraging her own heart to hope
that soon he would come to love her again. She
had gained his respect—but she would not stop
until she had his heart. It would take all winter
and more for him to learn all that she could teach
him. Time and the coming winter, when there
would be little to do outside the tipi, were her
allies.

Chapter 22

Snow drifted high all about the camp, making it almost impossible to walk anywhere in the village without the aid of snowshoes. There was no tobogganing for Flame now, nor for Shining Star, for the time was near for the births of their children. Winter had descended upon them early this year, bringing snow and icy winds whistling about the tipis, and it was harder than ever for the two women to get about in their delicate condition.

Flame felt so clumsy, so huge! Once seated, it was difficult for her to rise again without aid. It had been some time now since she and Night Hawk had been intimate, for their child was due almost any day now. For him to desire her now would be a miracle at any rate, for her stomach preceded her everywhere she went, and she waddled about like an awkward, misshapen duckling. Just when she had been making progress toward regaining Night Hawk's love and respect, her own body and child had put a halt to her schemes. Flame was sure he had been on the verge of declaring his love to her, but now even Little Rabbit looked better than she. With her stomach protruding, her ankles and face swollen, her awkward movements, she felt ridiculous!

It was nothing Night Hawk had said or done that made her feel this way, for in truth, he had been wonderful. Even as her figure burgeoned, he seemed to take delight in her, knowing that her increasing girth meant that his child was growing within her. His dark eyes shone with pride as he gazed upon her enlarging breasts, with their blue veins showing against soft white. At night, even now, he pulled her to him on the sleeping mat, stroking her stomach soothingly and massaging her aching back.

To lighten her burden, he had arranged to have Spotted Fawn, Red Feather's younger sister, come to their tipi each day to help Flame with the heavier chores. He took care to see that Flame did not tire herself overmuch, or lift and carry things that were too heavy for her. He pampered her outrageously, but Flame suspected that it was more for the benefit of his unborn child than for any affection he might feel for her.

If she could have seen into Night Hawk's mind and heart for just a moment, she would have known better. When it came to his wife, the war chief was as vulnerable as any man in love, for love her he did, with all his heart. It was this very vulnerability that made him wary of trusting his heart to her fully, that kept the words of love locked away inside until he was sure of her once more. She had played him for a fool once; he would not abide it a second time!

It was a dark, snowy night in late December, during the month the Cheyenne called The Moon When The Wolves Run Together, when Flame awakened from another dream. Her cry awoke Night Hawk, and when he could neither calm her nor understand her ravings, he became alarmed.

"Is it your time, Flame?" he asked, trying to understand. "Do you have pain?"

Finally she calmed enough to tell him, "No! No! It is Shining Star!"

"What of Shining Star?" His brow wrinkled in confusion.

"We must see if she is in the women's lodge, Night Hawk. You must take me there now!"

"If Shining Star is birthing her child, there will be little you can do for her," he said. "The others will care for her and the child."

"You are wrong!" Flame was becoming more frantic now. "I have dreamed of Shining Star and the birth of her child. She needs me, Night Hawk, or the child will be born dead!"

As she struggled to rise, her words finally penetrated his mind. "Come then. Let me help you to dress, and I will escort you to the women's lodge. We will see if Shining Star is there."

When they arrived at the lodge, they learned

that Shining Star had been there for most of the night. Night Hawk saw Flame into the tipi, then went in search of Stone Face, knowing his friend would welcome his company while awaiting the birth of his first child.

Flame went swiftly to the aid of her dearest friend. Long hours of labor had depleted Shining Star's strength, and still the babe refused to be born. Perspiration had wet her hair and face as pain after pain racked her, each one weakening her more. When she saw Flame, she gave her a weak smile, but it was a pitiful effort. "What are you doing here?" she asked, her voice hoarse with pain. "Has your time also arrived?"

"No, I have come to help you with the birth of your babe," Flame replied softly.

Another pain attacked Shining Star, and while her attention was taken, Flame motioned to Meadow Grass, who was attending the birth. Taking the woman aside, she whispered urgently. "The birth cord is wrapped about the baby's throat. This I have seen in my dream. It is the reason he will not be born. The cord will not allow the babe to turn properly in his mother's body. You must find a way of unlooping it, for the child chokes to death even now. Can you reach up inside and loosen it? Are your hands small enough to accomplish such a task?"

Meadow Grass gazed at Flame in wonder, and Flame had to pinch her in order to get the woman to respond to her query. "Yes!" she yelped in surprise. Then more clearly, "My hands are small enough, I think, if I grease them well."

"Make sure your hands are clean, and the

grease as well. Boil some water and wash your hands when it is cool enough, and boil the tallow as well, but be quick about it. We must hurry if the child's life is to be saved this night."

It seemed forever before Meadow Grass was ready. Grasping Shining Star's hands in her own, and disregarding the discomfort of kneeling so awkwardly at Shining Star's head, Flame talked quietly to her friend. She explained what Meadow Grass was about to do, telling Shining Star to try to relax and lie quietly if she could. They waited until the next pain had passed. When Meadow Grass slipped her hand up inside her, Shining Star cried out, involuntarily stiffening with the pain.

"No, Shining Star," Flame instructed softly. "Do not stiffen your body. Please, you must try to help us with this, for the sake of your child."

As Meadow Grass worked to try to find the birth cord and unwrap it from the baby's neck, Shining Star's grip on Flame's hands tightened, threatening to break the fragile bones. Flame winced, but made no objection. She crooned softly to Shining Star, trying to keep her calm, and prayed to every god she had ever heard of to help them deliver this child safely into his mother's arms.

It took three tries and what seemed a century before Meadow Grass succeeded in freeing the cord and turning the baby head first. After that, it was mere minutes before the child was expelled from his mother's body. The infant's face had a bluish cast to it that worried Flame, but when Meadow Grass had cleaned its little mouth and nostrils, and breathed softly into its mouth, the newborn drew in his breath and let out a mighty yell that threatened to waken the entire camp. Within a few heartbeats, its little face was a healthy red, and he was waving his arms and legs angrily as he cried lustily.

Flame nearly wilted with relief. Never had she felt such fear on behalf of another person! Never had she heard a sound as musical as this child's cries! Never had she seen anything as beautiful as the smile on Shining Star's face as she beheld her tiny, wrinkled son. Tears stung her eyes as she left mother and child to their first meeting and stumbled out into the cold dawn outside the women's lodge.

Night Hawk was waiting for her there, Stone Face pacing anxiously at his side. As Night Hawk pulled her near and let her rest against his strong body, she smiled tiredly at Stone Face's questioning look. "Your wife and son are both well, Stone Face. You have a beautiful, healthy male child."

To her surprise, tears shone in Stone Face's dark eyes. He came to her and took both her hands in his. "Thank you, Flame, for saving the life of my son," he told her in a voice grown gruff with emotion. "I owe you a debt I can never hope to repay. Please accept my apologies for the way I have behaved toward you these past moons. I hope you will once again grant me the privilege of calling you friend."

"Not one dawn has passed when I have not considered you my friend," she answered him easily, squeezing his hands in assurance, "but my heart is glad to hear your words."

When Stone Face had gone, Flame spent a quiet time alone with her husband. Together they stood and watched the sun rise over the glistening snow, turning the world first lavender, then pink, and finally golden with its blessed rays. With his arm wrapped tightly about her, they walked in silence to their tipi.

Later that same afternoon, Night Hawk knelt at Flame's feet, about to help her strap on her snowshoes. He had been strangely silent all day, casting her odd glances from time to time, as if he wished to say something to her but could not find the words. Now, suddenly, as he knelt before her, he burst out laughing. His dark head flew back, exposing his throat; and he laughed until he collapsed on the floor of the tipi, clutching helplessly at his sides as tears of mirth streamed down his cheeks.

"What on earth is wrong with you?" Flame asked in exasperation. She eyed him curiously, but laughing as hard as he was, he could give her no immediate answer.

Finally, he managed to choke out, "Your moccasins are on the wrong feet!" Off he went into further gales.

Hands on her hips, or what passed for her hips these days, she huffed, "It is no great wonder, Night Hawk! I have not seen my own feet in many moons now. They could have turned to pumpkins, and I would not know it!" Weary as she was, and as tired of carrying this child within her, she could find little humor in his words.

"They are not pumpkins," he assured her,

"though right now they look like small birds, each trying to fly in the opposite direction from the other!"

"It is not funny!" she pouted, smarting now at his insensitivity.

Swallowing back his chuckles, he nodded. "It is from where I sit."

She frowned down at him. "I am so glad that someone in this tipi can find something to laugh at these days."

He gazed at her curiously from where he sat, his dark eyes suddenly becoming serious, though the smile lingered on his lips. "Do you know that I have never found you so beautiful as now, when you are swollen with my child, your eyes spitting blue flames at me?"

She swallowed past the lump in her throat as his eyes declared more than his words dared. "And my moccasins on the wrong feet," she murmured softly, her heart calling out to him in silent plea.

His big hands came up to frame her bulging abdomen, and in a gesture of extreme tenderness, he lay his lips to her clothed stomach. Gently Flame stroked the top of his dark head, wishing with all her heart that this man could put aside his fears and love her again. Their child chose that poignant moment to kick both mother and father with a single movement, startling them both.

Night Hawk's eyes flew up to meet hers, and in that moment his fate was sealed. "I love you," he admitted helplessly. "You hold my heart within your keeping."

"I will guard it jealously and well," she vowed solemnly, "for there is nothing on this earth that I could treasure more. I love you more than my own life."

She eased to her knees before him, and they sealed their love with a passionate kiss, a kiss that held all the promise and desire they felt for each other. They held each other close, their hearts beating as one. It was a moment that would last forever in Flame's memory, all the more for what happened next. As Night Hawk helped her to her feet and prepared to strap her foot into one of the snowshoes, the first pain struck. Only Night Hawk's strong arms kept her from falling. Her eyes, wide with surprise and fear, found his. "The baby!" His words echoed hers perfectly.

Quite unlike the calm husband who had weathered Little Rabbit's time of childbirth so well, Night Hawk now came as close to panicking as he had ever done. Against all her protests that it was too soon to be sure if she was actually going into labor, he bundled her into his arms and carried her, wrapped in a warm robe, through the village to the women's lodge.

Once there, he was loathe to leave her, caught between wanting her safe in the women's lodge and needing to be with her. Standing outside the lodge, still wavering, the decision was taken from him when a second pain hit her. With a worried sigh, he left her in Meadow Grass's capable hands and went to find his friend Stone Face for some badly needed fortification.

Young, strong, and healthy, Flame was more

frightened than anything else. She was glad that Shining Star was still in the women's lodge, for she needed the support of her friend. Above all else, Flame wanted her mother at this moment, and Shining Star was the next best thing.

As the pains increased, Flame tried to concentrate on her vision of her young son, but the picture in her mind faded in and out on waves of agony. The bag of waters surrounding her child broke, and the pains came more regularly, harder and closer together. Hours dragged by, hours filled with pain and sweat and waiting. According to Meadow Grass's instructions, it helped to pant like a dog when the pains came, and she tried to relax and preserve her energy when they passed, but this was all so new to her that often she forgot. Fortunately, Meadow Grass and Shining Star were there to remind her, to soothe her with damp rags on her forehead, to talk her through the pains.

Toward the end, when the pain and pressure were almost constant, Meadow Grass placed a piece of deerhide between Flame's teeth, telling her to bite down upon it. It served the added purpose of keeping Flame from biting into her own tongue. Shining Star now stationed herself next to Flame, who was propped up on a roll of robes. She wound short lengths of rawhide around stakes driven into the ground and put the loose ends, into which knots had been tied, into Flame's hands. "Pull on these," she told her. Then she proceeded to talk softly, easily to Flame, speaking of the child soon to be born, of all the joy to follow the pain.

Flame barely heard Shining Star's words, but the tone of her voice was the only soothing thing about this entire situation, so she concentrated on it fiercely, drawing comfort from it as her whole world seemed to revolve in a circle of agony. Her stomach, her back, her whole body felt as if it were being ripped apart by a demon's hand.

Suddenly, swiftly, the pains changed and the pressure increased. As Meadow Grass crouched between Flame's legs, prepared to catch the child as it left its mother's body, she urged Flame to push with all her might. Once, twice, three times. Finally, on the fourth effort, Flame's son made his way into the world. He was squalling even before he was fully out of her womb, filling the air with his outraged cries before Meadow Grass had time to wipe his chubby red face free of the birth blood.

As she prepared to cut the birth cord and tend to the afterbirth, Meadow Grass laid the child gently upon Flame's stomach. Gazing at her son, her very own miracle, Flame reached out to touch his wet, dark head with trembling fingers. Awe filled her as she picked up one small, perfectly formed hand, staring at the five little fingers and their miniature fingernails. He wailed and kicked at her with a tiny foot, and she laughed aloud. "So now you can kick me from the outside instead?" she chuckled. "Something new for both of us!"

When he was washed and swaddled in a warm robe in her arms, she gazed wonderingly at him. Yes, this was the child of her dream. Already he

had Night Hawk's midnight dark hair and his
straight, bold nose. His chin looked stubborn,
but whether that came from her or his father, she
could not guess. Hazy blue eyes gazed back at
her, eyes she knew would not turn dark, but
would soon be as bright blue as her own. This
was her son, the proof and the product of the love
shared by her and Night Hawk, and her heart
swelled with love and pride.

At the moment of his son's birth, Night Hawk
was listening with dismay as a messenger, who
had only just ridden into the camp, told of the
disaster that had struck the tribe of Black Kettle
and their brothers, the Southern Cheyenne. A
moon past, a troop of soldiers—the very ones
from Fort Lyon who had offered them peace and
protection for the winter—had attacked and
killed many Cheyenne and Arapaho. They were
led by the white Eagle Chief's soldiers, the man
the whites called Colonel Chivington.

The Cheyenne and Arapaho had been camped
peacefully at Sand Creek when the unexpected
attack came. Most of their warriors had been
gone from the camp, hunting as the white soldiers had told them they could, and so they were
not there to help protect their families. The
Cheyenne chief, White Antelope, had been shot
down and killed while trying to make peace with
the advancing soldiers. He had been unarmed
and under the white flag of peace. The Arapaho
chief, Left Hand, also at first refused to raise
arms against the white soldiers, and was likewise
shot down, but he survived. So did White Ante-

lope's brother, Chief Black Kettle, who had tried to stop the attack by waving the American flag on a pole.

In the end, more than a hundred women and children had been brutally murdered that day, and almost thirty men. The bodies of the dead had been horribly mutilated, their scalps taken and their private parts cut off by the raiding soldiers. Babies, too, were butchered. The survivors of the attack, those who had somehow managed to escape, fled eastward through the bitter cold, with no blankets, no food, and no medicines with which to treat their wounded. For days they marched through snow and ice to reach the camp of their hunters.

Now word of the unwarranted attack and atrocities was spreading throughout the land, and many tribes were readying for war against the whites. War pipes were being smoked and battle plans made. The time for peaceful negotiation was past. The white men's words were worthless, nothing but lies. Now the tribes would have their revenge for the lives of their brothers, and the white men would pay dearly in the blood of their own people.

So it was that, with the angry words of the runner still echoing in his ears, Night Hawk named his firstborn son. The child would be called War Cloud, his name a reflection of the first rumblings of renewed war between the tribes and the whites that now echoed ominously over the land.

Chapter 23

Even in the midst of winter, with snow often as high as the bellies of their ponies, the tribes went to war against the whites. While the women, children and old men kept the camp running, protected by a few braves, the warriors rode out on their perilous raids. When they returned, there were always a few warriors who did not return with them, and others who were badly wounded. The slain were mourned deeply, the wounded gently nursed.

Sometimes when they returned, they brought white captives—but not often, to Flame's relief. She felt pity for the new captives, especially the women, but there was nothing she could do to help their plight. The children would be adopted and well cared for, but the women would have to find their own means of surviving. Flame was not about to do anything to jeopardize her newfound love with Night Hawk or her prestigious status within the tribe. Just as she had done when first captured, these women would have to learn to make the best of their situation, to adapt to their captivity, and to turn it to their best advantage if the opportunity arose.

Very rarely, the warriors would bring back a male captive. It always galled Flame when this occurred, for the man was never released or held alive as were the women and children. Male captives were brought back to camp only to be tortured to death in lengthy, horrible ritualistic slayings. Their agonized screams could be heard throughout the camp, sometimes for days.

Though the Cheyenne women participated in these tortures, Flame could not bring herself to harm one of her own people. While she knew that others frowned upon her refusal to do so, she stood firm. She did not try to interfere or intervene, but neither would she willingly participate in such barbaric acts or watch them. Because of her vision dreams, few dared to speak out against her for this. If Night Hawk was disappointed in her, he did not show it, nor did he berate her. He seemed to understand and respect her views, for which Flame was profoundly thankful.

Flame's heart was always in her throat when the warriors left camp, and there again when they rode back in. Always she feared that Night Hawk would not return to her, or would come back

mortally wounded. She did not fear for herself
now, as she might have in days past, for her own
revered position in the tribe secured her survival.
It was losing Night Hawk and his love that she
feared. Their days together were so very precious
to her now, and she could not bear the thought of
life without him.

When Night Hawk was not in camp, the days
seemed long and empty, even with War Cloud to
keep her busy. Their son was a healthy, bright
baby, a delight to both of them. It brought tears
to Flame's eyes to see the love and pride which
Night Hawk openly displayed for his son. This
was the way she had expected him to behave
when Little Rabbit's son was born, when she had
believed that Howling Gale was Night Hawk's
son. With his own child, Night Hawk was ever
tender and loving, taking time to talk and play
with him. Already he had made a beautiful
cradleboard in which Flame could carry War
Cloud, and he had carved several toys to fit those
tiny hands.

One of the most difficult things Flame had to
do, as a new mother in this Cheyenne tribe, was
to teach her son not to cry. It seemed so cruel! All
infants were soon taught to be silent, unless hurt,
as their crying could be heard for long distances
and might alert an enemy to the camp's position.
Basically, two methods were used. First the
mother would try blowing into the baby's face
each time it cried. The child would usually draw
in its breath and cease to cry after a few such
lessons. Most did not like this sharp gust of air in
their little faces, for it not only surprised them,

but tended to take their own breath away for a moment. It usually frightened them enough that they soon learned that this was the punishment they would receive for crying.

The second method was more severe, if the infant did not learn from the first. Each time the baby started to cry, the mother would pinch the child's nostrils shut and hold its mouth closed for just a moment. With its air supply abruptly cut off, the child would cease crying. Again, this was done until the baby learned that each time it cried, it would receive such treatment.

Even while she could see the necessity for it, Flame thought this treatment cruel, and she was glad that War Cloud learned quickly from the first and more gentle training. Only to herself did she admit that it was a blessing to have a quiet child. Many of her former acquaintances back East had such noisy children, and it was nerve-racking to have to listen to a baby crying continuously. Personally, she had often thought it easier to listen to fingernails scraping across a blackboard than to hear a baby cry for long.

Flame adored her young son, thinking him the most perfect baby she had ever seen. He was bright and alert, and so beautiful to look upon. For the first few days, she was constantly checking to be sure he was still breathing as he slept, and it was some time after she had him to herself in the tipi before she began to relax her vigilance.

Another small problem arose when she took War Cloud back to the tipi for the first time. Bandit, the pet raccoon, was curious about this new addition to his living quarters. Flame feared the raccoon might harm the baby with his sharp claws and teeth. Luckily, Bandit soon abandoned his curiosity in favor of his long winter naps, and by the time the next thaw came, Bandit was already accustomed to War Cloud's constant presence, accepting him without rancor.

Flame's occasional visions served the tribe well in those troubled days. Several times she saved the tribe or its warriors from walking unaware into disastrous situations. A few times she was able to predict exactly where the enemy was or would soon be, and in what numbers, with the aid of the old shaman's interpretations of her dreams. Once, her dreams had alerted the tribe to approaching soldiers. The village had been hastily moved to another, safer location before the soldiers arrived, and many lives were thus saved.

One night, Flame awoke once again from a vision of horror. Her heart thudded wildly in her chest, and she struggled just to breathe as the scenes from her dream replayed themselves vividly in her mind. There was a terrible battle. Guns roared and arrows pelted the air as Night Hawk's warriors fought against many soldiers. The warriors were badly outnumbered, outflanked, and deficient in weapons. She watched, helpless and horrified, as a soldier leveled his weapon and took careful aim at Night Hawk!

Even in her dream she cried out to her husband, trying to warn him of the danger, but he did not hear her. Terror clawed at her as she viewed the puff of smoke from the man's rifle, saw the bullet enter Night Hawk's body, witnessed Night Hawk's immediate jerk of pain and shock as the bullet tore through his side, and felt his agony as her own. Through a veil of tears, she saw him fall from his horse and lie unmoving on the frozen ground, his blood swiftly turning the pristine snow to crimson as the life flowed from his body. The dream ended there, and there was no way to force it to return, that she might know if he still lived or not.

Crying hysterically, she sat stunned and terrified. Over and over again, she screamed helplessly, "No! No! No!"

Unaware that her cries were loud enough to alert those in nearby lodges, she was even oblivious to Shining Star's arrival in her tipi. She sat sobbing and shaking as Shining Star took her in her arms and tried in vain to calm her.

"Hush, Flame. You frighten War Cloud with your cries and your tears. Hush now. Tell me about it. Was it another dream?"

Flame could only nod and hiccup. Through a jumble of words, only the words "dream" and "Night Hawk" came clear, but from Flame's violent reaction, Shining Star feared the worst and shared her friend's heartbreak.

"Oh, please! Please do not let this come true this time!" Flame begged, clutching tightly to Shining Star. "Please!"

By morning, Flame was more calm, if only from exhaustion. By now she had been able to relate her dream to Shining Star and Owl Eyes, but the shaman could not ease her pain by telling her more than she had already seen for herself.

Her story had traveled throughout the village, and all now wondered and worried what had befallen Chief Night Hawk. They could only wait and wonder and pray that the bullet had not taken his life.

For four long days they waited without word. Flame was nearly beside herself with worry, frantic to hear some news of her husband's fate. Finally, at long last, the war party rode into camp, weary and bedraggled and carrying their fallen and wounded brothers home with them.

Flame stood with Shining Star and waited as the returning warriors gathered at the center of the camp. Her anxious eyes searched for Night Hawk, but found Stone Face first. Together she and Shining Star fought their way through the gathering crowd toward him. It was then that Flame found her husband. Night Hawk's body lay strapped to his horse, his head lolling alongside the pony's neck, his dark braids half-hidden in the horse's mane. What she could see of his face was nearly as pale as her own. His dark eyes were closed, and he lay as still as death.

Her feet rooted themselves to the ground, held there by the greatest fear she had ever experienced. Shining Star's arm supported her, or she would surely have fallen, for her knees had no strength. A strange, keening whimper escaped her frozen lips, and she could not tear her eyes from the sight of her beloved husband's limp body. One trembling hand came forward of its own accord, reaching for him as tears raced unchecked down her face and her lips quivered around his name.

"Night Hawk!" It was a cry from the heart, a prayer, a plea. Though barely a whisper, it echoed about her, touching the hearts of all who stood watching.

With faltering steps, she approached his body. Just as she reached him, Stone Face was there, his arm replacing that of Shining Star. "He lives yet, Flame," she heard him say, though she could scarcely believe he spoke the truth. "He is badly wounded, but he clings to life."

Tearful blue eyes rose to his, searching for the truth of his words. "It is so," he assured her.

Staying at his side, she watched as Stone Face directed several men to gently lift their chief from his horse and carry him to the lodge of the tribal medicine man. When Flame would have objected, wanting Night Hawk taken to their own tipi, he told her. "He is still in grave danger, Flame. He needs the medicines and cures of Grey Fox."

Reluctantly she agreed, though she would make certain, in the days to come, that he had proper treatment and that she would be allowed to sit at his side when she wished.

Night Hawk's condition was extremely serious. He had taken a bullet in the side, just as she had seen in her dream, and he had lost much blood. For days he lay unconscious, so near to death that no one, not even Flame, could believe that he still lived. With other wounded warriors needing his attentions also, Grey Fox gladly allowed Flame to help tend to her husband, telling her what needed to be done and what signs to watch for.

When he thrashed about in his fever, Flame

held him down, calming him with soft words of love and encouragement. She bathed his burning body with cool water. Though it sickened her to look upon the torn flesh of his gaping wound, she learned to clean it and change the dressings, holding back the nausea that threatened her each time.

She sat with him almost continuously in those first vital days, leaving War Cloud in Shining Star's care. She barely ate or slept, except to nap fitfully at Night Hawk's side. She feared to leave him, lest he die, for she privately wondered if it were her very presence and the sound of her voice that were keeping him alive when he should have died from such a wound. As if to prove her right, the only word to come from his fever-cracked lips was her name—over and over again, like a litany of hope, as if he somehow sensed her presence and was clinging to it with all his remaining strength, trying to make his way back to her again.

Ten days after the return of the warriors, Night Hawk finally regained consciousness. His fever broke in the night, drenching him and the bedding. Flame was changing the wet robes beneath him for dry ones, leaning over him, careful not to disturb the fresh dressing on his wound. Upon feeling the slight brush of his dry, hot fingers on her arm, she started, almost losing her balance. Glancing at his face, she was surprised to find his dark eyes staring dazedly up at her, as if he could not quite focus properly. His lips parted ever so slightly as he rasped, "Flame."

A wondrous smile lit her entire face, and she

whispered back, "I am here, my love." With trembling fingertips, she touched his face tenderly.

His eyelids fluttered, as if they were too heavy to stay open for long. "Stay," he croaked out, his eyes adding what his lips could not form words to say. They spoke of pain, and love, and the lonely dark path of death that his feet had almost trod.

"I will," she promised softly. "Sleep, husband of my heart. Rest and grow strong again. I will be here at your side when you awaken."

From that night, Night Hawk began to recover. Seven days later he returned to their own tipi, carried there by his friends. His recovery was slow, but progressed nicely under Flame's watchful eye and dedicated care. Before long, he could sit up a bit, propped by rolled robes to prevent injury to his healing wound. As his convalescence lengthened, he became more and more impatient with his enforced inactivity, and it took all of Flame's patience and stubbornness to keep him still on his mat.

The one time he defied her and tried to get up too soon, he landed on his face on the floor of the tipi and had to have her assistance to get back onto his mat again. Her scowl matched his, and her look clearly stated what she thought of his foolishness. "If you tear open that wound again, I am going to ask Grey Fox to keep you in his tipi until you are well enough to walk from it unaided," she threatened, then said no more to him for the remainder of the evening.

At least War Cloud served to help keep his father entertained, for Night Hawk never tired of spending time with his son. Too, as soon as Night Hawk was well enough to have visitors, his fellow warriors and chiefs came often to speak with him. They discussed new battle strategies and included him in the planning of raids, which the other warriors continued during his recovery. They told him of battles he had missed, who had been injured or killed, how they and their enemies had fared in his absence, and generally kept him abreast of what was happening around him.

With each visit, Flame could see Night Hawk's impatience grow. He was aching to get back into action again, despite his brush with death. This, she supposed, was something she was going to have to get used to, being the wife of a war chief, but just now it was not easy to accept. After nearly losing him, she feared for him all the more.

Sensing her fear, Night Hawk sought to ease her mind. "Come here and sit beside me, where I can look upon your face and touch you," he said one day, after two of his fellow chiefs had left.

Doing as he bid her, she let him pull her small hand into the warmth of his. "I can see the fear that clouds your eyes each time we speak of raids and battles," he told her quietly. "I understand that it is your love for me that makes you worry so, as well as my wound that brought me so near death, but I am a war chief. As soon as I am well again, I will once more lead my warriors into battle. This is my duty and my privilege, to lead my men on such missions."

"I know this," she answered, her doleful eyes

dwelling on his face, "and I am trying to understand. I would not have you be a coward, Night Hawk, but loving you as I do, I cannot help worrying over your safety. Would you have your wife care less for your life?"

He shook his head and gave her a tender smile. "No. I would but ease your heart on this matter."

"How?"

He answered her question with one of his own. "Do you believe in the Great Spirit, Flame?" At her nod, he continued. "Then you must know that He looks after each of His children until it is their time to join Him in His home in the sky."

Again she agreed. "If this is so, then you must also know that He will not call me until it is His time to do so. Until then, I will return to you from each battle," he assured her. "Though I may be wounded many times before then, my feet will not tread the Path of the Dead until the Great Spirit directs them there, and when that day comes, there is no power on this earth or beyond it that will prevent it from happening. It does little good to worry over when or how it will be, for only the Great Spirit knows. All men's days upon this earth are numbered from their birth. Let us not dwell upon death, my love. Let us enjoy what time we have with each other and not let clouds of worry shadow the sunshine of our lives and our great love."

His wise words were a balm to her troubled spirit, just as he had intended them to be. When he was fully healed and well enough to ride once more with his warriors, Flame's heart, though sad, was not quite as heavy as before. She held his words within her heart, a talisman against her fear, a ray of hope to keep her until his return.

It held her in good stead, for the times ahead were troubled ones. The tribes continued to war against the soldiers, and many men on both sides were killed. With each raid, each successful rout and battle, Night Hawk's name became more widely spoken, on every tongue both Indian and white. Among the tribes, it was said with pride and reverence, for his fearlessness was fast becoming legendary.

Among the whites, his was soon a name to be feared and hated, for he was one of their most powerful enemies. Well versed in warfare, Night Hawk seemed to lead a charmed life, for despite his severe wound, he had recovered to fight again, more viciously than ever. He had an uncanny knack for knowing when and where his enemy would be, and how best to attack them. He was ruthless, wily, dangerous and fearless. His strikes could come as swiftly and accurately as those of his namesake, and often with less warning. Before long, the mere mention of his name struck fear into the heart of many a soldier.

Night Hawk—a deadly, almost ghostly enemy, fabled and feared by all!

Chapter
24

April brought spring thaws to the mountains and plains once more, and by May the land was green and glorious. However, this was the spring of 1865, and the war that had ravaged the country for four years had been won by the North at long last. May brought a sudden influx of added cavalry into the western territories, soldiers now free to fight in the escalating Indian Wars.

There had been heavy raids in the winter along the South Platte River, a combined effort of the Sioux, Cheyenne and Arapaho. In retaliation for the Sand Creek massacre, the town of Julesburg had been burned and its white defenders scalped, raising a hue and cry from the settlers in the western territories. There had been brief fighting around Fort Laramie. As the raids continued, miles of telegraph wire were destroyed and stage stations and wagon trains and small military outposts attacked. The tribes were successfully disrupting communications and food supplies to the West, and people were beginning to panic.

Now, as the numbers of soldiers increased, the tribes began to band together again. Spring saw a great gathering of Sioux, Arapaho, and both Northern and Southern Cheyenne. Large spring hunts were organized, and ceremonies were held day after day. Because of their large numbers, the threat of attack by soldiers was decreased, and it became a time of gaiety and festivities, as well as a time to organize successful raids and scouting parties against their white enemies.

Flame and Shining Star were enjoying this time of communion with the other tribes. They renewed friendships with other women they had not seen since the Sun Dance ceremonies the past summer. They gladly showed off their new sons and exclaimed over the other women's latest babies. The shared chores of scraping and tanning skins, and gathering firewood and berries and spring roots and plants, were much more enjoyable while they visited and gossiped with one another, working companionably with their infants strapped to their backs in convenient cradleboards.

Strange things were beginning to happen now, however. Evil, frightening things that threatened both Flame and her son. At first she thought it just an accident, when she returned to her tipi one day to find a rabid skunk inside. Bandit had the animal cornered, the two facing off against each other, and Flame had not known what to do. Foam was dripping from the skunk's bared fangs, and the entire tipi reeked of its malodorous spraying.

Night Hawk was gone, but one of the younger Cheyenne boys managed to kill the skunk with an arrow through the heart. The carcass was taken away and burned before any of the camp animals could become infected with the disease. The entire tipi had to be aired and cleaned with a special mixture of roots and plants to rid it of the stink. Many back-breaking hours were spent scrubbing robes and clothing free of the smell.

It was a little strange that no one else in the village had seen the skunk before Flame discovered it in her tipi, but she did not dwell on this too much at the time. It seemed just one of those freak things that happen once in a while.

Then, several days later, she was about to put War Cloud into his cradle and prepare the evening meal when an odd, dry rattling sound alerted her. Holding her son tightly in her arms, she barely leaped out of the way to avoid being struck by a rattlesnake. It had been lying coiled in the bed of the cradle! Thoroughly shaken, Flame ran screaming from the tipi. Again, in Night Hawk's absence, two young boys offered to remove the snake from her lodge.

It was many hours before she was calm again, and many more before she could cease to shudder each time she looked at her son's cradle and

thought what might have happened. How close
she had come to placing War Cloud into that
cradle on top of that snake! As small as he was,
War Cloud could never have survived being
bitten!

Now Flame could not help but wonder what
was going on. It seemed that someone was deliberately trying to harm either her or her young
son, or both. The incident with the rabid skunk
might not have been an accident after all. This
one with the rattlesnake certainly was not! There
was no way anyone would ever convince Flame
that the snake had crawled into her tipi and into
War Cloud's cradle on its own. Someone had
placed it there, just as they had probably put the
skunk inside the tipi.

Following these two frightening occurrences,
Flame became very cautious. Shining Star shared
her view that someone did, indeed, mean harm
to Flame and War Cloud. She too, kept a sharp
eye out for anything unusual happening around
the camp or anyone who seemed the least bit
suspicious. Of course, both women immediately
thought of Little Rabbit, but there was no way to
prove their suspicions, and they dared not accuse
the woman without some proof. Flame had not
even had any dreams to warn her of these dangers, or to indicate who might be behind them.

It had become a dangerous game, one Flame
dared not lose. She kept War Cloud close to her at
all times, never letting him out of her sight for a
moment. She developed a habit of looking about
her and not allowing her mind to wander as she
worked, staying constantly on the alert. Always,

she checked the tipi now before entering, making certain that nothing hid in the shadows before allowing herself to feel safe. When Night Hawk was not there, she kept War Cloud's cradle close by her side at night, and slept with a knife within hand's reach.

Night Hawk taught her how to use the knife most lethally, for he was furious upon returning home and discovering what had been going on in his absence. He did not seem to think that these strange happenings had been accidents either. Immediately he began to question those who had their tipis closest to his, and offered a reward to anyone who might give him any information or had noticed someone lurking about. Then he began to teach Flame how to defend herself with knife and lance.

Even with Night Hawk near, Flame found it difficult to relax her vigilance. Many times each night, she would awaken at the slightest sound and feel the need to reassure herself that War Cloud was well; even then she found it hard to fall asleep again. This loss of sleep and constant worry soon took their toll. Dark circles appeared beneath her eyes, and she began to lose weight. If this continued, she feared her nervousness and weariness would cause her milk to dry up and she would no longer be able to feed her son.

It was odd how each time Night Hawk returned, the incidents stopped, and whenever he left again, odd things would happen. "It cannot be Crooked Arrow," he told Flame, when she mentioned that she suspected Little Rabbit might be responsible. "Crooked Arrow has been on all our recent raids, and I would know if he were to disappear at any time. If Little Rabbit is doing these things, it is without his aid."

When the time came for him to lead his men on another mission, he held her close to his heart and told her, "Take care while I am gone, Blue Eyes. Remember all I have taught you and keep your knife at hand."

"I am afraid," she admitted softly. She raised her face to look at him. "Does that make me a coward, Night Hawk?"

Smiling down at her, he brushed her cheek with the back of his hand. "No, my love. It makes you a wise and careful mother. You would be a fool not to be fearful. Just do not let this fear master you. You must master it."

"How?"

"By being my strong and beautiful Firebrand and being very, very wary. We will catch this evil person, and he will be punished. You must believe this and be strong for our son."

Just when she had begun to think that nothing else would happen, Flame had another of her visions. It had been some time since she last stepped into her tipi to find someone had been there in her absence and that odd items were not quite the way she had left them. But for a while everything had been peaceful and she had started to hope that her antagonist had given up the game.

Then came the dream. In it she could not see the person who was entering her tipi, or even if it was a man or a woman. She saw only a hand reaching for her bag of acorn flour and dark fingers opening the drawstring. Then the intruder poured another powdery substance from his palm into the bag with the flour. Moving stealthily, the hand replaced the pouch and the intruder silently left Flame's tipi.

The next day, she and Shining Star took turns watching Flame's tipi, waiting to see who might try to sneak inside and poison the food bag. Whenever Flame had to be elsewhere, Shining Star kept vigil, but as careful as they tried to be, somehow someone still managed to creep into the lodge unseen.

Flame knew this the moment she entered her lodging. Nothing seemed amiss at first; it was just a strong feeling that someone else had been there, as if a scent of evil still lurked in the air. Walking to the sack of acorn meal, Flame now knew without doubt that the pouch had been tampered with. The tiny bit of feather she had wedged between the bag and the post it hung from now lay on the floor, unnoticed by whoever had trespassed here. Flame had deliberately placed the feather there, to know if anyone touched the bag. The acorn flour had been laced with poison, she was sure.

Nothing else in the tipi had been disturbed. Flame threw the flour away, borrowing a fresh supply from Shining Star. Neither woman said anything to anyone else. They merely went on about their daily work and waited to see who might seem overly curious or watchful. They especially kept a close watch on Little Rabbit, but the woman seemed as naturally spiteful as always.

When, a few days later, someone tried to kill Flame by throwing a knife at her while she was gathering wood with several other women, Flame was truly frightened. The gleaming blade had passed within a hair's breadth of her head. Had she not bent down just at that moment to retrieve a branch she had dropped, the knife would have entered her breast. Or had she turned about, it would have entered War Cloud's tiny body as he hung in his cradleboard on her back.

Even with the other women nearby, no one knew who had thrown the knife. None had seen it or even known what was happening until Flame screamed and they looked to see the knife still quivering in the bark of the tree just behind her. All rushed to calm her, to exclaim loudly over the attempt on her life, and to help her back to the village, for they could see how badly frightened their sister was. All of the women seemed genuinely concerned; certainly none of them seemed the least bit guilty. Neither was there any way of identifying the knife, for it was a common skinning knife, of the type used by almost every woman in the camp, unremarkable in any way.

It was Night Hawk who came up with a solution to their problem when next he returned and heard this latest news. Though it would not reveal who was guilty, it would surely put a stop to these attempts on Flame's life and against War Cloud. It was really remarkably simple, yet brilliant, and Flame wondered why they had not thought of it before.

"We shall spread the tale of another of your visions," he explained, as Flame, Shining Star, and Stone Face listened. "This vision will warn of another attempt on your life. While it will not show the identity of your attacker, it will show your escape to safety, while your attacker meets a violent death by his own scheme."

"But how can this work?" Flame questioned with a frown. "Will this person not realize that it is a trick, for who but he can guess what plot he might try next?"

A sly smile crept across Night Hawk's face, making his eyes gleam wickedly. "This is true. It is why we will speak of the dream, but not of the exact details. Let him imagine that whatever else he has planned will fail, causing his own death, or that it is some scheme even he has yet to devise, but which you have seen in your vision of the future."

"And he will be frightened because your dreams always come true," Shining Star added, clapping her hands in glee. "We must lead him to believe that if he does not attempt this treachery, his own death will not come to pass."

"If he does not know the exact nature of this dream or the plot it reveals, he will fear to try any sort of further attempt on your life, for fear it will be the one you have envisioned," Stone Face concluded. "It is a good plan."

They set their own plan into action the very next day. A few days passed without incident, then a few more. Night Hawk left on another raid, and in all the time he was gone, nothing odd or evil happened. When a full moon had passed, they knew that their scheme had been successful, and they could all rest more easily. Flame's life, and that of her son, were no longer in peril.

As if to add to her tribal status, and thus to her safety, Flame had yet another vision that made everyone tremble at the great powers she possessed. That summer, the Sioux were hosts for the annual Sun Dance ceremony, which Flame politely declined to watch this year. About this same time, the Cheyenne, in view of the increased raids and risks to their warriors, and because so many of their people were presently gathered in one place, decided to hold their Sacred Medicine Arrow ceremony. This was not an annual event, but a very important one, attended solely by the warriors.

During the four-day ceremony, the four sacred arrows were unwrapped by the Arrow Keeper, a particularly honored shaman of the entire Cheyenne nation. In a special part of the ceremony, the worn lashings were replaced with freshly blessed thongs. The feathered tips were carefully cleaned and reshaped; the shafts were repaired, but only rarely replaced, as these were such special arrows that there were only four in existence. The Cheyenne revered almost nothing more than these four all-powerful and important arrows.

These sacred medicine arrows were left safely in the Arrow Keeper's sole possession from ceremony to ceremony, and none other than he could claim or touch them until his death, when they would pass on to another chosen shaman of great power and status. They were to be kept hidden from sight until needed for the next sacred ceremony, guarded against loss or theft or accident.

The four arrows were kept wrapped in a special coyote-fur bundle, both the bag and the arrows most sacred and blessed. At this sacred ceremony, all the warriors and braves of the tribe would pass by to view the arrows, to make offerings and prayers for protection for themselves and their brothers during battle. Women were strictly forbidden to set eyes upon these sacred items, for fear that this would destroy their great protective powers.

But now, the sacred medicine arrows could not be found. The current Arrow Keeper had died suddenly and mysteriously, before being able to pass the sacred bundle on to his successor, or even to relate their secret location. The entire Cheyenne tribe was suddenly thrown into panic. What were they to do if they could not find the sacred arrows? Surely their entire nation would perish! They would be killed in battle and die horrible deaths lacking in honor if their sacred arrows could not be found. The protection of these powerful arrows was vital to their very lives.

Much to everyone's surprise, it was Flame who came to their aid. She had dreamed of a fur-wrapped bundle containing four old arrows, the tips of which were fashioned of stone rather than the metal that many warriors used today. They were bound in aged rawhide that obviously needed repair. They appeared to be very ancient.

Flame could not understand why she would dream of these four arrows. She had envisioned them hidden in a shallow hole near a place where three lone trees formed a triangle. A huge rock lay over the spot where they were buried. In the brief dream she had seen nothing else, no sign of any living person; she had sensed some importance to these items, but had seen no danger in her dream. Because she could not fathom what this vision might mean, and because Owl Eyes was not in his lodge when she went to ask him the significance of her strange dream, she soon forgot about it.

Only when the alarm went up throughout the entire camp that the sacred medicine arrows were missing, did she remember her dream and think to ask Night Hawk about these special arrows. "What do these arrows look like?" she questioned curiously.

Shaking his head worriedly, he replied, "I cannot tell you this. Women are not allowed to look upon them, nor to know about the ceremony."

"Are they old?" she persisted. "Four of them, with stone tips and frayed feathers and rotted bindings?"

A look of incredulous disbelief froze his bronze features as he stared at her. "Flame, how do you know of these things? What do you know of these arrows?"

"I have dreamed of four such arrows," she said simply, "though I did not know at the time what the dream meant, nor how important the arrows are to the tribe."

"Do you have any idea where they are?" he asked hopefully.

She nodded. "They are in the center of a triangle of trees, with a big rock over them."

"Where are these trees?"

"I do not know, Night Hawk. I am sorry."

Immediately he took her to speak with Owl Eyes. Though the shaman questioned her about her vision, she could recall few of the details, for it had been some time since the dream. Not to be denied the only means of finding the sacred arrows, Owl Eyes commenced to put Flame into a trance. Now, as he questioned her, the scene came clear once more, the details more pronounced. When he still could not determine the location of the arrows, he led her, still in her trance, into a hastily called council of all the chiefs. Before all of them, he asked her again about the arrows, and in her state of near-sleep, she recalled all that she had seen.

One old war chief of the same clan as the Arrow Keeper remembered one such place near their winter camp. It was a remote spot many days' ride from where they now were, but riders were immediately sent there. Several anxious days later, they returned, bearing with them the sacred arrows. A great cry of thanksgiving went up from the tribe, and Flame was proclaimed an honored Prophet of the People, most blessed and beloved by all for having saved the entire Cheyenne nation from certain disaster.

As soon as a new Arrow Keeper could be

chosen, the Sacred Medicine Arrow ceremony was held at long last, bringing a sigh of relief and a feeling of safety to the Cheyenne people, such as they had not experienced since discovering that their precious arrows were missing. All recognition for the safe return of their most prized possession was awarded to Flame. Her name went into their memories and their legends for all time as The Dreamer Who Found the Sacred Medicine Arrows, the only woman ever to have viewed them, if only in her wondrous dreams.

Chapter
25

Night Hawk's midnight eyes darkened, if that were possible, as he watched Flame's tongue snake out in an unconsciously provocative gesture to catch the honey that dripped from her fingers. His eyes lingered on her lips, still glistening with the sweet stickiness that clung there. The women had gathered honey this day, and Flame had just finished packing the last of their share into one of the leather holding pouches. Night Hawk had been sitting there watching her now for some time; the arrow he had been working on lay across his knees, completely forgotten.

Without a word, Night Hawk rose and crossed to the tipi entrance, where he tied down the flap in a manner indicating the desire for privacy.

Turning, he met Flame's curious look with a burning gaze. "Come." He held out his hand to her, nodding with his head toward their sleeping mats.

Surprise and delight made Flame's eyes go wide. Rarely did they make love now in the middle of the afternoon. Usually they were both much too busy, and War Cloud needed much of her attention since he had begun crawling about and getting into mischief. Just now, however, he was napping peacefully in his cradle, which he was fast outgrowing.

Rising, Flame started to hang the bag of honey on a peg with the others, but her husband's low words stopped her. "Bring it with you, wife. It is time your husband had a sweet treat of his own." His dark eyes gleamed with mischief, and her heart turned over in her breast as his gaze raked over her slim body.

As she walked slowly toward him, her hips swaying temptingly, his blood began to thunder in his veins. His hunger grew with every step she took. Reaching out, he took the honey bag from her and set it on the ground. Then his lean bronze fingers dealt swiftly with the lacings of her dress. Deftly, he removed it, and then her moccasins. She stood proud and naked before him, the fiery curtain of her hair her only covering. It fell like a sheer veil to cloak her bared breast, even as the rosy crests peeked through to tease him.

His wrists encircled hers, bringing her shaking fingers to his lean waist and the ties of his breechclout. "Will you return the favor, Blue Eyes?" he murmured.

She did so gladly, eagerly; and when he, too, stood in naked splendor before her, her hands slid up to caress the muscled strength of his broad chest. Her glimmering blue eyes adored him, admiring his smooth bronze flesh, feeling his heart beating wildly beneath her palm. Nimble fingers unbound his long dark braids, loving the way the loosened strands trickled through her fingers like an inky waterfall to frame the bold features of his face. Her hands wandered lower, teasing at his waist, skimming along his firm thighs, then trailing upward once more to find the hot, pulsing proof of his desire. Unconsciously, her tongue crept out to wet her honey-glistened lips, and he was reminded of his previous plans.

Lowering her to the mats, his dark eyes lingered on her silken skin, her tempting mouth and thrusting breasts. His lips swooped down to capture hers in a long, drugging kiss. "Sweet," he murmured, "but I would have more." There was a deliciously wicked twinkle in the depths of his dark eyes that thrilled her. It promised sensual delights, though she could only guess what they might be.

Long fingers combed through the bright strands of her hair, fanning it out about her head like a fiery halo. Smiling a secretive smile, he drew her arms above her head, palms up and open. The glow in his eyes grew brighter as this action caused her breasts to thrust even higher, as if in supplication of his touch. Slowly, teasingly, his fingers slid lightly down the length of her arms. His knees nudged her thighs apart, until she lay open and vulnerable beneath him. "Stay exactly as I place you," he said softly, his mouth hovering over hers. "Do not move unless I direct you to."

It was strangely provocative, this new game they were playing. Spread out beneath him, open now to his avid gaze, his every touch, Flame trembled in anticipation. Though her eyes widened as she saw him reach for the pouch of honey, she did not move. She lay perfectly still, her gaze flickering back and forth from his face to the pouch, as he slowly tipped the bag and thick, sweet honey began to drip onto her bare body. Carefully, precisely, Night Hawk poured the warm, thick honey over her breasts. It coated the pouting crests and flowed smoothly down the rounded slopes. A glistening pool formed in the hollow between her breasts. From there he ran a thin line down the center of her body to her navel, filling it to overflowing.

Never had she felt such warm, sensual pleasure! As the honey flowed gently over her, it created a trail of heat, like lava streaming from an erupting volcano. Everywhere it touched, it warmed, charting its own sweet path over her body, sensitizing her flesh wherever it went— over her breasts, down the concave curve of her stomach, through the thatch of red curls beyond, even to her toes. She gasped aloud as he raised her hips and poured the sticky mass over her thighs and between, bathing her femininity with the golden liquid. Lifting lids heavy with passion, she met his gaze and gasped again at the open hunger glowing in their dark depths.

He smiled, a wicked, devilish flash of white teeth in a bronze face. It was the face of a conqueror eager to ravish his prize. That she was a very willing victim was of no consequence. At this moment he was the master, about to enslave his beautiful captive and subjugate her to his powerful will. Beneath his heated look, Flame trembled, all too ready to submit herself to him, a sacrifice eager to be consumed in the fires of his passion. With a sigh, she offered herself up to him, willing him to seize that which he desired.

The exquisite torture began at her toes. Night Hawk took each in turn into the warm cavern of his mouth, licking at them with his tongue, suckling until she squirmed beneath him and begged for mercy. His mouth snaked a path of fire up her thigh, melting her bones as he lapped and nipped his way over her hip, bypassing for the moment the one place where she most burned for his touch. His tongue laved her stomach, delving intimately into her naval.

As her stomach clenched, Flame cried out and raised her arms to his head in an effort to ease the sharp torment. Instantly, his fingers grasped her wrists, returning her arms to their former position over her head, holding them there while his mouth worked its way slowly, tortuously over her ribcage, ever nearer to her aching breasts.

When she thought she would surely lose her mind, his lips closed over one turgid nipple. A whimper rose from her throat as he tugged at it, nipping lightly with his teeth, then soothing the slight pain with deft strokes of his tongue. He licked the honey from her breasts as a cat cleans its paws, his tongue and lips gliding down their slopes to the soft undersides and lingering in the valley between, savoring the sweet taste of her.

She was ablaze in sensual pleasure, moaning and thrashing beneath him, pleading for that final, ultimate joy of feeling him united with her—but his leisurely foray was not yet finished. His dark head moved between her thighs, and she bit back a scream as his hot mouth closed over her. Again and again, his tongue dipped into her, caressing, stroking ceaselessly. It darted swiftly, deeply, a hummingbird seeking nectar from the heart of the flower. Passion poured over her, overwhelming her in its tide as rapture erupted suddenly. Spasms shook her with unbelievable force, and still he did not cease. Twice more he brought her to that precipice of pleasure, and over the edge of ecstasy.

When at last he brought his body over hers, she was trembling violently, great sobs issuing from her. As his mouth claimed hers, she tasted the sweetness of honey and herself on his lips. With the last of her strength, she raised her hips to meet his first thrust, her cry of joy muted by his lips upon hers as their bodies joined.

Then they were flying together, the conquering hawk and his mate, soaring high over the mountaintops, higher than the clouds, straight up into the searing sun. They were spinning and whirling, melting into each other, blending until neither existed without the other, one in body and heart and soul. Forever joined in spirit, he was the Night Hawk with the brightest Flame to light his way. Together they blazed like the hottest comet, a shooting star, a magnificent, blinding, eternal Night Flame flashing through the endless skies, writing their destiny across the heavens.

All through that summer the tribes had problems, not only with the soldiers, but with groups of men traveling into their lands in search of the shining yellow rocks the white men called gold. While the Indians had little use for the yellow stones, not giving them the same value as the white men did, they resented this added intrusion into their sacred lands and through their best hunting grounds.

Still, they would often let the gold seekers go unharmed if the miners had something of value to trade for their passage and agreed to travel swiftly through the Indian lands on their way to this place they called Montana, where the gold was to be found. As long as they did not plan to settle here and build homes, or to build roads through the forests, they were often allowed to go freely through to their destination to the west.

This was the case with one particularly large wagon train of gold seekers that came into their lands in the latter part of the summer. For many days, a band of Sioux and Cheyenne braves harassed the wagon train, until finally they began to negotiate passage in return for a wagonload of coffee, flour, sugar, and tobacco. The delay of this group of white men soon brought an added advantage, for the Indians learned from them

that soldiers were even now attempting to build a
fort somewhere along the Powder River, right in
the middle of some of their prime hunting
grounds. This fort was to be called Fort Connor,
in honor of the Army general who was leading
these soldiers.

The tribes were incensed that the soldiers
would dare to build a fort in their very midst.
Councils were called, and it was agreed that they
would go in search of these soldiers and this fort
and drive them from these lands. Scouting parties were sent out, and riders soon returned to
report various troops of cavalry in several locations in the area. War parties formed and went in
search of these bands of soldiers.

Night Hawk led one of these war parties, once
again leaving his wife and son behind as he rode
at the head of his band of warriors. Flame sent
him on his way with a mixture of resignation and
fierce pride in her heart, for she still worried that
he might meet with harm and not return to her.
She no longer feared for her own safety, for since
the story of her dream about her attacker's death,
no further attempts had been made on her life or
that of her son. Little did she realize that she had
relaxed her vigil too soon.

Flame was sleeping peacefully in her tipi one
night, soon after Night Hawk's departure. War
Cloud slept contentedly in his cradle. Neither
stirred as two shadowy forms crept soundlessly
into the lodge. Flame never felt the sharp blow to
her head that would keep her from awakening as
the two intruders bound her and her son into
robes and carried them quietly from the tipi and

through the sleeping village. Neither did she hear the argument between her two assailants once they had mounted their horses and carried their chief's wife and young son far from the camp.

"I would have this woman once before we turn her over to the soldiers at the new fort," Crooked Arrow said.

"And have her recognize you?" Little Rabbit hissed. "What kind of fool do I have for a husband?" She sniffed scornfully. "You are the one who insists that we do not kill her, as I have suggested."

"She need not know who we are. If we do not speak, and bind her eyes, I can still have her without her knowing it is I," he argued.

"No!" Little Rabbit was adamant. "I have endured one husband who lusted after this woman over me. I will not abide another. If you take her, I swear to you that I will kill her when you are done, and the boy also."

Crooked Arrow sighed in frustration. "Your jealousy will mean the death of us yet, Little Rabbit. You know we dare not harm them. What of the woman's dream? Would you risk your own life in taking hers?" He saw the blood flee her face and nodded. "You, too, fear her visions, so do not belittle me for being cautious."

"There is nothing to prevent us from slaying the boy," she said.

"Nothing but what little honor I still possess," Crooked Arrow admitted derisively. "I have not yet sunk so low that I will take the life of the son of my people's chief, no matter how much I despise Night Hawk."

"Then I shall do so, if you have not the stomach for the deed."

"And what if the child is also one of the chosen Dreamers, as is his mother? Dare you risk that the woman has not passed these visions on to her son in her mother's milk?"

Little Rabbit did not respond to this, and Crooked Arrow pressed on. "We will deliver the two of them, unharmed, to the white fort, as we have agreed. It will be this way, or none. If you would return to the village and take them with us, speak now. If not, we will take them to the soldiers and be rid of them. Night Hawk will not find them there, and he will know nothing of our part in this. The woman will return to her own people, and she and the child will be forever out of our lives."

"We will take them to the fort," Little Rabbit agreed sullenly.

"Then we must hurry so that we can arrive at the fort while it is yet dark, and be back in the village before anyone knows we were gone. We must also say nothing of this fort we have happened upon, the same fort our warriors now search for and have not yet found. Flame must have time to be gone from here and back with her own people before Night Hawk discovers this place."

The sentry at Fort Connor could not believe his eyes—nor his ears. As he stared wide-eyed down at the wriggling bundle of robes just outside the stockade gates, he could swear he heard a muffled voice. The bundle was about the right

size to be the body of a young boy or small adult,
but it was hard to tell. It seemed oddly shaped.
The man frowned, trying to decide what to do.
How had the bundle gotten there, and when? He
had been on duty all night and had not heard a
single sound until just a few minutes ago, yet
there it was for all to see. Was this some sort of
Indian trick? His narrowed gaze scanned the
small clearing about the fort, trying to discern
any movement in the pre-dawn gloom.

He was still trying to decide what course of
action to take, if any, when his sergeant appeared
at his side. "What in Hades is going on out there,
private?" the officer asked. "Do I hear voices
outside the gates?"

"Yes, sir! Uh, no, sir! What I mean is, I don't
know what it is, sir!" The young man felt like a
fool, but he wasn't about to risk an opinion of his
own. "There is something outside the gate, sir,
wrapped in fur robes and making noise."

Looking where the private pointed, the sergeant peered at the bundle. "Any ideas, private?"

"No, sir. I ain't paid enough to think, sir. I just
follow orders."

The sergeant grinned at the younger man's
reply. "Then get your butt down there and open
those gates. I want to see what's in those blankets."

Disregarding his own advice to himself, the
private sputtered, "But, sir! What if it's some
kind of trap?"

"I thought you just said you didn't get paid
enough to think, private? If that's the case, then
you don't get paid enough to spout opinions

either. Now get down there and drag that bundle of fur inside so we can have a look at it. That's an order!"

A few minutes later, several men stood gaping in disbelief. Inside the robes, bound and gagged, was a young white woman! She was dressed Indian fashion, but her wary blue eyes and fiery red hair belied the sun-darkened skin. Next to her, lying cradled against her stomach, was a baby! Though the infant's hair and skin were dark, his blue eyes declared that he was at least part white, most likely the woman's child.

"Lord have mercy, Sarge!" one fellow exclaimed, finally finding his tongue. "It's a white woman!"

"A squaw!" another muttered. "What the hell's she doin' here, of all places!"

The soldier next to him nodded. "Maybe some buck got tired of her and decided to let her go."

"You're crazy!" his friend said. "They don't release their squaws. They either kill 'em or they trade 'em to someone else when they don't want 'em no more. And I hear they never give up their children."

"Then what's she doing here?" The other soldier argued. "Someone trussed her up like a Christmas turkey and dropped her off at the gate in the dark of night."

The sergeant finally took over, shaking his head at them in disgust. "The best way to find out is to untie her and take that gag off her mouth," he suggested wryly. "Instead of standing here gawking like schoolboys at your first dance, I suggest you do that. Now!" he barked as they failed to move fast enough to suit him.

Flame stared dumbfoundedly at the circle of soldiers surrounding her. What on earth was happening? Where was she, and how had she gotten here? Who were these men? Had soldiers attacked the camp while she slept? A million questions rushed through her aching head, but the answers eluded her. How could she not have known if the village had been attacked?

As the soldiers continued to stand over her, talking among themselves, she craned her neck and glanced cautiously about. Nothing looked at all familiar, except that she now knew she was inside some sort of fort. But how had she gotten here? The last thing she recalled clearly was going to sleep in her own tipi. Then she had awakened with a vicious headache, tightly bound and unable to see a thing. Her sole consolation had been discovering that War Cloud was with her, wrapped close to her and apparently unharmed. He lay at her side, cooing and sucking his fist hungrily.

As hands reached out to untie her bonds, Flame had to force herself not to cringe in fright. Fear leapt into her eyes for just a moment, and her heart thundered like a drum, but she fought it down again. She must not show these men that she was afraid. She would not! She must be brave in facing them. She had to gather her wits about her, and quickly, if she were to save herself and War Cloud from these soldiers—if she ever hoped to see Night Hawk again!

Chapter
26

After very little thought, Flame decided not to tell these soldiers that she was General Wise's daughter unless it became absolutely necessary. If she did so, they would surely send a message to her father, and as much as she wished to see him again, she did not want to jeopardize her chances of returning to Night Hawk. Her father would be sure to insist that she return home with him, and Flame did not want to do that. She wanted to find a way to be reunited with her husband. Of course, if it looked as if her life, or that of her child, were in peril, she would scream her identity long and loudly—but she would not do it unless she felt truly threatened.

A thousand thoughts flew swiftly through her

head, and Flame realized that she had few options and must decide quickly which to employ. These soldiers wanted to know who she was and how she came to be there. They were not just curious, for she could see the suspicion on their faces, as though they still suspected a trick of some sort. They wanted answers to their questions, and they wanted them now. They would not be put off for long.

Once more, the sergeant was leaning over her. "What is your name, Miss? You do speak English, don't you?"

Flame nodded, trying to buy more time. Suddenly a thought came to her. It was risky, but it might work! She would pretend to be hysterical, so distraught after her time with the Indians that she had lost all memory of who she was or where she came from! Who could prove differently? If they thought she had been so mistreated that she had blocked all memory from her mind, they could not expect her to be able to answer their questions. Also, if circumstances demanded, her memory could return as suddenly as it had gone, and she could still use her father's name for protection, if need be.

The problem would be acting her part with no mistakes. Only once had she actually met a person with this sort of memory lapse. He had been a patient of James's, and James had called the condition amnesia. The poor fellow had been wounded in battle and seen so many horrible things in his time as a soldier that his mind simply refused to accept it any more. While he could remember instinctively that he hated spinach, he could not recall his family or any of their names. His papers had revealed his name, and when his mother had rushed to his side, he did not even recognize the distraught woman.

Trying to imitate this condition would take great concentration, lest she give the game away entirely, but it was certainly worth a try. It would buy Flame the time she needed to decide what else to do to find Night Hawk or perhaps have him find her. If he could track her to this fort, she must be here, alive and well, when he came.

It took little effort, under the circumstances, to bring tears to her eyes as she gazed up into the face of the kindly sergeant. Allowing a whimper to escape, she then wailed, "Oh, dear Lord! I am safe! Please tell me that I am safe!"

The sergeant hunkered down at her side, a helpless look on his face as he tried to deal with this weeping woman. "Of course, you are safe, dear woman. You are at Fort Connor, with an entire troop of soldiers to defend you. Now tell us, who are you?"

Flame deliberately widened her eyes in a parody of despair. "I . . . I . . . Oh, God! I don't know!" she shrieked hysterically. "I don't know! I don't know!"

Horror in various degrees was reflected on each of the faces surrounding her, as these hapless men squirmed in their boots, not quite knowing how to react to her hysteria, nor what to do to make her stop. Finally, one soldier stepped forward, raising his voice to be heard over her frantic wails. "Sergeant, let me try to calm her," she heard him say in a deep southern drawl. "My sister used to go into fits like this at the least little thing. It's the shock of all that has happened to her, I'm sure. She'll be fine as soon as she is really sure she's safe."

Even as Flame wondered what a Southerner was doing out here on the western frontier, since she had heard that the North won the war, he knelt down and took her gently into his arms. "Calm down, now, honey," he drawled in a low, soothing tone. "Nothin's goin' to harm you any more. Don't you worry, little lady. Beauford Harris will take care of everything."

She faked a hiccup and raised wet-lashed eyes to his face. He was young, not more than twenty-five, with blond hair and blue eyes, and a rakish mustache decorating his handsome face. "But you don't understand!" she sobbed. "I can't remember who I am! I don't even know my own name!"

He rocked her within his embrace, as if she were a baby. "It's all right. The shock will wear off and you'll remember everything soon. You just have to give it time, honey."

He leaned back and tipped her face up again. "Now, why don't you come with me and I'll see if we can't get you something to eat and a place to rest. You'll feel better after that."

With a look so forlorn it would have done a basset hound credit, she nodded. Rising, she clutched War Cloud to her breast and prepared to follow Beau Harris to the mess tent. "Oh, hell!" he exclaimed upon noticing the baby once more. Then he apologized in true Southern style.

"Beggin' your pardon, ma'am, but is the child yours?"

Deliberately causing her chin to quiver, she looked down on War Cloud's downy head. "I—I don't know, but I suppose it must be. My, uh, my—" She broke off in acute embarrassment. Ducking her head, she murmured, "I think I must be feeding the baby myself, and will need to do so again soon."

Beau's face turned as red as hers, but he nodded his understanding. "We'll find you some place private, then," he assured her. "At least we won't need to worry what to feed the little tyke." With his arm at her back to guide her along, he asked, "Is it a boy or a girl?"

The answer was on the tip of her tongue before Flame realized that she was supposed to have amnesia. Just in time, she stammered weakly, "I don't know . . . I don't even know that," she sobbed. "But I know this child must be mine. No harm will come to my baby here, will it?"

"No, no," he reassured her soothingly. "No harm will come to either of you. I give you my word as a gentleman."

Flame had found a champion in Beau Harris. He was, indeed, a true Southern gentleman from the tips of his cavalry boots to the top of his aristocratic blond head. While some of the other men at Fort Connor did not hold the same respect for her because of her obvious association with the Indians, he always treated her like a lady and insisted that the others did also, like it or not.

His name for her stuck, and for lack of any other name to call her, she became known about the fort as Miss Honey. The old sergeant provided a surname when he compared her coloring to that of a red rose. So she came to be called Honey Rose.

Flame discovered that quite a few of the men at Fort Connor were former Confederate soldiers, most of whom had been prisoners of war. After the war ended, these men had joined the U.S. Cavalry, some voluntarily, but the majority coerced into it. Their two companies, consisting of almost two hundred men, were known as Galvanized Yankees. Quite rightfully, they felt that they should have been released to go home after the war, and they were resentful of this enforced enlistment in the cavalry.

Flame sympathized with them, having felt much the same when she first arrived at the Cheyenne camp. Of all the cavalrymen stationed at Fort Connor, she found them to be the most polite and gentlemanly in their attitude toward her. She supposed it had to do with their Southern upbringing, but she also realized that their attitude would probably change drastically should they ever discover that she was the daughter of a Union general, a man who had led many battles against them and their families. She found herself in the rather ridiculous position of needing their protection, even as she continued to lie to them daily.

Day after day, Flame continued her pose as the rescued woman who could not remember her past. The post commander was greatly aggravated that she could not recall any of the details of her capture or confinement among the Indians. Every other day he found time to question her about the tribe that had held her captive. How many Indians were there? How many warriors? What tribe were they? Did they treat her badly? Who was the brave who had captured her?

Always her answers were the same. She did not remember. Her body still bore the scars from the beating Little Rabbit and her friends had administered, and this, at least, convinced the commander that she had not been a willing victim. The bump on her head from Crooked Arrow's blow was thought to have caused her memory loss. The commander requested that the fort doctor examine her, which Flame allowed after much hesitation. The stretch marks on her belly, and the fact that she was breastfeeding the baby, also set to rest the question of whether or not the child was hers. She did not want to think what they might have done to her son if they thought that she was not his mother. Most likely, they would have killed the infant.

She was given a small tent to herself inside the stockade. Beau had insisted that her quarters be erected near his, so that if any of the less congenial soldiers got any ideas of visiting her uninvited in the middle of the night, she could call for help. She also received a cot and blankets, and Beau gave her a small knife for her protection, which she wore strapped to her thigh at all times.

Food was provided, and though most of the

men had little to donate in the way of clothing, they managed to give her two pair of breeches from a couple of the smaller men, and three shirts that hung to her knees. From the hide of a deer brought in one day, she fashioned a new pair of moccasins for herself and a tunic for War Cloud. A cotton nightshirt appeared mysteriously in her tent one day, the owner obviously preferring to remain anonymous, and from this Flame made several diapers for her son.

While Flame's past remained secret, she had many questions of her own, many of which could not be openly asked or readily answered, lest she expose her ruse. Knowing that a captive woman, fortunate enough to find herself rescued, would not be too curious about the tribes, Flame was forced to obtain her information by listening in on the men's conversations about various campaigns and confrontations with the Indians, all the while pretending ignorance.

To her dismay, she heard nothing of Night Hawk or his tribe. She did learn that several companies of soldiers were out of the fort at this time, including General Connor, and that they were reportedly attacking any and all Indian villages they happened upon. They were expected to return to the fort soon, and Flame could only pray that none of the returning cavalrymen would be men whom she knew, or who might recognize her.

The question of how she had come to be delivered outside the gates of the fort continued to be a mystery, though Flame had a strong suspicion that Little Rabbit and Crooked Arrow were responsible. Reason told her that whoever had done this had not wanted her or War Cloud dead, perhaps because they were frightened by her supposed dream. They had gotten rid of her in the only manner left to them without harming her.

The days wore on slowly, and Flame agonized over being parted from Night Hawk once again. She prayed that he would somehow find her and War Cloud soon, for escape on her own was practically impossible. She had no idea exactly where Fort Connor was located in relation to the Cheyenne village. Of course, the camp had most likely moved by now. She dared not attempt to strike out on her own with her infant son. There were too many perils waiting outside the walls of the fort, including soldiers, wild animals, enemy tribes, and miles of forested wilderness.

She did know that she had arrived at the fort at the beginning of September, and that each passing day brought winter closer. There was talk around the fort of the possibility of the cavalry being recalled to Fort Laramie before the snows made travel all but impossible. If she were forced to return to Fort Laramie with them, her masquerade would be over, for surely someone there would know her. It was even conceivable that her father might still be there, though it was unlikely. Could Night Hawk find her and War Cloud before they were lost to him forever? Each day she grew more worried and despondent. Would he never arrive to claim her and their son?

* * *

For days after arriving at the village to find
Flame gone again, Night Hawk searched, but
there was no sign of his wife and child. He was
like a wild man, like one of the Crazy Ones. He
ranted and raved and nearly tore the village
apart, then disappeared for many suns, only to
return weary and worn and without his little
family.

Despite Little Rabbit and Crooked Arrow's
vile declarations that Flame had once again run
away, taking Night Hawk's son and making a fool
of their chief, Night Hawk simply could not
believe that Flame would do such a thing. Not
this time! Not now! Not after having pledged her
love to him and surrendering her heart so completely. He refused to believe this of her.

A few of the villagers, mostly friends of Little
Rabbit and Crooked Arrow, preferred to believe
the worst of Flame. Most of the Cheyenne,
however, decided to reserve judgment, not wanting to condemn this woman until proof demanded it. They had come to love and respect her, and
her visions had many times saved the tribe from
certain disaster. Long since, they had ceased to
think of her as white. Flame was one of them
now, a Cheyenne, the wife of their war chief and
mother of his son, a chosen Dreamer to bless
their tribe. They felt her loss greatly, though not
as severely as Night Hawk. Until she was found,
they would try to ease their chief's troubled mind
and heart over the loss of his wife and son, and
they would pray for the safe return of their
Dreamer and friend to their midst.

Night Hawk did not know how or why Flame

was missing, but he was certain she had not gone
willingly this time. All of her possessions were
still in their tipi. None of her clothes, or War
Cloud's, were missing, except what they must
have worn on their bodies. As far as he could tell,
she had taken no food or provisions of any kind,
and her pony was still in the herd, with no other
horse missing either. The only thing he could
think was that whoever had tried so many times
to kill her had now taken her from the village. He
could only pray that they had not slain her or War
Cloud, fearing her vision too much to harm
either of them.

With only this slim hope to cling to, he continued to search for them. As time went on and his
search proved fruitless, he was forced to resume
his duties as war chief and hope to hear something of his wife and child from other tribes and
warriors. Worry caused him to neither sleep nor
eat properly. Soon he began to lose weight, and
dark circles appeared beneath his hollow eyes.
Only his responsibilities to his tribe kept him
from becoming too careless in battle, too reck-
less, as many days passed and still he heard no
word of Flame and War Cloud.

It was after a battle in which the tribes had held
many soldiers under siege, only to have fresh
troops of cavalry rescue their comrades at last,
that Night Hawk finally learned of Flame's
whereabouts. This came about quite by accident,
along with their eventual discovery of the location of Fort Connor. Under cover of night, the
soldiers slipped away from the Indians, but their

trail was easily read the next day and followed. It
led the warriors directly to the fort.

Undetected, the warriors spread out to encircle
the fort, keeping well hidden from the watchful
eyes of the white sentries. Scouts climbed high in
to the trees in the wooded area surrounding three
sides of the small clearing around the fort.
Others, Night Hawk included, rode their horses
to the tops of nearby hills, where they had a clear
view into the fort, though they were too far away
for their weapons to reach it.

Using a pair of captured field glasses, Night
Hawk scanned the interior of the stockade. Soldiers were milling about the yard, some eating or
resting, others checking their weapons in case of
attack. All along the walls, armed sentries were
posted. There were many soldiers in this fort, too
many for the tribes to attack just now.

As his gaze swept over the fort, noting the
locations of the horses and probable storage
areas for weapons, Night Hawk's sharp eyes
caught a sudden flash of red. Before he could
focus upon it, it was gone, but his heart began to
pound violently with renewed hope. It was just a
small glimpse, but he was sure the red had not
been the color of a shirt or blanket. What he had
seen had been the exact shade of Flame's bright
hair!

For many minutes he watched, scanning the
grounds again and again. Finally his patience was
rewarded. From a small tent, he saw his wife
emerge, War Cloud in her arms. His breath
caught in his throat, and his heart sang a glad

song within his breast. They were alive! They were well! They would soon be his once more, after nearly a full moon of separation.

Through the glasses, he saw Flame stop to speak with one of the soldiers. Whatever he said brought a sad smile to her face. When the man had walked away, Flame stood staring up, over the walls of the stockade, a wistful look to her features. She was looking almost exactly toward the location where Night Hawk now stood.

Then, as if she somehow sensed something different, he saw her stiffen. She stood there, gazing toward him, her bright head held aloft, like a doe scenting its mate. She stared, unmoving, a secretive smile slowly dawning on her lips, until the man returned and handed her a plate of food. Only then did she turn, reluctantly, with one last look toward the distant hillock, and enter the small tent from which she had come.

He was out there. Night Hawk had come for her at last. Flame was sure of this, as sure as she was of her love for him. When she stepped from the tent, she had felt his presence, like the warm kiss of a summer's breeze upon her skin. It would not be long now before she and War Cloud would be reunited with him.

Flame's only concern was how Night Hawk would accomplish this. There were more than two thousand cavalrymen in the fort at this time. Had he but arrived yesterday morning, there would have been only three hundred, but during the night General Connor had returned with his bedraggled troops. Many of the newly arrived men were wounded and starving, bone tired, but still able to fight. Indeed, they had been battling Indians for more than a solid month now, miles from the safety of the fort.

With sinking heart, Flame realized that the fort was too well fortified for the Indians to launch a successful attack against it. The warriors would also know this. How was Night Hawk to rescue her, in the midst of all these soldiers?

Had she been able, Flame would have simply walked from the fort and kept walking until she stopped within the safe haven of Night Hawk's arms, but this, too, was impossible. Having just battled with the Indians, General Connor was wary of an attack and had ordered that the gates of the stockade remain closed unless he commanded otherwise. Though the soldiers were as yet unaware of the warriors surrounding their fort, these men, fresh from battle, were armed, alert, and prepared to fight again at any moment. They had not yet had time to relax their guard.

Also, since the arrival of so many soldiers—some of whom had not set eyes on a white woman in many months, and others who, hating Flame on sight for her association with the Indians, eyed her small son with malice—Beau Harris had hardly left her side. He and several of his closest friends had designated themselves her personal watchdogs, guarding her more closely than ever in light of this new threat to her.

There was no way Flame could escape unnoticed to run to Night Hawk, as her heart so wished to do. She would simply have to wait for him to come to her, however he might accomplish it. She would be waiting, ever watchful and ready, now that she knew he was so near. It was with the aura of his presence surrounding her like a comforting blanket, that she settled herself until the time when he could once again steal her away from a well-guarded fort—only this time she would go with him most eagerly!

Chapter 27

Two days later, Flame was standing outside her tent talking with Beau, when a slight commotion at the gates drew their attention. "What is happening?" she asked nervously, not needing to fake her response. She had been on pins and needles ever since realizing that Night Hawk was near.

"Seems someone wants to enter the fort, and the sentry has to get permission to open the gates," Beau replied.

Evidently, permission was granted, for a few seconds later, the heavy gate swung open to admit a lone rider. He was tall, tanned, and dressed in a dusty cavalry uniform that had seen better days. As Flame waited, Beau went closer to discover why the man was here. When he returned, he said with a smile, "Good news! The lieutenant was sent ahead to advise us that a supply train is on its way to the fort, about a day's ride out. Lord knows we can use the supplies, with so many extra men to feed."

"Oh." Flame swallowed a sigh of disappointment, then felt her heart lurch suddenly as she watched the lieutenant slide gracefully from his horse. Surely her eyes were playing tricks on her, but she was sure that the man had just dismounted on the wrong side! With effort, she schooled her features into a bland mask, but her eyes remained trained upon the young officer.

Almost casually, he glanced her way, and Flame stifled a gasp. It was Night Hawk, disguised as a cavalry officer! So different did he look that she had almost failed to recognize her own husband! Her hungry eyes swiftly took in every detail of his appearance, noting the differences since she last saw him. He was thinner, his black eyes sunken and underlined with dark circles. Still, the uniform he wore was designed to fit a slightly smaller man. The jacket stretched tautly across Night Hawk's broad shoulders, the trousers fitting like a second skin over his muscled thighs. The brim of his hat was pulled low over his forehead in an effort to conceal his features.

In that one, brief glance he sent her, Flame had read the message in his eyes. *Be ready, Blue Eyes*, it had said. *You are mine, and I have come for you.* She had seen fierce determination glowing there, but she had not detected any anger in his look. For this she was profoundly grateful. Their love had stood the test, and he knew that this time she had not left him of her own will.

Curbing her impatience with difficulty, Flame returned to her tent. It might be a while before Night Hawk could approach her. They would have to be very cautious, especially Night Hawk. It was fortunate that no one else had seemed to notice his error of dismounting to the right of his horse, instead of the left as the soldiers always did, but he dared not make a more blatant blunder. Thank heavens she had insisted he continue his English lessons until he could speak fluently! Telling herself not to worry was like telling herself not to breathe; it simply was not possible with their lives at stake. Yet she trusted him, and she knew that he would find a way to take her away with him. He was here now, inside the fort, and she must wait until they could meet and talk and plan their escape.

She did not see him for the rest of the day. It was growing dark before she caught sight of him seated near a fire, talking and laughing and eating with several soldiers. At that moment, she was thankful for the evening shadows that concealed the shock she could not hide. She stared in stunned disbelief and horror. He had cut off his braids! His straight black hair was shorn short, brushed back on the sides and hanging only to his collar in the back. It was just a little longer than most of the cavalrymen wore theirs, since many of the soldiers tended to be a bit negligent about their grooming out here in the wilderness.

At that moment, Flame could have burst into tears. Night Hawk had been forced to cut off his long dark plaits in order to disguise himself as a soldier, and she knew what that gesture must have cost him. A warrior's braids were his badge of honor, a symbol of masculine pride in his noble ancestry. He would rather severe his arm than cut his hair. Yet he had done this in order to save her and their son! Her heart ached with love for him, that he would make such a sacrifice to have his family back.

He looked up and caught her watching him, her eyes shining with unshed tears as her fingers unconsciously stroked her own long tresses. A ghost of a grin crossed his face before he turned back to the fire once more.

Though the hour was late, Flame was still wide awake when Night Hawk slipped silently into her tent. The hand he placed across her mouth was an unnecessary caution, for she knew immediately that it was he. Before he could utter a word, her arms crept up to encircle his neck and pull his mouth down to hers. "I love you," she whispered. Then their lips met and clung in a long, joyous kiss of reunion.

Her hands stroked the planes of his face, as if memorizing his features in the dark. They touched the short, blunt ends of his shorn hair, and she moaned softly in renewed dismay. "Your hair," she murmured. "All your long, beautiful hair—gone!"

His soft chuckle sounded in her ear as he

nuzzled her neck. "It will grow again, I promise you. It was necessary for the disguise. I was fortunate that many of our warriors have taken soldiers' uniforms and horses in their raids. I borrowed the shirt from George Bent, and the trousers from Walks-Bent-Over. They are too short, but the boots hide this."

Her breath caught in her throat again as she told him of her fear for him when he had dismounted the horse from the wrong side. "You must take care, Night Hawk, lest someone suspect you. It amazes me that someone has not noticed that you wear no gun."

"Then I am glad I thought to borrow the saber from the brother of Fox Ears, and I have a new army rifle as my prize from our recent battle."

She sighed and snuggled closer to him. "Oh, Night Hawk, I have missed you so! It took so long for you to come for me."

"There was no trail to follow, though I searched endlessly. How did you come to be here? Who dared to steal you and our son away from my side? Tell me, and I will avenge you."

He felt her shake her head in the dark. "I know not," she admitted. "I was asleep in our tipi, and when next I woke I was bound in robes and lying outside the gates of this fort, War Cloud at my side. I would have returned to you, my heart, but I feared trying to find my way back through the forests. War Cloud is so young yet, and the perils were too great, so I waited here, hoping you would somehow find us."

He shifted, pulling her tightly to his side as

they spoke softly. "The soldiers did not harm you?" he asked, and she could feel his muscles tense as he awaited her answer.

"No. A few of them resent me, but others have kept them from harming me or our son. They might not have been so protective of me if they knew that I am the wife of the fierce war chief known as Night Hawk."

"They do not know of this?"

"They know nothing of my life with you, or of my life before we met." She went on to explain how she had feigned complete loss of memory. "It was a good plan, for if I could recall nothing of my past, they could not expect answers to their many questions."

"The spirits have blessed me with a wise and beautiful mate," he said with admiration. "Now we must find another excellent plan for getting you and War Cloud out of the fort. We have been watching, and the gates to the fort remain tightly closed. Do they suspect that we are near, and so they guard against attack?"

"I do not think the soldiers know that the warriors watch. General Connor is merely being cautious, for his troops have just returned from a battle with many warriors."

"This I know, for we were there. I am glad that we tracked them to this fort, or I might never have found you." He planted a light kiss on her brow.

"What are we to do, Night Hawk?"

He was quiet, thinking before he said, "Before many suns have passed, the soldiers will have to leave the fort to hunt and to bring water from the river. Perhaps we can go then, when the gates are again opened."

He felt, more than saw, her thoughtful frown. "Will they not send troops out to meet this supply train you spoke of? What will happen when they find you have lied to them?"

"But, wife, I have told them truly," he assured her, laughter in his voice. "There is a supply train but a day's journey toward the rising sun. Our warriors even now plan a raid. The supplies will never reach the gates of this fort."

He made love to her then, and stayed with her until dawn was near. Before he left her, he whispered low, "Keep War Cloud always with you, and watch for me. If they open the gates today, we will attempt our escape, but you must be ready to go without warning."

As Flame had predicted, troops were sent out from the fort to meet the supply train. General Connor hesitated to open the gates for any other reason, wanting to wait until the new supplies arrived safely. But when, by noon, the soldiers had used the last of their dwindling water supply, he was forced to rescind his order.

This was what Night Hawk had been waiting for. As the soldiers gathered their empty barrels and prepared to go to the river, Night Hawk approached Flame. He had forgotten to take into account Beau Harris's protective attitude toward Flame, however, and he soon found himself face to face with the determined young Southerner.

"I have come to escort the lady to the river," Night Hawk said, glaring at the blond soldier standing so near Flame's side.

The man returned his look and answered belligerently, "If she wants to go anywhere, I'll take her myself, Lieutenant."

Flame, War Cloud tied securely upon her back with a blanket, stepped forward and laid a staying hand on Beau's arm. "It's all right, Beau. The lieutenant and I became acquainted last evening, and I have asked him to escort me while I attend to my laundering. I am certain the lieutenant will see that no harm comes to me."

Beau turned pained blue eyes toward her, openly hurt that she would prefer another man's attentions to his own. In the short time they had known each other, he had become quite fond of her and had thought that she was beginning to return his feelings. "Are you sure you want to do this?" he questioned, hoping she would change her mind.

"Quite sure," she assured him, her small chin jutting outward in a stubborn gesture Night Hawk knew well.

"You'd better make damn certain Honey and her baby make it back here safely, or I'll have your hide, sir!" Beau warned Night Hawk, an angry glint in his eyes. "And it won't make a whole hell of a lot of difference to me if you outrank me or not, 'cause I'll enjoy taking your blamed head off your shoulders if you let anything happen to her."

Everything in Night Hawk urged him to meet

this man's challenge, but the gates were about to be opened, and he and Flame must leave now or risk missing their only chance of escape. With a final glare at Beau, he turned on his heel, expecting Flame to follow.

He almost jerked in surprise as she hurried to his side and placed her hand at the bend of his elbow. "White women do not walk behind their men," she explained softly. "They walk beside them, and the man usually offers his arm to guide her steps."

He eyed her skeptically, but said nothing as he lengthened his stride toward the open gates.

They made it through without mishap and walked slowly and calmly toward the river, where the rest of the men were filling the water barrels. Once there, Flame made a show of washing her clothing, while Night Hawk stood guard over her, his rifle resting in the crook of his arm. Beneath the brim of his hat, Night Hawk scanned the area, his sharp eyes noting every movement. There came a moment when everyone was busy, no one paying them the slightest attention.

"Now!" he whispered urgently, pulling her to her feet and shoving her ahead of him toward the cover of the trees as he guarded the area behind. "Run!" Soundlessly she ran across the open space between them and the first stand of trees, running as fast as her legs would carry her, War Cloud bumping along on her back. She ran without looking back, knowing that Night Hawk was close behind.

They had almost reached cover when Flame

heard a shout, followed closely by gunshots. Just as she entered the edge of the forest, she saw Night Hawk turn, drop to one knee, and take aim. With his confiscated rifle, one of the new repeaters, he fired off several shots. Flame did not stop to see how near their pursuers might be, nor how true Night Hawk's aim, though she heard at least two men cry out in pain. Night Hawk had told her to run, and she would run until she dropped before allowing the soldiers to catch her.

Suddenly she became aware of a new sound, beyond her own ragged breathing. It was the distinctive hiss and whistle of arrows flying through the air. Only then did she notice the warriors perched high on branches in the trees. As if by magic, Stone Face was before her, sitting astride his horse and leading two more. Someone, she knew not who, boosted her upon the back of the nearest mount. Night Hawk flung himself astride the other and they were racing through the trees, Flame clinging to the fluttering mane of her horse and War Cloud bouncing along in his make-shift blanket cradleboard.

They had done it! They were free! As their horses carried them swiftly to the top of the hillock from which Night Hawk had first seen Flame in the fort below, Flame began to laugh. Peals of merry laughter echoed off of the surrounding hills, bringing smiles to the faces of the warriors who heard it. She could have danced and sang and shouted her joy to the heavens. Her happiness showed in the glorious glow of her face and in the sparkle of her sky-blue eyes. It bubbled over in her infectious laughter, the smile that curved her lips, the exultation that radiated from her very being.

She stopped her mount on the crest of the hill, warrior husband at her side, the wind creating a bright banner of her unbound hair; as she gazed down at the fort full of enraged, befuddled soldiers, her triumphant laughter floated down to them on the wings of the wind. This day, one slight woman and one daring Indian brave had won their own small victory over their enemies.

If Little Rabbit and Crooked Arrow were surprised at Flame's return to the Cheyenne camp, they hid it well. Shining Star was ecstatic at having her friend home again, and it seemed the entire village breathed a collective sigh of relief to have their Dreamer back among them.

While Flame quickly settled back into her old routine, the warriors continued to plague the soldiers at Fort Connor and elsewhere in their territory. When, one day shortly after Flame's escape, most of the soldiers left Fort Connor and returned to Fort Laramie, the tribes celebrated their victory over the cavalrymen. They had sent them packing back to the safety of Fort Laramie.

The few remaining soldiers were a small problem, but the chiefs agreed that these men, too, must be forced to flee. They besieged the fort, cutting off all supplies intended for the hapless troops. Winter set in, and still the Indians held the soldiers prisoner behind the walls of their

own stockade. Soon the starving soldiers began
to desert the fort. One by one they sneaked away
under cover of night, preferring to take their
chances with the Indians and the winter wilderness than to slowly starve to death.

Many of these men managed to elude the few
Indians who now kept watch over the fort. A few
were not so fortunate. One such man was
dragged into the Cheyenne camp one day, led
through the village with a rope about his neck,
like a dog on a leash, while the Cheyenne cursed
and screamed at him. They threw rocks and
stones, and beat him with sticks as he stumbled
past them.

Hearing raised voices, Flame's curiosity was
aroused. Taking her fox cape from its peg, she
stepped outside the tipi to investigate this new
disturbance. Despite herself, pity welled up in
her as she viewed the skinny, dirty captive being
led to the center of the village. The man was so
thin that his ribs showed clearly along his sides.
He wore no shirt or shoes, and his trousers were
in tatters. Blood spattered the fresh snow where
he walked, for the tender flesh of his bare feet was
shredded.

So weak was he that he stumbled several times,
and when his captor finally halted near the
central fire, the man fell to his knees almost at
Flame's feet. He knelt there, head bent, wheezing
for breath. When at last he raised his head,
Flame gasped in dismayed recognition. The captive soldier was none other than Beau Harris!

Bleary blue eyes, as old as the ages, stared up at

her from a grime-coated face so thin that she wondered that the bones did not pierce his skin. He blinked, as if to clear his vision. "Miss Honey?" he murmured, not sure that she was truly there. Then he promptly lost consciousness.

Beau was dragged away and tied to a pole at the center of the village. Even as this was taking place, Flame hurried to locate her husband. She was going to see to it that Beau Harris was freed, and she would use all the persuasion in her power to accomplish this. The soldier had protected her, been kind and considerate, and she would not stand idly by and watch him executed.

Flame found Night Hawk at a gathering of the chiefs in the council lodge. Ordinarily she would not think to call him from such a meeting, but today she did not hesitate. He had no sooner stepped from the lodge than she told him, "Beau Harris, the soldier at Fort Connor who was so kind to me, has been taken prisoner. Your warriors have just brought him into the village." Her small chin jutted outward as she eyed him determinedly. "I want his life spared, Night Hawk. Beau protected me and War Cloud when others would have harmed us, and his life must not be taken in return for his kindnesses toward us."

Looking down at her, taken aback by her staunch defense of this enemy soldier, Night Hawk asked tersely, "This is the man with the yellow hair? The one who would have challenged me for you?"

Flame nodded. "Yes."

"He wants you," Night Hawk was swift to

point out. "I have seen his desire for you in his face. Why should I save the life of a man who desires my wife?"

His wife gave him a look that spoke of her disgust at this lame argument. "It matters not what Beau Harris may think of me, husband, for I do not return his feelings. You are my husband, the father of my child and the man I love with all my heart. Yet I cannot let this man, who gave me protection and shelter, meet death at the hands of our people. Without his help, War Cloud and I might not have remained safe until you found us. We owe him a great debt, and we cannot repay him with torture."

"He is yet our enemy, wife," Night Hawk argued. "If we free him, he will return to the cavalry. He will ride against us another time, perhaps hoping to kill me and take you for himself. Would you risk saving his life this day just to have him come against us as our enemy later? If the warriors have brought him here, he would easily be able to lead the soldiers to our camp."

"Your jealous words do you little honor," she answered, facing him determinedly. "The camp will move again soon, and the soldiers will not know where we have gone."

"One does not spare one's enemy and not live to regret it," he told her.

"Just speak with him, Night Hawk," she implored, her eyes going soft as she turned her feminine wiles on him full force. "Beau did not want to come west with the cavalry. He did not want to be your enemy. He was a prisoner in the big war between the white men. His people were badly defeated. After the war was over, all he wanted to do was to go home again to his family, but he was forced to join the cavalry instead. This was not his wish; he had no choice but to do this. If you were to free him now, I do not think he would rejoin the other soldiers. I think he would gladly give his word to go home to his family, as he wished to do before."

"I will think on this matter," Night Hawk conceded, "but do not think to sway my judgment with sweet words and soft looks, Flame. Your charms are many and delightful, but they will not serve to change my mind." His dark eyes gleamed as he bit back the grin that teased at the corners of his mouth.

Catching her lip between her teeth, she gazed up at him sheepishly. "Yet you still enjoy my charms, husband," she said, deliberately letting her eyes trail toward his bulging breechclout. "And you know that when I am pleased, I return the favor in full measure."

His brows arched as he returned her sensual survey. "You would bribe me with your favors, wife?" he asked softly, intrigued despite himself.

"No. I do not barter with my body, but a wise man knows that when his wife is content and happy, she is far more pleasant to be near than when she is displeased."

In the end, Night Hawk agreed to speak with the captive. Face to face once more with this white man who desired his wife, Night Hawk found it hard to listen with an open mind and heart, as Flame had asked him to do. Yet he did try, for Flame was right when she said that they owed Harris a debt, and Night Hawk's pride demanded that he honor that debt.

"My wife has asked that your life be spared," he told Harris, speaking in very precise, clear English.

"Your wife?" Harris asked weakly. He could not recall the last time he'd had a decent meal, or even enough tainted food to fill his stomach. The fort had been under siege for months now. Many of his fellow soldiers had already died of starvation, malnutrition, scurvy, and pneumonia as a result. Beau was certain he was not far from joining them, if these savages did not kill him first. Now, here was this war chief called Night Hawk, the very man who had taken Honey from the fort, saying some nonsense about his wife, and the possibility of his life being spared. What was going on here?

"My wife," Night Hawk proceeded to tell him. "The woman you knew as Honey Rose. Here she is called Flame."

Harris frowned, trying to concentrate in his weakened condition. "Honey is your wife?"

Night Hawk nodded affirmatively. "And the child with her is our son, War Cloud."

"Did I see her here earlier?" Harris asked, shaking his head to try and clear it. "I seem to recall seeing her, if I was not dreaming it."

"She is here," Night Hawk affirmed.

Now he turned the conversation away from his wife, resenting the fact that this man was so interested in her. "Tell me, Harris. If we were to set you free, where would you go? What would you do?"

The soldier's answer came readily. "I would go home, if I still have the strength to get there."

"Where is this home you speak of?"

"Far from here," Harris said with a wistful sigh. "It is to the east and south, in a land filled with beautiful lakes and moss-draped trees and the most fragrant flowers on earth. God!" he exclaimed. "I'd give anything to see it again, to hold my mother in my arms, to hear my sister's sweet voice, to know if Delia is still waiting for me."

"Who is this Delia?"

"She's my fiancée."

"Fee-ahn-say?" Night Hawk asked with a frown. "I do not know this word."

"My betrothed," Harris explained. "The woman who has promised to marry me, if I every get home again. Hell, she's probably given up on me by now and married someone else, with my luck. If they didn't get my letters, they probably think I died long ago."

"Do you care much for this woman?" Night Hawk was curious now. He was sure he had not mistaken the interest on Harris's face when he had looked at Flame, but if the man had a woman of his own waiting in his village, one who expected him to marry with her, perhaps he would not present a threat to Night Hawk after all.

"Yes," Harris answered softly. "All the time I was in that Yankee prison, it was thoughts of

Delia that kept me strong. As long as I knew that she was waiting, I refused to give up hope. Then I was drafted into the damned cavalry, instead of being allowed to go home!" His voice shook with anger and resentment. "It isn't bad enough that they ruined an entire way of life, burned and pillaged the finest homes and fields, and left folks starving and homeless. They won the blasted war! Why couldn't they at least let us go home to pick up the broken pieces of our lives and try to hold our families together?"

Night Hawk eyed him with open curiosity now. "You do not like being a soldier?" he asked. "If you were free to leave our village, would you not rejoin your fellow soldiers at Fort Laramie?"

"When hell freezes over!" Harris exclaimed vehemently. Seeing Night Hawk's confusion, he said, "No. Let them think I died out here. I don't owe them any loyalty. If you let me go, I'll head home again as fast as my legs will carry me there. I'll crawl home on my knees, if need be."

"And you would stay there?" Night Hawk persisted. "You would go and marry this Delia and never again enter upon Cheyenne lands, nor cast burning looks of desire upon my wife?"

Harris's eyes widened in surprise, and he sat mute, staring at the warrior. Night Hawk nodded. "Yes, I have seen the fire in your eyes when you look at Flame," he snarled, his dark eyes narrowing dangerously. "I know of your lust for her, and it angers me to have another man openly desire my wife. I would slay you without thought, but Flame has reminded me of our debt to you, for your protection while she and War Cloud were detained at the fort. Yet, though she begs for your life, I warn you—Flame is mine. She is the mother of my son. She will forever belong to me. Have no thoughts of taking her from me, or I will gladly drive my knife into your heart, soldier."

"She—uh, she wants to be here? To stay with you?" Harris questioned hesitantly.

Night Hawk drew himself up proudly. "Flame would rather forfeit her life than leave me," he told his enemy. "Did she not leave with me gladly when I came for her at the fort? Does this not prove the truth of my words?"

Harris considered this. "No offense, chief, but if I could hear from her own lips that she is happy here and doesn't wish to return to her own people, it would greatly relieve my mind."

"I will send for her now, that you will know that I have not forced her to say such words to you," Night Hawk offered. "I will let you speak with her alone, that you may believe what she tells you. In return I will have your word that you will leave this place if you are released, that you will go far from here and never return. If you promise this and are not true to your word, if ever I face you again in battle in your cavalry uniform, I will take great pleasure in killing you, Harris—and I will do so very slowly and in the most painful manner I can arrange. This I swear to you, upon my honor as a war chief."

Beau believed him. The malignant gleam in those black eyes warned him well. "I have told you the truth. I want no more of this land or its Indians or its stinking cavalry. If you let me go, I swear I'll hightail it out of this territory so fast, my feet won't even touch the ground. All I want is to go home and mind my own business and be left alone to live my life with the people I love."

"Is that not what we all wish?" Night Hawk answered gruffly. "We have tried to tell your white brothers this, but they do not hear our words. They want our land, and because they wish for it they believe that they can come here and take it from us. They come and destroy our land, burn our villages, rape and kill our women and children. All we, too, want to do is to be left in peace upon the lands that have been ours for longer than our ancestors can recall."

In that single moment, these two enemies, white and Cheyenne, shared a look of mutual accord. "I wish I could tell you that it would be that way again for your people," Harris said with a tired sigh, "but I don't think that is ever going to happen. White men are a greedy lot, Chief Night Hawk. They'll never stop coveting your land, never stop trying to take it from your grasp until they have stolen it all. The battles will go on, the blood will flow, lives on both sides will be lost, and may God forgive us all for the agony we bring upon ourselves and others."

Beau Harris was released soon after hearing from Flame that she was more than content with her life here among the Cheyenne. "I love my husband very dearly," she told him. "He is my life, my soul, the very air I breathe. Without him, I would not want to live."

She sent Beau on his way with a borrowed set of buckskin clothes, a bundle of food, prayers for his safety, and the hope that he would soon be reunited with his sweet Delia. "When you think of me, if you ever do, think of me happy," she told him, "and I will imagine you gladly wed to your sweetheart, dandling a baby on each knee. God speed and bless you."

Chapter 28

Spring thaws brought messengers through the many camps and villages. The white soldiers wanted to parley for peace with the tribes. A big talk was being arranged at Fort Laramie. Upon learning that their tribe was to attend the negotiations, Flame was torn between elation and dismay. At long last she would be returning to Fort Laramie, and if her father was not there, she would at least have news of him. However, if he were there, she was sure he would try to make her leave Night Hawk and return east with him. He would be hurt and angry when she refused to do so. It was a terrible dilemma.

Neither was Night Hawk pleased that the tribal council had decided that they would attend the peace talks. Was this a trick? A trap? Had Beau Harris gone back to Fort Laramie after all and told the soldiers all he had seen and heard in the Cheyenne camp? If he had, Night Hawk swore to track the man like a dog and tear his tongue from his throat!

Other unsettling thoughts plagued Night Hawk, too—thoughts similar to Flame's. His wife had been overjoyed when he rescued her from Fort Connor, but would she feel the same this time? What if her father, the general, were still at Fort Laramie? What if the soldier chief tried to talk Flame into going home with him to the East? What if Flame, upon seeing her father again, desired to go with him, choosing to leave Night Hawk?

Lying awake beside his sleeping wife, Night Hawk's arm tightened convulsively about her in denial. No! He would die before he let her go! Even if she desired to do so, he would forbid it! He would do everything in his power to prevent her from leaving him! She had pledged her love to him, and he would hold her to that promise, with force if need be. He could not believe that she would give up her child in order to gain a freedom she no longer seemed to care for, but he would use her love for War Cloud against her, if necessary.

Night Hawk's heart told him he was being foolish. Flame loved him. She would never choose to leave him; she would never leave their son. Still, his thoughts nagged at him endlessly, and he dreaded going to Fort Laramie for the talks. Perhaps he could keep Flame in the Cheyenne camp, outside the fort itself, and thus avoid any problems. Perhaps no one would even notice her there, with her bright, flame-colored hair that announced clearly her white blood. And perhaps he was deceiving himself in thinking that they could go to Ft. Laramie and not have someone remark upon his white wife.

Flame turned toward him, her arms hugging his lean waist. "You do not sleep, husband," she murmured groggily. "What do you think of here in the dark that keeps you from your rest?"

He answered truthfully. "Fort Laramie."

She nodded. "I, too, have doubts about this journey. I worry lest it be a trap, and I wonder if my father is yet there." Her fingers came up to wind themselves into his dark hair. It had grown long again in the past months, and now hung loose past his shoulders. Soon it would be long enough to wear in braids of a respectable length once more.

"Have you had no dreams of the treaty talks?" he asked hesitantly.

"No, but you know that I am not always blessed with the warning visions. They come when they will, not when I want."

"And if your father is there?" he questioned softly. "Will he challenge me for you?"

"There will be nothing to challenge, Night Hawk. While I would be glad to see him again, to visit with him, I would not agree to stay with him. You must know that I would refuse to leave you, for how could I exist without my heart, which is in your keeping always?"

Her loving words brought joy to his heart, and a measure of peace, but as he pulled her under him and began to make sweet love to her, he could not lay all his fears to rest. Something told him that there would be trouble ahead for them at Fort Laramie.

They arrived outside Fort Laramie in early summer, at the start of the month the white men called June. Dull Knife, Red Cloud, and many of the other chiefs were already camped there with their tribes. The treaty talks had not yet begun; there was a slight delay while they waited for other tribes to arrive.

At first everything seemed to go well. Flame was content to stay in the Cheyenne camp, slightly away from the fort. Night Hawk would meet with the other chiefs for talks that often lasted long into the night. He brought back the news that Flame's father had long since left the fort and returned east, and Flame was both saddened and relieved to be able to avoid the confrontation she had feared. Night Hawk also confirmed that Beau Harris had not been seen by anyone at the fort since deserting Fort Connor, which was now renamed Fort Reno. His fellow soldiers assumed him dead.

The trading posts and sutler's store were doing a brisk business in trade, and Flame longed to see the goods for herself. She had many fine robes to exchange, and wished to trade for cooking utensils, cloth, and needles and the like; but she knew she must not risk it. Shining Star offered to exchange Flame's robes for her, bartering well for a cast-iron cooking pot, two metal spoons, a supply of beads, and a length of red cloth. Night Hawk brought her several colorful ribbons for her bright hair. Flame forced herself to be grateful for their kindness and stayed strictly to the camp.

This proved not to be enough, however, for one day, as Flame was admiring Shining Star's newest purchases, Stone Face rode into camp as if demons were on his heels. Wheeling his horse to a stop before them, he blurted breathlessly, "They have arrested Night Hawk!"

Flame's heart stopped in her chest, and she came as close to fainting as ever in her life. "Why? How?"

He stared grimly down at her. "The soldiers are even now on their way to get you, Flame, and take you to the fort. Someone there has recognized you from before, when you were here with your father."

"How can this be?" she asked. "I have stayed in the camp all this time."

There was no more time for talk. The soldiers were there, riding directly toward her, their guns drawn to prevent anyone from stopping their mission. "Take care of my son," Flame told Shining Star. "Do not let him out of your sight for one moment."

To Stone Face, she said, "Do not attempt to stop this, my friend. I will go with them, and I will make certain that Night Hawk is released. Do not worry. Your chief will be back among you before the sun has set, or I will have someone's blood on my hands."

The soldiers were upon her, eyeing Stone Face with malevolent looks. "Sarah Wise?" the man in the lead addressed her. "We have come to take you to the fort."

By the insignia on his uniform, Sarah knew him as a major; from his arrogant demeanor, she knew instinctively that he was the cause of this trouble. She had seen his type many times before, growing up as she had with her father. This man had a lust for glory, and would let nothing stand in his way. It shone from his eyes like a beacon; it radiated from him in his very stance and the tone of his voice, which grated on her ears like gravel against tin.

"I do not know you, Major," she said, drawing herself up haughtily. "Why do you come here for me?"

Her attitude stunned him somewhat, and he needed a moment to regain his composure. Undoubtedly he had expected to find her reduced to a spineless idiot, or at least ready to throw herself at him in tearful gratitude. "One of our men has recognized you as General Wise's daughter, missing from Fort Laramie for almost three years now." He frowned, as if suddenly unsure of himself or his information, then rallied. "You need not fear coming with us. The warrior who has held you captive has been jailed in our stockade. He can't harm you any more."

"You, Major, are an ass!" she hissed, turning on her heel and walking from him.

He nudged his horse forward to block her way. "Where do you think you are going?" he asked curtly. "I have orders to bring you to the fort."

She glared up at him, shooting blue arrows of spite from her sparkling eyes. "I must see to my son, Major," she answered, enjoying the shock that flitted over his features. "When I have placed him in the care of my trusted friends, I shall then select my pony from the herd and ride to the fort with your soldiers."

"You needn't bother with your pony," he instructed her tersely, fast becoming irritated with her superior attitude. "One of my men will take you behind him on his horse."

"Have you no ears on your head?" she asked insolently. "I will ride my own mount. I will not be led into your fort like some unfortunate beggar." She stalked away from him, her back rigid and her eyes flaming, as soldiers and Cheyenne alike looked on.

Their arrival at the fort was that of a queen with her escort, as Flame sat straight and proud astride her pony. Her hair was a vivid banner blowing in the breeze, her pert nose was lifted high in the air, and her eyes gleamed with determination. Certainly, she presented anything but the image of a broken captive grateful to be rescued.

Major Danvers led her directly to the office of the fort commander, a congenial colonel who was trying desperately to organize the treaty talks. So far he had been very hospitable toward the gathering tribes—until Major Danvers had come to him with news of General Wise's daughter. The colonel had been forced to place Chief Night Hawk under arrest, much against his inclination, for he did not want anything to hinder the progress of these treaty talks. Lord in heaven, there were thousands of Indians camped around Fort Connor now, and more on the way! The last thing he needed now was to rile these savages.

The colonel found himself face to face with one very irate savage, within moments of her arrival. Flame marched into his office, planted both fists squarely on his desk, glared into his face, and demanded loudly, "I want my husband released, Colonel, and I want him released now!"

The startled officer stared back at her in confusion, his gaze switching to Danvers as he asked in a befuddled tone, "Is this General Wise's daughter, the woman you told me about?"

Before Danvers could utter a word, Flame announced. "Damn right I am, Colonel, and I'll have your head on a platter if my husband is not released immediately!"

Danvers bristled, and the poor colonel seemed about to pull his hair out. "Please, Miss Wise. Sit down and let's get this matter straightened out. I am sure we can come to some understanding if you will just calm yourself a bit."

"I am calm, Colonel," she retorted. "As calm as any woman would be upon learning that her husband has been arrested." She did accept the offer of a chair, however, for she was shaking so badly in her anger and her fear for Night Hawk that she feared her legs would not support her much longer.

"Now then," the colonel said, drawing a deep breath, "you *are* Sarah Wise, General Wise's daughter?"

"Yes." Her answer was clipped.

"And you were abducted from this very fort three years ago?"

"True."

"And the man we have arrested, this Chief Night Hawk, is the man who captured you?"

She gave a curt nod. "I want him set free. You have no reason to hold him here."

"He abducted you, Miss Wise, from this fort. That is reason enough," Danvers put in with a snide smirk.

Flame leveled a look at Danvers that should have shriveled him to a burnt cinder. "And my word alone will be reason enough for you to be digging latrines until your retirement, Major!" she snapped back. "You are the one who keeps reminding everyone that I am a general's daughter. I would advise you not to forget that fact yourself!"

The colonel cleared his throat and shot Danvers a warning look. Turning to Flame, he said calmly, "Young lady, I will admit to being more than a little confused at the moment. Why do you defend this savage who abducted you and forced you into a life of slavery? Do you fear him that greatly? Do you think that he will escape and find you again if you do not try to get him released?"

Flame nearly shrieked in exasperation. "Is everyone here completely deaf? Haven't you heard a word I have said?" She drew a deep breath and spoke very distinctly, as if she were talking to two morons—which, indeed, she was beginning to suspect they were. "Night Hawk is my husband and the father of my son. I am not some unfortunate slave, but the honored wife of a chief. I do not fear my husband, nor do I consider him a savage. I am staying with him of my own will, Colonel. I do not wish to be rescued by your soldiers, and I heartily resent your interference in my life!"

"But, Miss Wise, surely you realize our concern!" the colonel said, trying to pacify her. "What will we tell your father about all this?"

She met his look evenly. "Tell him the truth. Tell him you attempted to rescue me and that I would have no part of it."

"My dear girl," he groaned. "I can't tell him that!"

"Fine. Then I will!" she stated firmly. "Are your telegraph wires still connected and operating?"

"Yes," he conceded hesitantly.

"Then I will send him a message explaining everything, including the fact that I am dealing with brainless, braying asses who refuse to release my husband!" She looked down her slim nose at the two hapless officers. "Believe me, sirs, he will not be pleased to hear of your inept bunglings. Heads will roll before all is said and done. Obviously you have never dealt with my father when his feathers are ruffled, or you would grant my request immediately."

Danvers stuck his foot in his mouth again by threatening, "We could refuse to let you send a telegraph to your father, you know. We could lock you up and send you to your father by force, if need be."

Fire blazed from her eyes as she rounded on him. "I wouldn't try that, Major! There are thousands of Indians outside this fort who are none too happy at the moment that you have arrested Chief Night Hawk. They will resent even more your holding me. One word, one gesture, and I could have them all on your neck in the blink of an eye. Dead men win no glory, Danvers. Challenge me, and I will spit on your grave by the end of this day! This I promise you!"

The colonel glanced from one to the other in acute distress. Finally his gaze cut to Danvers with a look that clearly promised retribution for all the trouble he had caused. "Major Danvers, you will release Chief Night Hawk, with our profound apologies for his arrest, and you will see that he and this woman are escorted safely back to their tribe. Then you will report back to me." He sighed heavily, dropping his head to his hands. "Let us just hope that in stirring up this nice little hornet's nest, you have not done irreparable damage to our treaty negotiations."

Danvers' jaw dropped open as he stared at his superior. There was a look of disbelieving horror on his face, as if he had just seen his expected promotion taking wing. In fact, from the colonel's disgruntled tone, he would be fortunate if he remained a major after this disastrous episode. He had assumed that he would be greatly lauded for rescuing General Wise's daughter, not flayed alive by her sharp tongue, then shredded by his superior officer.

"And see to it that Miss Wise is allowed to send a message to her father before she leaves," the colonel added. "I assume, young woman, that

ou will advise your father of our cooperation in
his matter?"

Flame tempered her smug smile with difficul-
y. "Yes, Colonel. I will tell him of your consider-
tion in the face of having to deal with such a
umbling inferior staff. Also, I will make it clear
o him that I am staying with my husband of my
wn will, and that you did, indeed, do everything
n your power to dissuade me."

His brows rose as he stared at her. "You are an
mmensely stubborn woman, Miss Wise."

"Thank you, Colonel. My husband and my
ather would both agree with you, I am sure."

By nightfall, Flame and Night Hawk were both
ack in the Cheyenne camp, and word had
pread throughout the fort and beyond of her
reat bravery and determination in facing the
oldier chief. She had rushed into the fort like a
nountain lioness in defense of her mate, and
ome away victorious. Their pride in her was
oundless, and the entire tribe celebrated far into
he night.

Only one thing dimmed Flame's joy that eve-
ing. She had sent a message to her father, one
vhich had caused her great pain. She could only
ope that he would someday understand and
ccept her choice. Even as she sent him her love,
he knew that she would be hurting him terribly,
or she was his only child. It would break his
eart to learn that she was alive, yet chose to
emain with the Cheyenne. In hopes of temper-
ng his disappointment, she told him of Night
Iawk and War Cloud, and of her love for them

both, asking him to try to understand and forgive, and not to retaliate. She was happy and well, and she wished the same for him.

Late that night, with his wife curled tightly at his side, Night Hawk attempted to comfort her. "You were very brave today, my firebrand. The entire village speaks of your daring coup. Perhaps I should make you one of my warriors, for I hear your tongue and your temper are more fierce than any of our weapons. You have brought much honor to our lodge this day."

"I bring more than that, mighty chief," she answered with a grin. As he watched, she rose and drew from beneath her doeskin dress an ammunition belt filled with cartridges for Night Hawk's rifle. "I took this while the soldier was busy sending my message to my father and was not watching."

He laughed with her, his eyes filled with admiration. "You dare much, my lioness."

"I would dare anything for you, Night Hawk," she said softly. "Anything."

He drew her near to him once more, tenderly kissing her brow. "I would have spared you the pain of sending the message to your father if it were possible," he told her.

"I know," she whispered, tears filling her eyes. "I know, but at least now he knows that I am alive and well, that I am happy with my husband and son and not living in misery. Perhaps he will gain some comfort from knowing this."

It was a few days later that treaty negotiations fell apart, not because of the incident of Night

Hawk's arrest, but for other reasons entirely. It came to the chiefs' attention that the white men had already brought added troops into Indian country in preparation for building roads through land which the tribes had yet to agree to let the white men pass. This arrogance angered the tribes greatly, resulting in their swift departure and adamant rejection of all the white men had to say or offer. They would not parley with men who dealt unfairly with them.

To add insult to injury, the cavalry immediately began building not only roads, but two more forts in the Indian territory. All that summer the soldiers worked feverishly to build Fort Phil Kearny, and then Fort C.F. Smith even deeper into the Powder River country that was the home and prime hunting grounds of the Sioux and Northern Cheyenne and Arapaho tribes.

The tribes retaliated by constantly harassing the soldiers, attacking and waylaying their supply trains and luring the cavalrymen into open battle away from the security of their forts. Far into the fall, the warriors continued to raid and plague the soldiers, and when autumn began to show signs of giving way to winter, the tribal chiefs decided to set up their winter camps within easy striking distance of Fort Kearny, in order to further nettle their enemies. As they had done with Fort Connor, they intended to cut off all supplies to the fort and hold it under siege until the soldiers left or were all dead.

It was in early winter that Flame discovered she was again with child. War Cloud was now two winters of age, and she suspected that she had conceived almost as soon as she ceased to nurse her son. Night Hawk was pleased that she was to bear him a second child so soon, and Flame had to shake her head in amused exasperation at his blatant display of masculine pride in his own virility.

Then there came a further development, and though she regretted giving him more cause to prance about like a cock pheasant showing off his grand feathers, she could not keep such news to herself for long. Also, she could hardly wait to see the shock upon his face when she told him.

She waited until they had eaten their evening meal and were enjoying the quiet time afterward together. "Night Hawk?" she said, glancing at him as he repaired a halter for his horse.

He grunted an acknowledgment, his attention on the intricate braiding in his hands.

"I have had another dream," she told him casually. "This one is about the child I will bear you."

His head came up and he scanned her face for some clue. "Was it a good dream or a bad one?" he asked.

"I cannot tell, for I do not know how you will react to what I have seen." She had his full attention now, as she continued. "How do you feel about twins, my husband?" she questioned, hiding a grin.

"Twins?" he echoed dumbly, his jaw going slack in surprise.

She laughed openly now. "Yes, twins, you virile beast! You have gotten me with not one child this time, but two! I have dreamed of birthing two babies, a boy and a girl."

Night Hawk was stunned. Then he rewarded her with a smile that could have outshone the sun. "You are amazing!" he exclaimed. Coming to her, he grabbed her up and swung her wildly in a circle about the tipi.

"I was about to say the same of you!" she giggled joyfully, clinging helplessly to him as he whirled her round and round.

"Our people will shout your name to the skies, claiming you the greatest of women," he prophesied. "Already they revere you for your dreams, and now to bear twins to their chief!"

"It is not all that unusual, Night Hawk," she said modestly, wriggling down until her toes could once more touch the ground.

"Among the tribes it is a most rare and wondrous event," he told her, keeping her securely within his embrace.

Her smile matched his as all humility deserted her. "As we are rare and wondrous lovers," she declared softly, her eyes shining with love as she arched upward to bring her lips to his. "And so very blessed."

Chapter
29

The twins were born in early summer, a boy and a girl as Flame had predicted. Both the babies were very tiny, but strong and healthy nonetheless. Blue Wolf, the boy child, had dark hair streaked with red highlights, and eyes so deep a shade of blue that they appeared almost black. Sky Blaze, who Flame was pleased to have been able to name herself, had lighter skin and Flame's vibrant red hair, a startling combination with her large onyx eyes so like her father's.

While Flame was recovering from their birth, which had been remarkably easy despite the double effort, the entire tribe celebrated this unusual event. As Night Hawk had told her, the birth of twins within the tribes was a rare occurrence. Also, as he had predicted, Flame's status within the tribe rose even higher because of this.

She was soon up and about, glad to be able to move around normally once more. She had been even more rounded with the twins than with War Cloud, though she had thought it impossible, and it was a great relief to see where her feet were again. Night Hawk had teased her mightily that if she had gained much more weight, he would have to fashion a rope hoist for her inside the tipi. As it was, he had cleverly created a light, comfortable cradleboard capable of holding both the babies on Flame's back at one time.

Night Hawk also proved a remarkable help when it came to caring for the infants. He often took War Cloud in hand, taking the toddler about with him on his duties about the village, while Flame tended to the babies. War Cloud was not sure what to think of the two tiny invaders who had usurped his exalted position in his lodge, taking much of his mother's attention from him. The added attention from his father helped to quell any jealousy, however, and made War Cloud puff up with pride.

Many times, Flame and Night Hawk had to stifle their laughter at War Cloud's newly assumed self-importance, as Night Hawk pointed out to him how much bigger and stronger War Cloud was than his siblings, and how he would be expected to look after them and protect them from harm.

"If we are not careful, War Cloud will grow as vain as his father," Flame warned, her blue eyes twinkling with suppressed mirth.

"Let us just hope he is as wise and as brave as his sire," Night Hawk countered with a knowing grin.

"How humble you are, husband!" she teased, mocking him with bowed head and a giggle.

Night Hawk reached out and tugged lightly at her long braid. "A war chief has little need of humility, woman. He must be bold and daring, and count many coup."

She gave him a measuring gaze, letting her eyes rove his body. "Of course, it helps if he is also tall and strong and handsome as well," she said with raised brows, as if assessing his looks.

"Are you not the most fortunate of women to have found such a man?" he boasted, making her laughter ring out again.

"You are, indeed, most vain, my handsome husband," she told him, "and I am, indeed, a most fortunate wife."

The summer was spent replenishing their depleted food supplies, following the buffalo onto the plains, and raiding the three forts in the Powder River country. Earlier that spring, before Flame's twins were born, the white men had proposed another treaty talk at Fort Laramie. The United States Government was greatly concerned about the continued war with the tribes, especially in the aftermath of the Fetterman Massacre the previous December. In that bloody battle, some distance outside of Fort Phil Kearny, more than eighty cavalrymen had been led into a trap by the Indians. Not one soldier had returned alive.

Now the whites again wanted to bargain for peace, but Night Hawk wanted none of this. He and his tribe sided with Red Cloud's Sioux, saying that peace would not come until all the white men had gone from the Powder River country for good. So they stayed away from the talks and hunted game for their families instead. Later they heard that the talks had amounted to nothing more than lame words by the white leaders; they had missed little.

Twice that summer, Flame dreamed of raids on the forts that would result, disastrously, in many warriors being slain. Adhering to her warning, Night Hawk's tribe declined to participate in these two particular raids, trying to convince others of the danger also. Some listened; others did not. Again her visions proved true, but none of Night Hawk's warriors were lost in those battles.

One incident that summer would remain in the memories of the tribes for some time, to be chuckled over and retold over many a winter fire. Troubled over the iron tracks the white men were laying across some of their best hunting land, those tracks upon which the fearsome Iron Horse traveled, the warriors tried to think of some way of ridding themselves of this problem. After many unsuccessful attempts, they hit upon a plan that worked. The warriors pulled the bars of the tracks apart and waited to see what might happen. The train lurched from the tracks, its wooden boxcars tumbling after it and landing on their sides.

Following a slight skirmish with the white men on the train, the warriors ransacked the boxcars, finding all manner of food and cloth and other goods, as well as several barrels of whiskey. Drunk on the potent brew, the tipsy warriors then decorated their horses with the bright cloth and raced their ponies across the plains, whooping and hollering like children. Many a brave warrior held an aching head in his hands the next day, moaning in misery, and many a wife shook her head in wry amusement at his foolishness.

Flame salvaged what was left of the yellow cloth still tied to Night Hawk's horse, thanked him quietly for the coffee and sugar he had brought home to her, and gave him a stern lecture on the evils of strong drink. Then she left him to his misery and joined Shining Star to exchange tales with her friend over their husbands' childish behavior.

The following fall, just before the winter snows, the government again tried to parley with the tribes. This time they sent General Sherman to negotiate for them, but even his efforts failed. Red Cloud's Sioux and many of those who agreed with the Sioux chief, Night Hawk included, gave the same answer as before. They would discuss peace only when the soldiers were gone from their lands. Sherman and his fellow negotiators returned east again, telling the tribes they would come again in the spring to talk.

Meanwhile, Flame tended happily to her little

family's needs. As her children grew, she was kept busy sewing new and larger garments for them, as well as those for herself and Night Hawk. There were endless chores about the lodge, but she accomplished them cheerfully, a smile on her lips and a song in her heart as she watched her family thrive and grow.

The children were a joy to her, their bright inquisitiveness delightful to witness. When War Cloud reached three winters of age, she began to teach him English, much as she had done with Night Hawk. Her children would not be ignorant of their enemy's ways, or the white heritage that flowed through their veins from their mother's blood. Such knowledge might save their lives one day, and Flame felt compelled to teach them all she could.

The twins were crawling now, and Flame had her hands full trying to keep both of them out of trouble. Everything they could clutch in their chubby little fingers went immediately into their mouths. Already Blue Wolf had tried to cut his teeth on Bandit's furry tail as the raccoon lay sleeping in his log in a winter stupor. The infant had received a mouthful of fur and a nasty scratch from the irritated raccoon, and would not soon bother the animal again.

Sky Blaze had somehow managed to get into a pouch of dried berries and consume enough to give herself a tremendous stomach ache and resulting loose bowels. Flame had walked the confines of the tipi with the miserable baby all through the night. After several accidents down Sky Blaze's legs and the front of Flame's dress, and over Night Hawk's protests, Flame had torn her precious cloth into squares for diapers for the girl. The rest of the tribal mothers could put up with this nonsense of letting their children run free of clothing to cover their little bottoms, but she was going to flaunt custom and do things more sensibly.

When she insisted upon dressing Blue Wolf in the bright yellow cloth pants, too, Night Hawk nearly cringed in embarrassment for his youngest son. How humiliating for the son of a chief! Flame merely eyed him malevolently and told him bluntly to mind his duties as a warrior and let her tend to hers as a mother as she saw fit. She was sick and tired of having one child or the other constantly messing themselves, their clothing, their bedding, and her! Knowing when to retreat quietly, Night Hawk wisely backed down on this issue.

Twice more during those long, cold winter months, Flame had to nurse her husband's wounds. Even as she damned this stupid war, she was profoundly thankful that neither injury had been fatal. First he came back to camp with a bullet hole in his thigh, which kept him in camp for a short time—too short a time for Flame's peace of mind.

Shortly after his remarkably fast recovery, his horse slipped on a patch of ice and fell, pinning Night Hawk beneath the thrashing animal. Despite two cracked ribs and a wrenched left shoulder, Night Hawk continued to lead his men into battle, bemoaning only the fact that he had been forced to destroy his favorite mount, since the horse had broken its leg in the fall.

"I will have a difficult time replacing that big stallion," he grumbled irritably, trying to rotate the stiffness from his shoulder. "He was a rare animal."

Flame placed Sky Blaze in her bed and came behind him to massage his shoulder for him. "Then you had better hope that nothing such as that ever happens to me, dear husband, for I would be much more difficult to replace," she told him, bending to blow softly in his ear.

He laughed and admitted, "I could search the earth and never find another woman as stubborn as you, Firebrand, though I doubt we would have to put you out of your misery for a mere broken leg. However, while you were mending, I might require another wife to tend to your duties," he teased.

"I will shoot you with your own arrows, Night Hawk, if you even think of bringing another wife into this tipi."

Ignoring the pain in his shoulder and ribs, he twisted about and kissed the pout from her lips. "Never, my lovely Blue Eyes. Never," he promised, pulling her into the cradle of his lap. A little later, claiming the excuse of his injuries, he set her atop him and let her direct their lovemaking that night.

Sherman returned in May as he had said he would, and again treaty talks did not go well. The tribes were adamant, refusing to speak of peace until the soldiers left the forts along the Powder River. Sherman's hands were tied, for the Government was screaming for peace with the Indians. Finally he had no other choice but to order the cavalry to vacate the three forts in the area; Fort Reno, which had formerly been called Fort Connor, Fort Phil Kearny, and Fort C. F. Smith. This he did in mid-summer, and the tribes watched from the hilltops as the soldiers packed their wagons and horses and left the forts. In the wake of the retreating cavalry, the Indians celebrated by setting fire to the forts.

Out of sheer pique, and to further demonstrate their power in this situation, the tribal chiefs let the white peace negotiators cool their heels a little longer before finally consenting to sit down to treaty talks. It was November before the treaty was signed and peace reigned once more across the land.

It would be a short interlude, but Flame was content that she had envisioned this time of peace between the soldiers and the tribes. She had seen this in her dreams; it was to be. Now the tribes could go back to hunting game and raising their families without fear of the soldiers. Now her warrior husband would spend more time in the village, and with her and their children. Night Hawk would have time to teach War Cloud to ride his new pony, and to fashion a bow and arrows for his son and instruct him in their proper use. He could get to know his two youngest children, and they him. Life would be good again—at least for a while.

What Flame had seen in her dream of peace

was only a peace between the Indians and the soldiers. She had not envisioned that, now that they were not busy fighting the cavalry, the tribes would devote their war efforts toward their traditional enemy tribes. Long before the white man had come into their lands, the various tribes had fought one another. While some were devoted brothers, protecting and aiding one another, others were mortal enemies for all time. Through countless generations, there had always been warriors in the tribes, for there was always an enemy to fight.

Still, while Night Hawk continued to train with his fellow warriors and planned hunts and raids, it was a more relaxed time for them. They found time to laugh and play among themselves. Often she and the children would watch as Night Hawk trained his new stallion. They walked, they talked, they enjoyed life and one another.

It was the same throughout many a village. Families and friends now gathered again, some traveling to see relatives in other tribes whom they had not seen in many moons. Marriages and births were joyously celebrated, without the pall of death to overshadow the ceremonies. Wives did not worry constantly that their men would be killed or wounded, that they might soon be widowed and their children fatherless. Games of skill, or games just for fun were once again enjoyed. Everyone felt more secure, safer, happier. Perhaps that was why, when the attack came, it was such a surprise to everyone.

The Cheyenne had moved to their winter camp, and all had been peaceful for some time.

Winter was being kind for once, holding back its biting winds and deep snows and fierce cold, and allowing the braves to hunt for game. There was no shortage of food in this Moon When the Snows Drift into the Tipis. Not this season. The spirits were smiling down upon their children, sending them a mild winter.

The warriors organized a bear hunt. For days they sharpened their weapons and planned their strategies. They invited men from nearby tribes to join them, and held special ceremonies. At last they rode out, in high spirits, all of them reminding Flame of small children on their way to a party. In recent years they had found no time for such sport, but now they could relish it all the more. Very few of the men did not go on this hunt. Only those too old or too young, or those whose duty it was to protect the women and children did not go.

The men were not gone from the village for half a day, when, seemingly out of nowhere, a band of Utes stormed into the camp. It was a small party of warriors, but fearsome to behold in their warpaint as they rode whooping and shouting into the very heart of the village. Suddenly all was chaos as women ran screaming, trying to gather their children together and shield them from the hail of arrows showering the air. Those Cheyenne men left in camp ran for their weapons in a desperate attempt to defend their charges. Flames leapt high into the sky as fire arrows torched the tipis.

In the midst of all this, Flame was fighting down her terror. She did not know where to run, where to hide from this horror bearing down upon her people. Screams rent the air, and smoke billowed from several nearby lodges. She crouched just inside her tipi, guarding her three frightened children with only her knife and one of Night Hawk's spare lances for weapons. Not knowing how else to protect them, she had hidden all three of them under a thick pile of robes, instructing a trembling War Cloud to keep the two babies quiet and not to come out from the robes for any reason, unless she told him to.

Now she watched in terror as Owl Eyes was struck down before her eyes. The old shaman fell, a tomahawk buried deep in his skull. To add to the horror, the Ute warrior who had slain him then dismounted and swiftly took the old man's scalp. Flame turned and vomited on the ground beside her, fighting the dark veil that threatened to enfold her in its waiting arms. *I must not faint!* she told herself as she watched an enemy warrior attack a Cheyenne woman who was trying to flee him. *I must protect my children!* She closed her eyes in desperation as a young boy was trampled beneath the hoofs of a horse, his screams bringing tears to her eyes.

When she dared to look again, it was to see two Ute warriors bearing down on her tipi. Leaping from his horse, one of them came toward her, a terrible grin making a grotesque mask of his face. Flame went wild. With a primitive scream, she lunged at him with the lance, but he was too quick for her. He grabbed the lance, jerking it from her grasp and tossing it aside.

Then he was upon her, binding her arms

tightly to her sides when she would have stabbed him with her knife. He dragged her, kicking and screaming, from the tipi, handing her up to the other warrior waiting on his horse. The world spun around her as she was thrown stomach-first across the horse in front of the mounted Ute, but she continued to struggle. She thrashed wildly, trying in vain to dislodge the warrior's hold on her. In heedless fury, she sank her teeth deeply into the copper thigh near her face, clawing at his leg with her fingernails. The pleasure of hearing his howl of pain was short-lived, as he kneed his horse into a fast trot, knocking the air from her lungs.

As Flame glanced anxiously back at her tipi, where her children lay hiding, she screamed in unbearable horror as she saw the first warrior set a torch to the outer skins of the lodge. Smoke began to billow as the edge caught and began to curl. He was setting fire to her tipi, with her children still inside! Visions of small charred bodies shimmered before her eyes.

"No!"

It was a wail straight from her soul. With a strength born of fear and anguish, she wrenched herself loose, launching herself from the moving horse. Before her feet touched the ground, she was running—running swiftly back toward her burning tipi and her babies, her eyes wide with fright.

The blow from behind stunned her, making her stagger to her knees. Stars danced before her eyes and her head felt as if it were splitting in two. Still she tried to reach her children, crawling and clawing with all her remaining strength as the earth began to spin violently around her. Hard hands pulled at her, hauling her up again and away from her heart's goal. The last thing her wavering gaze beheld were flames licking greedily at the outer covering of her lodge—red, orange —and then she saw nothing but black—deep, dark, infinite black.

Chapter 30

Her eyes were wide open, staring eerily at nothing. She neither moved nor blinked nor spoke. She did not see the circle of strange faces peering down at her in concern; she did not hear their voices, spoken in a tongue she would not have understood could she hear them. In no way did she respond as they bathed her, dressed her in a clean doeskin dress and moccasins, and combed the tangles from her brilliant red hair. She was as if dead, and yet alive, for her chest rose and fell just slightly with each breath. Her spirit hovered somewhere between the land of the living and that of the dead.

For three long suns the Utes watched over this woman with the hair of fire, the one known as the

Dreamer, whom they had stolen from the Cheyenne camp. The raid that day had been specifically for the purpose of capturing this one woman. They had pillaged and burned and wounded others, yes, but their main purpose had been to bring this powerful woman back to their own camp, that she would grace them with her blessed visions from now on.

Now, as they gazed worriedly down upon her unmoving body, seeing her strange blue eyes staring upward at nothing, Chief Broken Thorn rebuked the two warriors who had brought her there. "You were not to harm her," he said sternly.

Bear Paw again explained. "It could not be helped, my chief. She was as a wild cougar, clawing and biting and screaming. My thigh will bear the marks of her sharp teeth for many moons. When she would have run back into her burning lodge, I tapped her but lightly on the head with my tomahawk."

Singing Bird, the chief's wife, spoke up in defense of the young warrior. "The Dreamer Woman has but a small bump on her skull, husband. I do not think she lies in this trance from the blow to her head. I think it is the shock of the raid and what she might have witnessed."

"What are we to do for her?" Broken Thorn wondered aloud, his eyes admiring the Dreamer Woman's fair skin and bright hair.

Singing Bird shook her head. "We must wait and hope that she awakens from wherever her

mind travels. She is young and healthy. Her body
is strong. We must hope it calls to her mind to
join it soon."

It was the next day before Flame awoke, blinking at the light streaming through the tipi opening into her eyes. Cautiously, moving nothing but
her eyes, she glanced about her. This was not her
lodge, she knew, but neither did she think it
belonged to anyone she knew. She remembered
hearing strange voices, a language unfamiliar to
her, and she recalled wondering if she were in
heaven—or perhaps in hell.

Her mind was slowly awakening from its sleep,
bringing with it visions of all that had happened.
With each passing moment, Flame recalled
more, reviewing the terrible scenes once again.
Horror invaded her soul as she remembered
running frantically toward her burning tipi, calling out to her babies. Her very heart ripped
apart, and her screams filled the lodge again
and again—long, agonized shrieks for the loss
of her children in such a terrible way! In her unbearable pain, her fingers reached up to claw
at her face. They tore frenziedly at her clothes
and her hair in an unconscious effort to create
enough physical pain to ease that of her broken
heart.

The next thing she knew, other hands were
pulling at her, shaking her. Strange faces swam
before her tear-filled eyes, foreign words assaulted her ears. Someone slapped her smartly across
the face. She gasped for air, suddenly unable to
bring enough into her heaving lungs. The lodge

began to darken alarmingly, the faces to waver before her. With a sob, she sank gratefully back into the blessed oblivion where pain and remembrance were held at bay.

When next she woke, the agony was still with her, ready to claim her in its relentless jaws the moment consciousness returned. It was not new to her this time; it was not so unexpected. Slowly she opened her eyes—and nearly shrieked as a brown face appeared over hers, peering down at her. The woman said something which Flame did not understand, and frowned when Flame did not respond.

The woman backed away, and Flame watched warily as she went to the fire and began ladeling broth into a bowl. She did not become overly alarmed until she tried to sit up. It was only then that she realized her hands were bound tightly to her sides and her ankles were tied together. Fear clutched at her, making her heart pound violently. Frantic now, she began to scream and wriggle against the bonds that held her. "Release me!" she shrieked. "I demand that you untie me!"

About to bring the bowl to her, the woman now backed away. She grumbled something, then fled from the tipi. Moments later, a warrior stepped into the lodge. He was older, his black hair streaked with grey, his middle beginning to paunch a bit over the waistband of his breechclout. He stood glaring down at her, obviously displeased with her display. "Silence!" he thundered, his booming voice filling the tipi.

Though she did not understand the word, his

tone was clear. Flame ceased her fit and returned his glare full force. "Unbind me," she demanded haughtily of this stranger.

He seemed to understand, if only from her thrashing gestures. With a warning in his eyes, he drew his knife and bent to cut the cords from about her body. Then he sat back and waited, the hunting knife held cautiously in his hand.

Flame sat up, briskly rubbing the circulation back into her limbs. She glared at him malevolently, feeling less vulnerable now that she could move about. "Why have you brought me here? Who are you?"

With hand gestures, he told her that he did not speak her tongue, asking her to repeat her question. She did so, now using sign language to communicate with him. "Who are you? Why have you brought me here?"

"I am Chief Broken Thorn, of the Ute nation. We have heard of your mysterious visions and have need of your dreams for our tribe."

She stared at him in disbelief as his words registered. For long moments she could not find her tongue, and when she finally did, she railed at him. "You have taken me from my village and murdered my children! How dare you ask now for my favors? You are crazy if you think that I will aid you with my vision, after what you have done to me and my family!"

"I know nothing of the deaths of these children you speak of," he told her with a frown. "They were not mentioned to us when we arranged for your capture. I am sorry if what you say is true, for I would not cause the Dreamer Woman such grief."

Something in what he said bothered her, but it took a moment to realize what it was. When she finally did, she gasped in outrage. "With whom did you arrange my capture, Chief Broken Thorn?" she asked with deadly softness in her voice.

She knew his answer before he gave it. "The terms were discussed with two from your own tribe," he said, watching her face closely for her reaction.

"Crooked Arrow and Little Rabbit." Two pair of hands signed the names at the same time.

Sparks of fire flew from her eyes. "Those despicable, lowly weasels! They do not deserve to call themselves Cheyenne! To arrange the abduction of their chief's wife, and the murder of his children! I will slay them with my bare hands if ever I see them again!"

Broken Thorn waited for her to calm herself, then signed, "I am curious. Why do they wish to rid themselves of one so valuable to their tribe? For many moons we have heard tales of the Dreamer Woman of Night Hawk's tribe. Your name is sung with great reverence in many camps. Why do Crooked Arrow and his wife despise you so?"

She answered him truly, seeing no harm in telling him the truth of the matter. "Crooked Arrow has wanted me since Night Hawk first discovered me. It galls him that he could not have me for his own. As for Little Rabbit, her jealousy of me has made her mind go mad. This is not the first time she has attempted such treachery."

The chief nodded his understanding, then added, "It is bad to have such traitors in the heart of a tribe. Very dangerous to many lives."

"If you know this, then you will also know that I wish to return to my village. You will let me go."

"No." He shook his head. "I understand your longings and your grief, but you must remain here. You will bestow upon our tribe the benefit of your great visions."

Flame surprised him by having the audacity to laugh in his face. "I will not dream for you, who are the cause of my great grief. I will not reward you for your treachery with my visions."

As she glared at him, he looked angry enough to strike her, but he did not. Flame could sense that he was holding himself back with great willpower. Then she saw his expression change, a new glimmer coming into his dark eyes. She did not have long to wonder what new thoughts had crossed his mind.

"I have just now remembered what the drums announced so many moons ago," he told her, a sly smile coming onto his face. "The wife of the Cheyenne chief, Night Hawk, was the bearer of twin children. Not only are you valued as a True Dreamer, you are also revered as the mother of these children. You are a rare prize, Dreamer Woman!"

Flame did not deign to respond to this dubious praise. When she did not comment, he announced, "We shall have to find you a new husband from our tribe. Yes," he mused thought-fully, "I think perhaps Bear Paw, who has already expressed a desire for you. He is one of the warriors who helped to capture you. He is strong and handsome and would father healthy chil-dren. If you refuse to grant us the wisdom of your visions, you can at least bestow upon us the honor of bearing twins to our tribe. Once you have more children to replace those you have lost, your heart will soften toward us, and then you may gladly dream your dreams for us."

All the hatred in her heart glowed from her flashing blue eyes. "I will kill myself before mating with such a vile dog!"

The chief rose to tower over her, his laughter grating on her ears. "The choice is not yours to make, Dreamer Woman." He left her with these words of warning. "It will do no good to try to flee, for I have stationed guards outside this lodge. I leave you now to consider your future with us. Matters will go much better for you should you decide to act with reason and proper respect. You will have a short time to ease your grief and resolve yourself to your new life. Then I will speak with you again."

Crooked Arrow was regretting his rash actions, regretting having made a pact with the Ute warriors. He had broken trust with his tribe in doing so, and this weighed heavily on his con-science. If only he had not listened to Little Rabbit's spiteful ravings! Since she had become his wife, Crooked Arrow's honor had been dent-ed and tarnished almost beyond repair or recognition. He could hardly hold his head up for the shame of what this woman had forced him to do.

No, that was not quite the truth of things. He should have known better, should have resisted her urgings and evil suggestions. He should have beaten her! Instead, he had become as weak and sniveling as she, and he had only himself to blame that he could no longer look upon his own face with pride.

He had made the pact with the Utes when he and Little Rabbit were coming back from a visit in another camp. The Ute warriors had come upon them suddenly, trapping them before they had a chance to flee. With their lives at stake, he and Little Rabbit had bargained for their freedom, bargained by telling the warriors about Flame's visions and the upcoming hunt when most of the Cheyenne warriors would be away from the village.

Now, Crooked Arrow was racing back toward the Cheyenne camp, having deserted the bear hunt. Not wanting to reveal his traitorous act, he had said nothing to Night Hawk or the others. He had slipped away unnoticed, hoping he could reach the camp in time to warn them of the imminent attack, if not prevent it altogether. If he could reach the Ute war party before they reached the village, perhaps he could offer them something else of value, though what he knew not, and stop this terrible thing before it happened.

He was too late. Crooked Arrow knew this the moment he topped the last rise. Smoke drifted toward him, stinging his nostrils, as his eyes scanned the scene below. Tipis lay toppled, some burned and others merely overturned. There was no sign of the Ute warriors; they had come and gone again, striking swiftly and fleeing. The only sounds to reach his ears were those of weeping women and barking dogs. The herd of ponies had been scattered, some wandering loose through the camp, others spread out along the floor of the small valley. He knew that the Utes would have taken as many as they could manage to herd along with them.

He rode slowly into the camp, sadly surveying the damage. He had known, of course, that the Utes would not simply ride into the village, steal Flame, and leave without wreaking further havoc. It was this that had caused him the most distress, for he had caused this misery to his entire tribe, not to Night Hawk alone.

Crooked Arrow searched for Little Rabbit, but failed to find her near their tipi. Spotting a group of women clustered near the center of the village, he approached them for news of his wife. When he drew near, he saw the women bending over Stone Face's wife, Shining Star. One held a damp cloth to a gash in Shining Star's head, as the woman sat weeping.

Though he hesitated to ask, Crooked Arrow said, "Has anyone seen Little Rabbit or Howling Gale?"

As one, they shook their heads. "Perhaps she is elsewhere in the village, Crooked Arrow," one of them said with a tired sigh. "Beyond all else that has happened this day, Flame has been stolen from us, and now her children are nowhere to be found. Shining Star rescued them from their burning tipi, and while she was beating out the flames, she was struck on the head. When she awoke, Night Hawk's children were gone."

"Was this while the war party was yet raiding the camp?" he asked with a frown.

"No," Shining Star moaned. "The Utes had gone. This was after."

Another woman began to wail. "Sweet Berries has died, her unborn child with her. Many of the women were wounded or raped. Owl Eyes lies slain outside his lodge, and Little Spotted Turtle lies close to death even as we speak. So much tragedy! So much to bear!"

Crooked Arrow hardly heard the woman's words. His mind was on what he had just learned of Night Hawk's children. If Little Rabbit was missing also, he would wager all he owned that she had taken the children. He had to find her before she could harm them, for he knew the workings of her twisted mind! In her madness, she would take great delight in torturing those helpless babies, merely because they were the offspring of her hated adversary and the man who had dared to choose another over her.

Leaning down, Crooked Arrow addressed Shining Star. "Have you sent word to the warriors about this attack?"

She nodded tearfully.

"You must tell Night Hawk, when he arrives, that I have gone in search of Little Rabbit and his children, for I am sure she must have taken them. I will bring his children safely back to him. Tell im I have sworn this on my life, as his boyhood friend. He is not to worry, but to go to the camp of Chief Broken Thorn to find his wife."

Before any of them could answer, he had pivoted his horse about and was gone, lost in the maze of lodges, winding his way out of the camp.

The Cheyenne warriors raced their spent and wheezing horses into the village they had left so few days before. Three new scaffolds stood a short distance beyond the last row of lodges, the bodies of the dead mounted upon them. Most of the lodges had been rebuilt, the women attempting to restore order to their lives as quickly as possible.

Night Hawk drew his stallion to a halt before his tipi. Even as he vaulted down and raced into the lodge, his mind registered its charred condition. It stood silent and blackened, an omen of what was to come.

Not finding Flame there, he was about to look for Shining Star when she ran toward him, her baby in her arms and a frowning Stone Face at her side. Tears raced down her face as she sobbed, "They have taken her, Night Hawk! The Utes have taken Flame!"

On hearing her words, his face paled. "And my children?" he asked, suddenly dreading the answer.

"Crooked Arrow has gone to get them back for you. Little Rabbit is also gone, and Crooked Arrow suspects that she has run away with them. He has sworn to return them safely to you, sworn this upon his life." She gulped back her tears, and added confusedly. "He told me to tell you to go to the camp of Broken Thorn to find Flame, though how he could know this, I cannot guess."

Night Hawk's face darkened like building thunderclouds. "I can. It was he who betrayed us! He and Little Rabbit must have told the Utes when the warriors would be gone from the village. They have brought this disaster down upon us, and they will pay with their lives!" he roared.

Stone Face agreed with Night Hawk. "There is no other way he could have known which tribe of Ute these warriors were from. We must make plans for an answering raid. We must save Flame and avenge our village."

"We must also find Little Rabbit and Crooked Arrow before they can harm my sons and my daughter," Night Hawk pointed out. "It will mean dividing our forces, but this cannot be helped."

As the two warriors walked away, intent on gathering their warriors and chiefs, Shining Star reached out for Night Hawk's arm, detaining him. "Wait. I know what Crooked Arrow has done, and it is too terrible to think upon. Yet I believe that he will do as he says. He will find Little Rabbit and bring your children back safely. He has sworn this on the memory of your boyhood friendship. Those are his words, Night Hawk, and I believe that he sincerely regrets all that he has done against you and the tribe. It is his way of restoring his honor and his pride in himself, which he has forfeited these past moons.

an you not trust him to do this, as he has
ledged?"

"You would risk the lives of Night Hawk's
hildren by asking him to trust such a traitor?"
tone Face gaped at her in shock.

"I love those children," she said tearfully, "as I
ove my own son, yet I cannot help but believe
hat Crooked Arrow is sincere in his oath. In my
oman's heart, I know this, though I cannot say
ow or why."

As she spoke, Night Hawk had been recalling
is lost friendship and all the days that had gone
efore, when Crooked Arrow and he were as
ose as brothers. There had been a time when
hey would have risked everything, done any-
hing, for each other. He wanted to believe that,
espite what he and Little Rabbit had done,
rooked Arrow truly repented of his crimes
gainst the tribe and his former friend. Night
lawk's heart cried out for this to be so, and he
nade a decision he hoped he would not live to
egret.

"Crooked Arrow will have his chance to prove
imself," he announced solemnly. "If he betrays
nis trust again, if he has not returned with my
hildren by the time we have rescued Flame, I
will personally rip his treacherous heart from his
ody and feed it to him. I will find him if I have
o track him to the ends of the earth. This I
ledge as his chief!"

Stone Face eyed his friend doubtfully, but said
nly, "Even should he return with the children,
e and Little Rabbit will still meet the anger of

the tribe. Our people will want revenge for th
lives lost in the raid, and for those who hav
suffered at Crooked Arrow and Little Rabbit'
hands."

"So it shall be," Night Hawk intoned, "but firs
we must return Flame to our midst."

Chapter
31

Crooked Arrow followed the tracks of the horse in the snow. He hoped he was tracking the right horse, Little Rabbit's pony, but it was hard to tell. They were fresh hoofprints, not more than a day old. This much he was sure of, even when they crossed older tracks, mingling with the prints of several other previous riders. He wished it would snow, just enough to cover the old tracks and make the ones he was following easier to read.

Whoever he was following was a lone rider on an unshod Indian pony, and the horse was carrying a heavy load. Of course, it could be a stout brave, or someone with a load of furs. He hoped it was Little Rabbit, with four young children.

He marveled that she could find a way to carry four active young ones with her and still maintain such a rugged pace through these forests and across the hills and rocks that marked the land. She had Howling Gale, who was now five winters old, and War Cloud, who was four; then there were the twins, who would be two next summer. He could only hope the two infants were not suffering for having been torn from mother's breast without proper weaning.

If only he could be certain it was she he was trailing. There had been many old tracks about the village, and several new ones following the raid. The Ute warriors had headed west and north, splitting their party a little way from the camp. The Cheyenne hunting party had gone north into the hills in search of bear. Of the remaining tracks, only three led east and south. He had first chosen those that led directly south, but when he caught up with the rider, it was a young widow who had decided to rejoin her own tribe after the raid, without waiting for an escort.

Now he was following one of the trails that led east, trusting that the delay had not cost him too much time—time for Little Rabbit to begin tormenting her young charges. So far he was heartened to find no evidence along the trail that she had harmed any of them—if this were indeed her trail he had doggedly followed for the past two days.

* * *

Flame was grief-stricken, but she was also anxious about her present situation. Chief Broken Thorn had told her the truth when he had said there were guards stationed outside the tipi. Two of the biggest, ugliest braves she had ever thought to encounter stood just outside the entrance. No doubt they would be replaced by two more such beasts at required intervals. She was trapped there, helpless to free herself against such brute strength—unless she used her wits and outsmarted her captors. Even if she failed to escape, perhaps she could delay their plans until Night Hawk could come for her.

The tipi flap was raised, and Singing Bird entered the tipi. Flame had learned that this was Chief Broken Thorn's wife. If that were the case, Flame was receiving preferential treatment, to be served by the wife of a chief. These people must be most anxious to please her. They must hope to win her approval, so that she would grant them a vision. Perhaps, if she were very crafty, she could use her dreams against them, frightening them into releasing her. If she waited a day or two, and planned her scheme carefully, perhaps she could lead them to believe anything she chose.

Crooked Arrow dismounted and carefully surveyed the small clearing. The traveler he was following had camped here the night before, and he was looking for signs of who that might be. A thin, nasty smile crossed his face as he viewed one slim set of moccasin prints, probably made by a woman, and several sets of smaller tracks, definitely those of children. He studied them closely, and was finally satisfied that there were four different sets of children's tracks.

To add to his conclusions, in the bushes to one side of the clearing he found two yellow cloth squares. He recognized these as the coverings made by Flame for her babies' bottoms even before he saw that they were thoroughly soiled by human excrement. His smile widened, though it never reached his dark eyes. Now he knew that he was pursuing the right rider. He would catch up with her soon. It would not be long now.

Flame did dream that very next night, her fifth in the Ute village, but it was not a vision she would speak of to the Ute chief. Her vision had been of Night Hawk, and of her children. It had not been just an ordinary dream, of that she was certain. This had been a true vision, and though it had brought her some comfort, it had also brought her pain and increased her fears for her babies.

She had dreamed that her children yet lived, though how they had escaped the burning tipi she did not know. She was only grateful that they had, for she had thought them dead, burned alive in the lodge. She had seen them riding through a dense forest. On the horse with them was a woman, and when the woman turned and Flame saw her face clearly, she had gasped in horror. It was Little Rabbit! Little Rabbit had her children and was taking them somewhere far from the Cheyenne camp, away from Shining Star and

Night Hawk and all those who would protect them from her evil schemes. How had this happened? How had Little Rabbit succeeded in kidnapping her babies? What did the wicked woman plan to do with them—to them?

Flame breathed a little easier when she saw the Cheyenne warrior following Little Rabbit. He was some distance behind, but fast gaining on her. He would save her children from harm! Then, when the picture of him came clearer, she moaned in dismay. The warrior was not Night Hawk, nor any of their valued friends; it was that scoundrel, Crooked Arrow. No doubt he was hurrying to meet his wife somewhere up the trail. They must have planned all this, to have Little Rabbit abduct the children and meet him later at a chosen place.

In her sleep, Flame frowned in confusion as the scene changed. What was Crooked Arrow doing? Why was he peering through the bushes at Little Rabbit? Why was he frowning so? Why did he not join his wife in the clearing and share the fire she had built for light and warmth against the night winds? Why did he not share with them the thick robes she saw piled at his feet?

Her attention turned to her children, and her heart cried out to them. She watched as Little Rabbit fed herself and Howling Gale from a pouch of pemmican, but when Blue Wolf toddled up and begged for some, she shoved him roughly aside. Sky Blaze sat softly whimpering and sucking hungrily at her thumb, a habit she had long since broken. And when Howling Gale would

have shared his portion with War Cloud, Little
Rabbit scolded him harshly, forbidding her son
to give food to "Night Hawk's brats."

Later, while Little Rabbit and her son were
snuggled between thick robes, Flame's own children shivered together under one thin blanket,
the same sweat-drenched blanket that had previously covered the pony's back. Surely they would
not survive the night this way! Even if they were
fortunate enough to live the night through, hungry and freezing, they were certain to become
deathly ill. Already they looked pathetically thin
to Flame's eyes.

Flame awoke with tears flowing freely, her
heart heavy with dread for the safety of her
children. Better that they had died quickly in the
burning tipi than to starve and freeze to death at
the hands of that demented woman!

It was almost dawn when Flame fell into an
exhausted, restless sleep. Again she dreamed, but
this time the visions were of her beloved husband. Night Hawk was rounding up his warriors.
He was surveying the damage to the Cheyenne
camp, and he was very angry. His dark eyes were
burning with hatred. Beside him, Flame could
see Stone Face, and for once his name fit him
perfectly. There was not a trace of compassion in
his hard features. To one side stood Shining Star,
looking on with worry lining her beautiful face.
Tears shone in her eyes, and she nervously fin-
gered the beadwork at the neck of her dress.

The vision shimmered as the picture changed,
and Flame saw Night Hawk standing alone and
staring despondently at the charred remains of

heir tipi. She was surprised to see that it still
tood, actually looking as if it were habitable.

Then her attention was wholly on Night Hawk
as a huge sob shook his broad shoulders. To her
shock and dismay, she saw him fall to his knees,
his dark head buried in his hands as he wept for
he loss of his family. Tears ran freely through his
ingers, dripping to the earth like salty raindrops
from the clouds. The heart-felt wail seemed to
ssue from the very depths of his soul, and it tore
at Flame's heart to hear such a mournful sound
come from him, from this brave, strong man
whom she loved so desperately.

She tried to reach out to him, to comfort him,
but he could not hear her words. His ears were
deaf to her; her hands could not touch him
through the veil of her dream. She heard him cry
out her name again and again, and she shared his
agony over their missing children. Then she
heard the words she so yearned to hear. Lifting
his eyes to the heavens, he shouted, "I will find
you, my love! I will come to you! Do not despair,
but wait for me, and know that we will soon be
together again, reunited with our children."

Flame awoke with hope in her heart and a
fierce determination to hold her antagonists at
bay for as long as it might take Night Hawk to
reach her. She never doubted that he would
come; she just did not know when.

Crooked Arrow frowned as he gazed up at the
night sky. While the gathering snow clouds
would keep the night from becoming bitterly
cold, the wind was gathering force. It was starting

to howl already through the tops of the barren
trees, beginning to bend the boughs of the whispering pines. There was the smell of snow in the
air, and all the warnings of a coming storm.

Crouched down in the bushes as he was, his
legs had begun to ache from staying bent in one
position for so long. He longed to move about, to
stretch his cramped muscles, at least to stand, but
he dared not—not yet. Little Rabbit had bedded
down for the night some time ago, but the
children were fretful. He feared they might hear
him approach and alert her to his presence before
he was ready. He must wait until they all slept
deeply before making his move.

The snow had begun to fall in fat white flakes,
driven thickly by the wind, when Crooked Arrow
crept softly into the clearing. He thanked the
spirits that Little Rabbit's pony knew his scent
and made no sounds of alarm. Quietly he knelt
beside his sleeping wife, studying her face and
wondering why it had taken him so long to see
the evil there. Even in her sleep, she looked
wicked and devious.

The sharp blade of his long knife glinted in the
light of the dying fire as he brought the razor-edge
to her throat. "Awaken and meet your death!" he
hissed into her ear.

Little Rabbit's eyes snapped open in immediate alarm. She lay stiffly, only her eyes moving to
find her attacker. When she saw that it was
Crooked Arrow, she relaxed and frowned up at
him, her tone harsh as she whispered, "What do
you mean by creeping up on me and frightening

ne so? Your joke is not laughable, Crooked
Arrow."

"It is not meant to be, wife, for it is no jest," he
countered with a sneer. When she would have
moved, he drew the knife more tightly across her
throat. "Your evil ways have come to an end,
woman. This time you have gone too far, and you
will pay with your life's blood."

Quite frozen now by his serious manner, she
stared up at him, eyes wide with fright. "Why are
you doing this? Tell me you mean only to frighten
me, for surely you would not slay your own wife
when I am even now carrying your child within
my body."

His laugh was low and dangerous, and he
shook his head at her obvious ploy. "You do not
bear my child, Little Rabbit. I know of the herbs
you take to prevent my seed from lodging in your
womb. Even if it were so," he continued almost
casually, "I would want no child that sprang
from your vile body, for the babe would be
tainted by your evil spirit. Night Hawk was wise
to cast you off as he did, but he was too soft. He
should have killed you long ago and saved me the
trouble of doing it, though I now do so with great
relief and pleasure."

There came no scream to wake the sleeping
children, for his stroke was swift and sure. Only a
long hiss of air from her throat and the soft gurgle
of blood was heard, and this only by Crooked
Arrow. When the last of her blood had ceased to
flow, when her heart had ceased to beat, he
dragged her body from the clearing and hid it

behind some brambles, so that the children would not see it when they awakened.

Then, one by one, he roused the four children. Carefully he bundled them into the thick robes he had thought to bring with him. Tying the two smaller toddlers to his back, he secured the two older boys on Little Rabbit's pony. With snow swirling so thickly that he could barely see to guide the horses, he started back the way he had come, through snow already to the tops of the horses' hoofs.

"Tell me of the dreams which have so disturbed your sleep," Chief Broken Thorn demanded. "Singing Bird has told me that you awaken in the night and thrash about in your sleep."

Flame threw a swift, killing glance at Singing Bird, who had spent the last few nights in the tipi with her, no doubt to report back to her husband. "If my sleep is broken, it is only dreams of my children's deaths that disturb me so," she fabricated, her face now an unreadable mask to cover her thoughts.

The chief scowled at her. "I have given you enough time to calm yourself. I give you only two days more to provide us with a vision."

Her answering smile was full of contempt. "You would dare to threaten me, Chief Broken Thorn?" she questioned haughtily. "Do you not fear that I might loose my mighty powers upon you and cast an evil spell upon your people?" Even in her present predicament, she enjoyed the stunned look that flitted across his face, and the way his wife turned almost white with fear. "What if I should conjure a great plague in my visions, and strike your tribe low with some dread illness that has no cure?" she taunted.

"If you possess such powers, why have you not yet used them?" he countered bravely, though she could still see the doubt lingering in his eyes.

"Perhaps my grief has been too great until now," she suggested slyly.

He was silent, thinking on her reply. "If you do such a thing, we will slay you without delay. Do you value your own life so little?"

"Your tribe would still die off from the face of the earth," she pointed out. "Nothing you could do would prevent this from happening once I have called upon the spirits to do my bidding."

Cornered, he backed down, trying instead to placate her. "We do not wish to harm you, Dreamer Woman. We ask only for a vision to lead our tribe, to keep us from harm, to protect our warriors in battle."

"And I ask only to return to my own people, to my husband."

Not wishing to argue with her or distress her further and risk her anger, the chief rose. "We will talk again later. Perhaps you will be of a more agreeable nature then."

Once more Flame had succeeded, if not in securing her freedom, in gaining herself and Night Hawk a bit more time.

A shout of alarm alerted her the next afternoon, and although Singing Bird berated her sharply and her guards would not let her past the entrance of the tipi, Flame watched through the open flap. When the older woman would have closed the covering, Flame threw her an evil glare that sufficed to cow the chief's wife into backing away.

Soon she witnessed what had caused such disturbance, and she had to bite back a sharp gasp as she saw Night Hawk ride into view. He was alone, unattended by any of his warriors, as he rode proudly and regally astride his new black stallion, into the very heart of the enemy camp. Even as she caught her breath at his daring, her heart sang a song of joy. He had come for her—at last!

Chapter
32

Night Hawk could not risk attacking the Ute village without first learning where his wife was being held, how heavily she was guarded, and what the danger might be to her life. He could send no one else in his place, for Chief Broken Thorn would suspect a trap if anyone but Night Hawk attempted to negotiate for her release. Flame was too important, too widely revered for them not to have heard of her. He was certain they must know of her visions, and that this was the real reason for their raid on the Cheyenne village. They would not have come so far and taken only Flame if they had not known of her worth. He could take no chances with her life.

He rode into the enemy camp alone, straight

and tall upon his stallion. He met the glares of hatred from his enemies and returned them with his own, his eyes stony black and glowing like polished onyx. His face reflected no fear, only contempt and determination as he rode boldly through the maze of tipis to the heart of the village.

The Utes could not believe their eyes, nor the daring of this Cheyenne chieftan. Had he no sense? Did he not fear them? They were astounded at his bold entry into their camp, alone and unfaltering. His courage was beyond anything they had heretofore witnessed. They watched in mute amazement and hidden admiration as he met their stares and continued riding unhesitatingly through their village.

Though he had not yet seen her, Night Hawk sensed Flame watching him. Then, from the corner of his eye, he saw her. Even as he drank in the sight of her in that short glance, his mind was noting the location of the lodge in which she was being held. He counted two guards, but knew there could be another inside the tipi.

All the while he worked his way slowly and steadily to the center of the Ute camp, his eyes seeming to stare straight ahead, he was watching and collecting invaluable information—how many warriors there were along his route, how many lodges, what type of weapons were displayed, where the largest concentration of force was likely to be.

Even as he saw the young warrior draw back the bow, he did not stop or draw his own weapon.

It would be fatal, both for him and for Flame. Night Hawk knew this, and he did nothing but try to keep from tightening his muscles in anticipation of the pain he knew was coming.

In the dead silence that followed his progress through the camp, the sharp twang of the bow sounded like cannon fire, the hiss of the arrow in its flight like a pit full of snakes. The arrow drove through the upper muscle of his left arm like a fist of fire, yet he did not flinch or hesitate. With no show of the pain he was feeling, Night Hawk calmly broke off the feathered end of the arrow and pulled the tip and remaining shaft through the bleeding wound. With admirable arrogance, he dropped the missile to the ground, he and his horse never breaking stride through the entire process.

As she saw the arrow pierce Night Hawk's arm, Flame caught her lip between her teeth to keep from crying out. His pain became hers, and she marveled that he could hide it from his enemies. She watched until he disappeared from view, then calmly seated herself on a mat near the fire, determined not to show her own anxieties to these people. If Night Hawk could display such bravery in the face of danger, then she, as his wife, could do no less.

Chief Broken Thorn awaited Night Hawk outside his lodge. All the grudging admiration he held for this young Cheyenne chief was carefully concealed from his features as he met his enemy face to face.

"I have come for my wife," Night Hawk announced clearly, ignoring proper protocol.

Broken Thorn did not attempt to misunder-
stand him, nor to pretend that he might not have
this man's woman. "You must be Chief Night
Hawk, of the Cheyenne," he said. "Come. Let us
talk within the comforts of my lodge, and warm
ourselves near the fire as we speak of this."

In the face of Night Hawk's courage, the older
chief disdained having any of his warriors follow
them inside his tipi. He, too, must show some
measure of valor before his people and this
daring young warrior. He would speak with
Night Hawk alone.

Inside the tipi, the two chiefs faced each other
across the fire. Night Hawk again was the first to
speak. "Your warriors have raided my village and
taken my wife. I want her returned to me."

Broken Thorn took his time in answering,
deliberately making the Cheyenne chief wait for
his words. "We will not readily part with this
woman, who is the Dreamer of Great Visions,"
he said at length. "Her worth is too great, and we
have risked much to gain her presence within our
tribe."

"She is my mate, and our children cry for their
mother," Night Hawk replied firmly. "She is not
yours to keep."

Broken Thorn nodded. "She is the bearer of
twins. This makes her value even more."

Night Hawk did not deny the chief's words.
"What will you take to return her to me? I have
many ponies. Though it is not usual to bargain
for one's own wife, I will pay to have her back."

Chief Broken Thorn shook his head. "No. She
will stay and be wife to one of our warriors."

"Then I demand to be paid what she is worth, if she is to no longer be my wife," Night Hawk stated stubbornly, stunning the older man with this sudden declaration.

"You expect me to pay for that which I already hold in my possession?" he asked in disbelief.

"Unless you would prefer that my warriors meet with yours to decide the matter. They are most eager to avenge the attack on our camp."

Broken Thorn thought but a moment. If this could be settled without bloodshed or threat of retaliation, so much the better. "I will give you two hundred ponies for her," he offered generously.

"Three hundred," Night Hawk countered, "and an added two hundred for my warriors, who seek recompense for damage to the camp and for the lives of three of our people."

"Why would you do this?" Broken Thorn insisted warily, suspecting some trick. "Why would you agree to part with such a woman?"

Night Hawk leaned forward, as if to divulge a confidence. "It is difficult, at times, to live with such a wife, knowing that she is often held in higher esteem than a war chief," he admitted ruefully. "She is often stubborn, and my pride cannot sustain such abuse."

This the older chief readily understood. The young Cheyenne was envious of his wife's status in his tribe. Five hundred ponies was a great number to pay for one woman, but she was the Dream Woman and the bearer of twins, after all. Not an ordinary woman by any means. Then, too, Broken Thorn could always regain some of his loss by requiring a bride price from Bear Paw. "It is agreed," he said at last. "You shall have your five hundred ponies this very day."

"No." At the dark look appearing on Broken Thorn's face, Night Hawk hastened to explain. "While I agree to the trade, I must wait to collect the ponies. I must gather a few of my warriors to help me herd them back to our village."

The older chief released a hidden sigh of relief. "I can allow no more than fifteen of your warriors to accompany you on your return, and we must set a time for your arrival, so that I know you will not try to go back on your word."

"I will return in ten suns' time, with fifteen men," Night Hawk agreed. "Now I must ask your word that you will not try to trick us or to delay payment of the ponies."

"You have my word of honor as chief of my tribe."

Night Hawk was not surprised to be followed as he left the Ute camp. In fact, he would have been surprised and distrustful had he not been trailed. Not deigning to look back and acknowledge his followers, he rode on, directing his horse toward his own camp. It was a long time later before his trackers finally turned back for the Ute camp, convinced that Night Hawk was, indeed, on his way home as he had said.

Flame stared at Broken Thorn in shocked disbelief as he greeted her with the news of her sale. "You lie!" she exclaimed excitedly. "Night Hawk would not do this thing! You have killed him and invented this tale to win my favor!"

Broken Thorn regarded her calmly, for he had expected such a reaction from her. "When he returns in ten suns to collect his payment, you will learn the truth of my words," he told her. "On that day, you will be joined with Bear Paw as his wife."

After the chief had left, Flame tried to reason calmly with herself, telling herself that this was all a trick, none of it to be believed. In the depths of her heart, she knew beyond doubt that Night Hawk would never trade her, not for a million horses, let alone a paltry three hundred! Reason told her that she had not really believed that he could ride into this camp, demand her return, and that somehow the two of them would ride out again together without incident. Night Hawk was up to something! This was all part of a larger plan to free her. He would be back. Her vision had shown her that they would be reunited once more. She would simply have to be patient and trust in him and in her dream.

Night Hawk's knife slid across the guard's throat, and the man dropped soundlessly at his feet. To one side, he saw Stone Face meet with the same result. Then, silent as a wraith, he slipped into the tipi where Flame awaited him. Singing Bird never felt the knife slide between her ribs.

Flame was awake before Night Hawk's light touch upon her arm. Without a word she followed him from the lodge, slipping from the shadow of one tipi to another as they made their way noiselessly from the camp.

When they had at last gained the safety of their

warriors, Night Hawk set three of them to guard her. Then, giving a signal, he led the raid on the sleeping Ute village. It was a short, fierce battle, but when it was finished, the entire camp was in shambles. Chief Broken Thorn and his wife were slain. More than two hundred Ute warriors lay dead. Of the hundred and twenty-three women, only about half had managed to escape with their children under cover of night. Some sixty women and children were taken captive by the Cheyenne warriors. It would be a very long time before this tribe of Utes dared to attack Night Hawk's Cheyenne again.

Night Hawk, Flame, and their warriors arrived back at the Cheyenne village in the midst of the worst snowstorm of the winter. Their horses could barely plow through the deep drifts, and the wind whistled about their heads like a singing demon. It was bitter cold, and they were thankful that they had been so near the village when the storm hit, or they might never have made it back alive.

On the way, Night Hawk had told Flame of her children, and that Crooked Arrow had pledged to find them and return them to the camp. In her turn, Flame related the details of her dream. Neither was completely comfortable, wondering if Crooked Arrow would honor his word. Upon arriving and discovering that Crooked Arrow had not yet returned, they were even more worried. The storm prevented them from doing so, or both would have left again immediately in search of their babies.

The snowstorm lasted for three more days, piling snow up to the bellies of the ponies and freezing wild animals in their tracks. By the time it abated, Flame was frantic with concern for her children. She and Night Hawk gathered supplies and prepared to ride out with several of their warriors. Though they had no idea where to begin their search, they vowed to look until they had exhausted every corner of the vast territory, or until they located their children.

They had just reached the edge of the encampment when one of the warriors gave a shout and pointed. A short distance away, two horses labored slowly and methodically through the deep snow. They could not tell at first who was riding the lead horse, pulling the other behind, for whoever it was, was so snow-covered and ice-encrusted that those watching could not distinguish whether it be man or woman, warrior or white.

They rode out to meet this rider who had braved his way through the storm. Two horse lengths apart, Night Hawk finally recognized the man as Crooked Arrow. But where were the children? Where was Little Rabbit? Had Crooked Arrow failed in his mission to find them?

Tied to the second pony were only thick rolls of fur, and suddenly an unthinkable thought occurred to Flame. What if Crooked Arrow had not been able to prevent Little Rabbit from slaying the children? What if he were returning only their lifeless bodies to them?

As they pondered all this, Night Hawk approached Crooked Arrow. The man was barely alive. His eyes were frozen open, his limbs so stiff they could not bend. Ice and snow coated his entire body, face and all. Only his mouth and eyes showed in his ghostly face.

Just as Night Hawk reined in beside him, Crooked Arrow slid from his horse. He lay on the snow-covered ground, his body still contorted grotesquely, his arms and legs still in the same positions as when he had been astride the horse. Swiftly, Night Hawk dismounted and knelt at Crooked Arrow's side. The warrior groaned something, his mouth and lips too frozen to form words.

"What do you say, Crooked Arrow? Tell me. Where is Little Rabbit? Where are the children?"

Leaning close to catch his words, Night Hawk strained to hear. "On horse," he heard Crooked Arrow whisper. He uttered one final word before he died, and Night Hawk turned pale upon hearing him groan, "Dead."

Before he could stop her, Flame was off her pony and tearing at the robes tied to the second horse. With a hoarse cry, Night Hawk grabbed her arm to prevent her from uncovering whatever horrors were hidden there. He was too late. The cord holding two of the bundles broke, and two small bodies tumbled to the ground at Flame's feet. Her frantic scream echoed off the snowdrifts as she stared down at the bodies of her two sons.

Then something miraculous and wonderful happened. The bodies began to wriggle, and seconds later two small, smiling faces popped up out of the deep snow where they had landed.

With a wild shriek of delight, Flame threw herself into the snow, hugging her sons to her as if she would squeeze the life from them herself, never wanting to let them go.

For just a moment, Night Hawk watched, a broad smile of joy and relief etching his face. Then he recalled himself and, walking to the opposite side of the pony, he untied the remaining two bundles. There he discovered his daughter and Howling Gale, safe and sound and glad to be free of their restricting covers. The reunion was complete.

Later, when they had time to review all that had happened, they thought that Crooked Arrow must have bundled the children warmly in the robes, making certain they were completely covered. Then he had managed somehow, with the last of his strength, to see them safely home to the loving arms of their parents. He had given his own life to complete his promise to his old friend.

Stuffed inside Crooked Arrow's tunic, they had found Little Rabbit's bloody headband, mute proof that he had honored his remaining vow. When he had uttered that awful word "dead," he had been trying to tell them that he had killed Little Rabbit. She would never again return to cause them tragedy with her mad jealousy.

Once more Night Hawk found himself responsible for his brother's child, for Howling Gale would now be in his and Flame's care. Their tipi would be overflowing with small children. They would raise Howling Gale as one of their own, loving him and raising him to be a fine, strong, honorable Cheyenne warrior, as proud and brave as his father and his uncle Night Hawk.

It was over. It was finished. They were all together, a loving family once more.

Looking out over the land, now budding and blooming with the advent of spring, Flame drew a deep breath and sighed. How sweet the warming earth smelled this day! How vibrant the greens and deep the browns, how bright the sunshine that touched the small valley where they were camped. Here and there, with a touch of blue and a splash of yellow, wild flowers were blooming. Bees hummed busily from blossom to blossom. The earth was alive with good things, growing things.

Happiness spilled over in her heart. This was the way it should always be, with sunshine and peace abounding. Her joyous smile reflected her contentment as she turned her gaze toward her children, all four of them. The twins were playing with a new puppy, laughing and chasing the roly-poly furball as fast as their chubby little legs would carry them, then tumbling into a heap as the puppy tripped them up. A short distance away, the boys of the village had organized a rousing game of stick ball, and War Cloud, Howling Gale, and Shining Star's Little Rock were right in the thick of it.

As she watched with a smile, enjoying the sight of the children at play, Night Hawk came up quietly behind her. Planting a swift kiss on the nape of her neck, he laughed when she squealed

n surprise. He gave her a quick squeeze, then
eleased her and held out his hand for hers.
'Come," he said. "There is a place I want to
show you."

"The children?" she asked hesitantly, not quite
over the fright of their abduction.

"They will be fine," he assured her with a
gentle smile. "I have spoken to Red Feather's
sister, and she will watch over them, for I know
how closely you watch them now." He understood her lingering fear, knowing that it would
soon pass now that Little Rabbit and Crooked
Arrow no longer lived to threaten their contentment.

He led her a short distance from the camp,
over a rocky footpath that wound up and through
several stands of trees. Turning, he swept her into
his strong arms and commanded, "Close your
eyes, and do not look until I tell you to do so."

Intrigued, she did as he ordered, snuggling
close to him as he carried her a little way farther.
Then he stopped. "Tell me what you hear and
smell, what you feel." When her lashes fluttered
slightly, he said, "No, do not open your eyes just
yet. Let your other senses speak to you, and tell
me what they say."

For the last few steps, she had been aware of a
muted roar, a kind of splashing and pounding
and trickling sound all combined. Now, still in
the cradle of his arms, she said, "I hear water,
and something else I cannot quite grasp, and the
breeze sighing through the tops of the trees." She
frowned slightly in concentration. "Though I feel
the sun warm upon my skin, it feels also as if it

were beginning to rain, for I can feel a mist upon my flesh."

"And what do you smell?"

He chuckled as she blindly sniffed the air. "Flowers!" she exclaimed excitedly. "I smell many flowers, mixed with the smell of the awakening earth. And I smell water nearby, and the sharp tang of pine trees."

"Very good," he said, letting her slide slowly to her feet. He turned her slightly in his arms, so that she stood before him with his broad chest shielding her back and his arms encircling her waist. "Now you may look," he said softly in her ear.

As her eyes slowly opened, she gasped in delight. Before her, in a small glade encircled by towering pines, was a tiny sun-sparkled lake, with water so clear it reflected the blue of the sky above—a perfect match for Flame's eyes. The pounding and splashing was made by water tumbling from rocks above, creating a little waterfall. Sunlight danced through the shower of mist rising from it, forming a pretty pastel rainbow. All along the gentle slope ringing the lake, flowers bloomed in a profusion of color. It was enough to stun the senses, so beautiful it brought tears to Flame's eyes.

"Oh, Night Hawk!" she breathed in awe. "The spirits have outdone themselves, to create such beauty! Never have I seen any place more lovely!"

"It cannot compare to the beauty I see when I look at you," he told her softly, bringing her to face him. "Alight with love and life, your eyes utshine the sky. Your skin is softer than the petals of the flower, your hair brighter than the fireblossom. Your love is warmer than summer sunshine, your voice more gentle than the whispering breeze. My soul basks in the tender glow of yours, and finds comfort there."

As he spoke, his lips and his fingertips gently roamed her face, touching tenderly upon her brow, her eyes, her sweet lips. His fingers released the thongs that bound her braids, carelessly tossing them aside as his fingers combed through her long waving tresses. Loosening the lacing at her neckline, he drew the doeskin dress over her shoulders, letting it fall at their feet. All the while, his lips played with hers, enchanting her with tiny nibbles and teasing tongue.

"It is too cool to swim, my love," she whispered. "The water will be as cold as ice."

"I did not bring you here to swim, Blue Eyes," he returned, laying her upon a bed of new grass, the fragrance of crushed flowers surrounding them. "I brought you here to make love with you, where the sunshine can kiss your body as I do. I want to love you here in this place that is so peaceful and private, where I can watch your eyes light up when I stroke you, where I can clearly see the wonder on your face as our bodies join."

There, in the quiet, secluded little glade, surrounded by the glories of nature, they made sweet, slow, passionate love. Afterwards, they lay silent for a long time, wrapped in each other's arms, listening to the songs of the birds and absorbing the serenity of the beauty around and within them.

"I feel cleansed," she murmured at length "Washed free of care and worry, bathed in love." She raised her head to better see his face as she confessed softly, "I used to think that our love would bind me, hold me where I did not wish to be; rather it has freed me, that my heart might soar true and strong with yours, my mighty Night Hawk. I love you with every breath in my body, every beat of my heart, and I never thought to be so happy. With the gift of your love, you have given my heart a glad song that will never die."

His dark eyes were gleaming with love, his smile a tender caress, as he answered truly, "You are the light of my life. Without you I would be lost in the dark forests where love and laughter do not exist. You are the torch to light my path, that the Night Hawk will not lose his way. I shall love you long after the mighty mountains crumble and the rivers cease to flow, until the end of all time and beyond. You are my love, my life, my heart—my own bright and beautiful Night Flame."

CATHERINE HART — Fire & Ice

Beautiful and spirited Kathleen Haley sets sail from England for the family estate in Savannah. On board ship, she meets the man who will forever haunt her heart, the dashing and domineering Captain Reed Taylor. On the long, perilous voyage, she resists his bold advances—until she wakes from unconsciousness after a storm and hears Reed's shocking confession. She then knows she must marry the rogue.

But their fiery conflict is far from over. Through society balls, raging duels and torrid nights, Kathleen seeks vengeance on Reed's brutal passions and his secret alliance with pirates. At last she is forced to attack the very man who has warmed her icy heart and burned his way into her very soul.

___4303-3 $5.99 US/$6.99 CAN

Silken Savage

Catherine Hart

Captured by a party of Cheyenne while traveling through Colorado Territory, beautiful Tanya Martin refuses to let her proud spirit be broken or her voluptuous body abused. But she has not anticipated the reaction of her heart to A Panther Stalks, the brave who has claimed her as his prize. Tanya soon becomes her captor's willing slave, overcome by a passion she cannot resist.

__4462-5 $5.99 US/$6.99 CAN

Dorchester Publishing Co., Inc.
P.O. Box 6640
Wayne, PA 19087-8640

Please add $1.75 for shipping and handling for the first book and $.50 for each book thereafter. NY, NYC, and PA residents, please add appropriate sales tax. No cash, stamps, or C.O.D.s. All orders shipped within 6 weeks via postal service book rate.
Canadian orders require $2.00 extra postage and must be paid in U.S. dollars through a U.S. banking facility.

Name_____
Address_____
City_____ State_____ Zip_____
I have enclosed $_____ in payment for the checked book(s).
Payment <u>must</u> accompany all orders. ❏ Please send a free catalog.

SWEET FURY

CATHERINE HART

...e is exasperating, infuriating, unbelievably tantalizing; a ...tle hellcat with flashing eyes and red-gold tangles, and if ...yone is to make a lady of the girl, it will have to be ...arshal Travis Kincaid. She may fight him tooth and nail, ...t Travis swears he will coax her into his strong arms and ...leash all her wild, sweet fury.

_4428-5 $5.99 US/$6.99 CAN

...rchester Publishing Co., Inc.
...). Box 6640
...ayne, PA 19087-8640

...ease add $1.75 for shipping and handling for the first book and ...50 for each book thereafter. NY, NYC, and PA residents, ...ease add appropriate sales tax. No cash, stamps, or C.O.D.s. All ...ders shipped within 6 weeks via postal service book rate. ...nadian orders require $2.00 extra postage and must be paid in ...S. dollars through a U.S. banking facility.

...ame_____

...ddress_____

...ty_____State_____Zip_____

...ave enclosed $_____ in payment for the checked book(s). ...yment <u>must</u> accompany all orders. ❏ Please send a free catalog.
CHECK OUT OUR WEBSITE! www.dorchesterpub.com